SAY NO
MORE

FORGE BOOKS BY HANK PHILLIPPI RYAN

The Other Woman
The Wrong Girl
Truth Be Told
What You See
Say No More
Prime Time
Face Time
Air Time
Drive Time

SAY NO
MORE

HANK PHILLIPPI RYAN

A TOM DOHERTY ASSOCIATES BOOK

NEW YORK

SAY NO MORE

Copyright © 2016 by Hank Phillippi Ryan

A Forge Book
Published by Tom Doherty Associates
175 Fifth Avenue
New York, NY 10010

www.tor-forge.com

Forge® is a registered trademark of Macmillan Publishing Group, LLC.

The Library of Congress Cataloging-in-Publication Data is available upon request.

ISBN 978-0-7653-8535-2 (hardcover)
ISBN 978-0-7653-8536-9 (e-book)

Our books may be purchased in bulk for promotional, educational, or business use. Please contact your local bookseller or the Macmillan Corporate and Premium Sales Department at 1-800-221-7945, extension 5442, or by e-mail at MacmillanSpecialMarkets@macmillan.com.

First Edition: November 2016

Printed in the United States of America

0 9 8 7 6 5 4 3 2 1

For Jonathan.
And Flo and Eddy.

Some of the greatest battles will be fought within the silent chambers of your own soul.
　　　　　　　　　　　　—Ezra Taft Benson

MONDAY

1

JANE RYLAND

"Did you see that silver Cadillac? What he did?" Jane Ryland powered down the car window to get a better look. "He plowed right into that delivery van! Pull closer, can you?"

"Anyone hurt?" Fiola kept her eyes on the cars stopped ahead of them in the Monday morning rush on O'Brien Highway.

Squinting through the sun's glare, Jane could just make out the Caddy's red-and-white Massachusetts license plate up ahead in the lane to her right. "I can't tell yet. We need to get closer."

"Should I call the cops?" Fiola asked.

"Hang on. W-R-C, one-R-four." Jane recited the license number while scrambling in the side pocket of her canvas tote bag for a pencil. No pencil. *Some reporter.* Using one forefinger, she wrote it in the dust of the news car's grimy dashboard, for once the miserable housekeeping of Channel 2's motor pool working in her favor. Then, before she remembered she wasn't in jeans, she swiped the leftover grime down the side of her black skirt. Nine-forty A.M., if the dashboard digital was correct. The time wouldn't matter, nor would the plate number, but it was all reporter reflex.

"Jane? Can you see yet?"

Fiola Morrello—*not* Fiona, as she'd reminded Jane a few hundred times already—had insisted on driving, even though she'd arrived in Boston only last week. Jane had protested once. Then, recognizing the sometimes-contentious reporter-producer dynamic, let her new producer take the wheel. That's why Fiola got the big bucks, right?

Jane was more comfortable being in the driver's seat, but the two new colleagues would work it out. Jane hoped.

"Almost." She leaned out the window, far as she could, her bare forearm braced on the sunbaked door panel. Their white Crown Vic inched ahead toward the silver car, Jane's passenger-side window scarcely moving closer to the driver's side of the Caddy. "Sure *sounded* bad."

The chunky new Cadillac had hit a green Gormay on the Way delivery van, the popular take-out restaurant a culinary necessity for college kids, as well as the darling of Boston's overscheduled millennials and overworked professionals. Including Jane. It was obviously the Caddy's fault, so the drivers should have been exchanging insurance papers and calling the cops themselves. Damage or not, that big new car had banged into the older van's rear. Jane had seen—and heard—the whole thing.

"Is the Caddy driver on his cell?" Fiola asked. "Or should I call?"

"He's just sitting there." Jane watched the man stare straight ahead, both hands clamped on the steering wheel, acting as if nothing happened. Good luck with that, buddy, she thought. You can't pretend a car accident away. "Why doesn't he get out? Check on the delivery guy?"

As they crept closer, Jane catalogued the driver's face, top to bottom, as she'd been taught back in journalism school. Middle-aged, Caucasian, widow's peak, grayish hair, pointy cheekbones, thin lips, clean-shaven.

"Is this a Boston thing? Ignoring an accident?" Fiola, keeping one hand on the wheel, had grabbed her phone. "What if he's hurt? I'm gonna call."

"Yeah." Jane wrapped her fingers around the door handle, ready to leap out if need be. The stoplight was still red, the ridiculously long wait at the intersection straddling Boston proper and neighboring Charlestown now working in their favor.

The Gormay van's driver-side door opened. Out came a man's leg—running shoe, khaki pants. The left-turn arrow light turned green. The cars on Fiola's left pulled away, headed toward Beacon Hill.

"What do we do?" Fiola said. "When the light changes in a second, we'll be blocking traffic."

"Don't move. The people in front of us can go." Jane twisted around, looked over the leather seat back. "No one's behind us. Light's still red. Go ahead, call the cops."

Another running shoe, another khaki leg. And then the face of the van driver, shadowed by the curved metal door open behind him. He stopped, both feet planted on the pavement, leaning sideways against the front seat. Hurt?

"That guy doesn't look right," Fiola said.

"Nine-one-one," Jane said. "Do it."

Three lanes of lights above them turned green. Instantly, a cacophony of horns began, each driver apparently compelled to remind their fellow motorists what green meant.

Their news car was kind of blocking traffic, but what if this was a story? The other drivers would have to go around while the accident scene got worked out.

The Caddy driver still stared straight ahead. Then, with a wrench of his steering wheel and a squeal of tires, he jammed the car into reverse, veered to the right, swerved forward and across the right lane, other cars twisting out of his path, honking in protest. With a clamor of horns complaining, he peeled away, fishtailed once, spitting pebbles. The big car jounced over a jutting curb as it lost its battle with the acute angle of the turn onto the cross street, and barreled through the graffiti-slashed concrete beneath the Green Line underpass. Jane could almost hear the roar of acceleration as the Caddy sped into the distance, vanishing into the gritty construction-clogged labyrinth of Charlestown.

"Are you kidding me?" Jane yelled at the universe, yanking open her car door, waving her arms, signaling *Go around!* to the driver now honking impatiently behind her. Though the van's rear fender hung distressingly askew, this wasn't newsworthy enough to make TV. Still, it was the principle of the thing. The Caddy hits a van, then tries to get away with it? *Middle-aged, Caucasian, widow's peak, gray hair, pointy cheekbones, thin lips, clean-shaven.*

"Hit-and-run?" Jane could hear the incredulity in her own voice. "Tell the cops—"

"I got this." Fiola, phone to her ear, pointed to the van. "Go check on the guy."

"I'll check on the guy," Jane said at the same time. So much for Jane and Fiola's plans. Their interview at the college would have to wait. They'd been early—imagine that—so there was still an acceptable window of not-quite-lateness. Jane trotted up to the delivery truck, looking both ways, then all ways, remembering she was a defenseless pedestrian navigating four lanes of determined chrome and steel. At least the other drivers, now veering around the two stopped vehicles, seemed to acknowledge the potential danger. Day one of her new assignment—two steps forward, one step back.

Maybe two steps back, she thought, as she saw the driver. A young man, arms sticking out of a pale blue uniform shirt, a thin trickle of blood down the side of his face, turned to her. He touched a finger to his cheek, then looked at the smear of red it left, frowning.

"Are you okay?" Jane could see the young man's body trembling. He opened his mouth, then said . . . something. Not in English.

"I'm sorry, I'm Jane Ryland. From Channel 2? My producer's calling nine-one-one. I saw what happened, okay? Are you hurt?"

The man pointed toward the back of his van. He wants to see the damage, Jane thought. Makes sense. Maybe he's in shock.

"Yeah, I know," she said, trying to look supportive and sympathetic. "Stinks. But come see. There's not much damage."

The man approached, crouched on the pavement, and ran his finger over the dent, leaving a smudge of red on the pale green paint. He stood, then rattled the twin chrome handles of the van's double back doors. They didn't open.

"Are you okay?" Jane persisted. "It looks like you're bleeding a little."

"Cops on the way!" Fiola's voice came from behind them.

"The police are coming," Jane repeated. Why hadn't he said anything? "Sir?"

Middle-aged, Caucasian, widow's peak, her brain catalogued again, *gray hair, pointy cheekbones, thin lips, clean-shaven.* She replayed the moment of the collision, the sound of it, the sight of it, making it indelible. *Middle-aged, Caucasian, widow's peak, gray hair, pointy cheekbones, thin lips, clean-shaven.* Yes, she'd remember the driver. She'd recognize him.

And she'd get Jake to run the license number through his magic cop database. Not that he was supposed to do that unless he was working the collision, which he wouldn't be, let alone telling her what he found. Not that she could use the information, or would even need it. But anyway. Be interesting to know.

Still silent, the food truck driver finally seemed to acknowledge her, his eyes wide, inquiring. A siren, faint but recognizable, materialized from somewhere behind them. The cavalry. She and Fiola could still make their interview, Jane calculated. After this tiny and unremarkable good deed. Being a successful reporter was all about karma.

Then the van driver pivoted, so quickly Jane stepped back, and with one thick-soled running shoe he kicked the white-walled left rear tire. He spat out a few words, almost yelling, in a language Jane didn't understand.

He kicked the tire again, then looked at her, palms outstretched. That, Jane understood. *What the hell? This is crazy.*

"Yeah, I know." Jane nodded, sympathetic.

"You?" The man pointed to her. He could talk—that was good. Not in shock.

"See?" He seemed to be searching for the word. "You see?" The siren grew louder. Any second now, the cops would be here, she'd be gone, and she'd never think of this again.

"Yes, I see. Saw." Jane held out both hands, nodding, smiling, the international language for "everything is going to be fine." With one finger, she pointed to her chest, then to her eyes, then to the place where the silver Cadillac had been. And then to the direction it had vanished.

"No question," she said. "I saw everything."

2

JAKE BROGAN

"Can't you lie low for a while?" Jake Brogan wasn't used to this, telling someone to duck and cover.

Grady Houlihan obviously wasn't used to hearing it. The kid fidgeted in the battered wooden swivel chair Jake inherited from the last detective assigned to sit at the corner desk, left row, in the BPD homicide office. Jake hoped there wasn't residual bad juju from that guy, now in disgrace somewhere, bitter that he'd been caught—by Jake—taking kickbacks. Jake had not only gotten the glory, but in a bit of copshop humor, he'd also gotten the guy's chair.

This corner of the now open-floor-plan squad room did have some privacy. Former superintendent Rivera had installed waist-high fabric dividers designed to "open up the place" and "prevent closed doors." The gray panels were now layered with push-pinned newspaper clippings, Red Sox schedules, hand-drawn maps, union announcements, and the occasional what Jane would call inappropriate cartoon. Moments ago, the other cubicled cops had acknowledged Jake's arrival with his young informant, but now ignored them, returning to paperwork and phone calling.

Jake watched Grady consider the "lie low" suggestion, and knew from experience—and years of reading criminals' body language—that the snitch had already decided the answer was no. How did someone so young get in so deep, so soon? But this was Boston, and traditions died hard. Sometimes young men did, too. Clearly Grady was worried he'd be next, and he might be right. Problem was, nothing Jake could do about it.

"Don't you guys have, like, a thing, a protection thing?" Grady's voice held a taut undercurrent, not quite a whine, not quite a demand, that Jake figured came from some bone-weary feeling in the kid that he was always on the losing side. Never getting the break. But that assessment was demonstrably not true.

Grady certainly'd gotten a break, big-time, when Jake arranged for his immunity in the Charlestown stabbing. And then the Hyde Park drug episode. That's when young Grady McWhirter Houlihan—white male, age 19, charged with felony firearm possession—had realized he could have a career simply listening, then telling the cops what he heard. Not the safest of jobs, but it was why he sat here at police headquarters sipping root beer instead of in the Suffolk County Jail awaiting trial. In one of those who-can-understand-how-a-criminal-mind-works situations, Grady talked only to Jake. Little did Boston's skulking lowlifes know how many of their colleagues were behind bars because of this kid they assumed was their friend. This time he was asking Jake to be *his* friend.

Yes, Suffolk County had "a protection thing." But for so many reasons it wasn't going to work. And that left Jake in a pile-of-crap situation. Law enforcement needed Grady for his entrée into the world of illegal chutes and ladders, for his clues to its transactions and its participants. But if he was in danger? What was Jake's responsibility to protect him?

"Jake? You hearing me? I'll go, like, anywhere. No big deal. You buy, I'll fly. I'm telling you, Jake, they're onto me."

"They?" Jake took a sip of rancid squad room coffee. D was bringing the afternoon Dunkin's and was late, as usual. Jake actually knew who Grady's "they" was—the Sholto operation, a Charlestown tradition in the most unpleasant of ways, a merger of the two most powerful families in the neighborhood. In a much-discussed union ten years ago, everyone knew, big gun Clooney Sholto, more reclusive than Howard Hughes and nastier than Whitey Bulger, had married the flamboyant Violet O'Baron, terminating an entire generation of intra-neighborhood warfare and competition.

With those wedding vows, the O'Barons' drug-and-money territory had ceded to the Sholtos. Now, with Grady's help, the impenetrable Sholtos—patriarch, wife, allies, and underlings—were in Jake's sights. No matter what the kid wanted, Jake would have to send Grady back on the street. No other choice. Though this choice sucked.

"The Sholtos? How do you know they're onto you?"

"Dude," Grady said.

"Indulge me," Jake said.

"It's like . . ." Grady blew out a breath, remembering. "I come into the room, they stop talking, they go out of the room." Used his hands to illustrate. In. Out.

Bitten cuticles, Jake saw, but no tattoos, no remnants of incarceration or indelible indications of gang affiliation. He could have been a regular college kid, except for a few disastrously wrong choices and the uncaring randomness of the universe. And an ironclad agreement with the cops.

"I leave the room, they go back in, start talking again. Dude. Somebody swiped my freakin' phone. When I found it—like suddenly it was on the table, you know? Like it was never gone." He held it up, the black plastic-cased evidence. "But I mean—why? Who? They're onto me, Jake. I gotta split, or I'm like—Jake. I scratched you guys' back, right? So now—we done. Call it a day."

Phones rang, doors slammed, cops complained. With the fragrance of bad coffee surrounding them and the August heat defeating the muttering air conditioners, Jake let Grady talk. The longer Grady talked, the less Jake had to, and Jake had no good news and zero options. With only casual attendance at high school, and two parents and two brothers already doing time, Grady didn't have many career choices. He possessed no skills, and no talent to speak of, except for a Boston-friendly demeanor—including ginger hair, green eyes, a stubby body comfortable on a soccer field or harbor trawler—and a good ear. Grady knew when to keep quiet, and, lucky for Jake and for the kid's so-far-pristine criminal record, when to talk.

Even so, Jake worried he'd become the kid's father figure. That was Jane's prediction. He should never have told her about the Houlihan situation, but too late to take that back. At least Grady didn't know about Jane.

The kid was Jake's eyes and ears in two big cases. After a back-and-forth with the DA's office, the department even let a couple of low-level drug deals Grady'd reported go through, to convince the bad guys there was no leak.

If Grady split, Jake was screwed.

One phone, insistent, jangled from across the room. "Somebody get that," a voice complained. "Somebody who?" someone else yelled back. "Somebody's not here," another called out. "Budget cuts." The phone rang again.

"Here's the thing, Grady," Jake began. "The budget for the Suffolk County witness protection program, such as it is, is part of the—"

"Hey. Grab one of these puppies." DeLuca's voice came from behind a flimsy cardboard carrier barely managing to contain three teetering Styrofoam cups. "If one goes over, it'll burn ya to death. Shoulda gotten iced."

Jake's partner shoved over a stack of paperwork on an unoccupied desk and deposited the coffees on the pitted surface. "Jake, you about done? Grady? Got one of these for you, cream, three sugars, like Jake said. But hey, you two about done with whatever you're doing? We have to—"

"Hey?" Grady stood, crossing his arms over his gray T-shirt. Looked at the wall. Ignored the coffee.

Grady and DeLuca had a push-pull relationship. If DeLuca didn't push him, Grady wouldn't pull out of the deal. But Paul DeLuca, Jake's longtime partner and at age forty-seven moving ever closer to his dream of early retirement, had no patience with snitches. "Rats," he called them.

Even in the situationally moral world of cops and robbers, DeLuca'd explained to Jake, you had to pick a side.

"What if I ratted you out, Harvard?" D put the question to him one late night last year, after a case closed, over a third Guinness at the Sevens. "Say, about Jane? It'd be the 'right' thing to do, I guess, but hell. Even though you went to that phony-ass school, we're partners. Partners don't rat."

DeLuca, though aware of law enforcement's need for the type of intel only an insider could provide, barely managed to hide his disdain for Jake's young informant. This afternoon's coffee had been Jake's idea.

"Hey, D." Jake removed his steaming extra-large from the carrier. The flimsy Styro cup, squeaking against the cardboard, seemed about to implode. "What up?"

"The nine-one-one came to a Brookline tower." D extracted a spiral notebook from the back pocket of his jeans and flipped through the pages. "From a cell. But turns out the vic—"

"Jake?" Grady scratched a cheek, making a red line on his pale skin. "You were saying?"

DeLuca took a step back. Dramatically gestured, yielding Grady the floor. "The vic can wait," D said.

"Look. Grady. Can you just lie low?" Jake paused. Started again. "Look, I understand. I'll put in your witness protection paperwork. But there's a waiting list, and the red tape's gonna screw us. There's no budget for it, Grady, that's the hard reality. I'll expedite. Best I can. But until then . . ."

"Dude. They'll body me before that." Grady muttered the words to the murky gray carpet.

"Kill you?" Jake narrowed his eyes. Options clicked though his mind, none of them workable.

"Whatever," Grady said.

"Jake?" DeLuca flapped his notebook against his palm. "We gotta go."

"Brookline?"

"Nah. Call actually came from Boston. The Reserve, doncha know. She's ours."

"Who?" Jake asked, collecting his phone and notebook. Grady would hear the answer, but no matter. It was nothing he wouldn't see on TV. *TV.* Jake's body registered *Jane,* even before his brain did. But she wouldn't be involved, not with her new assignment at Channel 2. "Who's the victim?"

"That's what we have to find out." DeLuca checked the cream-sugar markings on the side of one cup, then the other, selected the second one. "Dead woman, in a bathing suit. In a pool. No longer swimming."

"Drowned?" Jake asked.

"Like I said, Harvard." D toasted with his cup. "Let's go find out."

3

JANE RYLAND

"Where'd you get these crime scene pictures?" Jane Ryland whispered her question, hushed by what she saw. They'd shut the door to their shared office in Special Projects to keep out the inevitable snoops and gawkers.

Fiola used her mouse to click through a slide show of . . . well, some of it was hard to look at. "Rated V for violence," Jane had said when she saw the first picture. It had been fifteen minutes now. Nonstop. Relentless. Gruesome. But powerful.

"And Fiola." Jane turned to her producer, peering through the semi-darkness, pointing. "We can't possibly put *that* one in a TV documentary. I mean—the position alone. We'd have to blur it." She paused, assessing. "Blur it a lot."

"Yeah. Obviously. I'm just showing you what we're up against." Fiola clicked to the next photo. The hum of the computer, the flickering light, the glare of the shadows as the shots changed, it all separated them from the late afternoon newsroom hubbub. Their intentional sequestration somehow made seeing the heartbreaking pictures feel more personal. And even more disturbing.

"Like this one, big-time blur." Fiola changed the shot. "I got them from sources. Most of them. Not in Boston. Look at her. This is why we do what we do, sister."

In this one, the young woman's face had been cropped from the photo. After seven years or so in news, often on the crime beat, Jane had seen her share of escalatingly tragic and mind-bogglingly repugnant crimes. It never got easier. She'd never let it.

"And this one." Fiola clicked again. "Real people. Preventable. Every one of them."

A woman, again, this time showing a muscular bare leg, a chaotically rumpled skirt ripped along one seam, and her blouse, what was left of it, with a slash of blood across the recognizable Burberry plaid trim. The woman's arm dangled over the edge of the bed, fingernails painted pale pink, wrist graceful as a dancer's.

"Sexually assaulted. And survived," Fiola said. "Still unsolved. No surprise. We don't need to see her face, and that's a good thing. She'll be our—touchstone. The object lesson for our documentary. She's who every woman does not want to be, but who every woman might be. If this young student, only a sophomore in college, had reported her fears? Had gone to her school's dean, even. Or her campus police?" Fiola paused, letting Jane mentally fill in the rest. She clicked again. "Even when they do— well, here's one from Adams Bay College. Our only local victim, so far. The incident the dean of students was telling us about in the interview today. I kept wishing he'd go on camera."

"Poor girl."

"Yeah," Fiola said. "She was drugged, and traumatized. She quit school soon after. They often do."

Somewhere down the hall, trilling phones and raised voices heralded the countdown to the six o'clock newscast. But Jane's deadline was still a month away. The news director had allotted her—and new producer Fiola—thirty days to put together their hour-long documentary. "Get it on the air in time for back to school," Marsh Tyson had told them. "It's our gift to the students arriving this September."

Jane felt her third finger, left hand. Bare today, but where she some-times wore Jake's grandmother's diamond. The two of them had decided, over July 4th champagne and carry-out egg rolls and gloriously appropriate fireworks, that they should work on going public as a couple. Take their first steps. And that she'd be the one to—kind of—compromise. So she'd negotiated this new deal with Channel 2. She'd still do investigative journalism, still be on the air and get to participate in what could be an important documentary. But she made her position clear to news director Tyson—she was out of the breaking-news department.

"I'm going to have to keep some secrets," she'd told her boss. Jake's secrets. "If you can live with that? I can, too. If you can't? Tell me now. Because I can't feel responsible, or guilty, or like I'm letting you down."

"You're going to *want* to tell us when you hear a good story, I predict," Marsh had said, wagging a forefinger at her. "You're such a pit bull."

"Oh, trust me, I know." She shook her head, accepting it wouldn't be easy. "I'm an old dog—"

"Not that old," Marsh interrupted.

"Whatever," she said. Approaching thirty-four was approaching too-old in TV years, an industry that measured value on a sliding scale of youthful beauty. She'd be happy enough, she realized, to ease out of that losing battle.

"I know there'll be times when I'll be dying to call you with the scoop. But." She had held up her hand, shown off the engaged-to-be-engaged ring, just that once. Felt the weight of it, and all it meant. "For the sake of my future? I'll have to say no more."

Fiola interrupted Jane's thoughts. "What we need now are victims who'll go on camera. Can you hit the lights?"

Jane flipped the light switch as Fiola's slide show powered down. Blinking in the harsh fluorescent glare, Jane struggled to regain her emotional bearings, trying to shake off the disturbing aftereffects of her producer's photo collection.

Another relationship still in the experimental stage: hers with Fiola. Fiola, according to her impressive-looking resume, had started as main anchor at her hometown station, then moved through the ranks to become an experienced documentary producer in Washington, D.C. Though

Jane was confident of her own journalism expertise, she'd never done a story longer than seven minutes. Seven-oh-five—she knew its length to the second—when two months ago she'd revealed the biggest banking fraud in the history of Boston.

But now, instead of continuing to work solo tackling TV's relentless challenge of what-have-you-done-for-me-lately while juggling the boundaries of her relationship with Jake, Jane was assigned to Fiola's documentary team. Adding another unknown to the mix. One day at a time, though, and this was day one.

"Victims, yeah," Jane said, settling back into the swivel chair at her desk. "Who'll talk about their experiences, and what they learned."

That was nothing new, at least. Whether documentary, investigative story, or breaking news, TV was about getting real people to talk, to tell all to the camera.

Outsiders sometimes branded it a second victimization. A person's tragedy was bad enough, they argued, but then a reporter pesters them to talk about it? *It's learning from history,* Jane had debated with many a critic. How change was made. How justice was done. How more tragedies were prevented. It didn't make it fun. It *did* make it necessary.

"We can troll the listservs, Facebook, Twitter." Jane opened her computer screen, typed in "campus sexual assault victim" as she talked. "Say we're researching a documentary on—"

"I've already done that. See?" Fiola pointed to her computer screen, now a mosaic of multicolored shortcuts. "I set up this dedicated website with links to Facebook and Instagram, said we were looking for young women who'd talk about their experiences. I put in an e-mail and phone number. It's a special tip line that only rings on our desks. Let's see if we have any e-nibbles yet."

Drop-down menus flashed as Fiola moused through, checking for responses. "Nothing yet. But it's early."

"Only women?" Jane scooted closer to Fiola's monitor, read the website page again. "How about guys? How sometimes they're unfairly targeted? Unfairly accused?"

Fiola's scrolling stopped, fingers hovering above her white plastic computer mouse. After a beat, she started scrolling again. Didn't answer.

"I know it wouldn't be the main element of our story," Jane persisted. She was just as concerned and angry about campus sexual assault as anyone, but as a reporter, the best story was the whole story. They had to explore it. "And clearly it's usually the woman who's the victim. But it's a campus-wide problem. That's why 'he said, she said' campus assault stories are instantly suspect now."

Fiola opened her top desk drawer, the room so still Jane could hear the little wheels along the drawer's runners. Fiola took out a bag of pretzels, and, with a rattle of shiny foil, unzipped a pull tab. She waved the bag toward the closed office door.

"Can you open that door, Jane?" Fiola asked. "It's getting stuffy in here."

Fiola began scrolling her mouse with her right hand, popping little pretzels, one after the other, with her left. Fiola seemed able to eat anything, and did, incessantly, without it making a difference in her weight. Last week, the day they met, Jane had watched her eat a cheeseburger, then six pieces of sushi. For lunch.

The sounds of the newsroom floated back in as Jane opened the door. Reality returned. Crisscrossing theme music from the national newscast, audio from viewing stations, phones ringing, someone laughing.

Well, okay, Jane thought. Day one. Every big story had a ramp-up, of course, when every idea was on the table and every concept a possibility. You could always decide to cut an element, but the key was to consider everything. Discuss every angle, every point of view. Keep it fair and objective. The truth was the goal, silence the enemy.

"I'm just saying," Jane picked up as if there hadn't been a weird moment. "In light of everything that's already happened, I think we need to—"

The trill of Jane's desk phone interrupted her attempt at discussion.

"We'll do it properly, Jane. No worries. Your phone," Fiola said, unnecessarily. "Maybe it's a call from a victim. Better answer."

"This is Jane Ryland." Seemed like she'd hit a nerve with Fiola. *Huh.* If this new producer had some kind of agenda . . . Jane stopped her spiraling paranoia. It was early days. This was a solid story. Important. They'd make sure it was fair. Silence on the phone line. "Hello?"

"Jane Ryland?" A male voice, unfamiliar. Had a man responded to their sexual assault inquiry?

"This is Jane," she repeated. The man had asked for her, specifically, and her name wasn't on Fiola's website. So it couldn't be about that. "Who's this, please?"

"Assistant District Attorney Frank McCusker. From DA Santora's office."

Jane pictured the veteran legal insider, with his trademark suspenders and shaved head and imperious attitude. Dealmaker. Tough guy. She frowned, trying to parse out why he'd called her. He wasn't one of her sources. Usually an ADA would never talk directly to a reporter, let alone call one.

"Hi, Frank. What can I do for—"

"That hit-and-run this morning." He didn't wait for her to finish. "Thanks for the plate number. It'll help. Cops told us you'd seen the incident? The whole thing? You get a good look at the driver?"

Middle-aged, Caucasian, widow's peak, gray hair, pointy cheekbones, thin lips, clean-shaven. "What's the DA's office interest in a little fender bender?" she asked. She turned to Fiola, making sure she was listening. Fiola nodded, eyebrows raised.

"Can you come over, maybe now?" McCusker wasn't answering her question. "We'd like to chat with you about it, Jane."

Chat? She'd already given them the plate number. What nagged at her—she'd been on the job when she saw the accident. What if it somehow turned into a story?

Whatever ran on Channel 2's newscasts was public, and the DA could see that, like everyone else. But what wasn't on the air? Outtakes, raw video, what stayed in a reporter's notebook or in her head? That was never shared. So the highly unusual request for her to give additional information to the DA meant Jane would have to ask permission of news director Marsh Tyson, who'd have to get authorization from the station's owner, who'd have to get clearance from the station's lawyer. No matter how she personally felt about it—and she wasn't exactly sure how that was—no way could Jane unilaterally say yes.

There was no "chat." She was already second-guessing herself about having given them the license number.

"I'll have to get permission from upstairs," Jane said. She still wondered what could possibly be so pressing about the accident. What she'd witnessed hardly reached district-attorney level. It was barely beat-cop level. Which meant maybe there was more to it. Which meant it was her turn to ask some questions.

"Might help, you know, give me some ammunition, if you tell me what DA Santora finds so compelling about this. I mean—the Gormay driver must have described the whole thing. What'd he say?"

"We're getting a translator," McCusker said.

"Oh," Jane said, remembering. "Right."

Fiola leaned forward in her chair, elbows on knees, so intent she'd even abandoned her bag of pretzels. A scatter of crumbs and salt littered her desk.

"So. Tomorrow," McCusker was saying. "Call me before noon. We can subpoena you, you know, Jane."

Subpoena her? For a fender bender? "Yeah, you can try that, Frank." Jane kept her voice light so he'd understand she wasn't yanking his chain. They could be adversaries without being adversarial, and each of them was only doing what they were told. "But let's see what the command ladder says. Go from there before you drag me away in cuffs."

"Before noon." McCusker didn't sound amused. And hung up.

"Geez. Nice guy," Jane said, putting down the phone. "They threatened to subpoena—"

"I got it," Fiola said. "Did they want to talk to me, too? Since I was in the car with you?"

"They didn't say so." Jane shrugged. "Maybe they'll call you separately. Anyway, they wanted me to 'come over,' can you believe it? Can you see me deciding to sashay into Krista Santora's office and tell all? You'd be looking for a new reporter pretty fast."

"Well, I barely saw him anyway." Fiola swiveled back to her monitor. "I was driving."

"White, middle-aged, widow's peak, gray hair, pointy cheekbones, thin lips," Jane recited. "I looked right at him."

"Yeah, I know." Fiola clicked her mouse, and the slide show of victims paraded across her screen again, the light from the flickering colors playing across her face. "Thing is, that means he saw you, too."

4

JAKE BROGAN

"Is it murder if you kill a dog?" DeLuca complained as Jake knocked on the front door of 3140 Alcott Road.

Pronounced "Al-kitt," Jake knew. Their possible crime scene was an august brownstone town house in a quietly manicured cul-de-sac of The Reserve. Quiet except for the dog.

"Some lungs on that thing," Jake said. The dog's yappy barking came from the backyard. That's where the body was, dispatch had informed them. Seemed like no way to get there except via the front door, and now they were waiting for the beat cop to let them inside. "Not very 'Reserve.'"

No street signs proclaimed The Reserve, but ever since Jake was a kid, he'd been aware of the societal boundaries of this off-the-official-map enclave of blue-blooded affluence. His parents, most often his mother with her Dellacort heritage, had dragged him to "important" post-symphony-matinee or pre-library-lecture gatherings at the homes here of their "important" friends. Preteen Jake had played Ninja Turtles with the other children of industry and finance while the parents did whatever they did.

Jake had never been at this particular home, though. A cast-iron plaque named it The Morgan House, and a cornerstone carved 1893 gave it a birthday.

He knocked again. Nothing. Keyed his radio. "This is Brogan and DeLuca," he said. "On-site at the address." Static.

He let go of the radio button. "How about getting someone to let us the hell in?" he said out loud, though no one else but D could hear him. Budget cuts had ripped the understaffed dispatch, like everyplace else at the department.

"Try asking for Kearney himself," DeLuca said. "The new supe's always saying how we're in this together. Except, in real life, *he's* in his office, and *we're* out in murderland. Getting nowhere."

Jake looked up, saw three brownstone stories, polished windows, a flutter of curtains, slate roof, sky still bright with the last of the summer sunlight. No faces, though, no sounds from inside. Outside, no traffic, no horns honking, no tinkling ice cream truck music, no kids on bikes or laughter from backyards. A few silhouettes down the block, inquisitive neighbors, probably. And that dog. Jake held down the radio button again. "Requesting entry, please."

"The dog's gotta go." D leaned forward, balanced one hand on the brownstone wall, and pushed the branches of a spiky shrub away from the multipaned front window with the other, trying to get a look inside. He stood, defeated, brushed off his hands. "Can't see a thing."

The front door creaked open, Jake dismissing a brief imaginary vision of a black-coated butler bearing a silver tray. A uniformed cop stood in the entryway. Finally, some good news.

"Hey, Shom," Jake said. T'shombe Pereira was stand-up, and as close to making detective as anyone on the force.

"Right this way, Detectives," Pereira said, gesturing them into a shadowy entryway, black-and-white tiles, gilt-edged mirror hanging over a marble table. "She's in the back."

Jake stepped over the threshold, his eyes adjusting. He cased a twinkling chandelier, lights glowing. To the left, the living room, fresh flowers, fireplace, books open on a coffee table. A stairway to the right. Jane would call the carpet jewel-toned. A two-story wall galleried with photos. A long hall led to daylight at the end.

"You solved this yet, Shom?" he asked, mostly giving him grief. "Got a confession, cause of death? Signs of a break-in?"

"Not that we can tell. Front door was locked." Pereira pointed, then gestured down the hall. "No other way into the back."

"Who called nine-one-one?" Jake asked. Carpet continued down the hallway. No footprints in the center of the deep pile. Shom had kept to the edges, doing it by the book. The three filed toward the back of the house. The barking got louder

"Can't you shut that dog up?" DeLuca was scanning, assessing, same as Jake was.

"Looking into it," Pereira said. "Nine-one-one, I mean. The dog's above my pay grade, Detectives."

As the wallpapered hallway ended, Jake took it all in—décor, atmosphere, light levels, air conditioner humming somewhere, clean smell. Didn't smell like dog. Hmm. You never knew what might be evidence. As for the house itself, Jake realized he was "assessing" in an additional way. He and Jane had looked at a few brownstones together, pretending their venture into Realtors' open houses was simply a lark. An outing. Just for fun. It wasn't. Though Jane wouldn't wear Gramma's diamond ring in public—they'd talked about it again only the night before—their house-shopping was for real. Life was short, Jake thought, entering a pristinely white-cupboarded kitchen.

"Back there." Shom Pereira pointed toward sliding glass doors now opened to a flagstone patio and swimming pool, turquoise water glittering.

And next to the pool, the unmistakable juxtaposition he'd seen again and again over the past ten years on street corners, in blood-soaked living rooms, in a rain-sodden suburban woodland, even once, years ago, on a klieg-lighted high school football field. A dark shape on the ground, motionless, still, as if waiting for answers the victim would never hear. The attending shape of the medical examiner crouched over the body, ministerial, intent.

This scene—one like it unfolding every ten days or so in Boston, Jake and the other homicide detectives could recite the stats—was the beginning of a possible murder story. Soon that story would simultaneously

move backward to the past and forward to the future, and eventually some diligent law enforcement official would close the book on it. If they were lucky.

Often the scene was silent, whether reverent, or sorrowful, or tense, or all of the above. In this backyard, though, it was all about the dog. A white button eyed cotton ball—still yapping, one paw clamped on a yellow rubber toy—was tied to the leg of a black wrought-iron poolside chair with a strip of something pink and green.

"Sorry about the dog." The medical examiner looked up from the victim beside her, Kat McMahan raising a lavender-gloved hand in greeting as they approached, her back to the rectangular swimming pool. Under her white lab coat, Jake saw the ME's T-shirt of the day—this one more loose-fitting than usual. Above the logo of a nail-impaled tongue, a slogan read, "I Missed the Stones—Fenway 2011." Jake knew that T-shirt belonged to DeLuca. Decided not to mention it.

"She was going crazy," Kat continued, cocking her head at the dog. "Yelping and racing in circles. Her collar says 'Popcorn.' I sacrificed my scarf so she wouldn't bolt for the street."

"Be good riddance," DeLuca muttered, looking at the sun-dotted water. "Wonder if it can swim."

"What you got, Kat?" Jake pitched his voice louder than the dog's as he stepped closer to the body by the pool. The dead woman looked for all the world like a sunbather, sleeping prone, one hand just touching the edge of one of the blue tiles surrounding the pool. Not young, not old, dark hair splayed behind her. A hot pink, Jake guessed you'd call it, bathing suit, modest. Bare feet, painted toenails matching the suit. One flip-flop on, the other in the water. No blood, no gun, no signs of a struggle.

"Kat? Who pulled her out of the pool?" Would there be any reason not to?

The dog—Popcorn—kept up her side of the conversation as Jake took in the scene. He shrugged, bent down, untied Kat's scarf, and picked up the dog. Its yellow toy ball rolled away, and Popcorn quieted, blinked, looked into his eyes. Then she started yapping like a canine maniac. Her

tiny pointed teeth snapped at him, her ears flattened. The dog squirmed, a writhing ball of white fur, flailing legs, and thrashing paws, trying to escape.

"You kidding me, dog?" Jake held Popcorn out in front of him, trying to keep her sharp claws away from his face. Maybe she smelled Diva. *Diva'd eat this thing with one golden retriever chomp.* Kat was trying not to laugh, not succeeding. Good thing the public didn't see this side of law enforcement.

"Gimme that dog. She's only protecting—" DeLuca grabbed it, looking like a scarecrow holding a tiny lamb. The dog was instantly silent.

"How'd you—" Jake began.

"Do *not*—" Kat glanced at the pool.

"Dog's a witness, right?" DeLuca said. "Go on, Doc. Give us the scoop. Cause of death?"

Kat stood, eyeing DeLuca and the dog, then turned her attention to the woman on the pavement. The dog's owner, presumably. And D was right, the dog probably was a witness. If this was murder, some defense attorney'd figure out a way to use that. But that was down the road. Plus, if someone had a defense attorney, it meant there was a defendant. And that would be a good thing.

"Well." Kat took a deep breath, as she always did when making a prelim. "Too early to say. But she's wet, and she was in the pool. Her cell phone was, too. Anyone who's watched *Dragnet* knows the ME can tell if a person drowned."

"*Dragnet*?" Jake asked.

"Whatever," Kat said. "Drowning is an easy diagnosis. You can't get away with a fake drowning. So we have to ask—why was she dead in the pool?"

Jake thought about it. Fell? Pushed?

Kat kept talking. "Hard to dress a wet person in a bathing suit. Hard to dress a dead person in a bathing suit. Hard to—well, we can safely assume this is what she was wearing when she died. White, female, forty-ish, maybe younger, maybe older—have to look for plastic surgery. No

ligature marks, no blunt trauma, no stabs or bullet wounds. So. We shall see."

"Drugs? Alcohol?" Jake looked around. No glasses, no bottle. "Suicide?"

"Too soon to say," Kat replied. "Tell me if you find a note."

"ID?" Jake said. If the dog had a name tag, maybe it had a license. Which meant the dog-witness could be valuable after all. It could tell them her owner's name.

"That's why you get the big bucks," Kat was saying. "I've got the ambulance on the way. So. More to come."

"We'll check the house. Name'll be the least of our problems," Jake said.

"Someone coulda gotten through the shrubs, I guess." DeLuca held the dog in his arms as he scanned, doing a three-sixty. "Or jumped the fence. Gotta love mulch. Sucks for footprints."

"Who got her out of the pool?" Jake asked.

"Officer Reddington was the first here," Kat said. "Kevin. Came over the fence. Jumped in, pulled her out. She might have been alive. But she wasn't."

"Where's—" Jake began.

"He's outside. Still wet." Kat pointed toward the street. "He's got the phone, though it'll have to dry out. Told him to wait so you could talk to him. He's keeping the lookies away, too. College kid, a few neighbors."

"Detectives?" T'shombe Pereira stood in the frame of the open sliding glass door. A siren wailed in the far distance. So much for the neighborhood's afternoon of peace and security. Death had come to The Reserve.

"Dispatch traced the nine-one-one to a cell that pinged a tower serving this neighborhood," the officer said. "They're working on it. So far, door-to-door's got nothing. Except. Our victim is apparently named Avery Morgan. That's the same person who receives the mail here. And there's an open checkbook, her name, this address, with those textbooks on the coffee table."

"Thanks, Shom," Jake said. "Stay on it."

He turned to D and Kat, then to the body on the smooth poolside stones. Now she had a name, Avery Morgan. Morgan House, the place was called, and that could not be a coincidence. That meant their victim had an easily discoverable history. Connections. And discoverable enemies. Maybe this wouldn't be a tough one. It could happen.

"Too bad your townie informant has no pals in The Reserve." DeLuca's canine witness had fallen dead asleep in his arms, two back paws tucked under D's belt, a furry chin on D's forearm. "We could use some intel."

"Every group has a code of silence," Jake said. "It's a question of finding the weak link."

"Maybe the weak link was Avery Morgan," DeLuca said. "Sure wish this dog could talk."

5

WILLOW GALT

Was calling the police my first mistake? Willow tried to gauge whether anyone in Avery's backyard who looked up and across two rows of hedges would be able to spot her in the upstairs bedroom window, framed by ancient ivy and a ruffle of brand-new white curtains. She'd cross that bridge when she came to it. She'd done it enough, crossing bridges when she came to them, to stay in practice. But what she'd seen in Avery's yard was so disturbing. How could she not report it?

She examined the cell phone she'd used to call 911, one of her secret stash of prepaids. Even Tom didn't know she had them. But she was not about to cut herself off from the entire world, no matter what the two of them had promised or what deal they'd made. No one could erase the fact that she existed.

She *existed*. But in a different way now. "It'll be fine," Tom had reassured her. She could not imagine "fine." She wanted a pill. But she'd resist.

The phone rang, the jangle from their landline making her realize she'd been lost in thought. She let it ring. If it was Tom, he'd leave a message. If it was the police, they'd say so. Not answering it now would give her time to think.

Third ring. To get away from the phone, she went through the open bedroom door, down the carpeted hall, and into the "guest" room. As if they'd ever have guests. She tucked her hair behind her ears—she'd never worn it this long before!—and pressed her forehead against the window, feeling the cool glass. Two more people, maybe three, had arrived at Avery's.

So funny it was named "Morgan House" and Avery's name is—*was*—Morgan. They'd laughed about the coincidence.

"Fate," Avery had pronounced, and lifted a glass of prosecco, her Hollywood voice dramatic. "I was *destined* to be here. And you were, too, darling Willow!" She hadn't told Tom about their talks, and worried the chitchatty Avery might let it slip someday. Now that worry was over.

Others were beginning.

She and Avery had met just two months ago, after Willow saw a flash of dark hair though the backyard forsythia. She'd heard a voice call out, "Hello? Who's over there?"

The voice had parted the slender branches with one hand and peered through the greening leaves. Willow saw a woman about her size with a little white dog tucked under one arm. Pretty, Willow thought. Theatrical, in white pants and a paisley tunic.

"I'm Avery," she'd said.

"I'm Willow." She'd taken a step, one, or maybe two, toward the forsythia. The visitor might have thought it strange if she'd run away. Or worse, gossip-worthy. Safe enough to talk, just this once. She hadn't even stumbled over introducing herself as "Willow."

"Lovely name," Avery replied, using the entire musical scale for the three syllables. Willow listened to things like that. She'd thought about changing her own voice, just a little, in case. But that was difficult. As difficult as remembering you were someone else.

Willow had tried to smile and be neighborly, knowing she couldn't go any further. Risky enough having this encounter. Still, she longed for contact, for connection, for friends. They hadn't warned her it'd be like this, so lonely. Or maybe they had.

The next time she'd glimpsed Avery's dark hair, Willow had come back out, pretending she'd been planning to sit in her backyard anyway. Avery had slipped through the bushes, and they'd talked. Then had drinks by Avery's pool.

Now this.

Tom would kill her for calling the police.

The phone stopped ringing. Good. Willow listened for a message—but there was no voice. *Good.* They'd given up. Maybe it was a wrong number. Maybe she'd spooked herself again. Maybe.

Thing was. Someone, she honestly did not know who, had—Willow shook her head, envisioning it. Even now she could feel the memory changing. Fading. *Good.*

She wished she could un-remember all of it. The shape that came into the backyard earlier this afternoon. And the other shape, motionless, wrong, in the pool. Popcorn, barking incessantly, racing back and forth along the pool's edge. What would happen to the dog now? Willow still had a heart, and a conscience. They could not take that away.

But now the police were there, and they'd figure it out. They didn't need her. She'd watched an officer scale the back fence, hoist himself over the weathered wood, and pull Avery out, dripping and motionless. She'd try to forget that, too.

The sounds of the house surrounded her, the dull nothing of emptiness, the melancholy sweet fragrance of still-unpacked cardboard moving boxes. The last of the afternoon sun through the window made rectangular shapes on the off-white carpeting, like the hopscotch squares she and her sister had drawn on their suburban sidewalks so many years ago. Now here she was, in hiding. Not even Millie knew where she was or if she was alive. Instead of following directions and staying uninvolved, unconnected, and unremarkable, Willow had called the police.

She laughed out loud, her own rueful bark surprising her as it seemed to echo through the room. Of all things. She'd called the police!

Willow quieted. Listening. But no, there was only silence. She closed her eyes, weary and defeated. Tom would *kill* her. No. No. He'd understand. He'd have to.

When she opened her eyes, the shadows had moved, the hopscotch squares gone.

This time, she heard it clearly.

The knock on her front door.

6

ISABEL RUSSO

Isabel looked at the checkerboard of days on her August calendar, the one she'd found online and printed on the portable device set up by the coffee-maker on her kitchen counter. It was a high point of her day, she had to admit, when she got to obliterate another square, making a big black X to reassure herself she was one step closer to graduation. One day closer to leaving Adams Bay College, leaving Boston, leaving her old life behind and going somewhere, anywhere, anyplace no one knew her. Where no one knew what had happened to her. And where they never ever ever would. She would never say a word.

She stared at the remaining calendar squares. So many of them. Nine months to go. Every day at six P.M. she crossed off that day. If she did it in the morning, the day wasn't truly over yet, so the moment wasn't as meaningful.

Twenty years old, she thought, as she poised the thick black Sharpie over the square marked "Monday." *And I am counting the days until I can leave this apartment.*

Apartment. She looked around the little place she'd called home since she came to Boston going on four years ago, full of hope and excitement, full of her future as a performer or teacher or both. She'd gotten good news on the very first day, when she'd won the school's freshman hous-ing lottery and was allowed to opt out of Adams Bay's notoriously crowded dorms. Her mother, to her wild delight, had agreed to pay the extra it would cost.

At first, Isabel adored her new home base. She painted most of it pale blue, one wall pristine china white. Hand-stitched—because who has a sewing machine?—curtains from yards of blue-striped linen, installed with expandable rods from CVS. As inspiration, she arranged her framed posters of Maria Callas singing *Tosca* and Mirella Freni as Mimi, and in a fit of do-it-yourself fervor, successfully installed her little corner-mounted speakers. She put two potted scheffleras and a folding chair on her tiny wrought-iron balcony, a fire escape, really, overlooking Kenmore Square. She invited classmates to visit, and they'd drunk Nebbiolo and listened to her vinyl and compared, well, notes. The whole scene was cool, proof she was independent and free and grown-up and on her own.

Since last semester, though—last May, to be exact, one Friday night in May, to be horribly exact—her apartment had been all about allowing her to be apart: an apart-ment. She wished she could be apart from everything.

An e-mail pinged her attention. Professor Ruth Tully. Again wanting her to come to the summer semester's final Music Theory 301 classes in person, not rely on notes and online lectures. All the classes had video hookups for those who were disabled, or sick, or for when the winter weather was so miserable that attendance would be difficult for commuting students. The college-by-video thing was Isabel's lifesaver now. If Isabel didn't have to go outside—not set one foot outside, not *ever*, not *ever again* . . .

She pursed her lips, focused on the sunlight fracturing through the faceted crystal she'd hung from a thin wire over her kitchen window. Red, orange, yellow, green, blue, indigo, violet . . . silently she named the colors. The world was still beautiful, she needed to remember.

"Sorry, Professor," she typed. "I'll do video. Thanks."

Send. Done. With only a twinge of regret. Professor Tully was very sweet to care about her so much. Isabel wondered if she suspected something. Professor Morgan, too, sometimes inquired, wondering why Isabel was no longer attending her gatherings.

Obviously when a once-proficient classical music student vanishes from class, something is going on. But her professors, even well-meaning ones, could pry only so far.

Someday she'd be able to go outside again. She'd tried it already, several times. But when she stepped out into the hallway, or smelled the— anyway. It became surprisingly easy to keep to herself. Friends faded away, most of them. She ordered food from the delivery place, got books online, and sent assignments via e-mail. She had her music. She listened to her operas. She practiced her pieces. She could manage better in another reality. In someone else's story.

She would have transferred out of Adams Bay instantly, after the "event." But she'd have lost her tuition. And credits.

"You're fine. You'll be fine." She could hear her mother's voice. How could she know about "fine"? But then her mother, long-distance from St. Louis, had closed the door. And locked it. "We cannot afford it, not anymore. And we cannot tell your brother. It would kill him."

And there it was, the hierarchy, the family relationships in one little pronouncement. Who mattered, and who didn't.

Here at "home" she didn't have to touch anyone else. Or *smell* anyone. Or look into anyone's eyes.

Nothing had happened to "him," of course. She'd never say his name again. Never even think it. Never poison her mind with it. She'd make him a no one, a nobody, exactly as he'd done to her.

She looked up, glanced around as if someone could be watching. It always felt as if someone were, which was ridic. But Dame Callas's darkly disapproving eyes seemed to stare right at her, and Mirella's sweet expression had turned to pity. Isabel blinked, dismissing her fantasy. *They're only posters.* She looked at her watch. 6:30. Gormay on the Way would arrive in an hour.

She had time.

She clicked into Facebook, hit the bookmark for *his* profile. Smiling, smiling, smiling. It was like this every day. Why did she keep looking? She went to Instagram, checked his IG photos. She'd watched as his friend list grew, saw him amass endless "likes" with his stupid sports and silly pop concert tickets and dumb jokes. He'd gotten a new car, she saw, scanning the newest photos. Another new girlfriend. She was smiling, too, even kind of seemed familiar. She clicked away from the heart-twisting, stomach-turning site. *Enough.*

Her next stop was always the "help" sites. Somehow, not being alone in her grief was reassuring. Even though it should have been chilling. But she had to look, once a day, every day.

Sexually assaulted on campus? We want to hear your story.

The headline on the Facebook "WE CAN HELP" home page was so shocking, so surprising, so unexpected, she blinked at it, willing her eyes to go back into focus. The postage-stamp-sized icon was of a scale of justice. "Maybe you can prevent this from happening to someone else," the article began. "Make a difference," it said. "Take back the power."

"Click here," it said.

She looked up again. It *really* felt as if someone was watching. The back of her neck prickled, and she could hear the silence.

Click? She could not do it. Why should she? All these hours she'd spent, making this place her refuge. Give that up with a click? No. She'd created a tiny bit of peace out of her shambles of a life. No way would she ever relive or talk about it again.

Click?

But how could it hurt just to see? "Prevent this from happening to someone else," it said. She'd never wish her burden on anyone. Could she help instead? She touched her forefinger to the silver mouse. And pushed.

She steeled herself, waiting, not sure what to expect. Could they trace this? Know who she was? Should she close the computer, forget about it, fade to black? Maybe *this* was the biggest mistake she'd ever made.

She leaned her head back against the top rail of her kitchen chair, crossed her arms, felt the warmth of her bare skin. Briefly closed her eyes. *No.* The biggest mistake she'd ever made was going to that party. She shook her head, wondering. It was an odd relief, maybe, to understand that nothing worse could ever happen to her. Maybe that was her power.

Isabel paused, fingers poised over her keyboard. Thinking about the phone number now on the screen. Should she call? The atmosphere of the room changed—a flicker of shadow through the maple tree outside, then a single shaft of light glinted a rainbow on her keyboard, the spectrum of colors changing, dancing, playing across her fingers. Smiling in spite of herself, she looked up to see her little window crystal twisting in the resolute sunshine.

7

JANE RYLAND

"Your phone's ringing."

If Fiola was going to announce every phone call, Jane would not last long sharing this two-desk office with her.

"Yes, indeed," Jane said, forcing a smile, trying not to be dismissive. It was so late that the six o'clock news was already into the final sports segment. She and Fiola had handled a challenging day. The most recent challenge, the phone call from ADA Frank McCusker, followed by Fiola's "that means he saw you, too" remark, had engendered a troubling series of possibilities. More than a few times, Jane played back the hit-and-run episode in her head, trying to remember if she'd noticed the driver looking at her. Had he seen her? If he had, he might—might—have recognized her from her on-the-air days. Would that matter?

The phone rang a second time. Jane grabbed it before Fiola could say anything.

"Jane Ryland," she said.

Silence. Again. Was this McCusker? Playing psychological games? Making her wait to prove he was in charge?

"Hello?" She tried not to sound annoyed at the silence. Maybe it wasn't the DA's office. Anyway, it wasn't this caller's fault that she was feeling pressured, and unsettled, and, she had to admit, battling a few qualms after this first day on the new assignment with her new "partner."

"I'm calling about the . . . thing? On Facebook," the voice replied.

A woman. Responding to their campus assault inquiry. Jane sat up, bolt straight. Might even have made a tiny sound in reaction.

"What?" Fiola swiveled in her chair, scooted closer to Jane's desk. "Who?"

"I'm so glad," Jane began. She needed to sound reassuring, low pres sure, and avoid spooking the caller Into hanging up. This could be their first big get on the documentary. The caller could also be a nothing, a nut job, a phony, someone who'd misunderstood, or was curious, someone searching for attention or notoriety or airtime. Or, the worst possible scenario, someone from a rival station snooping on their investigation.

Open-ended questions, now, were the way to go. This might be a wacko, but it also might be a young woman who had suffered terribly. And had, in this one moment, decided to share her story. Jane was a good listener. She would listen.

"Thanks so much, I'm glad you saw that," she went on, keeping her voice level and gently supportive. "My name is Jane. Why don't you tell me a little bit about what happened? And why you decided to call?"

Fiola was scrawling on a yellow pad with a red marker. She brandished her note at Jane. "Put her on speaker," it said.

Jane grimaced, shaking her head. Held up a palm. *Hang on. I'll handle it.* And now she'd almost missed what the girl was saying.

JAKE BROGAN

"What good does an alarm system do if it's off?" Jake and D initially exchanged a thumbs-up after they did the prelim canvass of the Morgan House. Good news: They'd discovered the notebook-sized alarm system touchscreen on the right-side nightstand in the master bedroom. Bad news: They had to wait for the search warrant before they did any serious digging. They'd asked Judge Gallagher for it, out of an abundance of caution, in case someone else might be living here, someone whose defense attorney would object to whatever was discovered in a warrantless search.

D, as always, argued they could cite "exigent circumstances" and go for it.

"Search now, get the warrant later, ya know? Makes me cray-cray," D complained as they checked through the obviously empty house. They'd found a wire mesh dog crate in a pantry off the kitchen. Popcorn curled up with her yellow ball the moment after she skittered inside, then closed her eyes and zonked out. They'd have to do something with her, at some point. But first, the suspect.

"What's more exigent than this?" D, waving his arms in the direction of everything, was in full argument mode as they left the dog behind. "What if the bad guy's hiding in the bathroom? Ready to leap out and nail us? And we're like, wait, don't shoot, we're getting a warrant."

They could legally check through the house, arguing their suspect might be hiding there. But fearing the fruit of the poisonous tree, they'd stick with a legally unassailable search.

So plain sight it was, starting in the master bedroom, the epicenter, Jake knew, of many crimes. D slouched in the doorway, still pouting, as Jake scoped it out. Window overlooking the backyard, pool. Looking down, he could see Kat standing over Avery Morgan's body. Two EMTs had arrived, ready to transport.

Without touching the windowsill, Jake peered outside. Left, forward, right, back to the left. Could any neighbors see inside this bedroom? Maybe with, say, a telescope, or binoculars from a line-of-sight upstairs room? Avery Morgan's windows were wide open, no screens, and the last of the afternoon's breeze, such as it was, whispered against the filmy curtains.

He shook his head, answering his own silent question. No. No one could see in, not through the lofty trees in full summer leaf, not past the architectural angles. The only house in direct eyeshot was that tan brownstone across the backyard. Jake took out his phone again, clicked off a close-up shot to show the proximity. Then a wider shot to show the context. Whoever lived in the brownstone would be able to look down and see into the Morgan backyard, he bet. They'd go there next. See if anyone was home. Maybe that's who'd called 911?

He heard the click of a phone keyboard. Turned. D was texting. Now?

"D? You with me here? Anything wrong? Anything I can do to help?"

"Knock yourself out," D said. "I don't wanna touch anything—you know, screw up our case. I'm good."

"What's with you?" Jake asked.

"What what?" D said.

"Whatever." D, still focused on his cell phone, would tell him whatever it was when and if he was ready. No time for that now. Flowered rug, antique-looking dresser, a colorful quilt thrown over a rumpled king-sized bed. Was that indication of a struggle? Or simply someone who didn't make the bed? Maybe the bed had nothing to do with anything. That was unlikely, Jake had to admit. Sex was always a key motive. Having it. Or not. Wanting it. Or not.

One nightstand, not both, was stacked with books. That suggested only one person lived here permanently. Behind the books, the controls of what Jake recognized as a hard-wired alarm system. That meant oversight, records, and, potentially, video. Their last case had been solved by surveillance video. Maybe that could happen again.

Jake eyed the glowing keypad. He could hear D texting, so he touched the alarm's green rectangle marked "Security." Up came the familiar numbers, arranged like a telephone dial, ready to take the occupant's secret code. Jake didn't need a secret code to understand that the system wasn't on.

"Ready to arm," Jake muttered. Now, of course, D was looking at him.

"How much she pay for that?" DeLuca pointed to the keypad, shaking his head. His other hand still held his cell phone. "Though if she's home, I guess, no reason for it to be on. And Pereira didn't mention an alarm going off when he arrived. Even though the bad guy must have come in over the fence."

True about the alarm. But the fence?

"How do you know that?" Jake did another survey of the room, just in case, snapping off more cell phone photos for himself. Crime Scene would get the formal ones, the ones they'd enter into evidence if there was ever a trial, but Jake always felt grounded by taking his own.

"How else?" DeLuca shrugged. "The fence is the only way in, except for the front door. Telling you, Harvard, I know who did it."

"Great." Jake pulled at the already-open closet door, putting the hem of his black T-shirt between his fingerprints and the polished brass doorknob. Maybe it *was* exigent. Maybe a killer *was* hiding in the closet. Wouldn't be the first time. "Then let's call the new supe. Who'd have thought this police thing would be so easy? Who're you pegging for this?"

"Husband, ex-husband, boyfriend, ex-boyfriend," DeLuca said. He'd pulled a white handkerchief from the back pocket of his jeans and was using it to open the top dresser drawer. "Drawer sticks."

"D," Jake said.

"You touched the alarm thing. You opened the closet," D said.

"It was already open."

"So was the drawer."

It wasn't. "You okay?"

"Why do you keep asking me that?" D was texting again.

Back to the closet. The door of which had, indeed, been open. Clothes, a rainbow of colors, hanging in no particular order, but not disturbed. What had Avery Morgan been wearing before that bathing suit? And where were those clothes? Hard to put a bathing suit on a wet person, Kat had said. Maybe she'd been swimming, and had a seizure. Or heart attack. Maybe it was an accident, not a homicide.

Or maybe someone had held her under. Figured it would *look* like an accident.

D was probably right about the boyfriend/husband thing. They'd tell you that in every homicide squad on the planet. Probably even other planets.

They walked through the house, careful about their own footprints on the carpet, watching for indications of a break-in, or a scuffle, or something not quite right, but nothing. Bathroom, nothing. Tub seemed dry, walls of the shower stall room temperature. Maybe it'd matter. Maybe not. Spare bedroom, nothing plain-sight. The house looked grander from the outside than it did inside—only two bedrooms, one bath upstairs. Careful not to touch the polished wood banister, they'd gone back downstairs one more time, looking for . . . well, they didn't know. Jake couldn't help but price the place, knew Jane would have been doing the same thing. Seven hundred thou? Eight? He shook his head. Real estate. This was theoretically a great location, The Reserve. Now someone had died in the pool. Which was hell on property values.

"See anything?" Jake asked as they scouted the living room. Textbooks, stacked on the coffee table. History of La Scala. Puccini Librettos. "She's either studying music or teaching it," Jake said.

"Was," DeLuca said.

"Nothing looks stolen, you think?"

D shrugged. "Nothing in plain sight, Harvard. But—"

"So there wasn't a struggle. She wasn't afraid." Jake took a last—for now—look around Avery Morgan's house. He and D had only four unsolved murders on their history. The impossible ones. A drive-by shooting, a clammed-up neighborhood, two innocents in the wrong place at the wrong time. If this was a homicide, it wasn't that.

"This is not a random," Jake went on. "An affluent woman, seems like, in a fancy house. There's a reason for it, and where there's a good reason, there's a good solution."

"You're profound," D said.

"You're an asshole."

"As you often say," D said. "But you'll miss me when I'm gone."

8

EDWARD TARRANT

Edward Tarrant savored this part of the day, the edge of twilight, when he could be alone. He watched his newest student assistant close the inner office door as she left—she was here only for the summer, another silly cipher who worked in the Adams Bay dean of students' office as a way to offset her tuition. As if a soon-to-be junior—from Connecticut, was she?—could provide any actual help beyond getting lunch and coffee and making sure he wasn't disturbed unnecessarily. Manderley, her ridiculous name was, could barely make a decision about which calls to put through to him, let alone suspect what some of them were about. So his life worked. As indeed, he felt, it should.

The mahogany door latched itself behind her. Finally he was by himself, his office humming with the purr of his computer and the low rumble of the air conditioner. The plush carpeting that he'd installed last year had stayed pristine, the carved dark wood bookshelves were polished, the leather covers of the books they held were dusted and more than presentable. None had been read recently. He was more of an Internet fan these days.

Manderley. She'd be gone in two weeks anyway, when the fall semester started and the new recruits arrived. Fine, he thought, clicking closed the online issue of *Campus Security*. It was preferable to have someone who skated through the job without asking any questions. Someone who was two steps smarter might be a problem. Manderley had no idea about anything. Edward had a crew of others who did. But that was all information coming in, not going out.

And now it was quiet, his e-mails answered, the day's fires extinguished, including the visit from those two television women, Jane Ryland and the other one. Unavoidable. It was clearly more prudent to agree to an interview than to protest. He was savvy enough not to be labeled (and ridiculed) as one of those "refused to be interviewed" chumps. He'd handled it. In the end, sadly, oh so sadly, he'd declined, for privacy reasons, to go on camera. Then ushered the two zealots out the door. They'd tried to pretend they were objective, even sympathetic. Bosh. He'd never met—never even heard of—a reporter he could trust. He'd handled them.

Just like he'd handled yammering students complaining about their unfair and life-ruining Cs. Or about the roommate who was too dumb or stoned or noisy or quiet or rich or poor or whatever. These were college kids, for God's sake. They had to learn that life *wasn't* fair. Unless their parents were ready to join the endowment list. Then lives could be made a little more fair.

Today he'd had a triumph. He licked his lip, took a last sip of coffee from his ceramic mug. "Adams Bay College ABC," its decal read. With a predictable-looking school crest and the motto *Cras principes committitur hodie.* "Tomorrow's leaders start today." He'd secretly decided it meant "Crass principles."

Anyway, the triumph. The parents of an obviously hyper-hormoned coed who were threatening to take their precious daughter's tale to the "real police"—he stopped his recollections again, his memory tripping over the hated description. Real police. *Please.* He ran a tight ship, as his father used to say. And his helpers provided another layer of protection. Real police. Ha. They should have such connections.

But back to savoring the triumph. Yes, that was worth remembering.

It was always the girls blaming the boys and the boys blaming the girls for their own drunken or drugged-up escapades. Everyone needed to take a little responsibility. He'd used his most convincing arguments this afternoon for Rochelle's family.

Peer pressure, he gently reminded them. Advised them that Rochelle's life would never be the same if word got out. That it might be in her best interests—he always put it very gently—to keep silent about what she alleged had happened. Otherwise they might face investigations, inquiries, questions. Trials.

He'd used the same words with parents so many times, but he always tried to make the ominous litany sound spontaneous. A gift of knowledgeable and heartfelt information from a person who only had the student's best interests at heart.

When he questioned, he'd put a catch in his voice, a hesitation, as if he were taking a chance, risking embarrassment. Had your daughter been . . . drinking? Using drugs? What was she wearing? *Maybe she'd be thought of as a liar.* Those words, he'd whisper.

He waited through a thick parental silence this very afternoon, wanting to see how the family would respond. Sometimes there was a high-pitched refusal, a firebrand mother demanding justice or a swaggering father demanding revenge. Those, he sent right along to the "real police." And whatever they did, they did. Adams Bay had a few of those unfortunate incidents. He shrugged. ABC had a . . . a *typical* record. It'd look strange if it were perfectly clean. If that was how the family wanted to work it, fine.

But often, after the silence, after some anguished consideration, sometimes after a hushed little heart-to-heart with the girl—today it was Rochelle—the families would agree.

You're so wise, he'd assure them, to say no more about what may have happened between your daughter and the young man. I'll take care of her. I'll watch out for her. She can always come to me.

How can we thank you? they'd ask. Often, by this time, they were crying. However you like, he would say. He never needed to say more than that.

Almost before the phone had settled in its cradle today, he'd contacted young William's family to make sure they understood the trouble their son might be in—if he, Edward Tarrrant, didn't protect him. And, like so many others, he knew they would likely be so immensely grateful, they'd make it worthwhile. Again, not that he ever specifically asked for any reward. Of course not. But often, relieved and appreciative families could not resist making his life a little more pleasant. He looked at the shiny Italian leather of his new shoes. Nice. Appropriate for a man of his stature. He'd certainly earned them.

It was a bit of a—how would one put it?—a bit of a tightrope walk.

He smiled as he stepped to the window of his office and looked out over Kenmore Square. He could see one corner of the big Citgo sign, turned off this summer to save energy. Sixteen stories below, the bustle of the Fenway crowd and the swirl of students from Adams Bay and monolithic Boston University. He always raised a derisive eyebrow at BU, the megaschool next door. Adams Bay was in its shadow, architecturally, academically, geographically.

But Edward was a big fish in the Adams Bay pond. He liked it that way, he decided, looking out over his domain. If BU called him? He'd say no.

Cars battled across the three-pronged intersection, choosing the direction of Fenway Park, or Brookline, or The Reserve. He imagined a conversation, yet again, where he'd turn down BU. Cordial, polite, even magnanimous. "Happy to be considered," he'd say. "But Adams Bay needs me. I'm their fireman. When there's a public relations fire, I put it out." He would chuckle, and they would agree, and with regret they'd hang up, knowing what they were missing. Knowing they should have chosen him in the first place. They'd had their chance.

His phone buzzed. He looked at his watch. Approaching seven. It wasn't a lawyer, he reassured himself, taking the three steps across the carpet to his desk. Lawyers didn't work this late. He swiveled into the leather chair, got to the receiver before the second ring.

"Yes?" He recognized the answering voice, pictured the young man, one of his "helpers," as the young man delivered his news. Edward's eyes blurred, his book-lined office going almost out of focus as he assessed what he was hearing.

WILLOW GALT

If only she'd been taking a nap. If only she'd been watching TV, Willow thought, or in the shower, or in a million other places, anyplace but her own bedroom looking out the window. But no. No matter how you tried to create your story, how you tried to smooth the center and tuck in the edges and square the corners, life always took its own messy turn. She paused on the second-floor landing, hearing the *bing-bong* of the door-bell again, followed, again, by the knocking. She took a few more reluc-tant steps down the carpeted stairway, and as she got closer to the entry hall, heard the voices, too.

"Boston Police," one called out. Not *Come out with your hands up*. Or *We have a warrant*.

"Yes?" She stepped to the threshold, opening the front door only partway. Tried to make her body language say, *Go away*. Tried to think—*Do I need a lawyer?* But how did you ask that without making it sound as if you already knew the answer?

"Boston Police," the taller one said. He was so tough-guy, with that leather jacket, all angles, way taller than the other one. Hair unruly over one eyebrow.

"I'm Detective Jake Brogan, ma'am," the shorter one, the handsome one, said. He smiled, so she figured he must be the good cop. He wore a leather jacket, too, even in August. Probably a gun under it, she thought. She had done nothing wrong, though. She'd made the conscientious choice. She simply couldn't talk much about anything other than that. Anything at all.

"We're investigating an incident in the neighborhood," he went on. "May we come in? We'd appreciate a few moments of your time."

She felt the weight of his scrutiny, the way he noticed her hair, and her neck and her fingernails, and her bare legs, her bare feet. He was try-ing to look over her shoulder, too, inside the house. Not doing a very good job of hiding his curiosity. Maybe on purpose?

"What happened?" Willow figured that's what someone would ask, and it was true that she wondered. She knew the result of "what happened." But not what led up to it. Not exactly.

"Maybe we could talk inside?" The detective looked back over his shoulder, and Willow saw two blue-and-gray police cars, looking blocky and alien, like uninvited visitors who'd blundered out of their territory. There were no lights anymore, no sirens. She and Dunc— Tom—had been assured The Reserve was private, with "neighborliness" essentially frowned upon. If you have to introduce yourself, they don't want to know you, she'd been told. Someone—her heart lurched, remembering who—had teased her, saying that was The Reserve's motto.

Now here were the police, asking to come in, and there was nothing she could do. Tom. She could feel her entire being call out to him. But he wouldn't be home in time to rescue her, not today.

"Is everything okay? Is there danger?" She used her moment of looking over the officer's shoulder to search for inquisitive neighbors, still strangers, already gossiping about why two police officers were at her door. The dominoes, Tom called them, and if the dominoes started falling . . . it might be a good thing their cardboard boxes weren't all unpacked yet. She honestly yearned for answers. But these two, doing their job, could not be expected to give them. "Officers? Is there danger?"

"I'm sure there's not, ma'am," the tall one said. "And it's 'Detectives.' I'm Paul DeLuca, this is Jake Brogan."

"Homicide," Brogan said. He stood on the brick front porch, next to the white ceramic pot of multicolored daisies. She'd planted them herself, insistently cheerful. A couple of green flies buzzed past. A door slammed somewhere.

Homicide?

"Homicide?" She said the word out loud. "Oh, I—of who?"

She saw the two exchange glances. Clearly they had some shorthand, and whatever they were communicating meant Willow had no more time to stall. She had to decide, right now, what she knew, and when, and why, and whether they knew she'd called 911, and there was no way to do that, there was no way to know what they knew, and no way to anticipate.

There were too many silences, all hers, and she could not decide how an innocent person would behave, even though she hadn't done anything wrong and it should be easy.

"Ma'am?" Detective DeLuca had taken a step closer.

She held her ground.

"Did you call nine-one-one?" Brogan asked.

"We're willing to talk out here on the front steps," DeLuca added.

"Though I'm sure the neighbors will be curious," Brogan said.

"So did you call nine-one-one?" DeLuca asked it this time, and there was no way out of it now.

"And what's your name, please?" Brogan said.

Willow had made her bed. And now she'd have to . . . whatever the rest of it was.

"I'm Willow Galt." She felt their words pushing her, felt them closing in and the air closing in and the relentlessness of the outside world, and how you could never be in control, not at all. She'd thought she'd done a good thing.

"Come in," she said. Now she'd have to handle it.

9

ISABEL RUSSO

Isabel gripped the phone's receiver, stared at her bare feet on the kitchen's linoleum floor, and wondered how it would feel to hang up. She watched Fish swim another lap in his fern-filled aquarium. A room in a room. And neither of them, not Fish, and not Isabel, could get out.

She curled her toes, then uncurled them, waiting. *Should I talk to Jane?* she asked Fish telepathically. Fish seemed to say yes, and Isabel had to agree. She'd worked up the nerve to call, she'd managed it, even though it was hard to breathe as she punched out the numbers, and she was so happy with herself for that. It was a real step. Isabel wasn't used to talking with real people anymore, she realized, and that was silly.

"You saw our query?" Jane's voice sounded nice enough, it did, and not pushy or aggressive. "Thanks so much, I appreciate it. Want to talk a bit now?"

"Yes," Isabel said. Fish's golden scales sparkled.

"Okay, great." Jane's voice seemed so kind. "How can I help you?"

This was the moment. The moment Isabel had not faced since . . . well, since she'd told her mother, and then Edward Tarrant, and then . . . no one else, like he'd instructed. Not ever, not ever. Ever ever. But this wasn't telling, not exactly.

She chewed the inside of one cheek, acknowledging that tiny bit of pain. She wished she could see Jane. She was pretty sure Jane was the reporter she'd watched on the *Boston Register*'s video website maybe . . . a year ago? Brownish hair, TV-looking. Thirty-something. Like, famous.

But she hadn't been on the news recently, had she? Though Isabel had not paid much attention to the news over the past months. Real life was exactly what she longed to avoid.

"Yes, I saw the thing online. And it said—you won't tell?" Isabel had to be sure the reporter's query said "confidential." If it wasn't, she was hanging up, no matter what.

"Confidential, absolutely," Jane said. And she explained who she was, and where she worked, and what they were doing.

Isabel listened. Balancing, deciding. Could she get through the story? Live through it again? That was a challenge. Because she couldn't really remember, even though she'd tried to make herself do it, again and again, because she figured it must still be there in her brain somewhere. It happened, *that* she was sure of, and if she kept trying to remember, she'd eventually succeed. Wouldn't that have to be true? Even if she had been drugged. Which she had to believe she was. Sometimes it felt like she remembered, but it was never more than a wisp, a fragrance, a sound—and then it would vanish.

But she was the victim. She *was*. And if she was ever going to heal, maybe now was the moment to begin. She had, what, eighty more years to live, maybe? Was she going to spend them all in fear, hiding? She wasn't brave enough, or confident enough, to, like, carry a mattress to graduation in protest, like that girl in New York a few years ago. But sometimes there was a moment that changed your life.

Well, of course, Fish was saying. *It's already happened to you.* But maybe this was another one, she retorted. Some part of her had died. But some of her hadn't. She took a deep breath, turned away from Fish.

"Are you there?" Jane's voice broke her reverie.

"I was at a party," Isabel began. She'd tell the barest of facts. Just to see. Just to try it out. "There was a cute guy. Really cute, and nice. We talked about opera, we're both in—anyway. And he offered me something to drink. Everyone was drinking, and I was, too, but that doesn't mean . . ."

"Of course not," Jane said. "Go on, okay?"

"I can't believe I'm saying this." Isabel heard the change in her own voice as she heard her story through Jane's ears. "It sounds so . . ."

"It sounds true," Jane told her.

". . . abysmally typical," Isabel finished her sentence.

"It sounds true," Jane said again. "That's exactly why you're, forgive me, but so helpful. *Because* it's so common."

"So, okay. I drank it, not that fast, even, because I went to the bathroom in between drinking it. And he had a drink, too." Should she say his name? No. "And then I . . . I don't remember. And I woke up, in a dorm room, alone, *his* room, and the sheets were all . . . and I was all . . ."

She felt her voice trail off again. Felt her brain trail off, too. Saw the light change in the room. It seemed to dim, and go smoky-sweet, and close and dark, and smell like—and her skin was all like, it was all . . .

"Are you okay?"

"Give me a minute," she said. She looked at the almost-invisible pale hair on her bare arms. Sticking straight up. She could feel each one. Every single hair.

"I know it's difficult," Jane said. "You're very brave. I'm here. Long as you want."

Isabel saw a glint out of the corner of her eye. Fish, her one solitary goldfish, swimming around and around. I'm like you, Fish, she thought. Trapped. And swimming, swimming, swimming. Swimming to nowhere.

"No one believed me, I guess," she told the reporter. "Because no one did anything about it. That I know of, that is. And the guy who . . ."

She paused. Watched Fish, watched the water, watched her crystal in the window. Closed her eyes, briefly. And started again.

"The guy who," she said, "well, he's, he's in class, and in school. He gets new cars, and girlfriends, and 'likes' all over the place. Mr. Cool. Mr. Leading Man. He's all happy, and nothing happened to him, and the school knows, I know they do, because I told them, and they all know and everyone knows and it's not fair, it's just not fair."

And it should be all *about* fair. Isabel, frowning, almost getting a headache now, had never thought about it any other way. She knew she was right. This wasn't fair. There were consequences, and there should be, but why should all of them come crashing down on *her?* She'd been turned into the haunted one, the terrified one, the little hiding rabbit whose life and career had been ruined.

"You're so articulate," Jane was saying. "I promise you all of this is confidential, absolutely, until you give the okay. But we'd love—very much—to tell your story. I hear in your voice that you're—"

"Concerned," Isabel said.

"Concerned," Jane repeated. "And—"

"Angry," Isabel said.

"Angry," Jane said. "And I know you're also concerned and angry for your sister students who may have been, or may yet be, in the same situation. You know . . ."

Isabel felt the muscles in her hand clutching her cell phone, its smooth plastic case pressing against her face. Jane's silence felt like the reporter was deciding whether to say something. *Relax,* Isabel told herself.

"You know," Jane went on, "it could happen to another student. Tomorrow. Tonight. You can be part of the solution. Go on camera, and tell us what happened. Could you simply consider it? Could we talk about it? I'm not trying to push you, and please take your time deciding. I'm only making sure you know the great extent to which you could make a life-changing difference."

Go on camera? Isabel pictured herself on TV, standing up straight, in makeup, and a nice outfit, and telling the story. She turned to the now-opaque screen of her own little television. And yes, at that very moment, she could envision it. Yes. *Yes.* She would tell.

She stood up as she decided, her heart racing and the weight of her body disappearing. She could fly. She could touch the sky. She could shut down her computer and leave Facebook alone and never see his hideous hideous face again except behind bars, and she'd laugh as the jury sentenced—

She sat down, heavy again, on the flowered cushion of her kitchen chair. No. Absolutely not. Not on television, not in court. And, in about one more second, not on the phone.

"Hello?" Jane's voice. "Are you still there?"

"I can't," she said. It was too silly, too stupid, even more life-ruining than her life was already ruined. What was she thinking, calling this number? She'd hang up, right now. But Jane seemed nice, and she couldn't be rude to her. "I'm so sorry," she began again. "I never should have called. I can't come to your studio. I don't like to go outside. I'm so sorry. I look terrible. I haven't slept for—months. And I . . ."

"Listen." Jane's voice was low, intimate, as if Isabel were the only person in the world. "You don't need to come to the studio—we'll come to you. It won't matter how you look, because we'll electronically darken your face. It's all in silhouette. No one will know who you are, but everyone will hear your warning. You could save the next victim. You could change someone's life."

Could that be true? But this woman, no matter how nice she seemed, only wanted her to be on TV. She had to remember that.

"Tell me your name again?" Jane asked. "And at what college did your—incident—take place?"

"Adams Bay," Isabel said. She stopped. Had she said too much? Did they keep track of the reports, would the school have her name, could Jane learn about her "incident" now? The reports couldn't be public. Could they? She whisked a stray lock of hair from her face. It fell back across her forehead. When was the last time she'd looked in a mirror? Very very good question. "I never said my name. And I don't want to tell you. I just can't."

"That's fine. Whatever you want," Jane replied. "But so we don't lose touch. Maybe just give me your number, and make up a name, okay? And here, take my cell phone number. Okay?"

"Okay," Isabel said, and wrote it down. She didn't have to use it.

"What you could tell us is so important," Jane was saying. "Maybe call me tomorrow morning? Either way?"

Fish had stopped swimming. He hovered, motionless. Waiting, just like she was. But tomorrow would come, and then another tomorrow, and she'd cross off the days, and soon there would be no more boxes, and she'd graduate and have to go out into the world. How would she face it? What if she ran into—him—on the street? Or somewhere? *What if he does this to someone else? Would that be my fault?*

"Tosca," she said, looking at her poster of the brooding Maria Callas, pale and misunderstood and vengeful and doomed. She'd sung some of that role, last semester, in a student show. "Call me Tosca."

Her mother would appreciate that. She almost smiled. The Puccini heroine who threw herself off a balcony. *I've felt like that,* she thought, as she stepped to the window and looked down fifteen stories to the sidewalk below.

10

JAKE BROGAN

No one liked to talk about a potential murder. Even the most innocent of innocents seemed to go guilty. They might not be guilty for the reason the police showed up, Jake mentally smiled as he considered it, but they were guilty of *something*. Or thought they were. Somehow the crucible of a police badge brought out the tells of a guilty conscience like invisible ink held over a hot light. This Willow Galt was Exhibit A.

She'd led them into her living room, walls so spotlessly white Jake could almost smell the new paint job, furniture so new Jake imagined the plastic packaging might have been removed moments earlier. Galt had cleared her throat, then patted her hair, must have glanced at the desk phone three times already, then pulled out a cell from her back pocket. She clattered it onto a polished glass coffee table, gestured them toward matching flowered wing chairs, then perched, fidgeting, on the edge of a matching couch. Throat, phone, hair, fidgets. Tells.

They'd given her the barest of outlines. An unattended death in the neighborhood, they were going door to door, alerted by a 911 call. So far, the woman had not answered any of their intentionally unthreatening questions with anything but questions of her own. Who? When? How?

Once inside, Jake knew, she'd be more likely to talk. Something about being confined face-to-face with the cops—even in your own home, or especially there—put the pressure on.

So Jake took his time settling in. D did, too. Silence often guilted an interviewee into talking, filling the space to wallpaper over their awkwardness. The silence trick was so clichéd, employed by every fictional TV cop, he didn't know why real-life interviewees didn't notice it. *You don't have to talk,* that was the lesson. But no one seemed to learn it. Lucky for Jake.

He sized up the scene. Home alone. But wearing a wedding ring. No animals, no signs of permanence. No family photos, or stacks of old magazines, or collections or clutter. Maybe that was hidden.

Willow Galt's feet were bare, her toes in the thick pile of the creamy carpet, her legs tanned, some kind of floaty drop-shouldered white top over flowered shorts. Kind of California, he thought, but hard to pinpoint women by their clothes. Jane wouldn't have worn this outfit, though. She was a black T-shirt and jeans person. He'd see her in a few hours, their dinner plans on hold until he and D made more headway in this case.

The woman finally stood again. "Water?" she asked. She picked up the cell phone, jammed it into her back pocket again. "I could go to the kitchen and . . ."

She glanced toward the back of the house, as if yearning to get away. The moment she moved out of earshot, she'd be on that phone, Jake predicted. Who would she call? Maybe they should let her do it.

"No, thanks." Jake took out his notebook, rifled through the blank pages as if he were looking for something important—another TV trick people never seemed to connect with real life—simply to let more seconds tick by.

"Me either." D waited, too. "Thanks."

She sank back onto the couch. Put the phone back on the table. Scratched her arm, so fiercely it left red welts, as if raising some anxiety to the surface.

"Are you sure we're not in danger?" she finally said.

"To be honest, Ms. Galt, I don't know." Jake tried to lower what Jane called his police barrier, hoping to engage this woman, and, he had to admit, upset her at the same time. Sometimes it was effective to reassure a person. Sometimes it was better to put them off balance.

"You called nine-one-one, on that cell, was it?" He pointed. "We are grateful for that, ma'am. Thank you. Can you tell us exactly what you saw?"

Jake had no idea if she'd really called, but from the upstairs bedroom she'd have a perfect view, even with all the trees. Plus, this was no time to dance around the topic. A person was dead, and he needed to find out why. Was this Willow Galt in danger? Well, good question. How would *they* know? That's why they were here.

"I didn't . . ."

Jake watched her body lean away from them.

D cleared his throat. "We can get the ping from the transmission towers, ma'am," he said.

"I know on TV they talk about those 'burner' phones." Jake tried to sound sympathetic. "The bad guys use them, right? The prepaid phones? So the TV cops can't trace them?"

D interrupted, picking up the cue. "But that's TV, ma'am. In real life, we're smarter than that."

Jake didn't exactly relish the playacting that police work sometimes entailed. But human nature was tricky, and human emotions, and reactions, and what it took to get a person to talk. To tell the truth. In reality, prepaid cell phones were a bane. Cops could trace the pings from cell towers, and could tell which was closest to where the call came from. But the person who activated the phone didn't have to give a real name, and as a result, no name was attached to the number. Even if the cops could find where the phone was purchased, the trail ended there. Bad guys could use those prepaid cells and the good guys would never find them. Via those phones, at least.

If Willow Galt used a prepaid, why? And why not simply say, Yes, I called?

"But I thought . . ." Her voice trailed off, and she examined her phone again. Her blouse shifted across her shoulders, the red welts on her arms like stripes under the loose white fabric. "If someone used a cell phone that . . ."

"It's TV," Jake said. *Bingo.* She'd called. She'd seen something. So why not say so? "Think they'd really make a phone we couldn't trace?"

She could google this the moment they left, but they weren't leaving quite yet.

D shook his head, agreeing with Jake, equally amused by the silly TV viewers. "I mean, an untraceable phone? That'd be, you know, illegal."

That was pushing it. But Jake could always pretend it was a joke, if it came to that. It was all about getting this Willow Galt to talk. Especially after this perplexing five minutes of hesitation and reticence. What was the deal with the phone?

She picked up her cell again. "Um . . ." she said.

"Okay, terrific. Is that what you used?" Jake nodded. *Gotcha.* "It doesn't matter, and I'm not sure why you're concerned. We don't care how you called, ma'am. We do care what you saw. What you heard. What was that? Exactly?"

Almost eight o'clock now, on this soft August evening. The Galt residence—where was the husband?—had no air conditioner running. Jake looked past an open dining room, two candlesticks, white candles with white wicks on a dark oval table, four chairs, then French sliding doors open to a backyard, floor-to-ceiling screens gridding the green lawn beyond.

"I heard the dog barking," she answered. "Barking and barking. Popcorn never barks, so I looked out the window."

Jake waited, not wanting to interrupt her thoughts. She and Avery Morgan were not strangers. How else would she know the dog's name?

"And I saw—" She stopped. Clasped her hands in her lap, the knuckles whitening against her tanned fingers, that gold band shining on her left hand. She shook her head, as if answering herself. "Nothing. Just the dog. And I guess a, a dark shape. In the pool. Is Avery—" She stopped again.

"Avery?" Jake asked, this time out loud.

"Morgan," she whispered. "Is she okay?"

Jake waited, and D waited. At some point, he'd tell her, but she didn't need to be told everything. It was their job to get information, not give it.

"The doctors are there now," Jake said. True enough.

"You're homicide," she said, her eyes widening. "And that means Avery's . . ."

"I'm sorry." Jake shook his head. "For your loss. Were you friends?"

"We—no. Acquaintances."

Willow Galt hadn't asked, "Was it Avery?" Hadn't asked, "Who was it?" Or even "Where is Avery now?" Which meant she knew who was in the pool. Which meant she wasn't telling everything. Another concept TV viewers never seemed to grasp. It was really difficult to lie. Difficult to remember what you were supposed to say, and what you already said.

"Will you show us where you looked out the window?" Jake stood. "We need to see that."

"Now." DeLuca stood as well.

Willow Galt's blonded hair swung partway across her face as she got up from the couch, and she looked at the floor, not at them. Another tell.

She pointed the end of her cell phone toward a stairway. "Upstairs," she said.

"Was Miss Morgan a good swimmer?" Jake asked as she led them up the carpeted stairs. No art on the walls. Again, fresh paint.

"Swimmer? I know she didn't like—oh." They arrived at the landing. Three doors, one, leading to a bedroom, open. She pointed, then turned back to them. DeLuca was a full head taller, and she looked up to ask. "Did she drown?"

"We don't know, ma'am," DeLuca said.

She blew out a breath and gestured them into the bedroom—white again, closet door closed, mirror over a white dresser, nothing on the top. Queen bed, Jake calculated, white bedspread, meticulously made. Opposite of Avery Morgan's rumpled Bohemian quilts and pillows. Three windows across the back wall.

Jake questioned the woman with a cock of his head. *Out those windows?*

"Yes," she said.

Jake looked out and down. He could see a bit of the pool, dark blue now in the quickening twilight. Didn't see the EMTs, nor Kat, just a square of dark water, a patch of concrete, and the leaves of a too-close maple.

"Oh," he said, turning back. He'd remembered another puzzle piece he needed—the property records. "That place has got a plaque on the front: 'The Morgan House.' She's Avery Morgan. Was it a family home, Ms. Galt? Did she own it?"

"I don't know who owned it," she said. "We just moved here." She gestured to a stack of brown cardboard boxes. "As you can see."

"From where?" DeLuca asked.

"I'm originally from Iowa," she said.

He and DeLuca let that evasion go. For now.

Jake clicked off a few photos, the through-the-looking-glass images of the ones already in his phone. DeLuca was scanning the room as Jake finished. Signaled him with half a shrug. Nothing. *In plain sight,* Jake could imagine him saying. In plain sight did not help much if you were trying to figure out what someone was thinking. Nothing was in plain sight then.

"We need to find a next of kin, I'm afraid," Jake said. "Can you help us?"

"Avery wasn't married." She looked at her own ring. "That I know of."

"So *you're* married, Ms. Galt?" DeLuca had also noticed the ring on her finger. "When will your husband be home? We'll need to talk to him, too."

Silence. Sometimes police work was flash-bang, with squealing tires, drawn weapons, gunshots, adrenaline. Sometimes, like now, it was patience. But always, it was human nature—the turn of a head, a scrap of paper, a wrong word. Everything Jake saw and heard got tucked away, and mentally filed and remembered, rearranged and rethought for every moment of every day until one puzzle piece snapped all those random moments into the picture someone was trying to prevent him from seeing.

It was too early for that now. He and D were still collecting pieces.

Unless Willow Galt suddenly confessed, or ratted out her bloodthirsty husband or the drug-crazed boyfriend, the hidden blackmail note, the long-lost homicidal sister from Dubuque. On TV maybe. But that wasn't going to happen here.

"Husband?" Willow Galt was saying.

Jake's turn to be silent. He could wait.

"Yes," she finally said. "Tom."

"We'll need to come back to talk with him, and you, again," DeLuca said.

"Are you okay, ma'am?" Jake asked. They'd been at the Galt house for half an hour now, and with every moment, it seemed, Willow Galt was closer to tears. D's inquiry about a husband had pushed them even closer. But maybe she was upset about the death.

"I'm okay," she whispered.

Fifteen minutes later, armed with Galt's phone number and a promise that she'd call them if she remembered anything else, they once again stood on her front stoop, the door closed and locked behind them.

"Why didn't she just tell us she'd called nine-one-one?" DeLuca asked. "She's a piece a work. Geez, it's already dark. I need coffee before we head back to the scene."

"We'll find out," Jake said. "She's hiding something, that's for sure." He took an appraising look across the neighborhood, interior lights now blinking on as the evening closed in. Streetlamps glowing. The famous Reserve maples rustling in the quiet. Two cop cars still stationed in front of the Morgan House. "The Galts are new to The Reserve, though. That's a good thing. Maybe they're not so invested in the local code of silence."

"Sure wish that dog could talk." DeLuca opened the cruiser door.

"Don't need a talking dog." Jake slid into the driver's seat. "If those surveillance cameras at the Morgan place were recording on other days, we should know exactly who came and went. And when."

"That's a start, I guess." DeLuca yanked on his seat belt.

Jake keyed the ignition. "And a hell of a lot more reliable than a talking dog."

11

JANE RYLAND

"She says we should call her Tosca. *Tosca*. Yeesh." Jane swiveled her chair to face Fiola. The producer had been poised to snap up any tidbit she could glean from Jane's end of the phone call. Now that Jane had hung up, Fiola leaned forward, reaching out as if to touch Jane's arm.

"Did she say exactly what happened? Think her story will work for us?"

Fiola had twisted her cascade of dark curls into a bun on top of her head, jabbed it through with a yellow pencil. Until today, their first "interview" day, Jane had never seen her in anything but jeans. She fussed with the hem of her black skirt, twin of Jane's but maybe two sizes smaller.

"Will she go on camera?" Fiola went on, opening her top desk drawer again, this time pulling out a brown paper package, ripping it open. She poured several M&M's into her hand, then popped a few of the multicolored chocolates into her mouth. "I knew the Facebook thing would work," she said, chewing. "Is she a student? Got to love it. M's? For dinner?"

"No, thanks." Tempting, sure, but her dinner would be with Jake. And soon. Ish. "And yeah, she's a student at Adams Bay."

Jane turned back to her pad, flipping the spiral-bound pages. She didn't like to take notes on her computer, even though it was more efficient. Callers could hear the typing, and it often made them nervous. Especially if they were counting on being confidential. Half the time Jane had trouble reading her own scrawly handwriting, but it was better than having a source clam up.

She blew out a breath as she read over her notes. Had she been too aggressive with poor Tosca? Convincing reluctant people to talk, persuading them to go on camera—that was one of the worst parts of TV reporting. Jane had never quite come to terms with arm-twisting persuasion. Sometimes with an indecisive possible interviewee, especially a crime victim, it crossed her mind to whisper, *You know, you don't have to talk to me. You don't have to go on camera. Just say no, and I'll go away.* But then Jane wouldn't get the story. And someone else might.

Plus, how could she know what was in their minds? Maybe they *wanted* to talk. Maybe it would be beneficial for them to talk. Maybe convincing was exactly what they needed.

First do no harm, that's what doctors promised. Part of a journalist's job was the opposite: to *do* harm. But only to the bad guys. When it came to the good guys? Especially victims? All Jane could do was be careful with people's fragile lives.

"Tosca, huh?" Fiola took out a shiny black compact, checked her teeth, patted a foam puff across her nose, frowned into the tiny mirror. "Got to love that state of mind. A diva. And dead."

"Poor thing." Jane thought about the other person she'd tried to convince to go on camera today. "Did our Adams Bay guy say anything about—"

"Tarrant didn't say anything worthwhile about anything." Fiola snapped her compact closed, waved a dismissive hand. "He was a total jerk."

True, Jane remembered. "Mr. Big. Couldn't wait to get us out of there. Can you imagine being a college student who'd been assaulted? Or drugged? Trying to tell him about what happened at some vodka-fueled frat party?"

She shook her head, not waiting for Fiola to answer. "There has to be someone else at the college. Like . . . a rape counselor. Or whatever they'd call it. I think the feds require it now, under the Title Nine law."

Jane punched up the Internet, talking while she clicked at her keyboard. "That's who we should talk to. That's who's gonna know." Jane loved this part, when she got to learn the rules, to pull open the investigative doors, see what went on behind them. If you were going to discover where the system was broken, first you had to know how it was supposed to work.

She turned back to Fiola, now arranging her hair in the mirror she'd thumbtacked, precariously, to their wall. "I'll find out."

Jane looked at her notes again, thinking about "Tosca" and where she was, and what she said had happened to her. Why would she choose that particular name, a woman doomed by love and revenge? "She might call me tomorrow," she said. "Cross your fingers."

"Go on camera?" Satisfied with her hair, Fiola turned from the mirror. "You think?"

"Fifty-fifty." Jane wobbled a maybe hand at her. "But listen, where's Adams Bay's procedure for handling these things? Do you have their handbook, or whatever? Seems like the school didn't support her, and she's pretty clear the guy was never punished or anything. Oh." Jane held up one finger, then turned to her computer again. "The guy. She said he's on Facebook."

"Find him. We'll nail him." Fiola pointed at Jane's monitor. "Did she say his name?"

"No. But we couldn't say his name and not hers." Jane shook her head. "That'd be so unfair."

"*We're* not saying it," Fiola said, waving her off. "*She'd* be saying it. Tosca. Not us."

"That's—" *A lawsuit waiting to happen*, Jane didn't say. "Anyway. She didn't give me any way to find him," Jane lied. Not a chance she was naming a guy without . . . well, without a criminal conviction. She'd read that *Rolling Stone* disaster a few years ago. She'd read about Duke. And the kid at UMass Amherst who said his life was ruined by a false accusation.

She was convinced Tosca was telling the truth. Pretty convinced. But if Tosca didn't want to show *her* face, how could they show his? She and

Fiola could cross the fairness bridge later, though. No need to argue about identifying hypothetical student rapists. Now, at least.

"Hey, you two." Marsh Tyson, a cell phone in each hand, took up all the space in their office doorway. Jacket off, pale blue oxford shirt with white collar, yellow tie. "Burning the midnight oil?"

Jane smiled, trying to be optimistic. It was hardly ever a good thing if the news director wanted you. And it was never a good thing if the news director was at your door. It could mean an unpleasant assignment. Bad news. A lawsuit. Maybe all of the above. Harder to say no—or make up an excuse—when the boss was looking right at you.

"Hey, Marsh," Jane said. "Just working on our—"

"It's going great," Fiola interrupted. "We've got an Adams Bay student, a sexual assault victim, who'll talk on camera about what happened to her."

Jane felt her eyes widen.

"Jane's clinching it, tomorrow. But we are so rocking this," Fiola chirped.

Very high degree of chutzpah, for Fiola to take the credit for Jane's success, yet still make it Jane's fault if it fell through. Jane was glad this day was almost over. She hoped Jake wouldn't be too late, whatever he was doing. His text hadn't specified.

"Terrific," Marsh said. "But, Jane." He held up one of his cell phones. "Just got a call from the DA's office. ADA named Frank McCusker?"

"Yeah," Jane drew out her answer.

"You witness some kind of car accident?" he asked. "They want you over there, like, now."

"It was a—"

Marsh held up both phones, not letting her finish. " 'Parently you told them about it. Good for you. Said you had to talk to me first. Good for you. However, you *didn't* talk to me. Not so good."

"Well, just not yet, you know? Because I, we . . ." Should she have immediately gone to his office? Right then? ". . . I figured tomorrow would be fine."

"Well, the DA's office didn't think it was so fine. Neither did Barbara Dougan, or Allan Migdall."

The station's lawyer, the station's owner. "You talked to them? Tonight?"

"*I* figured tomorrow was too late," the news director said. "So did they. So off you go. McCusker's waiting for you at the DA's office." He stashed a phone into one pants pocket, pulled out a yellow piece of paper from the other. "Here's a cab voucher. Go."

"Is Barb Dougan coming with me?" Jane stood, clicked off her computer, grabbed her tote bag. "I'd feel better with a lawyer."

"Why would you need a lawyer? You do something wrong?" Marsh gave her a look. "Ha ha. Just go."

"And tell them everything? I mean, is it our place, as reporters? It feels like we're crossing a line, Marsh." Jane looked at Fiola, saw she was on her own. "What happens when we *don't* want to tell them something? Then they can say, *How about that other time, when Ryland came to our office? Why is there suddenly a problem?* See what I mean? What if they want me to testify in court? I mean, there's no way I'm going to do that."

"What's the big whoop?" Marsh put both palms up, stopping her words from reaching him. "We help them, maybe they'll help us next time there's a big story."

"But they won't. And anyway, that's not how it's supposed to work." Jane was fighting this losing battle without Fiola's help. But she'd go down swinging. "We do our jobs. They do theirs. Separately. Nobody 'helps' anybody. Plus, I won't get there till, like, eight-thirty."

"That's exactly when they expect you. And, Jane? Your job, right now, is to get over there and tell them what you saw. *Capisce?*" He turned away from her, then pivoted back. Held up a cell. "Call if you need me."

12

EDWARD TARRANT

"Avery Morgan? You sure?" Edward Tarrant waved the student who'd just arrived at his office to a seat in the not-quite-comfortable chair across from his desk. Frowned as he closed the door again. Frowned as Trey Welliver stumbled over the fringed edge of the oriental rug. At least he'd taken off his damn Sox cap.

Edward tried to remember to be cordial. After all, he relied on his helpers, kids like Trey who had some debts to pay.

"You sure?" he asked again. "Dead? In the pool?"

"Yeah. I mean, yes, sir." Trey looked a little green around the eyes, and his plaid shirt was coming untucked from one side of his jeans.

"How'd you hear?"

"You know. I was riding my bike, saw the cop cars. Ambulance. Detective car. I know where she, you know. Lives. Uh, lived. The Reserve."

"I'm well aware." Edward stood, pushing back his wheeled chair and coming around to the front of his desk. He crossed his arms, his fingers drumming his starch-stiffened shirtsleeves. "Did they say she was killed? Avery Morgan? What, exactly, did they say?"

"Say? There's no say. I just heard them talking. But there was a homicide cop, maybe two. One cop was even wet. Then I came here. You said tell you first."

"Correct." Edward jabbed one finger at the kid, emphasizing. "Good boy."

This was bad news, however. Very very bad. Avery Morgan, brilliant,

gorgeous, high-strung. Much pursued by drama schools across the country that were much bigger and admittedly more prestigious than little
Adams Bay. But they'd—*he'd*—won her over with the perks. And now she
was dead? Why? He had to figure out why before someone else did, and
before the story got out of control. Homicide cops meant murder, no
question of that. Which torpedoed another thought into the conversation.

"Press?"

"Huh?"

"Any press? Reporters? Anyone with a camera? Were they there? At
her house?"

"Um. Like I told you, I came here."

Trey's eyes didn't seem to be focusing, but what else was new.

Edward scratched at an ear, trying to remember it was an advantage
Trey had shown up, and not an annoyance. Trey's job, like the others',
was to keep Edward in the loop and allow him to get ahead of the curve. He
had to make a move, and now. He gestured to Trey. *Stay there.*

"Whatever," Trey said. The kid pulled out a cell phone.

"You expecting a call?" Another fire to put out. "You know they
can—" *Trace those things,* he didn't say. No need to spook the kid. Or
educate him. "Don't make any calls. And no texting. Just sit there while
I think."

Edward put a hand on his desk phone. His first instinct was to call
Avery, pretending he didn't know anything, see who answered. He took
his hand away. That might engender more questions than it answered.
Why was he calling? they'd ask. Why just then?

Plus, her death. Her *death*? He touched his fingertips to the sleek
wood of his desktop, trying to ground himself. No need to panic. Maybe
it was an accident, a fall, a heart attack. Like the kid said, in the pool. He
knew that pool behind the Morgan House. Homicide cops, though. That
meant real cops—*ah*—would be descending on the school any moment
now, and his office could be their first stop. At least now he could be
prepared.

How much time did he have to make this all work? He put out fires. And this was one hell of a fire. He needed to calculate the potential damage. He needed to check with campus police, see if they knew anything. Then shut them up.

He also needed time. There wouldn't be much of it.

Reaching under his desk, he clicked a hidden metal lever, eased open the narrow top drawer. Was about to pull out a—but wait. Not in front of the kid.

"Thanks, Trey, you can go." He tried to make his smile look genuine. "And see? This is exactly what I was talking about. No one knows you're here, no one will ever know. Just as I promised. Correct? It's no skin off your nose to tell me this."

Trey actually touched his nose.

"It's an expression," Edward went on. "Same as 'I'll scratch your back if' . . . never mind. I'll take it from here. And as always, this chat never happened. Right?"

"Right." Trey looked more confused than ever as he backed toward the office door.

Probably smoking weed again, Edward thought, trying to keep his patience. Or whatever they called marijuana this week. He raised both eyebrows, communicating, *If there's nothing else, get the hell out.*

As the door clicked closed behind Trey, Edward went back to the drawer. He eased out a thin book–sized square of wood, with rows of tiny twist-in metal hooks, each labeled with a narrow white numbered sticker, each holding an unlabeled brass key. He selected the one to 1606. Slid his "key board" back into the drawer, back into its secured place.

Down the empty hallway—no one. Around the corner—no one. Nothing but the dim incandescent bulbs spotting the tweedy carpet and a row of closed wooden doors, some with embossed slide-in nameplates, some with empty brass slots. He stopped outside 1606, listening for footsteps or the crank of the elevator. Nothing.

The brass holder of 1606 displayed the nameplate: Avery Morgan, Drama Department, Visiting Adjunct. He'd teased, "We should add a star," when he'd shown her the new office. "Lovely," she'd trilled. Before she realized he was kidding.

In the silence of the empty corridor, he took out the key and opened the door. Paused. Listened half a second. Nothing. Eased around the doorway and into Avery's office. Closed the door again and calculated his timing. Security would have to call him first, before anyone came up here. Then it'd take at least five minutes for whoever it was to sign in with the security guard. Then the guard would call the super to get the keys to Avery's office. But the super wasn't around, so the guard would call Tarrant's cell again. At that point, he could scuttle back to his office. Pretend he'd never left. The super had the only official keys, so that'd delay things even further. And if the cops wanted to see inside Avery's office, wouldn't they need a warrant? Another delay. He had time. But not much.

He tucked the contraband brass key into his pocket. Far as the college knew, *his* keys did not exist. But a firefighter like Edward needed keys. Some decisions simply had to be made.

He scanned Avery's shadowy office, the evening light coming through the open blinds allowing him to see as much as he needed to right now. Movie posters on the walls. Floor-to-ceiling bookcase, one side books, the other boxes of videocassettes. Which was—he shook his head. Problematic. Where could you play videocassettes these days? Maybe across the street at the journalism school. But there was no way he could look through tapes or tape boxes, not now.

A calendar was what he needed. Avery's calendar. Remembering not to touch anything—although, wait. What would it matter? You couldn't tell how long a fingerprint had been there. This was his school, after all, and Avery his colleague. And friend. *Hell with it,* he thought. *I can touch whatever I want.* He looked at his watch. But—quickly.

He flipped through the piles of papers on Avery's desk, mostly ripped-out magazine articles. No way to read them all now, or assess them. He paused for an instant, distracted by the fragrance of her flowery perfume, the scent of roses, perhaps captured in the tweedy upholstery of her chair or clinging to the crimson silk scarf draped over its ivory cushions. He shook off the memories, focused on the present. She was gone.

He focused on her desktop computer, the monitor sleeping and the screen black.

A white plastic mouse sat on a black foam mouse pad that read "Silver Screen," with a photo of . . . He squinted, identifying. Rosalind Russell. *Focus*, he told himself.

He jiggled the mouse. The screen saver came up, the roaring MGM lion. He extended his right forefinger. I'll wipe the keyboard clean, he thought. What was her password? He touched his finger to the keys: "one two three four five."

Incorrect.

Typed "Avery." Incorrect. "Silver screen." Wrong.

This was a loser of an idea. It would be undeniably suspicious if he were found in here. He stopped, assessing. Was there anything here that could tell him something? Anything that would incriminate him? He was haunted by those rows of videotapes, but there was no way to deal with them, unless he could somehow erase them all.

He could almost hear the time ticking by, could almost hear his office phone ringing. Although office hours were over, so if he wasn't there, he wasn't there. He pulled his cell from his pocket. If it rang, he could simply ignore it. Or answer. And say?

He shook his head, dismissing his hobgoblins. He didn't need to come up with excuses—he needed to come up with answers. Because the questions were already relentless. And he wouldn't be the only one asking them.

Will it be a black mark on the school? Who's going to deal with the press? With the students? Did the presence of homicide cops mean she'd been murdered? If so, who the hell killed her? Why? And where was the killer now?

He needed reassurance there was nothing untoward in Avery's office. If such a thing existed, he needed to find it before anyone else did, then decide what to do about it. His one opportunity was now.

He thought of all the occasions he'd visited the Morgan House, pre-Avery and after the college rented it to her.

And then she moved in, lock, stock, and—

He smiled. Extended his forefinger again. He tapped the seven letters, confident as a concert pianist. "POPCORN."

The Adams Bay seal appeared. Avery Morgan's computer was open.

13

JANE RYLAND

Jake hadn't answered her text.

Jane could only hope he'd eventually get it and understand she would be even later than he was. She grabbed the brass handle on the heavy glass door to the DA's office, yanked it open. Her stomach was rumbling in earnest now. She always kept food with her, almonds usually, since reporters could never know when they'd be starving, but she'd left them in her other tote bag. Fiola had the right idea about food stashes, at least. Though in a less healthful way.

The stuffy main hallway of One Pemberton Square was in half-light, doors closed. A row of framed drawings of stern-looking men, all high-collared and mustached, some with pipes, lined the wallpapered hall to room 412D. As she passed, the portraits changed to photos, men with shorter hair and Windsor-knotted ties, then, evoking Jane's thumbs-up salute, to a woman in a floppy-bowed blouse, followed by a darker–skinned woman with an artfully arranged scarf. The last photo on the wall showed a pale woman with a pageboy, careful makeup, and a pin-striped suit. Krista Santora, the current DA.

The hallway gallery had plenty of room for more photos. If Santora screwed up, or fell out of favor, or lost the next election, another framed face would take her place. Balancing law and order with power was always in the forefront for DAs. Keeping the public happy often meant putting miscreants away. Even if sometimes they were not exactly guilty.

"Jane!"

The voice came from behind a just-opening door, a few steps farther down the hallway. A pin-spot light hit McCusker—in his signature bespoke suit, expensive for a taxpayer-salaried employee.

"Thank you so much for coming this late. I'm sure you had other plans."

Anything but being here, Jane thought.

"No problem," she said.

Room 412D, institutional neutral with predictable furniture. Red accordion files lined the wall to the left of McCusker's desk, with cardboard boxes along the right. He pointed her to a ladder-back chair, its beige woven seat frayed and sagging.

"Apologize for the, uh, digs," McCusker said. "We use what we're given—taxpayer dollars and all." His phone buzzed, and he shrugged, apologizing. "Gotta take this."

"No problem," Jane said again. *Let's get this over with,* she thought.

Truth was, the hard line between journalism and law enforcement was a dilemma some couldn't understand. Both professions sought justice, but they required separate—sometimes opposite—ways of achieving it. Once a journalist took sides in a battle, or abandoned objectivity, it was impossible to be neutral again. That's what Jane thought, at least. Her boss clearly didn't.

McCusker was still on the phone, scowling, talking in monosyllabic code: yes, no, fine. "That's what I'm attempting to find out," he said. He flickered a glance at her.

She pretended to be looking out the open window. Across Pemberton Square, a few lights illuminated a row of windows in the limestone façade of the newish Superior Court. The night had darkened, finally, and the end of August had that tender feel of a closing, a change in the works, even though the breeze that riffled into the room still held the unmistakable warmth of a New England summer night.

She felt like a bug on a pin, caught and spiked and without any choice. Sometimes you made a debatable decision, took one little step over the line, and it seemed fine. Then, the next line appeared, a little more dim, and the next one even more so, and the next moment you were somewhere you couldn't believe you'd ever be.

She sighed. Maybe she just had low blood sugar.

The phone receiver rattled back into its port. McCusker cleared his throat, adjusted his yellow-striped tie, and looked at her across his desk, smiling. "Jane?"

"Right here." She tried to put a fraction of an edge in her voice, beyond reproach, but enough to telegraph she wasn't going to be a doormat.

"Good job on the fender-bender license number," he said. "We grabbed video from a couple of surveillance cameras in the area, but it's all black-and-white, and fuzzy as hell. So all we could get was that the car was light-colored and a sense that it was full-sized. Car was big. The delivery van's worse off than it seemed. The driver's okay, but the owner is pissed. Our focus is that it's a hit-and-run. Santora's hard-line about that, even though the property damage is not huge. Sets a precedent."

"Uh-huh," Jane said. So far, so good.

"What color was the car you saw?"

"Silver," Jane said.

"Make?"

"Cadillac." It was on the surveillance tape. They could figure that out, Jane knew, no matter how fuzzy it was.

"Yeah." McCusker nodded. "That's what we have, too. And a silver Caddy matches the license number you gave us. Which also gives us the driver. Well, the owner. That's where we are now."

"Great." She felt herself sitting up taller, optimism straightening her spine. Maybe this encounter wouldn't be so bad. "Another case successfully closed."

And then, before she'd even mentally formed it, the question came out. "Who was it, anyway? The driver. Where's he now? You charge him?"

"Well," the ADA said. "Thing is. The owner insists he wasn't driving. That he was out of town."

"Really?" Oh, right, Jane thought. As convincing as *I just had two beers, officer. I didn't see the speed limit signs. I thought I was in the turn lane.* That old story.

"That old story, right?" McCusker read her mind. "And that's why we need you to testify."

"Tes—?"

"—ti-fy," McCusker finished the word, nodding. "In court. Tomorrow."

"No!" She stood, fists on hips, and then sat down again. Put up both hands, conciliatory. She'd kind of yelped that *no*. "I mean . . ."

She paused, thinking about the instructions from Marsh Tyson. She'd help McCusker, because she'd agreed, reluctantly, to do that. But testifying was a different deal. Testifying was public. It would put her in a completely indefensible position. It would be precedent-setting for other journalists, too. She'd be held up as the Judas goat, the one who caved, even if it was her station's idea. Yes, she was still gun-shy over being unfairly fired, even though that was four years ago, and yes, possibly she was overreacting.

But no, she wasn't. Working reporters didn't testify in court. She'd agreed to help Frank McCusker, but she'd never agreed to sit in a witness box and point the finger at someone. She yearned for the station's lawyer, for anyone, to help argue her out of this. But she was on her own.

"Maybe we can avoid that," she said, trying to be part of the solution. "Why don't I tell you right now what the driver looked like? That's what my news director told me to do. I don't like it, not at all. But if I'm required to, I can describe him. To you. Not in court. He was—"

"No. Don't tell me." McCusker put up both palms, came out from behind his desk, shaking his head. "Really. Don't. The judge has ordered what's called a nonsuggestive identification hearing. That means you come to court, our suspect will be in the audience, or not, and you point him out. If you see him. Remember, he or she might not be there."

Middle-aged, Caucasian, widow's peak, gray hair, pointy cheekbones, thin lips, clean-shaven. She mentally recited the description, the face in her head as clear as it was the moment she'd seen the guy. She'd recognize him anywhere, no problem. But this seemed . . .

"Weird," she said.

"Not really." McCusker laced his fingers together, touched them to his chin, then pointed two forefingers at her. "It's all about the gaps in eyewitness identification. Eyewitness mistakes are the greatest contributing factor to wrongful convictions. True fact. People really think they know what they've seen. But so many studies, and overturned verdicts, prove they get it wrong. And if we showed you photos, like a typical lineup? You'd think it must be one of them, and your memory would change. Irrevocably. We now understand that's how people's brains work, so we can't have you subject to any kind of suggestion."

"Yeah, yeah, I've seen those studies," Jane said. The 60 Minutes experiments where the "crazy person" comes running into the classroom, and after he leaves, the descriptions of him are all over the map. And a couple years ago, a Boston reporter had revealed a case where cops used a phony suspect photo in a lineup to railroad an innocent person. But this was different. Completely different. "But I—I mean, I'm sure I'd recognize him."

"I believe you. That's why we need you. There's a defense attorney who's demanding the identification be unassailable. So—that's how it's done. Open court, face-to-face. Or, as I said, maybe not. Depending. It'll take only a few minutes."

"But why does it have to be in court?" She had to push harder. "Can't you show me a photo array?"

McCusker shook his head. "Wish I could. But defense attorney wants the nonsuggestive, and the judge ruled in his favor."

From somewhere down the hall came the Doppler hum of a vacuum cleaner. McCusker looked at her, his chest rising and falling, waiting for her response. Calculating his next move. Like a reporter trying to convince someone to talk, Jane realized. And now she was in the opposite role, the convincee.

"Let me just say . . ." McCusker's voice had a quiet but persuasive tone Jane recognized. Again, she'd used it herself. He sat on the edge of his desk, planted his feet. The toes of his wingtips almost touched Jane's black flats, and she pulled them away. "If you don't testify? He'll get away.

There'll be nothing we can do. The owner says it wasn't him driving. We think it was. You're the only one who can break the impasse."

"But it's only a—"

"There's no 'only a,' Jane. There's the law, and there's ignoring it. My job is to make sure reckless and dangerous drivers don't try to use the system to get away with doing damage and running away. You are all that stands between order and chaos. You saw him. You were honest and honorable enough to tell us that. Now you have to decide whether you are honorable enough to tell the court. To really make a difference."

McCusker's desk phone rang. Jane flinched, then looked at it with a flash of hope. Maybe it was a reprieve. Maybe something else had happened. Maybe she was off the hook.

McCusker ignored the phone.

"Jane?"

"What if I just said no?"

"Are you saying no?"

Could she even say no? People said no to her all the time, people like Tosca. And the Adams Bay guy this afternoon. What was Jane's response? To ratchet up the pressure. She began to grasp why people always trotted out the reporter's most hated excuse: "I don't want to get involved." Because talking made you involved.

But truth be told, she *was* involved. She couldn't "un-know" something that she'd admitted—volunteered!—she knew.

"That means he saw you, too," Fiola had reminded her. Now that was the least of it. If she pointed out this guy in open court, everyone on the planet, including the lawbreaking, scene-leaving, Cadillac-driving bad guy, would know who was identifying him. Jane Ryland, public figure, Channel 2 reporter. Jane Ryland, easy to find.

She sighed, wondering what she'd decide if she had the whole day to do over.

"Whatever," Jane said, giving in. But what was she giving *up*? "Tell me when and where."

14

JAKE BROGAN

"This is a sucky idea." DeLuca's protest followed Jake as the two of them turned onto yet another flagstone walkway, headed to yet another Reserve brownstone. "We got nothing, and we're gonna continue to get nothing."

Jake ignored his whining. They'd done well on this canvass, so DeLuca's complaint was not only annoying, it was unjustified. It wasn't always necessary to do a formal sit-down with a person, especially those who insisted they didn't know anything. But sometimes human nature, that need to show how smart we are, Jake reflected now, provided him with one tidbit, one morsel, offered up to prove the speaker wasn't completely out of the loop. Jake would put all those tidbits together, and up would come a blue-plate special of information.

Clearly he was hungry.

But Jake's point had been proved at each brownstone this evening. The wary but infinitely polite residents would first shake their heads, no, they hadn't seen anything. Or heard anything. And no, they really had nothing more to say. But when Jake pushed, just a bit, they unwittingly added their sound bites. No, they didn't really know Avery Morgan—but wasn't she a screenwriter from California? one asked. She had admirers, obviously, another said.

"Yes, so we've heard," Jake lied to the silver-haired woman in bright blue capris. His mother's age. "Can you point us in the right direction regarding the admirers?"

"Oh, dear no. Who knows about kids these days," the woman had said.

Kids, Jake thought. College kids? Came to see Avery?

"Did she have visitors from, uh, Boston University?" Jake asked at the next door, questioning a tight-faced woman in a flowered dress. She kept one hand on the doorjamb as she used a tanned leg to prevent a persistent tabby from escaping.

"BU? She taught at Adams Bay, didn't she?" The cat made a dash, orange-striped tail swiping, but the woman was faster. Scooped up the thing, which writhed and mewled. *Popcorn,* Jake thought. They'd have to do something about the dog.

"Did she?" Jake said. "Teach at Adams Bay?"

"I'm busy now," the cat person said. "I'm sure you can call the school."

"People come and go," said the guy with the pipe. *Who still smoked a pipe?* "All hours."

"Her Adams Bay students, you mean?" Jake asked. So Avery had visitors. They'd be on the home security video. If there *was* a home security video. "When? I mean, what times of day? Or was it at night?"

"We don't really watch." The man shook his head, puffed. "It's The Reserve."

One step at a time, Jake thought. So. Avery Morgan was a teacher at Adams Bay, which Officer Pereira had probably already discovered. But Jake and D now knew her students, or someone's students, had come to visit at all hours. They also knew Morgan's snooty neighbors might pretend to keep themselves hidden, but in reality very little got by them.

Jake turned the flagstone corner, headed to maybe the tenth place on the block. Streetlights were full-on now, the August moon a celestial peach. Yeah. Hungry.

"No one likes to answer the door in the middle of the night," DeLuca persisted, dragging his feet, voice pouty as a teenager's. "Much less talk to the cops."

"There's a possible homicide in their neighborhood, and it's like, eight-thirty," Jake said. "You got someplace to be?"

"We're on OT now," D said. "Unauthorized. Supe Kearney will freak." He pulled out his cell, texting as he talked. "I like the bucks as much as anyone. But I have a life. Dinner plans. Don't you?"

Jake did, happily, and he'd text Jane as soon as he finished with this door knock. D was right about the OT. Unlikely they'd catch a fleeing bad guy tonight, Jake had to admit, and even homicide detectives hungry for answers didn't—couldn't—work every minute of every day. Crime Scene was still at the Morgan House. They'd give that a good-night look before they called it a day. Start again tomorrow.

So far, no search warrant. All the personal stuff would have to wait. He might be off the clock, but he wouldn't forget about Avery Morgan. It was that personal stuff that got him. The books. Her garden. The little dog, snippy as the thing was, his crate broke Jake's heart. Avery's bed, somehow. Her home, unprepared for her absence, haunted him. She was gone, now, forever. But his job made him her champion. He wouldn't let her down. The clues to her death were there. Somewhere.

"One more house," Jake said.

EDWARD TARRANT

The footsteps were coming closer.

The corridor outside his office had been empty as he sneaked down to Avery's. All the other doors in the hall had been closed, no telltale strip of light coming from beneath any of them. If Mack was on his security rounds, he might or might not stop and look into this room—the room Edward had unlocked with a key he wasn't supposed to have. But what if the footsteps weren't Mack's?

Edward snatched at Avery's mouse, clicked the screen to black and the room to darkness. Had the monitor been on when he came in? He let his shoulders sag, hearing another footstep. The carpeting muffled the weight of it, so no way to know if it was Mack's heavy work boots or a student's rubber-soled running shoes. His eyes narrowed as he rewound the mental video of his actions. Had he touched anything?

And then, in the murky silence, surrounded by lofty bookcases and shapeless unfamiliarities and suspended time, he realized it didn't matter. No one but Avery knew how she'd left her office. And she certainly wasn't telling.

Now? Only two options. Hide, or stand his ground behind her desk. Hiding was absurd—he'd be caught, and the very fact he attempted it would strand him on shaky ground. The hallway footsteps were coming closer, the tread deliberate. Purposeful. But to what purpose?

If the door opened . . .

He'd left it closed but unlocked, assuming he'd be the only one to enter her office. If the door opened, letting in the light, he'd be cordial. Kind, with a tinge of amusement. He'd smile and say he was about to turn on the lights, that Avery had sent him on an errand for a forgotten . . . He thought back, envisioning how the room had looked when he'd entered. His fingers landed on the thin cloth on the back of the desk chair, unseeing. *Scarf.* Exactly. And she'd been . . . how would he put it? Embarrassed. To admit she'd left her door unlocked. Which, for flower-child-impulsive Avery, would be entirely plausible. Calling him, too. They'd been more than collegial. Everyone knew that. Avery was only in residence here because of Edward Tarrant.

Or maybe . . . and yes, here was the answer. His lungs filled again. He could breathe. In truth, Mack, or whoever it was, wouldn't bat an eye. He was Edward Tarrant, after all. Everyone knew who he was. Everyone understood his stature and access. How dare they question him? He had a right to be here.

He moved out of the sight line of the windowed doorway anyway. If the hallway person was simply headed to the elevator and happened to glance this way, no need to telegraph that someone was inside. His body clenched as he watched for an approaching shadow on the smoky glass. At least he'd see them first.

His ears strained at the silence, and he felt his eyes close. The darkness was unchanged. His eyes flew open.

What if it was the police?

The bottom dropped out of his gut. He'd been in such a control-freak panic—that's what Avery had always called him, he remembered, *control freak*, although she'd meant it in a very different way—he'd been in such a control-freak panic that he'd missed the key to all of this.

There was absolutely nothing on Avery's computer that would implicate him in any way about what happened to her. How could there be?

He paused. Could there be?

And then he realized the real danger of intruders or cops or investigations into Avery's death. They'd interview everyone, everyone she knew, look up calendars and e-mails, track phone calls and visitors and memos and meetings and appointments. "They" were cops. It wasn't like "they" were the public, or even snooping reporters, limited by the confidentiality rules protecting Adams Bay, a privately funded school that had no government requirement to hand over any documents or records. Cops could get *anything*. Anything that existed. Edward was savvy enough to know that even data one attempted to delete was still there, somehow, in the teeming maw of cyberspace. Everything existed.

The shadow appeared outside the door. Paused.

Edward marshaled his excuses, his explanations, and put on his welcoming administrative face. *Well, good evening,* he'd say. *What can I do for you?*

As if he didn't know what had happened to Avery. As if this were just another night. As if he weren't surreptitiously and probably illegally breaking into Avery's computer.

Because in truth? It wasn't only *her* computer he should be worrying about.

It was his.

JAKE BROGAN

"Send in the clowns," Jake muttered. The blocky news vans, three of them, now overlapped on the curb in front of the Morgan House. Nobody'd answered at the last door knock, and he'd promised D they'd wrap it up. And now? *This?*

Ever since he and Jane had begun their late night philosophical debates over the public's right to know versus the cops' right to investigate, and how each of them was only doing their jobs, he'd tried to temper his annoyance with "The Media." But those words still appeared, with capital letters, in his mind's eye. A cop's brain was a cop's brain, and not even Jane could debate *that* away.

First Amendment rights or not, press at a crime scene meant questions. Questions meant the circus was under way, with Jake forced to be the juggler. Balancing his silence. And his attitude. Because it wasn't that the police didn't know anything, it was that they simply weren't planning on telling any of it. But with cameras rolling, which was worse—cops sounding clueless, or as if they were keeping secrets?

Jake and D slowed their footsteps as they approached, but too late. The coiffed figures leaning against the logoed trucks bolted to attention and beelined toward the detectives.

"Freaking reporters," D said. "Anyone you know?"

"Hope not," Jake said. With any luck, Jane was at her condo or at his. When he had one second, he'd check his personal texts. Funny how that pressure was off, though, with Jane not covering crime anymore. She'd have pounced on this story: gorgeous dead woman in a ritzy neighborhood, connections with a local college, puppy as witness. Now he could tell her all about it. No more pretending, no more covering up, no more questioning himself about what to say and what not to say. They'd made the right decision. This would work.

"Jake!" A woman's voice, punctuated by her footsteps clacking toward them. Her photographer, trotting behind her, fussed with the camera balanced on his shoulder. They were still on the move when the reporter made the one-finger spiral for *roll tape.*

"Open season," Jake said.

"For bullshit," D said.

"Jake!" A guy in khakis elbowed in, and pointed his logoed wireless mic in Jake's face before the woman could. Another photographer lumbered behind him, eye plastered to the viewfinder. "Sean Callahan, from Channel—"

"I'm Roberta Spencer. *Ten News.*" The woman caught up, stuck her mic beside Sean's, shot her competitor a withering look. "Jake! Can you start over?"

Within seconds there were four of them, then five, jockeying for position on the narrow sidewalk, the molded logos encircling their microphones clicking together as they tried to get them closer.

"Do you *mind?*" one complained.

"Gimme a break," the woman said.

"Trying to do my job, you know?"

Jake raised his palm to stop their bickering, hoping his expression telegraphed *Shut up* without him having to say it.

"Guys?" he said. "Ready?"

Four spotlights, then five, clicked on, illuminating Jake and D in a pool of orange incandescence. Reporters' voices clamored against each other, vying for Jake's attention.

"Is she dead? Avery Morgan?"

"Can you confirm she's a visiting professor at Adams Bay?"

"We have not contacted next of kin." Jake could tell them that, try to keep her identity out of it as long as he could. "So we will not be confirming any names."

"We heard she was wet. Did she drown? Is it a possible homicide? Is that why you guys are here?"

"Homicide cops come to every unattended death, murder or no. Right, Jake? Is that the only reason you're here?"

"Is it suicide? If it's suicide, we're screwed."

"Yeah, we don't air suicides. Especially not the name. So, Jake, is it suicide?"

"Can you just let me talk? Jake? Was she having one of her student gatherings? Can you confirm she held student gatherings?"

Jake tried to hold back a smile, listening to the reporters think they were asking questions when in truth, like the residents he and D had just interviewed, they were giving him one potential lead after another. If he'd *asked* them for help? They'd have clammed up like . . . clams. He waited, hoping for another morsel.

"She was from California, we're told. Can you confirm that?"

Sean, he remembered. Khaki boy. Thank you, Sean.

"Where'd you hear that, Sean?" Jake asked.

"Can you confirm it?" Sean persisted.

"Can you?" Jake said.

"Can *you*?" The reporters moved in closer, cutting off the clearly unproductive exchange.

"Do you think The Reserve is in danger?"

"What would you tell the residents here?"

Fricking *always*, Jake thought, some jerk asks the impossible question. If we say no, there's no danger, that means there's got to be a reason why we think that, which means we know something. If we say we don't know, then there's a serial killer on the loose.

"Listen, guys?" Jake shook his head. "You can ask all the questions you want—delighted to stand here all night—but I've got nothing for you. And you're impeding our investigation. But word: If you use someone's name, or call it a homicide, that'd be a problem. We cannot confirm any of that. All information has to come from downtown, from the PIO, you know that. Call Karen Warseck, she'll be thrilled to help you."

"She's not there," a voice whined.

"Leave a message," DeLuca said.

"Okay. I *can* tell you one more thing," Jake said.

The reporters went silent, stabbing their mics even closer.

Jake stepped back. "We're eager for any information the public has about this, so as always, call the tip line," he said.

"Screw the tip line," one reporter replied.

"Yeah," D muttered. "And you stay classy."

"And we're done," Jake said.

By the time the reporters gave up, squabbling their way back to their vans, lights clicking off, Jake and D had managed to climb the front steps to the Morgan House, the cast-iron safety railings now yellowed off with crime scene tape.

"How'd they know she was wet?" Jake asked DeLuca as T'shombe Pereira let them inside. They still hadn't talked to the cop who'd pulled Avery Morgan from the pool. She was already dead, so he'd told Kat McMahan. "Maybe they saw Reddington, right? Wet? And figured?"

"Maybe. He's at HQ, writing his report, so says the text I got." DeLuca once again scanned the black-and-white tiled entryway. "We'll get him a-sap."

"Check it out. Crime Scene was here," Jake said, pointing to the living room. Fingerprint dust blackened the coffee table, the textbooks, the glass of the lithograph landscape framed over the fireplace. CS would have taken photos, too. Jake clicked off some of his own, adding to his personal backup collection.

DeLuca was texting again. "They're upstairs now," D said. "Nine thirty-five. I'm out of here in ten minutes, Harvard."

Jake started toward the stairs, then heard the sound from down the hall. From the kitchen.

"The dog," Jake said. "The dog. Is still in that crate. What do we do with the dog?"

"We're not gonna solve this tonight," DeLuca said. "Plus we got no next of kin."

"We've got to call Animal Control." Jake scratched his forehead, calculating. Even though the dog hated him, they couldn't simply leave the poor critter. Animal Control, though. He'd been to the city's animal shelter, rescued his own Diva three years ago from its dank concrete floors and bleak fluorescents. Though she wasn't Jake's favorite dog in the world, this sucked for Popcorn.

DeLuca shouldered by Jake in the narrow hallway, headed toward the kitchen. "I'm taking the dog," he called over his shoulder.

"You can't!" Jake followed him. That wasn't by the book. But hell. Did everything have to be by the book?

DeLuca lifted the metal latch on the crate, swung open the mesh door. The white ball of fur bounded out of the enclosure, almost leaping into DeLuca's arms. Barked once, a yip of triumph or fear. Or maybe relief.

"About time, I know," DeLuca was saying. "You'll be fine, buddy."

Jake had never heard that voice come out of his partner's mouth before, decided not to mention it. He opened the tall white cabinet closest to the crate, found a clipped-closed shiny paper bag with a smiling black Lab pictured on the front. He pulled it out. Half empty. Or, from Popcorn's point of view, half full.

"Food," Jake said. "Dog's probably hungry."

"Aren't we all," DeLuca said. Popcorn blinked her black-marble eyes at Jake, wary, but thankfully silent.

"We writing this up?" Jake asked.

"Writing what up?" D replied. "It's just for the night."

"True," Jake said. "And maybe Popcorn will talk to you."

15

WILLOW GALT

"I'm so glad you're home." Willow buried her face in Tom's shoulder, clutching his arm, breathing in his citrus and coffee fragrance, feeling the damp skin of his neck on her cheek. They'd be fine. They would. She'd done the right thing. The police were gone. She'd explained it all the moment Tom walked in the door. By the time they were climbing the stairs to their bedroom, together, her voice following him, she'd told him the whole story. Most of it. And now she was safe, safe in his arms.

"They hardly stayed ten minutes." Her words—fudging on the time just the smallest bit, but how could that matter—went into the wilting collar of Tom's pale blue shirt. She felt the knot of his loosened tie against her throat. He was home, and everything would be all right.

"Willow." Tom's voice had a knife-edge, her name a slash as he took one step away from her. "Why in hell would you do that?"

She *felt* his words, cutting through her very being. She couldn't move.

"Honey? I'm sorry." Tom came closer again, put his hands on her, one on each bare shoulder.

She could feel his heat as if he were the sun, her private sun. As long as he kept touching her, she'd be fine.

"I know it's nerve-racking for you," he said. "But why would you *call* the cops? It's the *last* thing . . . You allowed the cops into our house?"

"What else could I do?" She would float off the floor without those hands grounding her.

But Tom had turned away again, back to the window, flattening his palms on the pane, peering out.

Willow tried to look through his eyes, see the tree, Avery's backyard, the forsythia hedge, that dark blue watery corner of the pool. Her brain revved with anxiety. She needed another pill. Maybe she hadn't really seen it? But she had. Popcorn barking and barking. The dark shape in the water, and someone leaving. Maybe.

It was wrong, and awful, and she, a human being, could not ignore that.

"No one's down there now," Tom said, talking to the window. "Are you sure? What you saw? What time was it? What time did the police come?"

He turned to her, raking one hand through his hair. "Never mind. It doesn't matter. Because you called the police. Now we're on their radar. The person who calls is always a suspect, Willow. Haven't you learned anything?"

She felt her resolve failing, her knees unreliable. Should she have turned her back on Avery?

"I had to call, didn't I?" She needed to explain. "I had no idea she was *dead*. What if she wasn't dead? What if there was a burglar? The dog was so upset, and I'm here by myself, and—"

Tom touched one finger to her lips. "Shhh," he said. "You'll be fine."

He kissed her palm, then lowered her arm to her side. She stood, still feeling the ghost of his kiss as he moved away from her and went back to the window. He looked out again, his chest rising, then falling. With a quick motion, he pulled down the tawny raffia shade. The room dimmed, their personal night falling, as the raffia lowered inch by inch.

"It's all good." Tom was almost a silhouette on the shade, a lock of his newly grayed hair falling across his forehead. "But, honey? We *have* to keep to ourselves. That's why we moved here. That's why we chose this. If you hadn't gone to dinner at her house, you'd never have even known her."

He knew about that? She frowned, tilting her head, trying to remember.

Tom clicked on the nightstand light. "You told me, silly one," he said.

Maybe she had. "I can't cut myself off from the world, Tom," she whispered. "No matter what happened back home."

"We're not going to talk about that." Tom straightened the lamp shade, tilting the white pleated fabric. "This is home. All the other is gone, over, in the past. No, not in the past. It *never happened.* It's erased. We weren't there. I'm Tom, you're Willow, and so it shall be."

Willow. She'd bend like a willow in the wind. Whatever she had to do to survive, she'd do it. That's why she picked the name. And maybe Tom was right. Maybe she'd been wrong to call. Maybe someone else would have called, and then the police would have gone to someone else's house. But now she'd made her bed, *their* bed, and they'd both have to face the consequences.

"The police will come again. They said so." She felt the tears welling, tears of fear and uncertainty. "What will I tell them? What will you?"

Tom pulled the tie from around his neck, then silently coiled the strip of fabric around his hand, pulling it, striping his hand in red-and-black silk. Willow saw his fingers flex. Then he unwrapped the tie, one loop, then another, then another. Hung it on a steel hook next to his others in his closet, smoothed it flat.

"We'll tell them the truth," Tom said.

Willow remembered that first day she'd met him at the studio, when she was auditioning, and he was visiting, and it all had moved as fast as a movie script. He'd reached out for her then, and she for him. They could never resist, they couldn't stop touching or even standing next to each other, at the office, or at the beach, or even in the grocery, their force fields connected and braided together and they were one person. Soon after, she gave up her movie search, and he got deeper into it, and their life was happy and normal and California-fine.

Until it wasn't. Until they needed a new fine. And now—they'd lost it. Again. Because of her.

"We'll tell them *our* truth." Tom unbuttoned his shirt, one button at a time, as if it were a difficult task, important and significant. He turned to her, at last, his chest bare, tanned, the tails of his shirt loose and hanging over his khakis. "Our *new* truth. You were merely acquaintances. You saw the dog."

"Tom, I—" There was something wrong. She saw it in the set of his chin, and his stiffening shoulders. Maybe he was scared, too. And it was her fault. "*Heard* the dog, too," she said.

" 'Saw the dog,' 'heard the dog.' Fine. And that I'd never met her. I didn't know her."

"Okay," she said. Because now that was true.

"And that's all there is, right? Willow? All?"

"That's right. Nothing more."

Willow searched for the answer that would free them. Maybe she could un-remember what she'd seen. She pushed the vision from her brain, carapacing it over. If they asked—Can you identify the person? Even tell us whether it was male or female?—she could say, No, no I can't.

"Maybe it was an accident?" Her other fears were unspeakable. She would not bring them up, she would bury them, and not think of them. If it *was* an accident, this would all go away.

"An accident." She repeated the words to make them real.

"Maybe," Tom said. "So again. When the police call, we'll tell them the truth."

"I'm sorry, Tom. I wish—"

Tom stepped toward her, across the divide of their fear, pulled her, just like he was her California husband, to the edge of their bed.

She almost cried, with his touch, and the anxiety, and the uncertainty, and she felt breakable, not like a willow, not at all, she wanted their old lives, with sunshine and possibilities. And now Tom had his arm around her, and the night was soft, and they were together, even here, and it would all be okay.

"We'll tell the truth about your past connections with Avery Morgan, because they don't exist." Tom held her close. "Then they'll go away and find whoever killed her."

"Or whatever happened," Willow said.

"Right. Or whatever happened."

"The police will solve this on their own," Willow reassured herself, reassured them both, reassured the universe. "They don't need me. I won't have to say a word."

16

JANE RYLAND

"I remember him perfectly," Jane called over her shoulder. It had been a mistake to tuck the chilled bottle of rosé under her bare arm, but there was no other way to carry it and two wineglasses and two plates from her kitchen into the living room in one trip. "Hi, cat."

Coda looked up from her spot on the striped wing chair as Jane arrived, then stood, turned around, and settled into the upholstery again, wrapping her calico tail around her. Dismissing the humans, even non-cat person Jake, whom she usually stalked.

"We'll eat on the couch, okay?" She put the bottle and plates onto the coffee table, set the glasses side by side. "There's too much stuff on the dining room table."

"There's a table under all that?" Jake came into the living room behind her, holding silverware wrapped in napkins and two just-nuked Gormay delivery bags. "So you remember the hit-and-run driver. Great. Did Frank show you a photo array?"

"Nope. That's what I thought would happen, too, but McCusker wouldn't let me say a word about him. Here, let me help with that." Jane reached out for the steaming containers, put them on the table. "Weird it's from Gormay, isn't it? After this morning. But thank goodness for home delivery, or we'd never eat."

She took the silverware from Jake, made two place settings. "Anyway, McCusker told me the judge insisted on a . . ."

She paused, and stood in front of him, hands on hips. "Hey," she said.

"You okay? You haven't said a word about *your* day. Since the shower, I mean. Probably because I've been yammering about this car-accident thing ever since we got out."

"Nope, all good." Jake had pulled apart the clipped-together top of the insulated bag, and lifted out two plastic containers. "Whoa, hot!"

"Thanks," Jane said. Jake's hair was still wet, one sandy curl dropping a rivulet of water down his neck, his white T-shirt clinging damply to his chest. "You, too."

"I meant the food." Jake put the black containers on the table.

"You did?" Jane pretended to pout.

Jake leaned closer, smelling of her coconut soap. She couldn't help but melt as his kiss landed on her neck. She'd been in the shower when he arrived, and he'd joined her, making the whole thing take much longer than a shower should. Now in T-shirts and sweatpants, they'd finally gotten to their food, carry-out grilled salmon and asparagus. Brown rice. And chocolate cake.

Coda looked up again as Jake pried open one of the containers. "That cat can smell fish a mile away," Jake said. "Protect yourself."

They dumped the salmon onto the plates, and Jane padded into the kitchen with the empty containers, Coda trailing behind, predatory for leftovers. She and Jake had gotten into their rhythm, she realized, like an old married couple, in a good way, thigh to thigh on the couch, sharing wine and dinner, maybe watching a little TV. Comfortable. And now, with her new life-career decision, not even a guilt-inducing problem. They had separate jobs. Pretty much. She wasn't covering breaking news, so they'd promised each other—and their bosses—to keep it all compartmentalized. And so far, so good. It had only been a month, ish, since July 4th.

"Watch the news?" Jane curled up on the couch. She always sat to his left, an unspoken decision, like they'd been doing it for years. "Oh, wait, yuck."

She scraped the gray stuff off the bottom of her salmon. Balancing the goop on her spoon, she carried it into the kitchen for the always-ravenous cat so Jake wouldn't have to fight Coda for his food. "Cannot believe it's so late," she said as she returned.

Jake was aiming the remote at the TV, clicked it a few times. "Yeah, news is almost on," he said. "I'll mute it till then. Anyway, what'd he look like? The driver?"

"Middle-aged, Caucasian, widow's peak, gray hair, pointy cheekbones, thin lips, clean-shaven," Jane recited, poking at the salmon with her fork. "I've said it to myself a million times."

"Fiola see him?" Jake asked.

"She told me no." Jane picked up an asparagus stalk. "That poor delivery guy. Glad he wasn't the one who brought this." She gestured at their food with her asparagus. "That would have been bizarre. I mean, cripes, the Caddy just drove away."

"Jerk," Jake said. "Hit-and-run's like, well, he could get two years, if they find and convict him. You got his license plate? Stupid move on his part, as opposed to just owning up to a nothing accident, getting his insurance to pay. Bad luck for him you were there, Brenda Starr."

"Yeah, well." Jane contemplated her asparagus, thin and striped with grill marks, poked it into her rice. "What would you have done? Well, *you*-you, not police-you."

"There's only police-me," Jake said. "It's in the secret oath. So, in open court? Tomorrow? By yourself?"

"Do I need a lawyer? You think?"

"Do you have an extra thousand bucks?" Jake asked.

She poked his arm with one finger "No, seriously."

"No, seriously." Jake took a sip of wine. "If you needed a lawyer, the DA would tell you."

"Oh, right," Jane said. "Like he's out to protect me. I mean, do you think there's any . . ." She didn't want to say the word *danger*. It sounded way too melodramatic. People testified in court all the time, without ramifications. But there were also witness protection programs, and right now she could understand why someone would want to disappear after ratting out a bad guy. Still, this was only a fender bender. Though one that could lead to a two-year jail sentence.

"Honey?" Jake said. "You stopped in the middle of a sentence."

"Nothing," she said. "Maybe the station will send their lawyer. I'd feel better if . . ."

Jake had clicked up the TV volume. As she watched the screen, all thoughts of pending court appearances were overridden by Channel 2's swirling "Breaking News" graphic announcing *Death in The Reserve*. The Reserve was that ritzy neighborhood, right near Adams Bay College, where she and Fiola had been this morning. Death? What did "death" mean?

"Jake?" she began. "Do you know about this?"

The shot switched to veteran anchor Lisa Solari, wearing a camera-friendly black suit and sitting behind the neon-blue news desk. She spoke in portentous intro mode, her voice concerned, eyes locked on the camera. "For more on the possible homicide, we go to Sean Callahan with the latest."

"He's an idiot," Jane said. "A know-it-all who doesn't. One of the reasons people hate reporters."

"Welcome to my day," Jake said, pointing at the TV. "Young Mr. Callahan's my new best friend."

"Wait. 'Possible homicide'?" Jane stood, almost knocked over her wineglass as she focused on the screen. "Hey. That's you!"

JAKE BROGAN

It had almost been a relief, listening to Jane chatter about her fender bender. He'd been tempted to ask for the license plate number of that moron Caddy driver and run it, just for grins, see if he could make anything of it. But he hadn't asked, and now the subject was changed. Big-time.

Jane was still standing, her cute ass between him and the TV. He shifted on the couch to get a better view. Of the TV.

She turned, hands on hips. "Is there a murder? Why didn't you tell me? The Reserve? I was near there, with Fiola, this morning. When'd it happen? Who's the dead person? Is it a domestic? Or, oh, a suicide? Or hadn't you notified next of kin? That why they didn't say her name?"

Jake sighed at her barrage, *so* Jane, and clicked the TV back to mute once the story ended with the predictable "We'll keep you posted on any new developments." Which Jake truly hoped there would be. Though preferably not tonight.

"Yeah, well," he said. "Those are certainly the questions."

He watched her settle against the opposite end of the couch, crossing her legs under her.

"And you know what? This is terrific." She was still talking. "Now that we're out, ish, we get a whole new set of rules. So what's the deal with— what's her name? You know it, obviously. How did she die? *Hey.* Is there a killer on the loose? Now you can tell me everything. I love it."

"There's no 'killer on the loose,' Jane." He waved off the question with his fork. Always a reporter. "But off the record? Her name is Avery Morgan. We have no cause of death. Okay? And that's it. I can't tell you 'everything.'"

"Why not?" She had that Jane look, raised eyebrows and batting lashes, like *I'm so obviously right.*

"Because." He saw the flicker of the TV screen in his peripheral vision, now headlining some story about a person hit by a foul ball at a Red Sox game, and a pitching trade, which was pretty interesting, but he figured he should focus on Jane. And she was semi-right. They could risk being more open about their jobs. But some cop stuff had to stay cop stuff. And not just for investigative reasons.

There wasn't anything threatening in the Morgan case, that he knew of, but that was the whole point. He didn't know. Once he told Jane something, whether she kept it secret or not, he couldn't un-tell her. They'd changed the rules, all right. But as it turned out, they might have to discuss some new ones.

Which now he had to try to explain.

"Because I can't tell you anything that might put you in danger, honey. Can you get used to that?"

He clicked off the TV, popping the screen to black. Even at 11:30 at night, they needed to focus on this conversation. Jane already knew about his informant Grady, who'd just texted him with updates on the newest Sholto drug deal and the Morgan death. It worried him, Jake had to admit, that Jane knew who Grady was. That he was feeding Jake information.

"And because, if all goes as planned, you're going to be married to a cop. And everyone will know that."

"I know," Jane said. "And it *will* go as planned." She fluttered her ring at him, Gramma Brogan's ring. Then gave him two thumbs-up. "Married to a cop. Pension city. And great health insurance. Rocks."

"I'm serious." Jake took her hands, leaned closer, kissed each one. Maybe he was tired, and maybe because of Avery Morgan he'd been reminded, once again, of how short life was, and how it could be over in one unexpected moment, one wrong move or unwelcome visitor, one ill-chosen word.

"It's not an easy life." Jake heard the solemnity in his voice. "It's not predictable. *I* signed up for the danger. But what worries me every day—now you've signed up for it, too."

JANE RYLAND

What had gotten into Jake? He'd been teasing and low-key, slipping into her shower, and having a second glass of wine. But now he had that *I'm serious* look, his eyes narrowed and his jaw tight.

"Being a cop is no more dangerous than being a reporter," she said, half-smiling. "Usually. Sort of. Maybe." She looked down at her hand, fingers splayed. Gramma Brogan's emerald-cut diamond had fit perfectly without any adjustments. *Meant to be,* Jake had said. The ring, catching the light, was a symbol of so much. Jake's grandmother, and his grandfather, Commissioner Brogan, had handled their share of danger—the

Strangler, the Lilac Sunday killer, the rise of the drug lords and the fall of the Mafia, the Angiulos and the Winter Hill gang. Gramma still visited the commissioner's grave. So did Jake, a solemnly loving remembrance every anniversary of his death ten years ago. Two weeks ago, Jane had joined them.

Gramma, who still wore her wedding rings on a gold chain around her neck, approved of Jane. Showed her a photo of goofy preteen Jake in his grandfather's patent-billed police hat. *Take care of him,* she'd whispered.

"And if it's good enough for Gramma, it's good enough for me," Jane said. The cat leaped from her chair, bolted down the hall.

"What's with the stupid cat?" Jake asked.

"She's smart. Hates the phone." Jane reached down and hit the button on her landline. "Jane Ryland," she said. "I mean, hello." She could never remember how to answer the phone at home.

"Fee Morrello," the voice said.

"Fee—oh, hi, Fee," Jane said. Fiola. Fee. *Okay.*

"I thought that accident was a random hit-and-run, didn't you?" Fee went on as if they were picking up a conversation already in progress. "Like, the food truck guy just in the wrong place at the wrong time."

"It was," Jane says. "He was." She turned to Jake, shrugging.

"Aren't you watching the news?" Fiola asked.

"Uh, yeah . . ." They had been, but then Jake turned it off. Oh. *No.* Impossible. "You mean the body at The Reserve? Do not tell me—"

"Body? Nope, huh-uh. This is something else. It just came in, so maybe it hasn't been on yet," Fiola—Fee—said.

"Huh? 'It'?"

"Listen, I was down in the newsroom. Watching the feeds just for grins, and I saw video from another car accident coming in. Not where we were this morning, though, this was some street called Melnea Cass. Happened at eleven, around then. This time it's worse. The van's a mess. But it looked like the same truck, you know? As this morning?"

"A Gormay truck?" Jane asked. Fee was talking so fast, Jane had to untangle her words. "In an accident?"

"Yeah," Fee said. "I mean, it might not have been the *exact* same truck, no way to tell, but it was a—"

"A hit-and-run?" Jane stood, pacing away from the couch, dodging the empty plates and the empty wine bottle, facing the dining room, her back to Jake. She pictured this morning's scene, yet again. The food truck, the Cadillac, the pointy-chinned driver. The guy kicking his crumpled fender.

"Yeah, that's the thing. Didn't I say that? Exactly. But this time, I guess, no witnesses. I called the cops, but all what's-her-name Karen in the press office would confirm was the driver of the Gormay van was badly hurt. Might die."

"*Another* hit-and-run?" Jane turned and looked at Jake, wide-eyed.

"What?" he said, coming up beside her. "Hit-and-run what?"

"Apparently," Fee said. "I mean, yeah, definitely. But they're not releasing any identification info. Karen at the cop shop insists they don't even know his name, there's some hassle about the next of kin. But, Jane. What if it's the same guy?"

TUESDAY

17

JANE RYLAND

So much for no breaking news.

So much for sharing everything.

Jake had headed out at the crack of dawn, promising to see what he could find out and decide how much he could tell her. Problem was, if he eventually spilled the inside beans about the Reserve death, every cell in her reporter brain would be tempted to tell the news desk. That was exactly what Jane had promised she *wouldn't* do. And once she changed her mind, the news director would expect her to do it again. Jane pumped the metal walk-light button at the intersection of Cambridge Street and New Chardon again, hurrying it up so she could cross to the Dunkin' Donuts.

So, this wasn't going to work. Day two, eight A.M. Jane was already back in reporter mode. Maybe you couldn't simply "decide" your passion away. Her diamond winked at her in the morning sunshine, as if it were agreeing. She'd forgotten to take off her ring. She moved it to her right hand and turned it in a one-eighty, hiding the stone. She was being silly, she recognized that. The ring was still there, no matter how it appeared to the outside world. Reality was still reality.

She pursed her lips, concentrating, as she tried to dial her cell phone and watch for the walk sign simultaneously. Now she'd see whether her agreement to help the district attorney's office meant they'd scratch *her* back, too.

She'd talk to McCusker about last night's car crash. Then get back to

Channel 2. See if Tosca contacted her. And then, because she had no choice, show up in court at two. She'd be fine with no lawyer. She guessed. She needed coffee, maybe iced, on this wiltingly hot day.

Green light. Jane still looked both ways, trotting across the zebra stripes as she listened to the phone ring at the DA's office. Another car accident? With the same delivery company? She needed the police report of the second accident. The first one, too. McCusker'd better give it to her. After all, she was *involved*.

"Hey, Frank." She finally reached him after being tele-navigated through a maze of secretaries and gatekeepers. She opened the coffee shop door as she talked. "You got the report on the Storrow Drive accident yet?"

She covered the speaker of her phone as McCusker answered, quietly ordering her large iced with skim milk, no sugar, hoping McCusker couldn't hear. She could hear *him* fine. He was telling her no. Absolutely no.

"And what's more, Jane," he went on, his voice escalatingly dismissive, "you know better. It's under investigation. I wouldn't even be speaking with you if we weren't seeing each other later today. Two P.M. in Boston Municipal."

As if she could have forgotten. "But I'm also calling about—"

Her coffee arrived, and she acknowledged it with a smile. The barista raised a critical eyebrow at the phone clamped to her face. Jane tried to look apologetic. She hated to talk on her cell in stores, seemed so rude, but this was an exception. *Two hit-and-runs?*

"Jane?" McCusker took advantage of her brief silence. "Whatever it is, the answer is no. I'm clearly not supposed to be talking to you, but I was worried you were calling to cancel. Since you're not, we're done. 'Kay?"

"But there was another—"

"Not talking to you," he said. "See you later."

He hung up.

Jane stabbed off the phone, stashed it in the black hole of her tote bag, tamped down her orange straw against the plastic counter to break off the paper.

"So much for *that*." She jammed her straw into the clear plastic lid of her icy cup. The barista looked up, questioning. "Nothing," Jane said.

And so much for the mutual back-scratching Marsh Tyson had predicted. She'd told the news director this was a bad idea. That the DA's office only took information, they didn't give it.

But by the time she got to her office, Jane had a new plan. Fiola—Fee—wasn't at her desk yet. Jane swiveled into her own chair, carefully placing her mammoth iced coffee where she wouldn't knock it over with the phone cord. Dialed. Two rings.

"Hey, Karen," she said. "Jane Ryland at Channel 2." She slurped a sip, quietly, as the Boston PD public affairs officer protested. "Yeah, I know, Fiola called you last night, we're working on this together." Which was kind of true. "I'm just following up. Great that you're in so early, very impressive."

No response. So much for friendly.

"So, anyway. Do you have the police report from last night's accident? I know it should be public record." Which was also kind of true. "Only the accident report, I mean. Not the investigation part. And what's the victim's condition? Taken to Mass General or Boston City?"

Jane put the phone on speaker so she could flip through her snail mail and boot up her computer while Karen talked. Or more accurately, sneered. The veteran PIO was notorious for her instant denials. Why they called them public information officers Jane would never understand. They were rarely interested in making anything public.

"Jane, you know as well as I do," Karen Warseck said, "we've got nothing for you. I'm sure your colleague explained that it's under investigation. Certainly nothing happened between last night at midnight and now. And if it did? It's still under investigation."

Karen paused. "Unless there's something you'd like to tell us?"

Not a chance, Jane thought. Then she frowned, realizing where that question might have come from. Was that Karen's not-so-sly way of letting

Jane know she knew about her "talk" with the DA's office? On the other hand, the cop shop and the DA's office were notoriously contentious. Protective. Territorial. Which meant it was certainly possible that the cops didn't know Jane was giving information—under duress as it was—to the DA. Jane certainly wasn't about to offer that tidbit. She'd done enough of that for one lifetime.

Ignoring the PIO's question, Jane persisted. "Any ID on the victim?" If "nothing had changed" it meant the victim was still alive.

"What part of 'nothing for you' did you not understand?"

"Funny," Jane said. "So we'll follow up later?"

"No doubt," Karen said.

Jane heard the click of Karen's hang-up over the tinny speaker, then the drone of the dial tone. She poked the speaker off and sat back, shoulders sagging, trying to think. She stabbed her straw up and down in her iced coffee, now mostly ice. Heard the squeaking noise of plastic straw against plastic lid, couldn't resist doing it again.

"Having fun?" Fiola said. She waved a hand at Jane and the straw as she swept into the office.

"Hey, Fee," Jane said. She squeaked her straw one more time, just because. Fee wore all black today: skirt, silk shirt, linen jacket. It looked as if she and Jane had coordinated their news-predictable wardrobes. Jane was wearing her go-to-court pearls, though, and touching them reminded her. Today she'd be on the participant side, not the observer side. Which still ticked her off. "What's new?"

"I'm calling the cops about the Gormay thing." Fee parked her black handbag on the floor, kicked off her flip-flops, and slipped on black heels.

"I already did that," Jane said. "Nada."

"Jerks. You still going to court? Did Tosca call? Or anyone else?"

"Yes, no." Jane tossed her junk mail, slit open the one envelope that didn't look like it was addressed by a crazy person. Took out the white piece of paper inside. "And no calls."

"Anything on the news about last night's hit-and-run? Why didn't you turn this on?" Fee popped on their TV, kept the sound muted.

"Huh," Jane said. She looked at the white piece of paper. Looked at the envelope again. Her name, and Channel 2, and a postmarked-Boston stamp. "Lovely," she said. She held up the letter, showing Fiola its three-word block-lettered message. "Look."

"'Say no more'." Fiola read the note out loud. Frowned. "All in capital letters. Is there anything on the env—"

"No," Jane said.

The two sat in silence for a beat.

"Take it to Marsh Tyson," Fiola said. "Just so he knows."

"Yeah, I guess so." Jane replaced it in the envelope. "Either it's about the hit-and-run, or it isn't. Or it's about campus crime, you know? Or it isn't. Or it's one of the ten billion nutcase things people send to reporters every darn day."

"I know," Fiola said. "But you should take it to McCusker, too."

Jane put the envelope on her desk. Stared at it.

"Yeah," she said. "But it's got nothing identifiable. At all. Not even a zip on the postmark. So what could McCusker, or anyone, do about it?"

JAKE BROGAN

"What good does *that* do?" Jake probably shouldn't have said that out loud, but Austin the alarm kid was driving him crazy. SafeHouse Security, this business was called. Which, as far as Jake could figure, was deceptive advertising. The SafeHouse alarm system installed at the Morgan House certainly had not kept Avery Morgan safe. It hadn't taped any arrivals. Or departures. Hadn't warned the police of a break-in.

Earlier this morning, he and DeLuca had waited in the struggling air-conditioning of Judge Gallagher's chambers for two hours—DeLuca partially turned away from him on the waiting room's sleek gray corduroy couch, texting as if his life depended on it. Jake spent the downtime researching Adams Bay and making a list of to-dos in his notebook. Connect with the school's dean of students, some guy named Tarrant. Contact

Avery Morgan's fellow drama adjunct, Sasha Vogelby. He googled Willow Galt, too, and ran her through Facebook, but as sometimes happened, so far nothing. She was hiding something, Jake was sure. But then, so was everyone. Didn't mean it mattered.

Half an hour ago they'd handed their search warrant to SafeHouse's twenty-something receptionist, a grunge wannabe with cobalt-blue hair, who'd left them in the alarm company's chrome and glass lobby. Now she was back, and telling them the "vice president" had instructed her to "allow" them to see the video they requested. As if the warrant gave anyone a choice.

"Thanks so much." DeLuca saluted her with his Dunkin's large.

"And leave all liquids in the lobby," the young woman said, missing—or ignoring—his sarcasm.

"Are you ki—" DeLuca began.

"D," Jake said. D was no good until his third cup. This, sadly, had only been number two.

She buzzed them through the clicking locks of an electronically secured metal gate and led them down a corridor of closed doors to a closet-sized office with "Security" stenciled in black on the door. Windowless and hyper-chilled, the room's low-ceilinged walls were lined with darkened TV monitors held up by metal brackets, a carbon copy of every surveillance system Jake had ever seen.

"This is Austin," the receptionist said. "They're okay, Aus. Whatevs." And closed the door behind her.

A double-screen console took up the center of the room. Austin, a clearly beleaguered underling in wrinkled plaid shirt and random blue jeans occupying the room's only chair, guided them through the computerized records of the Morgan House security system. Which, as they watched screen after screen, showed basically nothing but black.

Now, after fifteen minutes of nothing, Jake couldn't stand it. "What good does it do to have a taping system if you have to turn it on?"

"It's just how it works," the kid said. "You wouldn't want the tape running all the time. Right?"

"Whatevs," DeLuca muttered.

"So it only tapes if the motion detector is set to run?"

"Or if we get a message to start the tape," the alarm guy said. "Remotely."

"So wait. The serial killer comes in, but there's no tape of that. Then you're supposed to say, hang on, let me start the video?" DeLuca stood, putting one hand on his lower back as if the effort of leaning over the screen was impossibly uncomfortable. "How much does this 'service' cost?"

"How would anyone know when to ask for surveillance video?" Jake interrupted. "Until it's too late?"

"There's a panic button," the kid said.

"It get pushed?" Jake asked. "In the last five months or so?"

Austin clicked his silver mouse, tapped on his silver keyboard, so work-worn the letters had disappeared from the keys.

If Avery Morgan had used the panic button, that'd certainly be in the records. Police—or someone—would have arrived, and there'd be an explanation. Which would be a lead. Which would point to a solution. A *possible* solution.

"Yes," Austin said. "I see a—"

Jake took out his spiral notebook. "What?"

"Oh. Heck." The kid stopped. Leaned closer to the screen. "Sorry."

"That's not good," D said.

Austin tapped the keyboard again.

"Austin? What exactly did you mean by 'heck'?" Jake asked.

"I mean, um, that was the wrong file." The kid kept typing. "Someone else's records. Let me try that again."

"Security," D said. "Awesome."

Austin shrugged, shoulders hunched, the black-and-white screens flashing and changing, code scrolling.

"All you usually need is the yard sign," he said. "Or a decal on the window. The bad guys see it's SafeHoused, they stay away. It's an Adams Bay house, anyway. They're the owner. The college, I mean. Ask *them* how they like it."

Jake lowered his notebook. He'd assumed Avery Morgan owned the house. "Say again?"

"Nope, no panics." Austin tapped more keys. "In fact, far as I can see . . ." More tapping. "She never turned on the video. She'd have to put in her password, but she never did."

"What was it?" DeLuca asked. "Her password?"

"It's secret."

"She's dead."

"Still secret."

"Listen," DeLuca began.

"Do you know what this warrant means, Austin?" Jake, interrupting the fencing match, pulled his copy from his jacket pocket. His phone was buzzing, and a text pinged in, but he had to ignore it for now. "It means, according to a Suffolk County Superior Court judge—wanna see it?—it means *nothing* is secret."

"Dead, not dead. The warrant don't care," DeLuca said.

"Popcorn," Austin said.

18

WILLOW GALT

"I'm going for a walk." Willow trotted down the stairs after her husband. As he'd gotten dressed for work, in the navy suit and striped tie suitable for the accounting job they'd found for him, she'd yanked on a black sleeveless knit dress and flat shoes, then packed what she needed in a woven gypsy bag she'd kept from California. She could no longer see anything unusual in Avery's backyard—no police, no guards, not even crime scene tape. No dog, either. What had happened to the dog?

What worried her more: What if the police were now watching *their* house? Or following *them*? She was paranoid, sure, but was it paranoia if it made sense?

"Willow." Tom shook his head, continued down the stairs. "If you're not here, the police will just come back."

"Okay, you got me," She smiled, trying to act natural. "But, sweetheart? I really don't want to face them alone. Bad enough that you're working late tonight. Maybe I'll stay out, too. Have dinner somewhere."

Willow had to make Tom believe she was not only dodging the police, which was true, but also that taking a walk was her only agenda. Which wasn't true.

"What's gotten into you?" Tom asked. "Did you sleep at all? Honey? You go for walks every day. You don't have to ask permission to do anything. Why is this a big deal?"

"Oh, Tom, what if we have to leave again?" She couldn't hold it in. Couldn't. She was exhausted, drained, hadn't slept, not a minute. "What if they've found us? What if they killed Avery as a warning that *we're* next?"

She had to stop. Her brain was going too fast. "Or by mistake? Thinking she *was* me?"

"Willow, honey. Willow. We don't look the same as we did, you and I." Tom put down his briefcase, gestured at her. "Look at your hair. Your eyebrows. Some mornings even *I* don't recognize you."

She looked nothing like the old Daniella, she knew that. But they couldn't change Dunc's—*Tom's*—cheekbones, and even his gray hair didn't make him someone else.

"Exactly!" She was almost crying now. "That's how they could have made a mistake! Because we don't look like we used to! And—"

She stopped, mid-tirade, with yet another fear. What if the police suspected *her* of killing Avery? She hadn't, of *course*, but how would she defend herself? It would all come out. She thought of yet another undefendable horror.

"What if they try to blame *you*?" Her voice tensed to a wail. She could hear it, but couldn't help it.

"Me?" Tom came closer, gently smoothed her hair away from her face. "Oh, honey, don't do this. Okay?"

"But Roger—" She almost choked on the name, couldn't say it, the name of the man whose fault this whole hideous thing was. The head of Untitled.

"Roger Hayden can't hurt us," Tom said. As if he'd read her mind. "He's in custody. In California. Remember?"

"But what if Hayden helped the feds somehow? Like we did? What if now—he's free, too? What if he found us? We ruined his life. Don't you think he'd want to ruin ours? That's why we're—" She waved an arm, flailing, gesturing to everything. "Right? Right?"

Willow felt her heart race again. It got worse when she saw Tom's face change, his forehead furrow. Because it proved he was considering what she'd said. As he should. Yes, Tom had made some mistakes, huge ones, but only at the behest—demand—of studio head Roger Hayden.

And when it got too much for Tom's conscience, he'd taken the studio's books, the real ones as well as the duplicate ones, to his lawyer, and then to the feds. Untitled Studios collapsed, with Roger Hayden, threatening his eternal revenge, taken into custody. Soon after, the two of them, accountant and actress, were federally reborn as Tom and Willow Galt.

Now she'd blown the whole charade. But what else could she do? Avery was a friend. Kind of. She second-guessed herself, regretting. Keeping quiet was always better. She'd remember that now, forever and ever. Never say another word.

"Tom. What if it gets out that I'm talking to the police? What if someone takes a photo and puts it on TV? What if the police start looking into our background? What if they find out who we really are?"

"You're making this up. All of it." Tom hefted his briefcase, as if to signal their "discussion" was over. "Don't get hysterical, honey. Avery Morgan is dead. It's sad, but she can't be connected to us. It has nothing to do with Roger Hayden, and he can't find us. The police will solve their case, and go away."

His face had softened with a curve of his eyebrows, the hint of a smile. "Honey? Of course you're upset. Anyone would be upset." He tucked his arm around her waist, walked her to the front door. "But don't make it more than it is. Deal?"

Outside, the beginnings of a summer morning—an insistent cardinal, the rustle of elm trees, a white butterfly dancing across their tiny front lawn. Together they looked left, then looked right, but they were alone. No police, no sentries, no lurking guys in pretending-to-be-civilian outfits. Willow could almost breathe.

"See? There's no one waiting to pounce." Tom clicked his remote at their silver car. "Okay? You okay?"

"I'm okay." She waved as he backed out of their driveway. Tom was much better at this than she was. He didn't need pills, like she sometimes did. He'd been fast asleep last night, this morning really, when she'd sneaked out of bed and locked herself in the guest bathroom.

She'd balanced on the cool molded edge of the white porcelain bathtub, turning the heavy black pages in her scrapbook.

Contraband, certainly—beyond contraband, and into land mine. Time bomb. She'd retrieved the scrapbook from its safekeeping place under the guest room mattress. Even Tom didn't know she had it. In the safety of the white-tiled bathroom, she'd paged through, seeing her childhood. Millie. Her California home. And the studio.

She turned the page, knowing what was next. The photo at the Untitled annual party, the photo of her and Dunc. On the very day they'd met. This captured moment was a treasure, her *treasure*. She would *not* rip that photo to pieces. She couldn't.

But in the same photo, a smiling Avery Morgan. Even though Willow had never met her back then, she'd recognized Avery in the photo because she'd looked at it so many times. She'd never thought it would matter. Now it proved their real identities. Proved they'd all worked at the same California studio. Proved a past. The photo blew their cover and ruined their new lives and ended their safety.

If the police searched their house, they'd find it.

She could not destroy this book, not ever. She *needed* it, to remember Duncan and Daniella. But even the possibility of discovery meant she had to get it out of the house. Had to hide it. Somewhere safe, and, equally important, somewhere she could retrieve it when the time came.

And, thanks to Avery, *poor Avery*, she knew exactly where that would be.

EDWARD TARRANT

He wasn't gawking, not like some feeble-minded, tabloid-reading lowlife fascinated by death. This was purely business. Edward had every right to be at the Morgan House. He would decide how to present himself when he arrived. If he decided to arrive.

Edward stepped up his pace as he crossed Brookline Ave and turned into the leafy boulevard that marked the edge of The Reserve. A couple of silvery airplanes on the westbound takeoff pattern from Logan left slashing contrails across the cloudless blue sky. He remembered that opening day of school in 2001, when the planes stopped, leaving Adams Bay and all of Boston in eerie silence. He remembered the days, just at spring break, after the Marathon bombing, when the streets went empty, save for jungle-camouflaged National Guard members and their menacing German shepherds. What happened to Avery Morgan wouldn't stop air travel, or clear the streets. But it might prove equally earthshaking to *his* life.

An imaginary conversation began in his head as he squinted into the morning sunshine, the irritating red light at Regatta Road slowing his progress. Did you kill Avery Morgan? some cop might ask. He could feel his blood pressure rising as he contemplated the audacity of that question. But the answer was no, he hadn't killed her. And that was the truth.

Next question: Did you know anything about it? The light changed as he measured out his answer to that one. No, he didn't, he'd say, and that was probably true. It might have been a vagrant, or a hophead, some dope dealer. Or some sob-story-telling stray, some random roustabout who bighearted Avery had allowed inside. Or hell, it might have been the next freaking Boston Strangler.

This chaos, and the inevitable questioning to come, threatened to upset Tarrant's personal applecart beyond repair. Unintended consequences. He'd brandished that phrase to so many of his students. *What you do has consequences, and I'm the one who will tell you what they are.* He smiled, even now, remembering their anxious expressions and dawning understanding.

And there it was, the Morgan House, a block away now. Red brick, with black wrought-iron fencing, knee high, around its patch of green lawn. Tarrant's office paid for that damn lawn. The yellow crime scene tape, festooned like a macabre holiday decoration, looped through the curved iron and draped across the front door. A barrier to keep out intruders.

But he wasn't an intruder. He was the landlord. And possibly the best defense was a good offense. Should he approach the cops? Calculating, he adjusted his tie, loosening the paisley silk, feeling his starched shirt collar fail in a puff of August heat.

A sound behind him, and as he stepped into the shade of a Reserve elm, a white Crown Vic slid by, as obvious a cop car as any he'd ever seen, two figures in the front seat, windows closed. The car eased by him, slowed, pulled to the curb across from the Morgan House. The doors remained closed.

Do you know Avery Morgan's password? He felt his expression change to reflect his infinite skepticism as he mentally practiced his response. No, he'd answer, certainly not. And that would be a lie, but an unprovable lie. The cops could never know he'd guessed it.

If they took her computer, though, he might be screwed. Might be better for him to go back and take another look. Only Mack had seen him the night before. Mack, who'd respectfully tipped his ball cap to Tarrant, then continued his security rounds. Edward hadn't even needed to try out his excuses. Mack had simply accepted he was where he should be. After all, Mack hadn't known Avery was dead. Just another evening at Adams Bay.

Edward had been so spooked, though, he'd bolted from the room, controlling every muscle to keep himself walking at a leisurely pace, not giving in to his instinct to sprint back to his office as fast as he could.

He knew exactly what he was afraid of. What he was looking for. The video he'd taken down from YouTube but couldn't bear to destroy. Who else had a copy? Could be anyone. Could be no one.

Did that video also live on Avery's computer? Had she also kept it as a souvenir? Of . . . him?

Edward's skin had tingled as he'd clicked open one set of his own files last night, then another one, going deeper into his computer. He'd been an idiot to keep it, a sentimental fool, but how did he know it would ever matter? Maybe it wouldn't. But if the police found it, it could certainly put the lie to "We were simply colleagues" and "We never socialized."

Before the cops asked him, he definitely had to decide how he'd characterize their relationship.

Behind his locked door and back in the darkened privacy of his office, heart rate down to semi-normal, he'd clicked the "play" triangle before he had a chance to second-guess himself. He needed to look at the video through a cop's eyes, not his own, and see what someone else would see. He was a pro, he could do that, he knew what they'd be looking for.

The music on the video blasted, so loud it had banged off the walls of his office. He stabbed the mouse to mute the sound, then eased the volume up to bare-whisper level. The lighting at the party was tantalizingly random, he remembered as the scene unfolded, fat candles flickering shadows on the round poolside tables, a scattering of paper lanterns dangling from the trees in Avery's—the Morgan House's—backyard. A few heads bobbed from the shallow end of the pool. Slashes of underwater lighting proved they were wearing bathing suits. Beer bottles, wineglasses, heads thrown back in laughter. He tried to see the summer gathering without the filter of death, without the filter of what had happened—how? why?— in that very same pool.

He'd pressed his fingertips into his forehead, watching the students singing into their beer bottles. Then Avery herself, in a white dress, her hair held back with a pink ribbon, sipping from a yellow plastic cup. Someone's shadow moved across her shoulders. Someone who'd stepped away as the camera moved closer. *His* shadow. *His.*

He watched as the camera zoomed in on Avery, her eyes shining, candlelight softening her face. She turned to smile at him. He'd seen it on video a hundred times, knew the camera never really included him, but still felt his throat tighten every time he watched, absurdly fearing the student using the camera would somehow move it, just enough to reveal him next to her.

The same student who then posted it on YouTube. Edward had called him in, "asked" him—the word with infinite subtext—to take it down, to protect the school's reputation, and Ms. Morgan's, and, more pointedly, the student's own. The student, wisely, agreed to delete it. Edward had asked for the original, too. Couldn't be too careful. And no student was going to refuse Edward Tarrant. Especially not Trey Welliver.

Edward had made his own private copy before Trey deleted it. Had Avery made one, too? Had Trey? Had anyone else? The video ended, snapped to black.

Edward had started it again from the beginning, scouring for anything he might have missed. And trying to memorize it. Because, certainly he'd have to delete it. Soon.

But he didn't. Couldn't. Not the night of her death. This last memory of her? Of what they had? She'd embraced it, he'd seen it in her eyes.

And now, standing a block from the Morgan House in the next morning's light, watching two obvious detectives get out of their Crown Vic, he pivoted and, again using every bit of his willpower not to run, headed back to his office.

19

JANE RYLAND

"Do you know what they called it? How they slugged the story?" Jane asked Fiola, who was behind her as they headed down the station's cheerless back stairway. Jane had realized they didn't need the cops' report to get the scoop on the Melnea Cass Boulevard crash. All they had to do was screen the footage in the station's video computer. *Take that, Karen Warseck in PR.*

She stopped, hand clenching the rusting metal banister. Felt the weight of what they might be about to witness. "We're the only ones who'll see both accidents, you know? And we might be able to tell if it's the same guy."

Fiola nodded, silently for once, and Jane imagined her producer's brain doing the same calculations as her own. They'd first seen the delivery guy about this time yesterday morning. With a banged-up van, a cut on his forehead, indignant and unhappy. This time, what if he'd died?

Or maybe it was someone else, another victim. Which would mean . . . "SAY NO MORE," that stupid note had warned. About this? Or something else? Or nothing?

They yanked open the glass door to ENG Receive. "ENG" for electronic news-gathering, "Receive" because that's where the breaking news video feeds came in.

Jane didn't bother to sit. She leaned over, planted her fingers on the grimy keyboard, and typed in her password, then narrowed the search to the past twelve hours. Fiola hovered next to her.

"Think the slug is hit-and-run?" Jane typed those words into the search window as she spoke them. Blank screen. "Melnea Cass Boulevard." Nothing found. She typed "Cass car accident." Nothing.

"Car ax?" Jane typed, trying the newsroom shorthand.

The computer pulled up the video, and the first frame appeared. Night, which made it harder to see, and also easier. Harder, because everything in the background was dark. Easier, because whatever the camera lights hit blossomed into bright colors and sharp focus. The video swayed and jounced as the running photographer approached the action.

Police had already arrived, the swoop of their wigwagging blue lights and powerful flashlights illuminating the demolished Gormay van. The van had smashed into the metal lane divider, the hood crunched against the unyieldingly thick steel pole of a highway marker. The front end was crumpled almost flat, air bags exploded, headlights shattered, the camera's powerful spotlights reflecting some sort of liquid leaking onto the dark pavement. Smoke from the engine, or steam.

"No EMTs yet," Jane said. "That means the victim is still in the front seat."

"Yeah," Fiola said. "Apparently the overnight stringer heard it on the police radio and was like, right there. Got lucky."

News-lucky, Jane thought. Only reporters could get away with calling a possibly fatal accident "lucky."

The cops had blocked off traffic as the photog swung around to get an establishing shot behind him—the lengthening row of glaring headlights, impatient drivers already honking. The yellow numbers of the video's electronic time-of-day code ticked by in the screen's upper left: 23:22:03.

Swish pan, back to the scene. Two officers, uniforms, at the open driver's-side door of the van. The passenger door was open, too, and the camera moved to show a cop's body extending into the front seat.

"They don't know if he's dead yet," Jane said.

The photog held his shot steady, waiting. Jane had to give him props—a sweltering night, a heavy camera, all to tape an incident that could turn out to be nothing.

It didn't look like nothing.

"Hear that? Sirens," Fiola said.

In seconds the whirling red lights of the ambulance appeared, brighter and brighter, speeding the wrong way on the highway and pulling up to the car. A scramble of running EMTs, cops, a stretcher. More lights. The siren unrelenting, horns in the background. Traffic coming the opposite direction slowed, gawking at the glare and chaos.

"Jerks," Jane said. But she couldn't take her eyes off the screen. At this point, in video-time, the police hadn't known the condition of the driver. So Jane and Fiola were watching with knowledge that those who'd actually participated didn't have.

"They say people are riveted by car accidents because it reminds them they're safe. *It wasn't me,* they think." Jane shook her head. "But *we* put it on TV. Unless there's a bigger point, like drunk driving, or texting, I've never understood that."

"Can you tell? If it's the same person?" Fiola's shoulder touched hers as they stared at the screen.

"Hang on. I'll pause it when—" Jane clicked the mouse as the victim's face came into view. All movement stopped, a freeze-frame of disaster. The man's face obscured by red, dark murky red in the artificial incandescence of the camera spotlight. EMTs stopped mid-motion, arms reaching out, stretcher in midair, one uniformed young man's expression—fear, or concern or doubt—captured in that single instant. When Jane pushed "play," the commotion would start again. Strange to remember that at the time this was shot, reality was unfolding, with cops and medics trying to save a life and control traffic and figure out what happened. Now she and Fiola could stop time.

"Can you tell?" Fiola repeated her question, this time in a whisper.

"Yeah," Jane said.

JAKE BROGAN

"You never know what's going to matter," Jake said as he shut the cruiser door behind him. So yeah, he'd taken a resident-only parking spot on Alcott Street. The Reserve residents should be happy he and D were making sure no serial killer was loose in their neighborhood.

He'd left Jane this morning, quietly as he could, still asleep with that cat curled up on her back. Ten o'clock now, so she was probably at work. He'd text soon. Maybe call, hear her voice.

But first, the victim. If she was a victim.

That text he'd gotten in the SafeHouse office was from Kat McMahan, informing him and D that water in Avery Morgan's lungs proved she was alive when she hit the water, and she'd drowned. But why?

"Know what I mean?" Jake went on as D approached. "Even though that piece-of-work alarm company had no video, we still got—"

"Buncha crap." D joined Jake at the curb.

"Hey. We know there's no video for us to screen. And we got her password. If we're lucky that'll be her password for everything."

Jake scanned the sunlit street, the lofty elms making shadowy patches on the sidewalks. Some guy a block away stood at the striped crosswalk, staring at them. People were relentlessly curious. He and Jane had discussed it, how onlookers—like TV viewers—were fascinated by the disasters of others. But the man turned, sauntered away. Okay, then.

The crime scene tape still marked the Morgan House, the plastic sagging as it always did with the weight of morning dew and pestering breezes. And snooping neighbors. Sometimes people tried to steal the yellow tape, use it for decorations in their kids' rooms. Jake shook his head. Death as entertainment.

"Speaking of her password," Jake said as they crossed the deserted street. "How's the dog? If we can't find relatives, we're going to have to call the shelter at some point."

"What dog?" DeLuca said.

"Good one," Jake said. They approached the front door, knocked.

"Hey, Shom," Jake said as the front door swung open. He held up the warrant, showing the officer on scene the magic key to unlocking the case.

"Step aside, bro," D said. "It's open season."

"Anything new?" Jake asked.

Shom explained that Crime Scene was running fingerprints, and it'd take a while. But it took five minutes, maybe less, for Jake to get into Avery Morgan's laptop, a silver sliver of metal on the narrow desk tucked under her bedroom window. "Gotta love Popcorn," Jake said.

Another ten minutes, and Avery Morgan's life was revealed, easy as scanning computer files and calendars. Once in, nothing was password-protected. Avery Morgan, age forty-six, once married, once divorced. Moved here from California, hired as adjunct professor, got use of the college-owned Morgan House as a perk. Taught performance drama and opera twice a week at Adams Bay. They read e-mails from summer students, asking for grade changes. E-mails from a movie agent, Allan Underwood in Los Angeles, telling her that the options on *Callas and Pablo* had expired. "We tried, sweetheart," the e-mail said.

He read it out loud to D. "Sweetheart?" Jake said.

"Possible." DeLuca had yanked out the six dresser drawers, dumping the contents onto a chair. He'd rolled the bedsheets into an oversized evidence bag and the thin quilt into a separate one. He'd flipped the mattress over. Now it balanced, not quite back in place, on the wooden slats, one corner snagged against the padded headboard.

"Or maybe it's just Hollywood movie crap," Jake said. He clicked open a file labeled "Untitled," said, "Yeah, she writes screenplays, looks like." He scanned the opening page.

Exterior, night, winter. A college campus, urban, unnamed. CARISSA, a beautiful young student, runs down the front steps of a vine-covered brownstone into the snow. We see she is barefoot.

Jake clicked down farther, lowering himself into the swivel chair, skipping ahead.

DEREK pulls CARISSA'S white T-shirt over her head. Close-up of her bare skin, DEREK'S hand caressing.

CARISSA'S voice: "No."

DEREK: "*You know you don't mean that, babe. You don't really mean no.*"

" 'Crap' is right," Jake muttered.

D was pulling stacks of folded sweaters from the closet, pawing through them, adding them to the tumbled pile of clothing already on the chair. "We got nada here. No hidden notes, no secret files, no clandestine photos or love letters with freakin' pink ribbons. Nada."

D added a pile of white things to the mountain of possessions. "Screenplays, you said? Easier if this *was* the frigging movies. Been a clue, like, under the mattress or something."

Jake clicked the script closed and opened another screen, pulling up the contacts list on Avery Morgan's e-mail. He searched for "Galt." Nothing. Typed in "Willow." Nothing.

"Guess we could e-mail all of her contacts," Jake thought out loud. "Or, if we had a thousand years, read everything in the computer."

"Only *her* stuff in here." DeLuca, ignoring him, closed the closet door, surveyed his handiwork. "No men's clothing. No weapons, anything like that. Nothing hidden behind the posters on the walls. Lemme check the bathroom, though. Medicine cabinets are my favorite. People always forget."

"I star-six-nined her landline," Jake said. "Nothing there. We'll get the records. But, hey. Adams Bay. Her e-mail address is dot e-d-u. She has an office there, dollars to doughnuts. That's where her stuff is. Hope I-T can dry out her cell. We need to contact her last caller."

"Hi, who is this, please?" DeLuca pantomimed a phone call. "Thank you so much, sir. You're under arrest."

"It could happen," Jake said. "Off to school we go."

20

ISABEL RUSSO

"He's not coming *here*—he couldn't be." Isabel Russo lowered her binoculars and said the words out loud, though no one but Fish could hear them. She whisked the pebbly rust-red pellets from her bare arms. She'd been resting her elbows on the metal rails encircling her little balcony as she focused in on the street below. Fifteen stories up, she had a perfect view, usually a bustle of students and tourists and baseball fans, the Green Line trolleys racketing by.

People hardly ever looked up. Most kept their eyes forward, or down, or focused on the screens of their cells. She took a deep breath, smelling the green of the summer leaves, and the hot gray pavement, even a faint pink scent from some distant garden. Being outside, even this far, made being alive bearable. She could pretend she was part of the world. Watch the seasons change, see the different light, feel the rain in her hair.

She relied on her binoculars. The ones she'd once happily carried to symphony performances and the Boston Lyric Opera, the time they sang *Otello* on the Boston Common. Even sitting far back in the students' cheap seats, the binocs had allowed her to perceive the love and joy on the performers' faces, the intensity, the power. Being in a crowd like that now? Even the idea made her kinda queasy. She balanced herself against the wobbly railing again, recovering. She was fine.

Now without her binoculars, she watched the world in real size. How the pedestrians moved in a flow, the rhythm of the morning. Fifteen stories below, the traffic light changed, a horn honked, cars surged forward. The world was going on. Without her. Was that fair?

Because her situation, her solitude, was not her fault. Should she call Jane, that reporter? She'd been chewing on that question, mulling it over, imagining outcomes, ever since their phone conversation yesterday. Jane had been . . . persuasive. And it was verging on possible that what she'd said was true. Maybe, if Isabel talked to her, talked to anyone, it would help her feel safe.

She lifted the binoculars to her face again, canceling reality, more comfortable in her own private experience. She could make out faces now, her once-classmates, and strangers. And, yes, she did, she looked for "him," every day. She'd marked the days on her calendar, a red dot under the black X's, with the exact time, on the days she'd caught a glimpse of him. Alone, or in a pack of guys, or his arm linked with some girl's. She'd see him all the time, going into the library or Java Jim's. Nothing he ever did was predictable. So she had to keep watch.

"Keeping watch," she said out loud. Then sang the words, "Keeping watch!" Trilling a full C octave, "*Sorvegliare!,*" imagining *Tosca* from her balcony.

Tosca. Should she call Jane?

Wait. On the street.

Isabel adjusted the focus of the binocs, twisting the ridged plastic dial, not moving the lenses from her eyes. Clearly—two hundred times more clearly than her regular vision, to be exact—it was Edward Tarrant, strolling up Brookline Ave. Behind him, a woman with long blond hair wearing a black dress, carrying a huge tote bag.

Tarrant. She narrowed her eyes, watching.

His office, in Colonial Hall, was across the street from her building, next to the yellow bricks and flower-filled stone pots of Adams Bay's Endicott Library. Not that Isabel hadn't tried, once, maybe twice, to see into his window, but the angle was wrong. She'd never seen him walking up the Ave, hadn't seen him in person since that day in his office, last May to be exact, last May twenty-first, to be even more exact.

He stopped now, at the crosswalk in front of the drugstore. The woman was right next to him, and he waved her to go ahead as the walk light changed, and she lifted her hand like, thank you, as they crossed the street. Were they together? But the blonde went through the big revolving doors and into Endicott Library. Tarrant entered Colonial Hall. *Lucky woman.* Edward Tarrant was someone she'd be better off not knowing.

"He's going to his office, Fish," Isabel said. "Ready to ruin someone else's life."

JANE RYLAND

Jane had to get back outside. Into the sunshine. Out of the dingy half-light of ENG Receive, away from the sirens and blood and destruction. And away from that three-word note she'd received, even though it was probably nothing. Any good reporter got such things. After all, their jobs required them to make some people unhappy.

But the crash video—there was no uncertainty about that. She and Fiola could turn it off, fade it to black with the click of a button, but they still had to handle the reality. The man, bloodied and motionless, was certainly not the same man she'd consoled at the fender bender.

Now she and Fiola were approaching Cuppa Joe's, brainstorming it.

"You think it could be coincidence that there'd be *two* accidents, hit-and-runs?" Jane held the coffee shop door open. "Both with Gormay trucks? How can that be?"

Fiola shrugged. "Why would the driver think he—or she—could get away with it?"

"Large skim iced latte," Jane said to the barista. She turned to Fiola. "You? My treat."

"Caramel mochaccino," she said. "And a chocolate croissant."

Jane pulled out her cell, thumbed in a search as the barista waved them to the waiting line. "Hit-and-runs," she typed. "Unsolved."

"Look at this," she said, showing Fiola her phone screen. "This says last year in Massachusetts? Almost eighty thousand hit-and-runs. And *most* are unsolved."

Their coffees arrived, Fiola's huge croissant taking up all the room on a section of waxed paper.

"Your coffee," Fiola announced.

"Thanks. Drunk drivers, unlicensed drivers, texting drivers." Jane stabbed a straw into the lid of her plastic cup, intent on her search. "Lots of reasons to run from an accident. That's why the DA is going crazy over it."

"Maybe someone was out to get Gormay," Fiola theorized as the door to the coffee shop slid shut behind them. "Or the drivers."

"Huh." Jane played out that scenario, taking her first icy hit of caffeine. "Maybe that's why our Gormay driver looked so frightened."

If she were a street reporter, she'd call Gormay—silly name—and get a comment. She jiggled her ice, thinking. Two hit-and-runs on the same company's vehicle? And now one of the drivers might be dead?

"If we could get the victims' names," Jane said as they walked, "maybe we could figure out who's behind it. Whatever 'it' is."

"And maybe our opening-of-school documentary could go on the air next year instead." Fiola was frowning. "You sure you're up for this, Jane? Maybe you want to go back on the street? I'm sure Marsh and I could arrange it."

"No, no." Day two, and her producer was already second-guessing her commitment. "Can't wait to do the Tosca interview. If she calls. Here's to that." She toasted Fiola with her coffee as they waited to cross Cambridge Street.

"I'm curious, too, though, gotta admit," Fiola said. At a break in the cars they scurried across, ignoring the light, got safely to the sidewalk. "If the second guy lives," Fiola went on, "he might be able to describe the car. Or the driver."

Middle-aged, Caucasian, widow's peak . . . Jane stopped, mid-sidewalk, so quickly Fiola almost slammed into her. Luckily their coffees had lids.

"Listen. What if I identify the guy this afternoon?" Jane's stomach flipped as she remembered her two o'clock obligation. "If they have the right guy for *our* hit-and-run, all they have to do is find where he was, or where his car was, last night at eleven twenty-two."

Fiola nodded. "I see where you're going."

"If the same driver caused both accidents . . ." Jane tried to figure out what that might mean. Wondered whether anyone at Gormay had gotten a note warning "SAY NO MORE."

"Maybe an insurance fraud thing?" Fiola said. "McCusker'd eat that up."

"Yeah," Jane replied. McCusker. Which reminded her, again, of the journalism quicksand she'd landed in.

"Thing is." Jane held the door for Fiola as they went inside. "It's not only the stupid letter. Now I also have to decide whether to tell McCusker we've got video of that second hit-and-run."

The door slammed behind them, and they were back on the job. No more stalling.

"You know what, Fee?" Jane tossed her empty coffee into the security guard's wastebasket. "Getting involved stinks."

ISABEL RUSSO

Should she get involved? Isabel "took a walk," as she called it, to figure that out. Circling her apartment, fifty-one times, she'd decided, was sufficient exercise for each morning. She did yoga, did stretches, she was still in fairly good shape, even without going to the gym, like she used to. Or running, like she used to. Now, wearing her running shorts and shoes and purple Nike top, she did "circuits" of her apartment. Sometimes, before dawn and before anyone could possibly be awake, she'd put on her running shoes, go out in the hallway, and run, very softly, thirty-five times, up and down. No one had ever seen her, but it made her heart beat so fast to do it she almost couldn't, and avoided it until her body cried out for motion.

But today she would stay inside. She started at her refrigerator, then took the seven steps to the living room, trotted between the couch and the coffee table, turned right at the TV, passed the couch again. Thinking about Edward Tarrant, on *his* walk, outside, able to go wherever he wanted.

Down the hall on the right side, passing the too-small bathroom, into the bedroom. Down the right wall, turn past the bed, past the footboard, up the other side, along the back wall, down the hall again. Sometimes she sang, top of her lungs, doing her circuits until she sang an entire aria. Often *"O mio babbino caro,"* one of her favorites, so anguished, pleading for her true love. *"Nessun dorma,"* too, though a song for a man. Puccini made her feel strong, and even potentially triumphant. *"Vincerò,"* the final exultant word. I will win. *"Vincerò"*: *I will win.* Would she win this time?

Sometimes she walked, making the time go by. Sometimes she marched, trying to laugh, trying to remember the days when life had no baggage. Sometimes, like now, she couldn't resist, had to think about "him." Like that day, just yesterday, how he'd looked, strutting up the street. How he'd probably not even recognize her if he saw her again.

Not even recognize her?

She'd recognize *him*. For sure. As her steps quickened, she remembered every Facebook posting she could. She'd scoured the Internet, sometimes staying up all night doing it, finding photos and videos, from Facebook and Instagram and sometimes Snapchat. She'd copied each one, with ritual and reverence, and saved it, with all her notes, to a special file. A file she labeled "Someday."

Someday. She felt her frown deepen as she began the next circuit, approaching the refrigerator, and the days-to-go calendar she'd magneted to the fridge door. She'd be out of here, soon, someday soon, soon she'd cross off today on her calendar and then Gormay would arrive and—

She stopped, sank to the floor in the middle of the kitchen, feeling the cool hardness of the linoleum against her bare thighs. Her rainbow crystal caught the light, played it over her skin. As she looked up she saw not the crystal, but her cell phone, on the kitchen table, the black sliver of technology that could connect her to her future. Was Someday now? All she had to do was pick up the phone.

She reached toward it, then let her arm fall back to her side. She wanted justice, no matter what Tarrant had instructed, no matter what her mother did, no matter what anything. But how could that happen without letting everyone know how dumb she was?

"I wasn't dumb!" She surprised herself as the words came out, so loud and biting and bitter in the silent room. But she was right. She wasn't dumb. She was . . . harmed. And if she didn't have the courage to say so? Whose fault was that?

A scene began to emerge, the role she'd play, the lines she'd say and the lines she wouldn't. It would be . . . embarrassing? Silly? Pitiful? To admit how she was not exactly stalking him, but keeping a special file. So she wouldn't say that. She didn't have to tell everything.

She felt herself smiling, felt her posture changing to inhabit the role, become a . . . she selected each word, carefully. "Quietly suffering ingénue." She smiled, adding one more. Quietly suffering but "crusading" ingénue. She would keep some secrets, thank you very much. About her personal life, she would say no more. That wasn't—how had Tarrant put it that day?— relevant.

Her face changed. She could feel the frown return and the muscles in her back stiffen. What was "relevant"—she spit out the word in her head— what was relevant was that she was raped, assaulted, drugged, violated. She piled the disgusting words on top of each other, building her case and her wall of anger and revenge.

Tarrant had ordered her to stay quiet. She didn't even want to remember the conversation he'd had with her, and later, with her mother. He'd ordered them never to mention "his" name. And she'd agreed.

Well, she could do that. Exactly as she'd promised. And still win. The ingénue-feeling returned, and with it a tantalizing hint of the future, her happy future, her safe and powerful future. Her freedom. This would be her first truly starring role.

All she had to do was call Jane Ryland.

Call Jane and say yes.

And, she thought, *Vincerò!*

21

WILLOW GALT

Willow Galt pushed through the revolving doors of Endicott Library, smiled at the auburn-haired librarian behind the curved mahogany front counter. Her arms goose-bumped with the blast of air-conditioning as she entered the library's main hall, and she clutched the tote bag tighter.

Maybe this was risky. She'd imagined a dark enclave, musty shelves, an air of forgetting, and of the forgotten. But a bright-lighted display of "Books to Take to the Cape," festooned with fishing net, took center stage of the first-floor great room, an array of pastel-covered novels with Adirondack chairs and flip-flops on the front, the kind she'd read—was it only last year?—as her final summer as Daniella ended three thousand miles from here. No time for that now, for froth or romance.

She turned right, determined, toward the elevator. Seconds after she pushed the "up" arrow, it arrived, onyx doors sliding open with a soft welcoming ping. Empty. Willow slipped in, pushed a black button to close the doors, then the white one marked "3."

She could almost feel heat from the book she carried in her bag, feel its power and its secrets.

The rattle of the cables began, a smooth ride, past 2, and then, with another soft ping, stopping on 3. The doors opened. She and Avery had never been here together, though they'd talked of it. And now here she was, by herself, *because* of Avery. In so many ways.

Floor three was designed for academics, Avery had explained, and for storage. One long metal table lined the wall nearest the elevator, a row of chairs, empty—*hurray*—along its edge. The rest of the room was crowded with ceiling-high gray metal bookshelves, each row double-sided and crammed face-to-face-to-face with bound manuscripts, maybe ten shelves deep, Willow estimated, crowded together and accessible only by turning a spoked metal wheel attached to each side.

"A graveyard of blood, sweat, and fears where no one ever goes," Avery had proclaimed, describing the student papers she'd read and evaluated, and how they were stored on the third floor of Endicott. "If I have to read another thesis on 'Strong Women in Puccini' I'll . . ." Avery had laughed again, that laugh, taken another swig of wine. "Their parents pay all that money. But no one ever looks at them again."

No one ever looks at them again. Willow could hear that voice, almost as if, now, Avery was giving advice from the grave.

She put her tote bag on the long table, then counted four shelves from the front, because Tom's real birthday was in April. Clamped both hands on the stubby handle of the turning wheel, and cranked to the right, once, twice, saw the bottom edges of the shelves slide noiselessly across metal runners set into the floor. Two turns, then three, revealed a narrow mini-corridor, walled by hundreds of bound manuscripts. Each bore a catalog number of some kind, written in black or white ink, depending, on the lower spine.

She stood, feeling the silence, thinking of needles in haystacks. Haystacks no one would even think of searching. She had no connection with Adams Bay, no reason to be in this library. There would be no record of her being here. This was a haystack in a haystack. She counted four sections toward the wall. *There.*

She heard her heartbeat, or felt it, or imagined it, as she unzipped the top of her tote bag and reached in. She felt the still-cool black leather, held it in her arms, clutched it to her chest. With a deep sigh, she imagined bougainvillea and California sunshine, neither of which she was likely to ever see again. Four rows in, four sections down, four rows up.

Remembering to keep the manuscripts in order, she extracted two of them from their place on the shelf, then two more, then two more. Placing her treasure flat against the back of the shelf, she then replaced the manuscripts where they belonged. One after another she walled up her scrapbook behind all the other volumes, not even its top edge showing, obscured by the other books.

She stared at the place where her scrapbook was, memorized the numbers on the spines of the one to its left and to its right. Whispered them. Then, fearing her sorrow and the distractions certain to come, pulled out her wallet and a pencil to write them . . . uh, *where*? On the back of her new Social Security card. She wrote the numbers, smiled, and returned it to its place behind her new driver's license and her new health insurance card.

"Stay safe," she whispered the words to her scrapbook. "I'll come back and get you when I can."

JAKE BROGAN

"Where the hell is she?" Jake, muttering, used the side of one fist to bang on the front door of the Galts' brownstone. They'd been heading for Adams Bay to follow up on Avery Morgan, but instead Jake turned their cruiser up Ionian Street to the Galts'. He needed to chat, one more time, with Willow—the woman who'd called 911, but wouldn't discuss it. He scratched his head, waited for sounds from inside. Movement, or a television being turned off. Heard nothing.

Maybe Ms. Galt was simply an innocent Good Samaritan. And he was making too much of it. But if that was the case, why all the mystery?

"No car in the driveway," D said, joining him at the top of the front steps. "Newspaper's gone. They're probably not home."

"I see why you get the big detective bucks," Jake said. "So. My online search. At first run-through, picking the low-hanging social media fruit, there's nothing about the Galts. So far."

"Why do we care?" D lifted one corner of the woven welcome mat, though it didn't say welcome, let it fall back onto the porch. "No key. They suspects?"

"Everyone's a suspect," Jake said. "We'll come back."

"Ve'll be back." D did his Arnold imitation, then chuckled as if he'd never said the line before. He stabbed at the air, punctuating his words. "Ve vill hunt you *down*."

"Good one," Jake said. "Too bad about Avery Morgan. She might have hooked you up with her Hollywood crew. You'd dig a whole new career, right?"

D stopped, looked at him, shrugged. Turned away, headed toward their cruiser.

"What's wrong?" Jake called after him. D probably needed more coffee. *He* sure did.

By the time they found a semi-legal parking place in front of Colonial Hall, fortified themselves with dark-roast larges, and gotten the attention of name-tagged Mack at the security desk—"Security Desk" was spelled out on a black plastic placard in front of the bespectacled guard—it was almost eleven.

"Detective Jake Brogan, here to see Edward Tarrant." Jake held up his badge wallet.

Mack sat up straight, squared his blue-uniformed shoulders, pushed his wire-rimmed glasses higher on his nose.

"You got an appointment?"

"Nope," Jake said. "Is he here?"

"I'll have to check." He pointed a yellow pencil at a wooden bench along the wall across from them, a curved dark wood settee bookended with elaborately carved lion-head armrests. The brick wall behind it displayed a painted shield, some Latin phrase in gilt letters encircling it. "You can wait on the lion bench."

Rent-a-guards were always a trip. He and D exchanged amused glances as this one turned to his phone console. Jake always figured it was better to start out letting guys like this think they had some authority. If Mack let them do what they wanted to do, couldn't hurt to let him think he'd allowed them to do it.

But they weren't going to sit on any bench. They waited at the desk, Jake leaning on it with one elbow, D focused on his texting. As usual.

"In a meeting." Mack wheeled his swivel chair away from the console and closer to them, but still held the phone receiver, its twisty cord stretched to full length. "He says, what's it about?"

"We say, police business." Meeting, my ass, Jake thought. Two detectives show up at your office, you don't give them the in-a-meeting dodge. Unless you're stalling, or guilty, or an asshole. Or all three.

"Mack? I'll take this, okay?" A voice from down the hall.

Jake looked up to see a black-suited woman, white hair curly and wild, purple glasses perched on the top of her head. She hurried toward them, her mouth a red slash, her high heels tapping the wooden floor. She looked at Jake, then D, then back at Jake.

"Detective Rogan?" She chose Jake, offered her hand for him to shake, smilingly hospitable.

"Brogan," he said. "And this is my partner, Detective DeLuca."

"Ah. *Brogan.*" She glanced at Mack, rolling her eyes. "Apologies. I'm Sasha Vogelby, head of the Drama Department here. Mr. Tarrant sent me. He very much regrets—"

The woman stopped, mid-excuse. She must be reading the expression on my face, Jake thought.

"Anyway," she said, her smile plastered in place. "Mr. Tarrant asks, will you please come up to my office? He'll finish his meeting as quickly as he can, and then join us."

As they headed for a bank of silver elevators, Ms. Vogelby's skirt swishing in front of them, Jake realized what had *not* happened this morning. Mack the guard had not asked, "Is this about Avery Morgan?" Sasha Vogelby had not looked weepy, or red-eyed, or even downcast, had not inquired about the woman Jake assumed was her colleague. Could they not know Avery Morgan was dead?

Possible, Jake answered himself. Which meant the next half hour or so could be pretty interesting.

22

JANE RYLAND

"I'll take the stairs," Jane said as Fiola stabbed the "up" button in the station's glass-walled lobby. Channel 2's elevator was notoriously unreliable. Jane had once checked the inspection record, handwritten in spidery script with what looked like a fountain pen, and it appeared no one from the state's Inspectional Services had checked the thing since the blizzard of 2000. Stairs were healthier anyway, and she had to get exercise somehow, since her gym attendance was equally out of date. She yanked open the heavy metal stairwell door and held it ajar with her back, about to wave to Fiola, who'd snagged a *Register* from the stack on the guard's desk.

"Fee? Anything in the paper about The Reserve?" Jane asked.

"Hang on." Fiola flapped open the paper just as the elevator arrived. "See you in a sec." She stepped inside and the doors closed behind her.

"It worked? Amazing," Jane muttered. She entered the windowless stairwell of pitted metal banisters and scarred walls peeling their once-green paint. Tromping up the stairs, she tried to focus on how many calories she was burning per step. Her buzzing phone interrupted the count.

"Jane Ryland." She made it to the landing, grabbed the newel post, swung around the corner to the next flight.

"Assistant District Attorney Frank McCusker," she heard. "You're sprung."

Jane stopped, mid-step, mid-stairway. "Sprung?"

"Yeah. As in, off the hook. In the clear. Excused. You're livin' right,

Miz Ryland. The driver of the Cadillac has come forward, turned himself in. So all good, we got our man. The judge is aware, nonsuggestive ID session is canceled, life goes on. Justice served."

Without me, Jane thought. She felt her shoulders sag, almost imagined a black cloud lifting to the ceiling and floating out through the air-conditioning vent. She didn't have to say anything. If that letter *was* a warning about her testimony, now it didn't matter.

"Terrific," she said.

"We'll let you know if we need any more," McCusker went on, "but at this point, seems slam-dunk. I mean—this guy's all 'I'm doing the right thing' and about his 'guilty conscience,' I don't know. Some bullsh—" Jane listened with amusement as the ADA apparently reconsidered his language. "Whatever. He's here. He's making a statement now."

"Who is it? Did he say why he ran?"

"All I can tell you, he's cooperating like a good little criminal," McCusker said. "I foresee a plea, probation, and some kind of restitution. And on we go."

Goodbye, widow's-peak-and-cheekbones guy. Goodbye, nasty letter. "Middle-aged guilt, I guess, right?"

"Middle-aged?"

Jane heard the confusion in McCusker's voice.

"Yeah," Jane said. "Maybe older."

"Uh, no." McCusker paused, cleared his throat. "The driver is barely twenty-five. That's why he skedaddled. He thought his insurance rates would kill him."

Jane stared at the blotchy wall, then sank to the middle stair, sitting with her feet planted on a lower step. *When in doubt, don't say a word,* an irreversible law of the universe, she knew, and *I should have kept my mouth shut* the wail of regret from centuries of rueful chatterboxes who realized, yet again, they should have left well enough alone. *Know when to shut up,* her father used to tell her and her sister.

Now, with her one throwaway question about middle-aged guilt, Jane had said too much.

"Jane?" McCusker's voice dragged her back from her spiral of remorse. "You with me?"

"I lost you for a second—bad connection," Jane lied. "I'm in the stairwell, and on my way to the office. Want to call me later?"

"What do you mean, 'middle-aged'?" McCusker's voice had an edge to it. "Can you hear me now? If we've got the wrong guy—"

Jane grabbed the banister, hauled herself to her feet. If she kept quiet, she was letting an innocent person plead guilty to something. She'd seen the driver, completely, consciously, indelibly. He was not a kid.

"Does your guy know *I'm* a witness?" Jane asked.

Silence. "I'm not sure I can reveal that," the DA finally said. "Why?"

Her turn to be silent. She'd had that one moment of freedom, of relief that she no longer had to rat out a bad guy in front of a courtroom audience and a defense attorney and who knew who else. The bad guy had presented himself to law enforcement. Good news, except it was the wrong guy. Cue the quicksand.

"The driver I saw was definitely older."

"Shit," the ADA said.

Jane opened the door marked "Floor 2," saw the hallway outside the Special Projects Unit and its framed posters of network shows, some of which had already been canceled. Only the smiling stars remained on display, all photoshopped and flatteringly lighted, blithely believing their shows would never become victims of bad promotion or bad writing or bad ratings.

Had Jane gotten it wrong, too? For a fleeting moment, she almost hoped so. Hoped that possibly, in the heat of the moment, she'd made a mistake. She sighed, shaking her head. In hard reality, there wasn't any heat of the moment. She wasn't wrong.

"You sure?" McCusker went on.

"Yeah. The man I saw was definitely—"

"Again, don't describe him," the ADA said. "We'll hold this guy, nonetheless. But as for you, it's back to plan A. Be in courtroom 206, at two. If we've got an innocent person confessing to a hit-and-run, that's a whole 'nother problem. We'll see who you recognize. If anyone. Remember, the driver, the one who confessed at least, may not be in court."

So near and yet so far. She continued toward her office, dragging her feet, wondering, again, about that stupid letter. Wondering about bringing the station lawyer to court with her to make sure she didn't say more than she should, though it might already be too late for that. But there was one more thing she had to ask McCusker.

"Why would he confess?" She'd broken a big story a few months earlier where a confession was key. As long as she was hopelessly ensnared in this, might as well get some answers. "Did he confess to the other hit-and-run, too?"

She paused in the hallway, eager to hear the answer. Two hit-and-runs by the same guy? That'd be a story.

"'Other hit-and-run'?" the ADA asked.

Jane opened her office door. Fiola had the phone tucked between her cheek and shoulder, apparently taking notes on her computer. That white envelope was still on Jane's desk. She'd tell McCusker about it in person.

"Jane? What other hit-and-run?" McCusker repeated.

"Sorry, I'm still in the stairwell," Jane tried the lie again.

"Very convenient," he said. "Well, listen, Jane. If you can hear me? Two things. One? See you at two. And as for the 'other hit-and-run,' that's one phone call to the cop shop. So again, thanks for your help. We do welcome it when the media steps in to help law enforcement. Much appreciated."

"Gah." Jane stuck her tongue out at her cell phone as she clicked him away. Fiola hung up her call at the same time.

"Who was that?" Fiola asked. "Listen, I've set us up with the campus big sisters, so we'll get a bunch of good stuff from them. SAFE, it's called. They're like, advocates, buddies, support systems. Victims, too, some of them." She rubbed her palms together. "They're happy to give us the scoop. Don't you love it when someone spills the beans?"

"Yeah," Jane said. At least Fiola didn't know about the DA's phone call. Far as this afternoon was concerned, nothing had changed. "That'll be great. When?"

Jane's desk phone trilled, the double ring that meant an outside call.

"Now what?" Jane picked up the receiver. "Jane Ryland." Better not be McCusker again. Like, asking if the station had raw video of the other hit-and-run. *All* she needed.

"Jane?" A woman's voice, tentative. "It's Tosca."

23

EDWARD TARRANT

Edward Tarrant let the receiver clatter back into place, knowing that the phone call from Sasha Vogelby signaled the opening curtain of an imminent and all-important performance. He needed to remember that knowledge was power. In this case, right now, he had the balance of both.

He knew Avery Morgan was dead. Trey Welliver clearly had no idea what happened, though thank heaven the boy had shown up with the news. Sasha didn't know, or she certainly would have asked him about it. College police were not in the picture. Even though the Morgan House was owned by the board, it was out of their campus-only jurisdiction.

Edward prayed with all his being that Avery's death was an accident. That soon, today, they'd confirm that, and this would all be over.

But certainly Avery Morgan's death was why the Boston Police detectives were now at his door. The damn *homicide* detectives, which seemed to put the lie to his hopes of an accidental drowning.

Because of that, he'd sicced the deferential but persuasive Sasha on them, stalling. He needed to regroup, yet again, even though he'd spent hours the night before staring, alone, at his—their—bedroom ceiling, plotting moves and strategies and outcomes.

He could not afford to have Adams Bay involved in a scandal. And he, personally, could not afford to be its cause. The terrifying possibility that Avery's death might detonate both bombshells was what kept him restless, awake, and calculating the damage.

He pressed his fingers to his forehead, trying to hold in his brains.

He'd steeled himself for a flood of phone calls after last night's TV news-casts, even as shallow and unrevealing as they were—her name had not been used—but thank God for summer break and the diaspora of most faculty and staff. There'd been only a brief snippet in the *Globe* and *Register,* and again no name. Maybe the press was also waiting for the word on suicide.

He paused, considering. Then contemplated the uncomfortable real-ity that he actually wished a "friend" had killed herself. But had she?

A wine-fueled Avery herself had divulged to him that her star was on the wane in what she called Tinseltown, and gushed her intense grati-tude for the sinecure that Adams Bay—and Edward—offered. Apparently, though Avery hadn't elaborated much, there'd been some embezzlement blowup with the head of the studio, with Avery a casualty. An innocent ca-sualty, she'd wailed, hanging on to his arm. Had she truly been distraught? Depressed? In danger? He'd thought she was simply being dramatic.

He realized he was still standing behind his desk, staring at the now-silent phone. Where the hell was Manderley? Of all the days for his as-sistant to be late. But maybe for the best. Keep her out of this. No need to have her spreading rumors among her little friends.

Sasha would have taken the cops into her office by now, and stalled them with whatever prattle. But she couldn't stall forever. His "meeting" would have to end. And soon. They were the cops, after all. *Homicide* cops.

But he needed time. He needed to write a statement of sympathy for Adams Bay president Reginald P. Buchholz to issue, soon as they could reach him in the south of France, where he summered with his family.

Family.

If only Edward had gone with them this year as usual, the dutiful son-in-law, right after spring semester's end. But no, this year he'd stayed in town, and then . . . Avery.

Problem was, the moment he contacted Reg Buchholz about Avery's death, Brinn would also have to know *all* about it, and ask him *all* about her, thinking she was being compassionate and wifely, and possibly in-sist on coming back to Boston. He'd been so exquisitely delighted that

Brinn Buchholz Tarrant had agreed to leave him behind for the summer. And now this.

Did Avery have family? The question saddened him, somehow, with a pang of conscience. He had no idea.

Why did Avery Morgan die? How?

The next time his phone rang, shrill and strident, it would signal the beginning of the endgame. He took a deep breath, steeling himself for the attack and defense ahead. He was a firefighter. He'd put this one out, too.

JAKE BROGAN

"Look at this." Jake kept his voice low as he showed the cell phone screen to DeLuca. They were sitting—they'd had no option—on a foofy couch in Sasha Vogelby's office. She'd left them, bustling out for coffee. Jake tried to refuse, telegraphing they wouldn't be around long enough to drink coffee. But D accepted, and turned out that was for the better. Jake used the downtime—*Tick tock*, he thought, imagining Edward Tarrant's "meeting"—to dig further into Avery Morgan. After finding her on Google this morning, he'd checked her bio on the various Hollywood sites. Now he was following up her connection with Untitled Studios. "About our victim," he continued.

D had clicked off his own phone, stashed it in his jacket pocket.

"What?" D squinted at Jake's screen. "My eyes are going. Gonna need cheaters, so says Kat. But what does she know?"

"She's a doctor. Just saying," Jake said, taking back his cell. DeLuca's clandestine relationship with medical examiner Kat McMahan was as under the radar as Jake's with Jane. Their mutually assured destruction had ensured mutual silence about their professionally improper liaisons, Jake's with a member of the dreaded media, DeLuca's with a law enforcement colleague. "Anyway, seems like there was a big embezzlement scandal at the studio where Avery Morgan freelanced. Untitled, remember?

From the quotes the feds out there gave, sounds like there was a confidential informant. What if the informant was Avery Morgan?"

D examined his fingernails, moving his hands closer to his eyes, then farther away. "That's why she moved here, you think?"

"Could be." Jake stared at the screen on his cell. What'd they do before they could run someone's life history from their phones? It was either amazing, getting a pile of work done without even going into the squad, or it sucked, since you were expected to be on the job every second of every day. Still. He'd much rather have the instant access.

He checked his watch. Almost noon. California cops would be on the job now, but the US Attorney types not until nine West Coast time. They'd know the deets about this. And they'd have to supply them.

"Talk about a code of silence," Jake said. "What if it wasn't someone in The Reserve who Avery Morgan ratted out? What if it was someone in Hollywood?"

"Avery Morgan?" Sasha Vogelby appeared in her doorway, holding a white ceramic mug in each hand.

"You know her?" Jake stood. Now was as good a time as any. He took the offered mug of coffee, signaled D to do the same. Best not to give someone bad news when they could scald themselves in reaction.

"Well, who doesn't?" Big smile from Vogelby, opened arms. "She's a joy, a complete joy. Her students a*dore* her."

"She a professor here?" DeLuca was playing dumb, Jake knew. They were well aware she was a visiting adjunct. The two of them had instantly found her on the college's summer program site.

"Visiting. An adjunct." Vogelby, smiling, raised a correcting finger. "I'm the head of the Drama Department. As you can see."

She walked toward her desk, gestured at the engraved nameplate, and then at a row of framed movie posters along a red-painted wall. "Yes, that's me. Ah, I know, once an actor, always an actor. But, alas, when the parts became, shall we say, fewer and farther between? I devoted my life to teaching the 'younger' generation. Acting, and costuming, and stagecraft."

"Terrific," Jake said.

"Yeah," DeLuca said. Took a sip of coffee. They both put their cups on the low table in front of the couch.

Vogelby blinked at them, silent. Then her eyes narrowed. "Why were you talking about Avery?" Her hand flew to her lips. "Oh. You're *homicide detectives*."

She lowered herself into her chair, then instantly stood again. The chair rolled back, banging against the metal bookcase behind her, its motion teetering some slender glass figurines lined up in front of the books. One crashed to the floor and rolled out of sight under the desk.

Vogelby did not go after it, but stared at the two of them.

"Is she . . . ?" The woman's voice had dropped to a whisper. "Was she . . . ?"

"I'm sorry for your loss," Jake said. In all the years, he'd never come up with a better response than the now-cliché. "I'm sorry" wasn't personal enough, "it's terrible" was too emotional, a simple "yes" could sound insensitive.

Plus, this stage of an investigation was always tricky. The ME had deemed Morgan's death a drowning, but not homicide—yet—which meant there weren't really "suspects." But some tests were still pending, including for drugs, so homicide was still on the table. Which meant everyone was a suspect.

Sasha Vogelby had covered her mouth with both hands, as if to prevent herself from saying something, or maybe to keep her emotions in. She sank into her chair, staring into the middle distance, past Jake and D and past the open office door.

"It was my idea, inviting her to Adams Bay." Vogelby sighed, rested her forehead on splayed fingers. Looked up at them through an array of knobby silver rings. "How? Did she die? Where? When?"

"We're investigating," Jake said. "Please be assured—"

"Are the rest of us in *danger*?" Vogelby's eyes widened. She sat up straighter, reached for her phone. "I need to alert—"

"We'll do the alerting, thank you, ma'am," Jake said.

"That's why we need to talk to the dean." DeLuca looked at his watch.

"If that's who you're about to call, feel free," Jake added. "If it isn't, please wait."

"I feel so guilty." Vogelby took her hand away from the phone, was almost talking to herself.

"Ma'am?"

"It was supposed to be a *fabu*lous experience. And now it's a *tra*gedy." Vogelby took a deep breath, as if pulling it all in, the sorrow and the surprise. "All the students a*dor*ed her. They were always coming to her house for parties, and gatherings. Script readings. Rehearsals. She gets that *lovely* home, and the pool." She stopped. "Got, I mean."

"So you've been there," Jake said. "When were you last at her house?"

"You certainly can't think . . ." Vogelby stood, her head dropped back and her eyes raised to the ceiling. Then she fluffed her silver curls and touched the glasses on top of her head, adjusting. Cleared her throat. "I'm sorry. I know you must ask, officers."

"'Detectives.'" DeLuca could never resist the correction, even in times like this. Jake ignored him, as always.

"So when were you last there?" Jake persisted.

"Oh my goodness, I could check." She selected a stack of papers on one corner of the desk, flipped through the pages. "I'm sure there's a record of . . ." She looked at the two detectives with an apologetic half-smile. "I'm so sorry, I'm not trying to be difficult. I simply am—*dev*astated. Upset. Concerned. And . . . a little, discombobulated, I'm afraid. Forgive me."

"Did she have any students who were special friends?" DeLuca asked.

"Or any she complained about?" Jake added. Discombobulation was the perfect time to ask questions. The less a subject or witness was focused, the more off balance and uncalculating, the more honest and uncrafted an answer they might give.

She looked up from her papers, frowning.

"What?"

"Who would go visit her? Is that typical, for a professor to have parties?"

"Adjunct," Vogelby said, glancing at DeLuca.

"Adjunct." Jake smiled, oh-so-patient. "So, you said parties? How did students get invited, do you know? Which ones?"

Vogelby's back stiffened. "We're meticulous about privacy here at Adams Bay." She put down her papers. "I'd certainly need to ask for parental permission before we released any student's name."

"Not if they're over eighteen," Jake said. Not threatening, simply providing a fact. "And certainly not if they're over twenty-one."

"I'll have to think about that," Vogelby said.

"We'll wait," DeLuca said.

Her shoulders dropped, her mouth twisting in thought, the red lipstick changing shape. After a beat, she picked up the phone, waited, poked three numbers. Waited. "Mr. Tarrant?" she asked, her voice blank and emotionless. "Are you free?"

She paused, listening, nodding, at one point glancing at Jake and D. She put down the phone without saying goodbye. "Mr. Tarrant knows about Avery," she said. "There are—things to take care of, as you might imagine," she added. "Family."

Jake raised his eyebrows, couldn't hold back his skepticism. Who'd told Tarrant? But he'd honestly been surprised the buzz had been contained even this long. Though reporters had to wait for next of kin and Kat's determination whether suicide was the cause of death, the spreading rumors about Avery Morgan would be impossible to prevent. Problem was, if it was murder, the killer would now be regrouping, creating alibis and getting stories straight. Exactly what Jake could not allow to happen.

"We don't need to 'imagine.'" He stood. Enough of her stalling. "And you'll need to give us her family information."

"As a result," Vogelby went on, as if Jake hadn't said a word, "Mr. Tarrant says, please leave a card, and he'll contact you. As soon as possible."

"When?" D asked, draping one arm across the back of the couch, signaling he wasn't planning to leave.

"How about now?" Jake said. "Now is better."

24

JANE RYLAND

"Do you swear to tell the truth, the whole truth . . ."

Jane couldn't take her eyes off the court clerk, diminutive in a navy dress and mismatched jacket, her right hand raised, palm forward, just as she'd instructed Jane to do. Jane felt the seat of the witness chair against the back of her legs, knew that in thirty seconds she'd be asked to—

"Please be seated." The clerk gave Jane a fleeting smile. Maybe she'd recognized her? And then turned back to her own seat in front of the judge's bench.

Jane had covered many a trial in this very courtroom, 206 of Boston Municipal. But now *she* was the center of attention in the raised witness box. On this side, the dark wood was scuffed and dented, damaged by the restless feet of countless fidgeting witnesses and defendants.

Judge Francesca Scapicchio looked down from her higher vantage point. The Scap, as whispers called her, was carefully lipsticked, perfectly postured, hair in a gray chignon, the fluted edges of a pale green scarf showing under her black robe. Red nail polish.

"Let's wait one moment, Ms. Ryland," Scapicchio said, her voice low, then rustled through some papers on her bench. A tyrannical, no-nonsense judicial veteran, The Scap had once telephoned a newspaper reporter and yelled at him for calling her "feisty."

Jane was happy to wait. *Take all the time you want,* she thought. She could wait forever, if need be.

Half an hour ago, she'd shown the "SAY NO MORE" letter to ADA McCusker, who'd examined it at his desk, frowning.

"This is why I asked if your suspect's lawyers knew it was me who's testifying," Jane said.

"Huh." McCusker had turned the letter over, then the envelope. "No markings, postmarked Boston, nothing traceable. No way to know if it's connected, Jane."

They'd sat in silence, McCusker staring at the letter, Jane's toe tapping the office's thin carpeting.

"You worried about this?" he finally asked.

"No. Well, maybe. I don't know." How was she supposed to answer that? "I get weird mail all the time. But . . ."

"Okay." McCusker put the letter back into the envelope. "Never mind then. You go home. We'll take the guy's confession. Santora's cracking down on hit-and-runs, but this one's not a biggie. We'll go with what we've got, see what the judge says."

"But you might have the wrong guy." Jane had tried to follow his reasoning. "You'd accept his confession, knowing that?"

McCusker shrugged. "Up to the judge. I could compel you to testify, of course. Your lawyers could fight it. We could make it a big public deal. But, hey. I'm the good guy. If you feel you're in danger, I'll make it your call."

He stood, handed her the letter.

She didn't take it. She stood, too, looking him eye to eye. "You'd let an innocent person be convicted?"

"If you don't testify, we got nothin'." McCusker put the letter on his desk. "Guy confessed. Why would he do that? Maybe you're wrong."

"I'm not wrong."

"Your call," McCusker said.

Now, in the witness box, she tried reassure herself. McCusker's "your call" was an impossible decision, but she couldn't let an innocent person be convicted. And McCusker was right. Why would he confess?

But she had a more immediate dilemma: Soon she'd be asked to look at each person in the courtroom and, maybe, point out someone. A guilty person. Her hands clenched in her lap, the bottom of one thumb rubbing against the top of the other, her feet planted flat like she was a kid called to the principal's office. An ancient air conditioner struggled in a casement window, once-blue velvet curtains optimistically drawn aside, giving the relic some room to combat Boston's relentless August.

"All you have to do is tell the truth," the news director had assured her. "And show that letter to the DA. You'll be fine."

She'd be fine? As if they could know. ADA McCusker was now seated at one of the lawyers' tables, turning pages in a loose-leaf notebook.

She stared at her hands again, couldn't seem to unclench them. How many witnesses had she watched in this very box? How many personal Rubicons had been crossed from this very spot, how many bridges burned, how many lives forever changed? Now, with the rows of audience members in front of her, the gravity of her words to come weighed heavy. She might be about to accuse someone of a crime.

Strange, though. As a reporter she did that all the time. She did her research, produced her investigations, put her story in the paper or on TV. Naming names. She didn't need to swear to tell the truth for television—she simply did it. Why did this feel so different?

Also strange, now that she thought about it, telling the truth was exactly what she was asking Tosca to do. She'd pressured the young woman a bit, she had to admit, and was thrilled when Tosca had agreed to be interviewed tomorrow.

Jane hadn't told her anything that wasn't true, of course. Tosca's disclosures could certainly make a big difference, would change lives and reveal some frightening realities of college life.

But now, as the one who had to answer questions instead of asking them, Jane felt a twinge of regret for her manipulation. *You'll be fine*—she'd actually said those words to Tosca.

Turnabout was fair play, she guessed. Still, with the lawyers waiting at their identical tables, court officers guarding the doors, the American and Massachusetts flags side by side and the darkly oil-painted portraits of John Jay and James Madison staring at her, it felt like—

"Miss Ryland?" Judge Scapicchio asked, her voice low but now amplified by the courtroom sound system. "Are you ready?"

ISABEL RUSSO

Who would be calling her? Isabel, startled by the ringing phone, lost a pink flip-flop as she scrambled back through the window, one foot poking through first, the other keeping her balanced on the ribbed metal floor of the balcony. She'd left her lunch, half a tuna sandwich on a paper plate, on the table outside, next to the flapped-open book she was reading, a biography of Maria Callas. The phone rang again. Her landline. That's what made her skin crawl.

No one ever used this phone, an old-fashioned brick-red wall phone left over from the tenant before. Her mother had insisted she keep the hardwired system. "In case of emergency, for heaven's sake, Isabella!" Had something happened to her mother?

She trotted the two steps to the wall, her mind racing, every possibility dire. Maybe it was some Adams Bay thing—a change, or demand, or calamity. The school's admin office had this number, and it was the one in the student handbook, not that any student ever called her. No student called anyone, for that matter. They were all about texting. What if the caller was Edward Tarrant, telling her—her brain clamped down at the thought, and her fingers touched the red plastic.

"Hello?" Her kitchen reeked of tuna fish, disgusting, suddenly, and she was off balance in one flip-flop and one bare foot. "Hello?"

No one on the other end. Only a crackling, staticky sputter, then a muffled murmur of "hold music," as if she had called someone and they'd put her on hold. She frowned, studying the flat red receiver. Then smiled, rolled her eyes at her own ridiculousness.

The one thing her paranoid self hadn't considered. The one thing that made sense. Wrong number. Or sales pitch. Didn't matter. Someone she didn't care about.

She hung up, embracing the sound of the handset settling into place. She'd clean up the tuna fish stuff—not really so disgusting—go back outside, and live inside her book. It was for opera history class, happily, so she was actually studying. She was up to the part about—

But as she closed the dishwasher door, the phone rang again. Maybe a salesperson? And since she'd answered the phone the first time, now they knew they'd reached someone. That meant there'd be a human on the other end.

She grabbed the receiver, ready to order them to leave her alone. She didn't want to buy anything. Unless they were offering freedom. In which case she'd pay anything.

"Hello?" The music, volume up a little louder this time, was all she heard. *So* insane. As if she had nothing else to do but answer the phone. "Hey," she said, hearing her annoyance over the muted music, "you have the wrong number. Okay? Don't call anymore."

She slammed the phone back into place. At least it wasn't her mother, or anything about her mother. And it wasn't Tarrant, or anyone from Adams Bay.

"Geez," she said out loud. The sound in the empty kitchen made her think about how long it had been since she'd had a real conversation. With a real person, face-to-face. The Gormay delivery guy didn't count, even though she had to admit she looked forward, in a way, to his arrival. It wasn't always the same person, but often it was. The young man with the red hair and the kind of seen-it-all face. He knew her only as "Isabel with the grilled chicken or lasagna." But she knew his whole name, Grady McWhirter Houlihan.

She'd gotten up the courage to ask his name the night he forgot her salad dressing. She'd told him it was okay, but he'd made a special trip back to bring it to her. And after that, they'd chatted each time, about music, and the weather, nothing big, just . . . being themselves. She'd even invited him in, once, her insides fluttering. He'd stayed at the door, seemed to recognize, somehow, how skittish she was. Isabel and Grady, she thought. But there would never again be a man in her life. Never, ever, ever.

"Are you kidding me?" She said it out loud as the phone rang again, almost as if it were making fun of her.

"Good luck with that," she told it. She stood, hands on hips, staring it down. Waited one ring, then two, then three. She had the power, she realized. Just don't answer. *Take that, whoever.*

The ringing stopped, the message system taking over. Fish swam in a frantic circle, acting like the phone upset him, too. "Could that be?" she wondered aloud. "Do fish think?" She grimaced, embarrassed by her thoughts, and by her talking to herself out loud. Clearly she was losing it.

Maybe she really was. What if? She sat in her lone kitchen chair, thinking about solitude, hearing the rush of the Kenmore Square traffic through her open window, the hum of the fridge and the drone of her brain. She was . . . This was . . .

A tear laced down her cheek. She felt it before she even knew she was crying. She feared the world, and feared the time, and feared whatever would happen to her next. She talked to a *fish*, for Lordy's sake. She was Isabel, talented and even pretty, and now, she was like a lost child, defeated by one adversity. One huge adversity, yes, but others had survived, hadn't they? She wished she hadn't promised to stay silent, but Tarrant had assured her silence was the prudent thing. Prudent.

Well, she was—she stood, whisked away another tear with a determined palm—finished with prudent. She'd handle her own life, she'd—she felt her heart beating so hard she had to touch one hand to the kitchen table to steady herself. Yes. She'd do it, she'd go out out out—*out*—and be herself again. For a start, she'd call Professor Tully, and actually attend class. In person! She'd call Professor Morgan, too, who'd complimented her and encouraged her.

And she'd . . . *ha.* She'd listen to the message, because what if it really was something important or life-changing? She smiled, imagining. Say it was Gormay calling. She strutted to the phone, imagining the scene. It would be Grady from Gormay, and he'd say, *Oh, I was just inquiring about your order.* And, he'd say, *Wondering if you'd like me to bring it a little earlier? Or later?*

Oh, she'd laugh and toss her head. *What a lovely idea. Can you bring enough for two?*

She tapped her message-retrieval code into the keys, EGBDF like the scales, and heard the message thing whir. It was a salesperson, no doubt, so she'd simply delete it. And, now she thought about it, maybe see what she could do about her hair. Jane and her producer, Fiona something, might be coming. Even though she wasn't going on camera, she should look nice. For when she finally told her story and saved her own life. *Yes, Isabel,* Grady would say. *You're . . .*

She paused her invented dialogue mid-scene to listen to the message.

Music. The same caller. She started to hang up, annoyed but relieved it wasn't Mom or Adams Bay, then stopped, the receiver held midway between her ear and the wall. Music, recognizable now.

She clamped the phone back to her ear, eyes screwed shut, blanking out everything but the sounds from the phone, coming from somewhere, from someone, meant only for her.

A flush washed across her face, then a chill, her knees gone unreliable. She tapped the phone keys, 2-2, to replay the message from the beginning. And then again. She steeled herself each time, disbelieving, but needing to hear the whole message. The crazed scherzo of strings, then a swelling of orchestra, the opening measures of . . .

"O Scarpia, Avanti a Dio!" She heard it, perfectly, clearly, almost as if someone were raising the volume as the climax of the opera continued. So intense, so fiery, lasting less than a minute, but Isabel felt her lips mouth the words along with Anna Moffo—she'd recognize the lyric soprano's voice anywhere. Moffo as Tosca, the doomed and deceived lover of Cavaradossi, the victim of the evil Scarpia. *"O Scarpia,"* the line Tosca wails in anguish, hitting that piercing high C before she flings herself to her death over the parapet of the Castel Sant'Angelo. "We will meet again before God."

And then the music stopped.

Tosca. Who knew she was Tosca? And why would they call to torment her?

Isabel stood in her kitchen, alone alone alone, one foot in a flip-flop, one foot bare, the summer breeze teasing her white curtains and twisting her crystal in the open balcony window as she clutched the now-silent phone.

25

JAKE BROGAN

"About freaking time," Jake muttered as he and D were led down the carpeted hallway, a corridor of closed and numbered doors, toward Edward Tarrant's office. Sasha Vogelby, several steps in front of them, had called Tarrant back, and in a hushed but insistent voice relayed Jake's admonition that with or without his permission, they were on their way to his office. At which point the woman turned the charm on them.

"Mr. Tarrant will be happy to see you now," she'd gushed. As if it were his idea. As if his happiness mattered.

"Piece of work," D said, keeping his voice low. "You think she really didn't know? About Morgan?"

"She's an actor, right?" Jake muttered.

"Gentlemen?" Vogelby stopped halfway along the hall, in front of a closed office door. "All set?"

Jake didn't like her. He couldn't help it. He knew that was a pitfall for cops—personal feelings should never get in the way. But a layer of yellowing disdain kept threatening to tinge Jake's response to this woman. Her obsequiousness toward Tarrant, her ivory tower existence, her flouncing around this insular and otherworldly environment. He knew it well from his Harvard years, had experienced the same entitled atmosphere, the higher learning and know-it-all swagger drawing a hard line between us and them, campus and townie, the educated and the not-so. DeLuca still tormented Jake about his educational background.

"Set?" DeLuca repeated in reply to Vogelby's question. "We were 'set' when we arrived, about half an hour ago."

"Thanks, Ms. Vogelby," Jake said. Good cop. Might as well be.

They lurched through preliminary small talk, Jake taking in the opulence of Tarrant's office. Must make quite the salary, Jake figured, he'd check the records. After he heard the dean's oh-so-sincere eulogy for the "intensely talented" and "much-admired" Avery Morgan, Jake had another on his personal list of "not-guilty but not-likable."

Could Tarrant be the killer? Strangulation was most often a man's crime. The strength it took to wrap your hands around the victim's neck, the intensity of the proximity, the willingness to get that close to your prey. Feel their breath on you, match their struggle, hear their last gasps. It wasn't as instant—or pretty—as in the movies. Drowning, though, that could be a woman's crime. Especially if Kat found there were drugs involved.

Sasha Vogelby had retreated to a shadowy corner, dwarfed by the ceiling-high bookshelves behind her.

"We're sorry for your loss," Jake said again. They hadn't been invited to sit, and Jake now looked pointedly at the two chairs across from Tarrant's desk.

"Thank you." Tarrant, big shot, gestured to the expensive-looking upholstery.

"Were you particular friends with Ms. Morgan?" Jake said after he and D had sat, taking out his notebook, mostly for show. D did the same, and licked his pencil tip like a two-bit comic cop. For Tarrant's benefit, Jake knew.

"'Particular'?" Tarrant seemed to taste the word, testing it. "We were colleagues, certainly."

Jake waited, silent. Waited for Tarrant to fill the space. A shadow passed by the frosted glass of Tarrant's outer door, then his phone buzzed. "No calls, Manderley," Tarrant said into the speaker.

Manderley. Jake clicked his pen, wrote it in his notebook, figuring he'd spelled it correctly. Jane'd love that name. But whoever Manderley was probably knew more than she—*she?*—was aware. He'd check with her, for sure. Calendar, schedules, phone calls. A secretary knew them all.

Tarrant, hands steepled, stayed silent. Fine, Jake thought.

Changing tactics, Jake leaned forward. "How did Ms. Morgan come to be associated with Adams Bay, Mr. Tarrant? Did she have family? Where was she from? And where were you, sir, yesterday from noon until approximately six P.M.?"

Take that, Jake thought. He heard a sound from the back of the room, turned to see if Vogelby wanted to say something. She coughed, twice, covering her mouth. "Sorry," she whispered.

"Sir?" Jake prompted Tarrant, as D shifted again in his apparently uncomfortable chair. Though Jake's wasn't bad.

"Ms. Morgan came to us from California," Tarrant said. "She lived outside Los Angeles, if I remember, in a suburb called . . ." He shook his head, then spread his hands, apologetic. "As for her personal information, I must admit I am not clear on the protocol. I've put in a call to our president, Reginald Buchholz, but, alas, he is out of the country, and I fear the time zones don't work in our favor."

"Alas," DeLuca said.

"I fear—" Jake paused, but not quite long enough to be nasty "—the protocol of the Boston homicide division takes precedence. Sir. I'm sure there's a personnel file, and that's what I need. We *don't* need the permission of the college president, although I will want to talk with him. So." Jake gestured to Tarrant with his ballpoint. Clicked it. "You'll provide that information, as well as more. Was she married? Divorced? Did she have a boyfriend, for want of a better term? Or girlfriend?"

Tarrant cleared his throat. "Might I ask you, Detectives, whether the school should put out some sort of alert? Do you think there's a danger to students, or faculty, or anyone else in the neighborh—?"

"We don't, Mr. Tarrant," Jake cut him off. "We would have mentioned that right off the bat. I *can* tell you there were no signs of forced entry, no struggle, nothing out of place."

Tarrant's eyes widened. "Are you thinking she knew her killer?"

Jake saw Tarrant's face change. Did he exchange glances with Vogelby? Hard to tell.

"Or could it have been sui—" Tarrant stood, his fingers poised on his sleek black desk blotter. "Could she have—" his voice dropped to a whisper "—killed herself?"

"It's all part of the investigation, sir." Jake flapped his notebook shut. Sometimes that made subjects more relaxed, as if the "real" interview were over. The real interviews were never over. "So. Personnel file. Ms. Morgan's contact information. Her acquaintances and relationships. As well as President . . ."

"Buchholz," Vogelby's voice came from the back of the room. This time they *did* exchange glances. Tarrant glared at her.

What was between those two? Jake needed to split them up.

"While we were waiting for you, Ms. Vogelby described student gatherings, parties, maybe rehearsals, at Ms. Morgan's home," Jake said. And under the bus she goes. "The house was part of her salary?"

"Part of her employment package, yes," Tarrant said, sitting again, leaning into the dark brown leather. "Use of the house. And yes, there were—I wouldn't quite call them 'parties.'"

Tarrant shot Vogelby the glare again. "But certainly Ms. Morgan encouraged students to participate in group gatherings at her home. I understand they did rehearsals there, little theatricals. She was our resident expert in performance, with a specialty in opera. So obviously her students would congregate there—not unlike other professors having teas, or sherry with poetry readings. That sort of thing."

DeLuca coughed, which Jake thought unnecessary. But funny. D was not big on poetry. Or sherry.

"We'll need the names of her students," Jake said. He nodded at D, whose notebook was still at the ready. "Especially those who were familiar with the house."

"I *told* them, Mr. Tarrant." Sasha Vogelby's voice again. Jake turned, watched the woman take a few steps closer to them, her white hair emerging from the shadow of the shelved leather volumes. "I told the detectives we'd have to get per*miss*ion from the families to release their names. It's a classic *privacy* situation."

"It's a possible murder situation," DeLuca said.

"Were *you* ever at Ms. Morgan's parties?" Jake looked at Tarrant, then Vogelby, then Tarrant again. "Either of you?"

26

JANE RYLAND

Was she ready? Jane tried not to laugh out loud at the judge's question. This was the world's most horrible idea, Jane sitting in open court, faced with six dozen spectators, and expected to point to the driver in a hit-and-run accident. Ready? Yeah, she was ready. Ready to bolt straight out that big double door, uniformed guards or no, and head for the hills.

"Yes, Your Honor," Jane said. "I'm ready."

"Mr. McCusker?" Judge Scapicchio pointed a scarlet fingernail at the assistant DA.

Jane watched McCusker stand, slowly, and smile at her, the practiced expression of reassurance he must have used before on countless nervous or reluctant unfortunates in her position.

Jane heard a low rumble from the audience, as a few dozen people murmured what they probably thought was softly to each of a few dozen others.

"Spectators, you will remain silent during this hearing," the judge said. "Any outbursts, any discussion or reaction, and I'll have you removed from my courtroom. And held in contempt. Am I clear?"

Silence.

"Thank you, Your Honor. Now. Ms. Ryland." McCusker turned some pages in his loose-leaf binder.

Jane waited, her world on pause, wondering how she must look to the spectators, each and every one of whom was staring at her. Well, all but one, and he was looking at the judge. She felt herself gulp, and tried to pretend she wasn't nervous, because there was no reason to be nervous. Except, there was.

"Ms. Ryland," McCusker said again. "Where were you on the past Monday morning at approximately nine-forty?"

Jane swallowed, wished for water. Her brain was somehow short-circuiting on this simple question. What did he mean by "where"? Did he mean—in a car? In Boston? On O'Brien Highway?

"I was in a car, on O'Brien Highway." She heard the quaver in her voice. *Get a grip, Jane.* "On the Boston side," she added, sitting up straighter. *She* wasn't on trial, after all.

"Were you driving?"

Just answer what you're asked, the station's attorney had instructed her. "No."

"You were a passenger."

"Yes." This would be over soon, just a memory, and she and Jake would laugh and go on with their lives. The dark-haired defense attorney, still seated at her table, appeared to be listening intently, fiddling with a hoop earring. But Jane could see the woman had a cell phone in her lap. On. Was she texting?

"What was the weather?"

"Sunny."

"And did you see anything unusual?"

Unusual? Well, was a fender bender unusual? Not in Boston, that's for sure. *Just answer, you dingbat,* she told herself. "I saw a car rear-end a van. There was a red light, and the van had stopped, and we had stopped. And then the car hit the stopped van."

"How did you see that?"

"I looked out the windshield. And then out my window. The passenger-side window."

"I see." McCusker nodded. "The window was open?"

"Not at first, but then I opened it."

"And what kind of a car, if you know, did you see hit the van?"

"A Cadillac. I recognized the—" Just answer the question. "A Cadillac."

"Color?"

"Silver."

"And you took the license plate."

"I did," Jane said. She heard the audience murmur, saw a few people whisper to their neighbors behind raised palms.

"Why was that?" McCusker raised an eyebrow, smiling.

"I'm a reporter," she said. "I guess it's habit."

"I see. What did the driver do then?" McCusker's voice was smooth, and he ran a finger down his yellow pad.

"He . . ." Jane paused, picturing it. "He sat there for a moment, in the front seat. Then he drove away."

"A hit-and-run," McCusker said.

"Mr. McCusker." Judge Scapicchio's voice did not conceal the rebuke. "There's no jury here. And no need to characterize."

"Thank you, Your Honor," he said. "Ms. Ryland. Did you see the driver of the silver Cadillac? Did you look at him?"

"Yes." Her heart started beating, so fast it surprised her, so hard it almost made her gasp. *Say no more,* she thought. Right. It was about to hit the fan. And no question that lawyer was texting.

The audience murmured again, as if they, experienced courtroom observers, knew precisely what had to be coming next—the big climax, the big identification, the pivotal Perry Mason moment.

But then the door to the courtroom squeaked open, and all eyes turned left, all heads swiveled to watch the late arrival. A prune-faced man in a dark suit hustled past the court officers, scanned the audience, quickly, then slid into a pew close to the door. A broad-shouldered court officer took a tentative step forward. He approached the newcomer, then seemed to decide there was no problem. Prune-face wasn't the driver, Jane thought, though he had gray hair and looked kind of familiar. Lawyer, maybe.

"Now, Ms. Ryland?" McCusker cleared his throat, and the audience's attention swiveled back his way. "Without pointing to him or her, if the person you saw driving the car in question, the silver Cadillac, is in this courtroom, could you please tell me that?"

The audience leaned forward, as one, anticipating, as if the closer they were to Jane, the sooner they'd hear the answer.

"And," McCusker continued, "again, not by pointing, but by simply saying yes or no." The ADA smiled once more, swept a hand toward the audience behind him. "We don't want any mistaken identities."

Jane narrowed her eyes, wondering if that was some kind of crack. She'd been fired from a TV job because she refused to reveal the name of a source—and as a result, most of Boston believed she'd made a mistake in publicly identifying a bad guy. Since then she'd worked to redeem her image, and thought she'd finally succeeded. All she needed now was McCusker reminding the whole world about one of the worst moments of her life.

But maybe that was her own paranoia. No reason for McCusker to needle her, after all. She tamped down her probable overreaction, wondering how she must look to the spectators, each and every one of whom was staring at her. The defense attorney, too, as she fiddled with her other silver earring.

"Go ahead," McCusker said. "Please take your time."

Now or never. Jane scanned the audience, left to right, squinting a bit in the spackled lighting of the verging-on-seedy courtroom. The state moguls had slashed funding for courthouse renovations before they got to this one, and as a result, the walls were dingy, the curtains dingier, and the lighting even dingier. The driver wasn't black, or Asian, not dark-skinned, not female, so those people she could easily skip. She took herself back to that moment on O'Brien Highway, imagined herself looking out the right-side window of the Channel 2 car, seeing the man with his hands on the wheel. *Middle-aged, Caucasian, widow's peak, grayish hair, pointy cheekbones, thin lips, clean-shaven.*

But here in courtroom 206, in the rows of lined-up possibilities, she saw middle-aged but not gray hair, Caucasian but chubby, widow's peak but wide lips, face after face the wrong shape or the wrong color or the wrong gender. Face after face, linking their eyes with her, as eager with anticipation as a—

"Ms. Ryland?" McCusker interrupted her thoughts. "Have you—"

"Let her look," the judge interrupted. "This is your show, Mr. Mc-Cusker. We're in no rush here. This is the justice system."

Jane looked again, right to left. Scanned every face, chanting her description mantra silently to herself. She dismissed the professorial type in the blazer. The white-hair in the short-sleeved madras. Could any human being reliably do this? Recognize, without mistake, a stranger they'd seen for less than a minute? Maybe she'd been too quick to rely on her own perceptions. She kept looking, examining each face, feeling all those eyes on her. It wasn't the fidgeting teenager. Not the preppy with the popped collar. Not the bespectacled pin-striped suit.

He's simply . . . not there, she realized. And of course he wasn't. They'd told her the driver might not be there, explained that's what made the identification fair. Were they trying to trap her? Seeing if she would choose someone who looked similar, and thereby prove she was unreliable so they could righteously nail the person who'd confessed? But she *was* reliable, and as certain as anyone could be of what she'd seen. Not recognizing anyone proved she really did have the correct description.

All eyes were still on her, each person leaning forward at exactly the same angle, hands on thighs, and with exactly the same expression, eyebrows raised and mouths slack, as if awaiting the announcement of a lottery winner. Or in this case, loser. Even the defense attorney had turned to look at the spectators. Courtrooms were theater, Jane realized, the theater of reality, and the same way spectators gawked at crime scenes and rubbernecked car accidents, this audience had gathered in this courtroom to watch whether a fellow citizen would be pointed out as criminal.

But wait.

She tried not to smile as she looked at the only person who now was stolidly not looking back at her. As if that ostrich technique would avoid her scrutiny. Pale brown hair, curly, a baby face. Even from here she could see freckles. She'd taken Psych 101. Easy enough to figure that was McCusker's not-guilty guilty kid.

Wait, Jane thought. *He's confessed. For whatever reason, he wants us to think he's guilty.* So what she was really doing here was providing evidence that the person who'd confessed wasn't the real driver. In this peculiar reality, the point was for her to help the DA prove the defendant was *not* guilty.

"Ms. Ryland?" The judge leaned forward from her higher perch.

Jane turned to her, smiling apologetically, then tried to erase her expression. She wasn't supposed to feel any emotion about this. It was a simple question: Was the driver here in the courtroom? And the answer was simple, too.

"Sorry," Jane said. "But I don't—"

"Objection!" The prune-faced newcomer jumped to his feet in the audience before she could finish, his face reddening, even his scalp turning red under his thinning white hair. "Objection!"

The judge banged her gavel. The court officers moved forward, one putting a hand on his holstered weapon. The crowd buzzed, a million cicadas, all eyes now riveted on the man. Jane turned to McCusker, her eyes widening with her question. *Who is this guy?* The man had taken a few steps toward the bar separating audience from courtroom. Fifteen seconds had passed, less.

"I'm Randolph Hix, Your Honor, and Mr. McCusker knows perfectly well who I am and precisely why I'm here." He turned, faced down the court officers, pointed at them with an accusatory forefinger. "And you two know me perfectly well, too. Thanks to my colleague Ms. Obele here"—he pointed to the dark-haired lawyer—"I'm here to insist we call this train wreck to a halt. Your Honor, I refuse to point out my client, for reasons that are more than obvious, and if Your Honor is a party to this, this manipulative charade and complete travesty of—"

Whatever else he was saying was lost in the crashing of the judge's gavel and the now-unrestrained curiosity of the chattering audience. Jane clutched the sides of her chair, watching whatever drama this was unfold, deeply wishing she could pull out her phone and roll some video of this whole thing. Randolph Hix, that's who that was. She hadn't recognized him instantly. The once-headline-happy attorney had dropped off the legal radar several years ago. Maybe made all the money he needed. So what was he doing here? Who was the woman lawyer? Jane looked again at the curly-haired, baby-face kid who'd ignored her. He'd now fixed his sights on the protesting Hix. But then, so had everyone else.

McCusker turned to the judge's bench, entreating, his voice raised to trample Hix's demands.

"Your Honor, talk about a travesty!" McCusker's voice, plump with scorn, escalated into outrage. "Bursting into your courtroom like this? With proceedings under way and a witness sworn? This is—"

Hix waved him off, infinitely dismissive. "*This?* Is clearly actionable. To the fullest extent, Your Honor. Learned counsel *never . . .*" Hix continued with his objection, now jabbing his finger at McCusker, his voice heavy with sarcasm, a twinge of a Boston accent thickening "never" into "nevah." He paused, eyes to heaven, as if the whole episode were simply too egregious to comprehend. "We understood, we were *assured*, by Mr. McCusker himself, that Ms. Ryland was here only to—"

Scapicchio's gavel continued its drumbeat, but the audience hubbub and babble went on unabated. Finally the judge stood, still banging, eyes shooting flames.

"Not. Another. Word. From either of you." She pointed to the audience with her gavel. "Nor from any of *you*. Am I making myself understood? Or I will clear this room."

The courtroom hushed, including center-ring combatants McCusker and Hix. Each man's chest was rising and falling. It was impossible to decide whose face was redder. The audience seemed to settle in, perhaps hoping they'd get a better show than they'd expected.

"Approach please, *counsel*." The judge, with an edge of disdain, gestured the two seething lawyers toward the bench, including the no-longer-texting Ms. Obele, then turned and nodded at Jane. "I apologize, Ms. Ryland. You're excused."

27

JAKE BROGAN

Jake waited for the answers, trying not to smile as he imagined the inner struggles of the pompous ass Edward Tarrant and his annoyingly theatrical colleague Sasha Vogelby. He loved it when he posed a simple question and the people he asked couldn't seem to figure out an answer.

It was easy to come up with the truth. Only a lie was difficult. And, as apparently in this situation, a lie that had to be corroborated by people who couldn't compare notes was the most difficult of all. Jake enjoyed the silent attempts at communication between these two. Communication that couldn't possibly be successful.

"So, you're thinking about whether you'd been at Ms. Morgan's parties," DeLuca said. "I must say I'm not sure why you'd have to do that."

"They weren't parties. And I'm not 'thinking,'" Tarrant said. "Of course I've *been* there. It's an Adams Bay property, and I was instrumental in providing that housing to Ms. Morgan. I've probably been there more than she has, come to . . ." He paused, huffed out a breath. "Be that as it may. My answer, which I most assuredly did not have to 'think' about, is yes."

"I have, too." Sasha Vogelby slid a cell phone from her skirt pocket, then replaced it as Tarrant glared at her.

Were they texting? Couldn't be, Jake thought.

"Exactly when?" Jake asked.

"Now *that* I would have to think about." Tarrant looked at his watch, as if to communicate how little time he had.

Jake got the hint. Jake didn't care. "Do you have a key to the house?"

"Or do you need to think about that?" DeLuca said.

"Of course I don't." Tarrant was clearly not a member of the DeLuca fan club. "As for the dates, I'll have Man—my assistant check the calendar," Tarrant went on, addressing Jake. "It must have been some sort of school affair, gathering, whatever."

"Me, too." Vogelby stepped forward. "Probably the same event, whatever it was. Avery was always having—"

She stopped.

"Yes?" Jake said.

"Nothing."

"You can go, if you like, Ms. Vogelby." Jake knew she'd be more cooperative away from Tarrant's supervision. "We'll be in touch."

Jake saw how she glanced at Tarrant before she bolted from the office. The door clicked closed behind her.

"Just a few more things, Mr. Tarrant," he said. "We've asked the surveillance company—you're aware there's an alarm system with surveillance?"

Tarrant blinked. "Yes, certainly."

"So you know, then, we'll be able to collect all the video of whoever came and went from the Morgan House. In fact, that's already in the works," Jake lied. Turned to DeLuca. "It'll be ready soon, correct, Detective?"

"Far as I know," DeLuca said, nodding, seamlessly playing along. "But, Mr. Tarrant? Speaking of video, do *you* have any? Of Ms. Morgan?"

"Good thought," Jake said. For all his quirks, DeLuca was a solid partner. "Or of those parties?"

"They were *not*—" Tarrant began.

"Rehearsals, then. Are there videos or pictures of them? Students these days photograph everything." Jake turned to DeLuca, wondered why he hadn't thought of this earlier. "We should check YouTube."

EDWARD TARRANT

Damned cops. He, Edward Tarrant, had nothing to do with Avery Morgan's death, nothing whatsoever, and yet these two, questioning him, were making him feel not only guilty, but as if he were participating in some sort of cover-up with Sasha Vogelby. No wonder she'd failed as an actress. She couldn't even keep an expressionless face as these two bozos clumsily attempted to elicit information. And unless she was deliberately playing the role of a guilty person, she was certainly acting—if you could call her pitiful performance "acting"—like she was terrified. He wished he'd been able to strategize with her, not that there was anything to strategize.

Which reminded him of his wife. And of Reginald Buchholz. Father-in-law. And boss. Which reminded him he hadn't even crafted the school's formal public relations response. Which reminded him someone had probably killed Avery Morgan, because there were homicide cops in his office, and that the inevitable avalanche of reality was one loose pebble away from burying him alive.

Vogelby had just fled, lucky woman, and now the cops were asking about video. First the surveillance video, for God's sake, which he'd certainly be on. He should have thought of it, but who knew it would matter? Could they actually get that from SafeHouse?

And now they were talking about YouTube! He'd been smart enough to wipe that party video off the face of the Internet, and they couldn't look at his computer without getting a warrant. By which time he'd have erased his last pictures of Avery. He felt a pang of sorrow. Unusual, but he was tired, and pressured, and in an excruciating situation. Still, better to be safe. If that was even possible now.

"Ah, video," Edward said. "There *was* one on YouTube. Because of my role here, I had it taken down. Because it has AB students in it."

The look on this cop's face was absurd. As if he'd trapped Edward like some sort of insect. Pathetic, those two, the preppy one so smug and entitled, and the skinny one sarcastic. *Real* cops. He couldn't believe he had to deal with this. He had so many other fires.

"We've got a state-of-the-art I-T division," Brogan was saying. "Even if it's been removed from YouTube, it's never really gone. We're the police, Mr. Tarrant. We can get whatever we want."

Edward wanted to kill these assholes. He'd fight them instead, and win. Using their own damn rules.

"With a search warrant or a subpoena," he said. He couldn't resist, even though it was showing his emotional hand a bit more than he ought. "I know the system, too, officers."

"'Detectives,'" DeLuca corrected him. "Is that a problem? If you have a video, and I now assume you do, why can't we see it? Is there something on it you'd prefer not to be public? We're not the public, Mr. Tarrant."

Edward imagined that video, let it play out in his mind yet again. What was there to lose? The camera never actually revealed him. Nonetheless, if they questioned others at the gathering, they'd certainly place him there. Would that be a deal-breaker? It was easily explainable. Had he somehow revealed their relationship? That he could not remember. He ran his tongue over his front teeth, contemplating.

A knock at the door. "Yes?" he said.

A reprieve, whoever it was.

JAKE BROGAN

Jake almost laughed out loud at the relief on Tarrant's face. Whoever was knocking on his office door was clearly Tarrant's lifeline. Any interruption gave the guy more time to figure out his next move.

Amusing how these blue-blazer types always thought they were in control. Sooner or later, they'd realize the cops were in charge. Only a question of how to get to yes. Right now, Jake needed to get there a little faster. This guy was clearly trying to keep that YouTube video from them. Which meant that video was exactly what they wanted.

A young woman opened the door, white female, approximately 19 y-o-a, Jake's cop brain catalogued.

"Yes, Manderley?" Tarrant's voice oozed charm. "What can I do for you?"

Again Jake stifled a grin. Manderley's baffled expression telegraphed that the Tarrant she knew had somehow been replaced by a polite duplicate.

"Just, um . . ." The girl, a leggy fawn in the headlights, looked at Jake and D, eyebrows knitted. *She's forgotten her skirt,* Jane would say. "To see if you need anything."

"How nice." Tarrant couldn't have sounded more chivalrous. "I'm fine, right now, and hold my calls, please. Ah, unless it's President Buchholz. You'll put him right through, naturally. Or my wife."

Manderley, nodding, closed the door behind her.

"Your assistant?" Jake said. *Wife?* Jake tucked that nugget away. "And her last name is?"

"Rosen," Tarrant said. "Why does that matter?"

"Everything matters," DeLuca said.

No need to antagonize this guy, Jake thought. His Grampa Brogan had always advised him to use a person's own power as leverage. Gramma Brogan still told him, "You'll catch more flies with honey."

"Thank you, sir," Jake said. He'd combine both methods. "I know you're concerned about your campus. It's a difficult situation, and I'm sure you have many compelling responsibilities. So we're grateful for your help. As for the video, we'll get it, sooner or later, so we'd be appreciative if you'd simply show us. It will give us valuable insight into who knew about Ms. Morgan's home, allow us to watch her interactions. Listen to her. Our goal is not to embarrass any students, or to harm Ms. Morgan's reputation, sir. Our goal is to solve this case, and if it *is* a homicide, bring to justice whoever killed Avery Morgan. I know that's your goal, too."

Tarrant eyed his computer. *So that's where the video is.* Jake could almost watch the man's thoughts marching though his brain, the options getting weighed, the outcomes calculated. Jake had seen this before, the turning point in a case, the moment when a subject decided he'd be worse off by stalling and might as well join the good-guy team. He'd even seen bad guys make that decision. They were the only ones who ever regretted it.

Now Tarrant was tapping at his keyboard, and moving his silver mouse over a thin black pad.

Jake, waiting, glanced at D, who raised a silent eyebrow.

"It is indeed my goal," Tarrant said, not looking at them, talking slowly as he tried to mouse and talk at the same time. He paused, turned to look Jake square in the eye. "Certainly I want justice for Ms. Morgan." He put a hand on each side of his monitor—Jake noticed there was no wedding ring—and swiveled the screen toward them. "Best I can do, gentlemen."

Jake stood, and D hovered behind him as Tarrant double-clicked the white triangle over the video. The pictures, full-color and full-screen, exploded into reality. A peal of girlish laughter, startlingly clear, came from off camera. Night, twinkling lights in the trees. Swimming pool in the background, and center stage, a woman.

"Is that her?" Jake asked, pointing.

"Yes." Tarrant leaned forward, an inch, didn't take his eyes off the screen.

The woman, in a white top, her dark hair pulled back in a ribbon, sat with one arm draped across the back of her white plastic chair. Attractive, Jake thought. Caucasian female, dark hair, age approximately forty-five, maybe older. The woman in the pool, come to life.

A drink was in front of her, hard to tell what, in a yellow plastic cup. Another cup was to its left, but no one sat in the corresponding chair. The armrests of Ms. Morgan's chair and the empty one were close together, touching, Jake noticed.

"Who are all these people?" Jake asked. The others surrounding Avery looked young, though it was increasingly hard to tell these days. "Are they students? Which ones? Are they in her classes?"

DeLuca flapped his notebook to a new page. "If you can point to them one by one, and identify them. Also if there's anyone you *don't* recognize. That's important, too."

Sounds of splashing and laughter provided a festive background, accompanied by the thumping bass of some unidentifiable rock music. It was impossible to clearly make out the faces of the students, if that's who they were, in the shadowed pool.

"You can pause it, if you want," Jake said.

Tarrant clicked the mouse, stopping the video. "None of this is about 'wanting.' I *cannot* give you their names. Even those over twenty-one are Adams Bay students, and as such, are entitled to privacy protection. What's more, FERPA specifically prevents—"

"What-pa?" Jake hated jargon, especially as an excuse rattled off by a pretentious academic.

"The Family Educational Rights and Privacy Act. FERPA. It expressly prohibits colleges from releasing certain education records. But, frankly, I'm not sure why their identities matter."

"They matter if Avery Morgan was murdered." Jake didn't try to keep the contempt out of his voice. "And that means—"

"Well, of course," Tarrant tried to interrupt.

"And that means whatever privacy rules you've made or think you understand disappear into college handbook limbo." So much for honey. Jake had completely had it with this guy. "Now, sir? Please start the video again. We'll need to watch the whole thing. And then we'll do it again, with the names. All of them. I can pick up this phone and get a warrant faster than you can say 'contempt of court.'"

Jake ramped it down, de-escalating. "And happy to do that if it'll make your decision easier to sell to your boss. Clear?"

"A court order is a court order," Tarrant said.

"Great," Jake said. "When was this taken, anyway? There's no date stamp."

Tarrant clicked his mouse, and the party hubbub echoed through the office again.

"In May, I think. Before the end of the spring semester," Tarrant said. "Avery Morgan arrived in . . . February, if I remember correctly. I could look it up."

"Do," DeLuca said. "And the identifications?"

Tarrant shook his head, reluctant again. "Well, even if I agreed. I can't possibly recognize every—"

"Mr. Tarrant?" Jake kept his eyes on the video. This was a flat-out party, far as he could see. It looked nothing like a rehearsal, or a formal lesson of any kind. Why would they have characterized it that way? Maybe because "Party with the teacher" was not something they'd want in their school brochures. Underage drinking was even more problematic, and there was no doubt that had taken place—Tarrant had just admitted that some of the attendees were under twenty-one.

For now, Jake would ignore it. Let this guy also think Jake hadn't noticed the ubiquitous beer bottles. Or the yellow cups. "We're in a 'sooner or later' situation here. That means, sooner or later, you'll have to tell us."

"You indicated you could get a warrant." Tarrant's voice had turned taut, taunting. "So do that."

DeLuca took out his cell phone. "With pleasure."

On the video, the atmosphere seemed to shift. Shadows moved through the background, the once-raucous music stopped.

"Avery, watch this!" A voice, off screen, cried out. "You ready?"

Avery Morgan twisted in her chair, following the changing sound. With a blare of orchestration, a new selection of music blasted over the scene, and a line of students, some wearing bathing suits and others in cutoffs and T-shirts, all carrying drinks, danced—Jake guessed it was dancing—in a line in front of the camera. Some were singing, a few pretending their beer bottles were microphones. Avery Morgan stood, applauding, then adjusted her long skirt, picked up her drink, and stepped out of the picture, leaving the camera lens trained squarely on the teenagers' antics.

Kids these days, Jake thought. Calling her "Avery." His own college interactions with professors were formal and arm's-length, certainly never first-name. Appropriate or not, it did look like these students, if they were students, were having fun, animated and enthusiastic, arms linked, lost in their performance.

Had any of these students been "special" friends of hers? Did any of them know more than they realized? Morgan called out to one of them, a young woman, then hugged her. Had any of these people been inside her house, that night, or before? Whose drink had been parked next to hers? Did any of these revelers know she was now dead? Had one of them caused her death? Killed her?

Avery Morgan walked through the picture again, briefly blocking the camera shot. She laughed apologetically and fluttered a playful wave at whoever was taking the video. She stopped at the edge of the screen, then beckoned to someone, smiling.

"Over here!" Jake heard her call out.

Tarrant tapped the mouse, stopping the action. "That girl comes into the shot, they hug, then the food and beer arrives, then it ends." Tarrant looked at his watch again. "Gentlemen? I have an appointment out of the office, so . . ."

DeLuca clicked off his phone. "Warrant's in the works."

"We'll need to see the rest, Mr. Tarrant," Jake said. Passive-aggressive tactics might work on students, but not on them.

Tarrant moved the mouse, and the video flickered back into life.

In one quick move, DeLuca leaned forward, close to the screen, squinting. Momentarily blocked Jake's view.

"Jake," DeLuca said. "Look."

"I can't, long as you're in the way," Jake said. D leaned back, and Jake watched the scene continue. A delivery person had appeared, carrying what looked like three pizza boxes stacked on top of each other. On top of that, a brown paper bag, almost obscuring the delivery person's face.

But not quite.

"Holy sh . . ." Jake said under his breath. *Grady.*

28

JANE RYLAND

I'm excused? As the meaning of the judge's words sank in, it was all Jane could do not to leap up, dash from the witness box, race out the door, run home, and dive under her comforter. Three-thirty in the afternoon was too early for a glass of wine, but she was spent and exhausted. She'd awakened every hour on the hour the night before, taunted by the glowing green numbers of her alarm clock, terrified of being late, her restive dreams full of winding dead-end corridors and unopenable doors, of unfindable addresses and incorrect clocks. But she'd promised McCusker she'd meet him in the DA's courthouse office after her testimony, and then needed to get back to Channel 2 and Fiola.

Home wasn't an option.

She left the courtroom, trying not to run, and hustled past the burly court officers, ignoring the stares from the still-silent audience, their curiosity so piercing she could almost feel it against her back.

Once in the clear, thankful at hearing the door shut behind her, she paused for a moment in the silence of the frescoed hallway. And then with a lifting heart, she realized. *I'm done. This is over.* Say no more? She wouldn't have to.

Allowing herself a brief smile of relief, Jane trotted down the wide staircase to the lobby. Welcoming the caffeine, she grabbed a sludgy but convenient courthouse coffee from the weird guy at the snack bar. She wondered what happened after she left the courtroom. Why had Hix arrived? And who was the earringed Ms. Obele—some kind of legal lookout?

She'd ask McCusker for the deets. Least he could do, after all this, was give her the scoop.

Coffee in hand, Jane trudged back up the curved marble staircase to the second floor, lamenting her too-high heels, the pressure of the witness box, and the loss of her day. But she'd gotten a reprieve from having to rat out a criminal. That part of her life was finished. She was never going to divulge another word to law enforcement again. Except to Jake, of course.

Unlike in her dream, she easily found the door marked "District Attorney," which in real life had a doorknob, and entered the office. Empty. Empty reception area, empty couch, three empty chairs, empty reception desk. Fine. She'd wait.

Plopping onto the couch, muscles deflating, she pulled out her phone. Maybe call Jake? And certainly Fiola, see what the plans were to interview Tosca. That part of her life seemed so easy, suddenly, so risk-free.

But not, of course, for Tosca. It all depended on whether you were the questioner or the questioned. She let out a breath, stared at the blank wall, realized that for the first time in eight hours she wasn't quaking with apprehension.

She could close her eyes, just for a moment.

"Jane?"

McCusker. She bolted to her feet. Had she been asleep? Didn't matter. "Hey, Frank. How'd it go?" Reached for her coffee, took a sip. Still hot, so maybe she hadn't been asleep.

"It's complicated," McCusker said, beckoning her to follow him. "We can talk in my office."

She shadowed him down a narrow hall that smelled of old paper and older coffee grounds. The crackling overhead fluorescents only highlighted the grunge. Inside McCusker's office, stacks of file folders lined the yellowed walls. She surveyed the place, a cell-sized cubicle, one four-paned window curtained with forlorn translucent nylon.

"Taxpayer dollars," he said, one hand waving to encompass the shabbiness. "At least you can't do a story about how District Attorney Santora is overspending on office décor." He pulled a manila file folder from his shiny black briefcase, opened it, pulled out a photograph. Didn't show it to her.

"Listen, Jane," he went on. "Thanks for taking the stand this morning. You did us a solid. But, you're sure about who you saw driving that car?"

"Yeah," she said. The only visitor chair in the room was stacked with files. Not that she wanted to sit. She was leaving, soon as she could. "He was—"

"It was nine A.M.," McCusker interrupted, then leaned back against the edge of his desk. "The sun was glary, there was heavy traffic, lots of distractions, you had to look through two car windows. Yours and his. It all occurred very quickly. Eyewitness identification is notoriously tricky. You're absolutely sure?"

"No question." And there wasn't any question. As she'd scrutinized the courtroom audience, she'd held that image of the driver in her imagination. No one matched. She'd know the driver if she saw him. And she hadn't seen him in court. "I'm a reporter. This is what I do."

McCusker looked at the photo in his hand, turned it toward her, held it up between his thumb and forefinger.

"This is the person who confessed," he said.

Baby-face kid.

"No way." Jane shook her head. "Never saw that guy in my life. Well, until today, when I saw him in the audience. He was the only person not looking at me. Who is he, anyway? And, listen, Frank, can I just say? The man I saw was middle-aged, white, widow's peak—"

"Don't—" McCusker tried to interrupt.

"Pointy cheekbones, thin lips," she finished before he could stop her again. She'd braved the stupid identification hearing, and it had resulted in a nonidentification identification. She didn't see the actual driver in the audience, didn't recognize the kid who confessed, so now she could go home.

The ADA stared at her, still holding up the photo.

"You sure?" he said.

"How many times do you want me to reassure you? I'm a very reliable witness." *Shut up, Jane.*

"Tell me about that other accident." He slid the photo back into the file, slid the file back into his briefcase. "The later one. On Melnea Cass. Did you happen to see that one, too?"

McCusker's desk phone buzzed. "Excuse me," he said, and turned, facing the wall as he talked.

Thank goodness. Jane brushed her palms across her cheeks, smoothed her hair behind her ears. She needed a shower, and a nap, and then a glass of wine. Maybe a back rub, or whatever else Jake might have in mind for tonight's entertainment. What she did not need was another dilemma, another decision about where reporters drew the line at giving information.

Had she seen the second accident? Well, she had, in a way. The aftermath. On tape. And Channel 2 still had the raw video of it. But to get it, the DA would have to subpoena it, and the station would fight it, as they always fought subpoenas. Whatever video didn't get on the air was never shared with anyone, even law enforcement, without a subpoena. To circumvent such controversies, every station she'd worked for simply destroyed the raw video, erased the tape, or deleted the digital file. Or said they deleted it.

So if she *had* seen it, and the video was gone, what was the point of saying so? And she hadn't seen the actual accident. She tried to take another sip of coffee, but her paper cup was empty.

McCusker hung up the phone. He still looked impeccable, tie immaculate, even after the harrowing—for Jane—day in court. "Jane? Did you see that one, too?"

"I didn't see the accident happen," she said. That was true.

"I'm sure you didn't." McCusker aligned a few yellow pencils on his glass-topped desk, putting all the erasers in an even row. "Good answer. But you know perfectly well what I'm asking. Nevertheless. Tell your station to expect a subpoena."

29

JAKE BROGAN

"Could you believe it was Grady Houlihan in that video?" Jake said.

He and DeLuca were about to jaywalk across Beacon Street toward their cruiser, dodging the Kenmore Square pre-game traffic.

"You heard from him lately?" DeLuca frowned as a car of boisterous Red Sox fans made an illegal left turn. "Grady?"

"Had a message yesterday night." Jake began to step off the curb, then decided against it. "He was updating on the Sholtos, says their drug sales will go into high gear once fall classes start. Molly and poppers, he says. Roofies. Knew about Avery Morgan, too."

"Kills me," D said. "When I was that age it was all weed. Quaaludes, if you were a stoner. Now that stuff's for punks. Molly and poppers. Roofies. Shit."

Jake knew Grady used the delivery job to infiltrate local campuses without being noticed—and a good idea it was—but the last person Jake had expected to see in the Avery Morgan video was his CI.

"Clooney Sholto, there's an asshole. His son Liam, too," Jake said. "Selling drugs to college kids. There's a legacy. I told Grady, don't say anything. Just listen."

"And then inform us, right?" D said. "That's why they call them 'informants.'"

"Freaking witness protection budget." Jake, wanting to remain alive, checked both ways for traffic. Remembered Grady's apprehension the day before. "My fault, you know? If the kid gets hurt while we're

Jane shrugged, smiling, weary. "Above my pay grade," she said.

She tossed her empty coffee cup into a black metal wastebasket, where it landed with a soft thud. Now it was her turn to ask questions. She would check the court records, the docket file containing all the official reports and maybe even evidence, and make copies of everything the moment she finished here. But might as well get the scoop firsthand.

"By the way, who *is* the guy who 'confessed'?" she asked. "Did he own the Cadillac? Did he confess to the second hit-and-run, too?"

"It's complicated." McCusker sat behind his desk, picked up one of the pencils, rolled the others into a drawer. "That was part of what the judge and I were discussing. Why I was delayed. Why she sealed the court records." He pointed the pencil at her. "But we'll find the bad guy."

"Sealed? Why?" Jane was so close to the door, and almost home free, but she couldn't help it—once she was onto a story, she had to know how it ended. Getting court records sealed was a difficult burden. A judge had to be convinced there was a threat, or some crucially private information that needed to be concealed. That keeping the records secret outweighed the public's right to know. "Will you at least tell me—"

"We'll be in touch," McCusker said. "All I can say."

"Great," Jane said. *You owe me,* she didn't say. She put her hand on the doorknob.

"And I'll let you know when your next court appearance is," McCusker said.

He didn't even try to hide his smirk. She took her hand off the knob, faced him square-on.

"What 'next court appearance'?"

"Yours," the DA said. "When we find the real driver. Because, Jane? You're the only one who saw him."

"But—"

"You said it yourself, Jane. You're a very reliable witness."

waiting for the DA's office to get its act together? Why is it always about money?"

"It's about business." D said.

"Wonder what Avery Morgan's business was. Talk about assholes. Tarrant, I mean. I'd like *him* for it, big-time, if he didn't have an alibi. His colleague is dead. Maybe murdered. Hard to believe he tried to stall about naming the kids in the video."

"'I don't recognize them all'?" D imitated Tarrant's mannered accent. "Bull. Shom's checking them out."

"Think Tarrant's lying about Grady? That he doesn't know him?"

"Fifty-fifty." D pointed to the sidewalk opposite. "Now."

As they headed for the cruiser, Jake mentally reviewed the personnel records Tarrant had finally handed over. They revealed Avery Morgan moved to Boston from an L.A. suburb earlier in the year. No husband, no next of kin, but there was a social, a landlord reference, and a California address. Good leads. And that intriguing Untitled Studios connection. Had Avery Morgan been a whistle-blower? A rat? Had she moved from California to distance herself from the bad guys? Jake had called the US Attorney out there before he and D were even out of Colonial Hall.

"Hold on." Jake stopped in the middle of Beacon Street. A guy in a speeding Volvo slammed the horn, had to swerve to avoid them. A middle finger extended from the driver's-side window as the car careened though the yellow light.

"You're gonna give me a heart attack," D said. "Can you tell me whatever it is on the sidewalk? So we'll survive to discuss it?"

"Yeah, D. We suck." They stepped onto the curb together, then separated for their cruiser doors. Jake clicked the car open, and both slid inside, slamming their doors simultaneously. Jake cranked the AC. Then, with the twist of a knob, turned it off.

"Hey, gimme a break," D said. "It's a million degrees in here. Suck? We suck?"

"Yeah. So we're getting out," Jake said. "We're going back to Tarrant. I've got one more question for him."

WILLOW GALT

Never say another word?

She was *never* supposed to say another word? About who she truly was, or where she came from? How was that humanly possible? Willow had whiled the day away, browsing the Kenmore boutiques, pretending to be normal. Pretending to be carefree, having a lovely snack at Galatea. But as she sat at the raffia-topped sidewalk table, watching the fans elbow their way to the Red Sox game, she knew it was no good pretending. She and Tom were in real danger.

Avery's killer had struck in error. It had to be true. The killer had been sent to track down Willow and Tom. Why didn't Tom realize that?

She lifted her iced tea. The cubes rattled against the glass. Her hand was shaking.

She stopped, tea in midair. Should she get her scrapbook back? Anyone could find it, anyone! By simply moving a book, there it would be, so obviously out of place. And then they'd read it, and wonder—and then find her! She could not breathe. She could *not*.

Her heart pounded with the relief of the pending reunion with her darling scrapbook. Her life. Her history. She tucked a twenty-dollar bill under her dripping tea glass, then walked away, fast, faster, fast as she could, looking down at her feet, her new black shoes—-all her clothes were new—seeming unfamiliar against the also-alien Kenmore Square sidewalk. She felt someone close to her, and stopped short, almost banging into a man at the curb.

"Oh, sorry," she apologized, frazzled, to him, a lawyer, maybe, in a blue summer blazer. He was frowning, seemed annoyed. She looked out over the traffic-clogged street, saw two guys a block away trying to jaywalk across.

"Only in Boston." Willow smiled, gestured at the jaywalkers, tried to be polite. "In California, we obeyed—" and then she stopped talking.

Stopped talking because she wasn't supposed to talk about California.

Stopped talking because she recognized the jaywalkers. And they were coming her way. Straight toward her. She saw their cruiser behind them, parked on the street. She knew the tall one's angular walk. The cute one seemed to be pointing toward her.

"Are you okay?" the man said. "Are you lost? Where are you headed?"

"I'm fine." Willow's heart pounded so hard it threatened to choke her. *Lost.* He didn't know the half of it. Everything was lost. "Have a nice day." *Or whatever you say.*

"You, too," the man said.

Willow didn't have time for niceties. She took her eyes off the cops, just for a second, scanning, calculating escape routes. They'd been following her! Had they seen her go into the library this morning? Had they already been in there?

What if there were surveillance cameras inside? What if they had taped her every move? What if that librarian at the front desk had told them everything?

What if her book was *gone*? The world almost went black, but she reeled herself in, fighting for balance.

"Shut up," she said out loud.

The cops had stopped, right in the middle of the street. They'd tried crossing against the light and were stranded on the island dividing the lanes. Cars, a billion of them, darted and swerved in all directions.

She felt the panic spiraling in her chest, felt her brain churning at light speed. Move. She had to move. There were so many people, and it'd be easy enough to melt away. The man in the blazer was nowhere in sight.

She ducked into the Java Jim's, where the wave of cinnamon and cheap milk nearly knocked her over. A life-sized cardboard cutout of some uniformed baseball player, all huge muscles and toothy grin, almost made her shriek in fright. Did the place have a back door? Where were the detectives? Oh, no, no, she'd gone into a *coffee* shop, and cops . . .

The ladies' room sign pointed her toward the back. But if she went in there, she'd have to come out. She couldn't stay in the Java Jim bathroom forever. This was dumb, truly dumb. Bracketing her hands against her face, she peered out the front window. They were still on the traffic island. She had time.

The library was three doors to the right, she knew, next door to the Adams Bay administration building. She'd . . . she'd . . . She untwisted her silk scarf, wrapped it over her hair—well, no, no one was wearing a scarf, it was August. And what if the police had seen the scarf?

She dropped it on the coffee shop floor. Maybe if they came here, asking questions, they'd see it, and decide she was somewhere inside.

But she wouldn't be. She slammed out the front door, keeping half an eye on the cops, who seemed to be talking to each other while the traffic went by, and ran, lungs bursting, toward the library.

Hand on the door. Pull the door open. Pull again. Again. What? "Closed," the sign said. Closed. Summer hours.

Was she screaming? She wasn't, she wouldn't, but the library was closed? Could that even be? Or was it a ruse? A *closed* library? A closed *college* library? At 5:25? No. No. They were clearly clearly waiting for her, waiting for her to come back, and they'd closed the place so that when she arrived, no other people would be around to interfere. It made blazing sense. They'd investigated her, they knew who she was, and Tom. It was her fault, all her fault, for calling the police in the first place.

She pulled out her secret phone. She always carried one with her, in case. Cops still on the street. Arguing, now, it looked like. Good. Gave her some room.

She couldn't dial and run at the same time, so she tucked herself into a narrow alley, an arm's-width strip of open space between the dry cleaners and the liquor store. She dialed Olive's number, Olive, three thousand miles and three time zones away. Go through, she prayed, go *through*. She had to talk to someone, had to. Witness protection was to hide you from the bad guys, not from your friends.

The phone rang, a second time. Willow, leaning against the bumpy concrete wall, pictured dear Olive Brennis, the agent who'd helped them create their new identities. Olive was her lifeline. Her security.

A voice cut through her haze. "Yes?"

"It's Willow," she whispered. "Daniella." She thought about Tom, and their new home, and their promises. *I am Tom and you are Willow, and so it always shall be,* he'd said. She was so sorry. She could not do it. She could not stay here. She was too afraid.

"Yes?"

No turning back now. "Get me out."

30

JANE RYLAND

"Tonight? They want to talk to us tonight?" Jane hadn't gotten one step into their office before Fiola stood up and blocked her path.

"Now, actually." Fiola gathered her briefcase. "I know you had to go to court—can't wait to hear about it, naturally—but frankly, you lost us five hours of documentary time. So unless you had other plans for the evening?"

"No, no, it's great." Fiola's attitude was oozing negativity, and Jane's energy reserves were running on empty. But juggling was her life. She could juggle some more. "Sure."

By the time they raided the station's vending machines—coffee and apple for Jane, peanut butter crackers and Dr Pepper for Fiola—navigated the Channel 2 parking lot, and hit the Storrow Drive rush hour, it was pushing six o'clock. Jane had texted Jake. Their dinner, and whatever else, sigh, would have to wait. No answer. He was probably out, too. She needed to tell him about her day in court, and a lovely dinner and glass of wine would make that even more satisfying. Maybe they'd call Gormay. Then she shivered, remembering.

"Did that Gormay driver live? The Melnea Cass guy?" Jane asked. Fee had insisted on driving, so Jane once again looked out the passenger-side window. Unnerving, now, to think about that hit-and-run. If their stop for coffee yesterday had taken five minutes longer, or shorter, if there hadn't been traffic on Storrow, or if they'd stopped at the light at

Cambridge Street instead of Fiola's blasting through the yellow, they wouldn't have seen it at all.

Life turned on those little moments. *The Bridge of San Luis Rey.* You never knew whose life you were entering. What change your existence would make.

"No idea." Fiola brushed cracker shards off her black silk blouse. "Damn. That'll leave a mark. Anyway, the SAFE women will talk at the library, on background. When the time comes, they'll get someone to go on camera. Library closes at five, summer hours, but one of the librarians lets them in. So, good for us. Hang on."

"Wait, Fee? Don't turn here. There's gonna be—"

Fiola ignored her, taking the off-ramp to Kenmore and funneling them into the molasses of the Red Sox traffic. Jane would have gone around, up to the next exit.

"Red Sox," Jane said. "That's what I was trying to tell you. We're doomed."

They inched through the horn-cacophony of game-goers, past the funky restaurants, coffee bistros, and persistently hip but ephemeral boutiques, then finally past the ivy-twined brownstones of Boston University and Adams Bay.

"Parking?" Fiola asked.

"Not a chance." Jane scanned the bustling intersection. She pointed. "There! Car doors open—are they getting in or out?"

"Out," Fiola said. "Keep looking."

Jane did. Right at the two men exiting the car. Holy—*Jake.*

"Jake!" She buzzed down her window, delighted, a peal of laughter escaping before she could stop it. Paul DeLuca, too. "Hey!"

But every horn on the planet started up, paving over her words. Jake and DeLuca didn't even look around as they jaywalked—*typical,* she thought—across the busy street. She hated when he did that, striding across so confidently, as if all the cars would stop for him. Could she get out, maybe? Run and grab him?

She yanked out her phone. So funny—easier to call him.

"Who?" Fiola asked. "You see someone?"

"Yeah . . ." Jane tried to dial and talk at the same time. Fiola had no idea about Jake. That'd be an interesting conversation. At some point. "A pal," she said.

Her call went straight to voice mail, meaning he must be on a case. She watched the two men dodge moving cars, making their way toward a yellowing brownstone. The Adams Bay admin building.

"That possible homicide in The Reserve," Jane said out loud. "The one on TV. Wonder if the victim was connected with Adams Bay?"

"Maybe the SAFE people will know," Fiola said. "Keep an eye out for parking. We're almost late."

She'd tease Jake about seeing him. The glimpse was a kind of gift, a little secret moment when the universe worked in her favor, reminding her that life was good and there was more to it than work and bad guys and car accidents and victimized college women. And that she was lucky.

They found a spot behind Uno Pizzeria. Jane messaged Elaine Whitfield-Sharp, the SAFE group's leader, that they'd be there in ten minutes.

Many members of SAFE were victims of sexual assault on campus, Fiola had told her. Jane had a couple of close calls herself in college, that was for sure. Fifteen years ago, when times and laws were different.

"Fee?" Jane asked as they unbuckled their seat belts. "Anything . . . happen to you? Back in college? I mean, I've wondered why you picked this topic. In particular."

Jane hesitated, worried she'd crossed a line. They were colleagues, not friends.

"One in four?" Fee said. She pushed open her car door. "I bet it's more like four in four."

"So . . ." Jane didn't know what to say. One in four college women were sexually assaulted on campus, or forced to have sex without consent. That's what the newest statistics said. They'd talked about naming their documentary that: *One In Four*.

"Can we not talk about it now?" Fiola slammed her door, leaving Jane inside. Then she opened it again, leaning in. "I'm sorry, Jane. Really. It's just—in the past."

"Of course," Jane said. "I don't mean to . . ." But Fiola had closed the door again. So there was *that* answer. Did it make for a conflict? Not necessarily. And that's why more than one person worked a story. Jane got out and joined her producer on the sidewalk.

Boston was having one of its gorgeous pre-sunsets, the sky golden blue, somehow, sunbeams edging the drifts of clouds. They stood for a moment, silent.

"You okay?" Jane said. "You ready for this?"

"More than ready," Fiola said. "Let's go help these women change their world."

JAKE BROGAN

"D. Look." Jake nudged DeLuca with an elbow. They'd made it to the second traffic island, skin of their teeth, and now stood stranded as a wave of NASCAR wannabes barreled through the almost-red traffic light and into the heaving chaos of Kenmore Square. Horns blared nonstop, as if that would enable anyone to move any faster.

He pointed, directing DeLuca's attention. "By the library now. That's freaking Willow Galt. Hand on the door, see?"

"So what?" D said, shading his eyes with one palm. "Yeah. She lives, like, two, three blocks from here."

"But what's she doing at the Adams Bay library? She's got nothing to do with Adams Bay."

"You watch too many TV shows," D said, waving it off. "Hardly a big deal to be in your own neighborhood. She's walking the other way now, anyway. Not going in."

"Whatever," Jake said. "We still need to talk to her again. And I don't watch too much TV." Which wasn't true, of course. *Jane*, he thought. *Wonder what she's doing right now.* "Come on. Let's make a break for it."

Mack the security guard was still at his front desk post in Colonial Hall, turning the pages in some tabloid-shaped newspaper.

He looked up, finally. Expressionless, as if he'd never seen them before.

"Detective Jake Brogan?" Jake reminded him. Couldn't believe this guy.

"We were here, like, seven minutes ago? With Edward Tarrant?" DeLuca shot him a look. Jake tried not to laugh.

"He's gone," Mack said. "Sir."

"Gone?" That was the last thing Jake expected. How could he be gone?

"How could he be gone?" D asked, dismissing this preposterous response. "We've been here the whole time. He didn't come out the front door."

"Exactly." Mack gestured to his right. "There's a back, gentlemen."

"Sasha Vogelby?" Jake predicted that if one had scrammed, they both had. Were they together now, somewhere? Why?

"Ditto." Mack gestured exactly the same way, toward, Jake assumed, a back door. "Should I give them a message? *Sir?*"

DeLuca's phone rang—the theme from *Jaws*. He yanked his cell from his jacket pocket. "Gotta take this," he said. And turned away.

"Thank you, *sir*," Jake told Mack. "We'll be in touch."

DeLuca lagged behind as Jake headed to the car. *Lots of to-ing and fro-ing today.* That's how Jane sometimes characterized his policing process. Door knocks, waiting, driving, more knocking, more waiting. Lots of unhappy people.

TV police were always in car chases, shoot-outs, hostage situations. Big high-caliber action. Jake was perfectly content with asking questions. Every time he'd been involved in so-called exciting stuff, someone got killed. And the victims weren't always the bad guys. It was better on TV, he thought. Fantasy death. The murders got solved in fifty-two minutes.

The good guys lived happily ever after. That's not what happened in real life. Not often enough, anyway.

Whenever Jake was summoned, someone was already dead. Now he and D had to find out who did it before anyone else got killed. Sometimes that happened. Sometimes it didn't. Never in fifty-two minutes.

Jake pulled out his phone as he neared the cruiser. Then paused, startled, as he looked at the windshield. Had they gotten a parking ticket? Why in hell would any sane meter person give them a . . . but no, what was tucked under his driver's-side windshield wiper was on lined paper, not heavy orange stock.

He grabbed it. DeLuca was still deep in his phone conversation. Had Tarrant left them a note? Vogelby? A frightened insider hoping to sneak them information? Should he be careful for fingerprints? Jake unfolded the paper and saw, in black Magic Marker, the crude drawing. Of the letter B? Like a capital letter B. *B?* he thought. *What's B?*

And underneath, a J. A capital J.

B? J? Jake frowned.

"What's that?" DeLuca had stashed his phone, peered now over Jake's shoulder. "Aw," he said. "She's tailing you, dude. True love."

"True love?" Had D lost his mind? "What's 'B'?"

"Turn the paper, moron." D took it from him, angled it. "That's a heart, asshole. Not a B," he said. "And a J. And since I get the big detective bucks, I deduce one Jane Ryland was in the neighborhood."

Jake burst out laughing—for the first time that day, he realized. So, not an informant. Right. Not a scrawled B. It was a heart. Signed J.

He tucked it into his pocket as he scanned Kenmore Square. Was Jane still here? Where? There was movement across the street at the library door, but then the door closed.

"Hey, Romeo." DeLuca plopped onto the passenger seat as Jake got behind the wheel. "What were you going to ask the elusive Mr. Tarrant, anyway? Last I heard you were saying we suck as cops."

"Yeah." Jake cranked the ignition. The cool blast of the AC flooded the car. "Here's why. I wanted to ask him the question we forgot." He shifted into reverse. "That video of Avery Morgan, and all her students. We asked him to name the ones he could see. But how about the one we couldn't see?"

"Huh?" D yanked his seat belt over his shoulder, clicked it. "Couldn't see?"

"Yeah," Jake said. "The person who shot the video."

31

JANE RYLAND

A young woman in jeans and black peasant blouse, her curly hair in a random twist, unlocked the heavy glass door of Endicott Library to allow Jane and Fiola inside.

"Elaine Whitfield-Sharp," she said, holding out a hand. Looked them in the eyes, assessing. "With a hyphen. Elaine is fine."

The woman was ten years younger than Jane and Fee. Okay, fifteen.

"Thank you so much, Elaine," Jane began. "I'm—"

"Yeah," Elaine interrupted Jane's attempt at nicety. "I know who you are. And you're Fiola. Fee. Let's talk, two minutes, before we go upstairs." The woman stopped them inside the library's front door. The three of them were apparently alone in the strangely empty library great room, all hunter green and richly oiled pin-spotted portraits, lace collars and pinched mouths, a room designed to be full of people, now abandoned. Rows of glistening wooden tables stood empty, as if all the students had dashed away for dinner, or fun, or whatever students did, abandoning their studies for another time.

"We meet here because it's deniable," Elaine said. "No one notices if you go to the library. And Ashley Masse at the desk closes for us, says it's for 'summer hours' or 'dinner' or whatever Ashley can concoct to give us some privacy. The school doesn't know. Like they even care."

"So we'd like to—" Fiola began.

"You have no hidden cameras, correct?" Apparently Elaine wasn't ready to cede the floor. She eyed the two of them, not trying to hide her suspicions. "I'm even concerned about notebooks. We're intense about privacy."

"I understand," Jane said. This was make or break. Either they got Elaine's trust, or they didn't. "This is simply—"

"Background," Fiola interrupted. "We're only here to listen, to hear your thoughts, and what—"

"What you think can be done, perhaps," Jane put in. The producer/reporter dance was a constant one.

"Fine. This way, then." Elaine pointed them to a short hallway, a single elevator. The door opened and she pushed the button for 3. "We're in the stacks—no one ever goes there. It's like an academic graveyard. All the dissertations are stored up here, master's theses and PhD stuff. Years of work, not to mention obscene tuition, now mostly gathering dust. Perfect meeting place, though."

They watched the lighted numbers change, silent. The doors opened onto a room full of industrial shelving, row upon row of binders and metal-clamped papers. It reminded Jane of her own journalism thesis, "Pretty Crazy Girl," about reporter Nellie Bly, titled from the 1887 newspaper headlines about Bly's groundbreaking undercover investigation of an insane asylum. Far as Jane knew, it remained untouched in her college library. Maybe she should browse through some of these, see what kids were researching and writing about now.

Jane's favorite research discovery about her role model: Nellie's real name was Elizabeth Jane. Jane's full name was Jane Elizabeth. Sometimes the universe had a sense of humor. She shot a glance heavenward. *Thanks, Mom.*

"Everyone?"

Jane and Fee stepped back, at the same time, as Elaine explained who they were and what they were doing.

Ten women, by Jane's quick count, sat around a long table scattered with coffee cups and soda cans. Three other folding chairs, battered beige metal, were empty. How could silence instantly feel so awkward?

"So it's only preliminary, understood?" Elaine wrapped up her brief introduction. "No names, no notes."

She glanced at Jane and Fiola.

Both nodded, confirming.

"I—" Fiola began.

"We—" Jane said at the same time.

"And," Elaine went on, giving them an I'm-not-finished eyebrow, "Ms. Morrello has given me her word you can say what you want without fear of attribution. Right, Fiola?" Elaine paused, holding out her open palms toward the group. Nods all around, including Fiola's. Elaine dragged a chair away from the table, sat next to the wall. "Okay, then. Agreed. No names. Who wants to start?"

Jane felt ten pairs of eyes on her, but heard only silence. Mentally she assigned each one a name, trying to keep them straight. The dark-skinned brunette in the white T-shirt and oversized round eyeglasses at the end of the table could be "T-shirt." Sitting next to her was "Ponytail," with chestnut hair and in a skinny-striped tank top. "Headband," an oddly elegant blonde wearing a headband and pearls. "Yale," supershort hair in a pink Yale sweatshirt with matching pink lipstick. And "Red," a waif of a girl in a Red Sox baseball cap.

College girls, Jane thought. We didn't look like this, but we had the same experiences. This backdrop of scholarly effort made the scene somehow ironic. Shelves holding what college was supposed to be, a table of women illustrating what it actually was.

"Could I—ask a few questions?" Jane pulled out one of the folding chairs, gestured Fee to sit in the other, hoping to break the ice. Sometimes it was easier to get people to talk about someone other than themselves. If a subject was reluctant, sometimes addressing a hypothetical was effective. A wide shot instead of a close-up. "When you first came to Adams Bay, were there any, oh, assemblies, or convocations about potentially iffy, um, social situations?"

No one spoke, but a couple of the women shrugged. Looked at the table. A few took sips from their Starbucks cups. Okay, then. Pressing on.

"Was there, like, a handbook of rules of conduct? Or, where to go, who to tell if . . . something happened?" Jane felt about a million years old—how was thirty-four suddenly ancient?—and realized she didn't have the vernacular anymore. How did young women talk about this? Probably more straightforwardly than she did. She started again.

"Were you cautioned about sexual assault? Guided? Warned?" This was the topic, after all. Why they were all here.

"I'll start." Corner of the table. *Yale*. "I'm—"

"No names." Elaine stood, arms crossed. "Okay?"

"'Kay," Yale said. "I mean, okay. Not that my name is Kay." She laughed, just once, but it was enough. The atmosphere changed.

"Okay, not-Kay." Jane, smiling, tried to look patiently encouraging.

"I felt so pressured," not-Kay began. "They told us—just say no. Make it clear. So I did. I said no. I said it again and again, but . . ." She paused, her face reddening. Pressed her lips together. "I ran. And got away. Barely. But that jerk—" She shook her head. "Whatever."

"It's okay," Ponytail said, reaching over to pat her arm.

"Like hell it is," Headband said.

"We don't need to talk about our personal situations yet." Elaine made the time-out sign. "Fiola, you said you wanted to know how we take care of the newcomers each year. Why we formed the group?"

"Yes, so—"

"I'll start," Ponytail said. "When we got here, they told us a lot of stuff." Heads nodded around the table. "But it wasn't real life."

"We found that out, like, on our own. Luckily, you know, roommates talk. And friends."

"We don't make a big, you know, freaking deal about it," Yale said to the tabletop, then looked up at Jane. "We're just, like, sick of it. And the pressure and the fear."

"We don't, like, march in protest, or shame guys who are assholes."

"We should," Ponytail said. "Seriously."

"That'd backfire." T-shirt shook her head, took a sip from her paper cup.

"Why, because we're the problem?" Yale cocked her head, derisive. "*We* are so *not* the problem."

"Back on topic," Elaine said.

"We just—protect each other, okay? Make sure we go places with buddies. We're not against having sex. We just want sex when we agree, not when we don't."

"Half the time, the guys wouldn't even call it rape." Ponytail waved a dismissive hand. "They're like, it's fun. It's sex. It's, you know, what people do. Which is nuts."

"We haven't really gone public, you know." T-shirt seemed to be the most frightened one of the group. "We just deal with it. Like, in-house."

"In-house?" Jane asked. "Are you all in a sorority? Or do you live in the dorms?"

"Some do, some don't," Elaine said. "It's not a sorority thing, or a nonsorority thing. It's a woman thing."

"A safety thing."

"We've written to the school. Called, too. Talked to Edward Tarrant. He's the dean."

"Jerk," Headband said.

Tarrant was the man she and Fee had interviewed yesterday, the patronizing dean of students who'd drawn a hard line in their discussion—no names, no specifics, many platitudes.

"We know him, yes," Jane said. "Why a jerk?"

"You know him?" Elaine's voice went taut. She narrowed her eyes at Jane.

"We interviewed him," Jane explained.

"Why?" Elaine asked.

"What'd *he* say?" Headband again. She touched her pearls, pursed her lips. "Probably something about how *all* campuses are dealing with this 'problem.' How Adams Bay is no different from anywhere else. Did he tell you how many calls he gets from women? Complaining? And their parents? And what happens to them?"

"Like what?" Jane said.

"Like nothing," Elaine said.

Nothing? Jane had a flash of impatience. They'd promised to keep this confidential. If there was all this hesitation, what was the point?

"Uh, listen, Elaine," she began. "If we're going to understand—"

"No." Elaine shook her head, cutting Jane off. "I don't mean 'nothing' in the sense of we're not going to say anything. I mean it like—we report to him what happens. Every time. We *have* to put it on the record. But then nothing *happens*."

"He's dismissive and disrespectful," Yale said. "He says he'll take care of it. He says—"

"Do you tell him the boys' names?" Fiola asked.

"Of course," Elaine said. "And they're *men*."

"You said 'parents'? Call?" Jane longed for a notebook. She and Fiola would have to talk the whole thing through the minute they got back to the station. Compare mental notes and re-create the conversation. Make sure they didn't lose any of this.

"He wants to 'protect the school's reputation,'" T-shirt was saying.

"Which is bull, because what about *our* reputations?" Red pointed to herself. "Our lives?"

"Did any of you go to the police?" Jane scanned the faces, each one looking at her, one teary-eyed, a few stoic, two looking down at the table.

Yale shook her head. "It'd be a mess. I mean, then what? A big investigation, or a trial, all public, and all over the news, and what good would it do?"

"Victims don't always look hurt," T-shirt said. "You know?"

"'He said, she said,' they can say." Headband made quote marks in the air. "Or, 'It's difficult to judge.'" She puffed out a derisive breath. "Bull."

Jane thought about the police photos Fiola had shown her—the ripped clothing, the grotesque positions, the splayed limbs. The young women in this room hadn't been killed. But their lives were forever changed.

"Disgusting," Ponytail said. "But we decided to, to use our shitty experiences as a lesson, and a weapon, and use what we know to prevent it happening to anyone else."

"So, buddies. Teams. Partners. We watch each other's drinks."

"We go to parties together. Like tomorrow's student welcome party. We won't go alone. Or let anyone else go alone. Or leave alone."

"We made a creep list, too," Headband said. "So we can keep track."

"Man!" Ponytail said. "Um, I'm not sure we should—"

"It's all off the record," Jane reassured her. A creep list? That was irresistible. A list of names, on paper or a computer somewhere, of college students who were suspected—or guilty—of sexual assault? Lawyers would go ballistic, never allow it to be used in court. But then, she wasn't a lawyer. Journalists had different rules.

"Can we see it?" Might as well go for it, Jane thought. She wished Tosca were here. Maybe she was? If not, she should find out how to connect her with these young women. And what if whoever attacked her—allegedly attacked her—was on the creep list?

"No way," Elaine said.

"Why not?" Headband said.

"What would you do with it?" T-shirt asked.

Jane and Fee exchanged glances. They didn't have to discuss anything to agree this would be a pretty interesting item to have. Jane's brain was already calculating how she could track down student disciplinary hearings, or administrative actions, suspensions, or expulsions. The privacy laws would make it all semi-impossible. The college was not required to release—could not even consider it—personal information on student discipline. The reports the school was required to make under Title IX regulations could not include student names. Only if there was an open hearing or a public document would they be able to discover whether any student, male or female, had a pattern of sexual misconduct. So yeah, what would they do with the list?

Jane decided not to answer, maybe let that question percolate a bit. "Well, let me ask you this. You said there's a welcome party tomorrow."

"Yes, big blowout," Yale said.

"Crazy-full of the new students." Headband.

"School-sanctioned?" Fiola asked.

"No," Elaine said. "It's like a tradition. School kind of ignores it, so they don't have to deal with it. Almost the end of summer semester, beginning of the fall. It's at the Spotted Owl—you know it, Fiola?"

"I, uh . . ." Fiola looked at Jane.

"Fiola's new in town," Jane said. "But sure, over behind Fenway Park. So, are you all going?" She looked at each woman, questioning. They all exchanged glances, seemed to agree.

"We have to," Elaine answered. "Part of our . . ."

"Mission," Headband said.

"Passion."

"Responsibility."

Documentary, Jane thought.

"Is there room for another guest or two?" she asked.

32

JAKE BROGAN

"Who keeps calling you?" Jake had been tempted to go lights-and-siren to get the hell out of Kenmore. His growing annoyance—with the traffic, with the unhelpful attitude of Edward Tarrant, and with the possible murder of Avery Morgan—was intensified by the insistent tuba notes of DeLuca's *Jaws* ringtone.

Whoever was calling his partner was relentless. Jake tried to ignore it, tune it out and focus on his own life. He finally made the turn onto Charlesgate Road, heading for HQ and his desk, more coffee, and possibly a moment to connect with Jane. He and D had a load of stuff to do. Track down the students in the video. See who knew who. Follow up the leads in Avery Morgan's personnel file. Handle the authorities in California, who should be calling him back.

If Avery was an informant, it would color this whole investigation. But he couldn't confirm that without info from the West Coast. And no way he would pull an all-nighter over this. Detectives were real people, with real lives and real schedules. The BPD resisted paying overtime. So, all good. It was either Jane's condo, wine, and, eventually, sleep. Or his own place, some kind of dinner, sleep.

"No one 'keeps' calling me." DeLuca clicked off his phone. "I have a life outside of work. Like you do, right, Romeo?"

Before Jake could answer, the tuba rumbled again from DeLuca's pocket.

"I rest my case," Jake said.

D gave him the finger, talked into the phone. "DeLuca."

Then silence.

More silence.

"D?" Jake said.

"Hang on," D told him. And to the phone, "You sure?"

"D?" Jake said again.

"On it," D said. He hung up, took a deep breath.

Jake knew it. All those phone calls? All those conversations? *No one? Bull.* Something was up with DeLuca, big-time. And he was about to hear it.

"D?" Jake stopped at the light on Mass Ave, watched the shopping-bag-toting tourist parade saunter by. *Jane, wine, whatever, sleep.*

"Lights-and-siren, bro," DeLuca said. "And turn right. Now."

EDWARD TARRANT

No wonder he hadn't been able to reach Reg Buchholz. No wonder he hadn't been able to reach his wife. Edward Tarrant flew down the Mass Turnpike, weaving his SL past the morons who insisted on clogging the left lane and making driving impossible for everyone. Green numbers on the dashboard's digital clock taunted him, valuable time ticking by. Buchholz was treating him like a peon. A lackey. Not with the respect due a colleague and goddamned son-in-law.

Edward had tried to call them, warn them, let them know about the Avery debacle, and that he was handling it. Certainly that was his responsibility. He'd assumed they simply hadn't gotten his messages, or hell, were drinking at some vineyard, or touring cathedrals. But now he knew Buchholz hadn't responded, and his wife hadn't responded, because instead of calling him back, they'd decided to return to Boston. Without telling him. Until they reached New York.

Edward downshifted, the motion punctuating his memories, and veered across three lanes to the airport exit. Manderley had left a message before she left—early, naturally—saying President Buchholz and Mrs. Tarrant were flying back from France. And they'd arrive at Terminal C, 8:23 P.M.

All he needed. *All.*

Moreover, he was supposed to pick them up? At the airport? Had they never heard of a taxi?

He rolled down a window, left the AC on, tried to adjust his attitude, adopt the role of attentive son-in-law. Husband. Responsible college administrator. Power broker.

Yes. He nodded, agreeing with himself. It would be better to have President Buchholz on campus. Better to have *him* publicly handle the Avery situation. Better to keep himself, Edward Tarrant, behind the scenes making sure everything worked.

"Make it work," he said out loud. His words floated out the open window, dissipating into the fumes and exhaust.

He'd shaken off the parasitic Sasha Vogelby. Why that woman insisted on sticking to him, burr on tweed, he'd never understand. I know you're upset, he'd told her, trying not to look at his watch. Go home, have a glass of wine. And then, good Lord, she'd asked him to come share it. It was all he could do not to laugh. He'd peeled her away, figuratively, insisting they'd talk tomorrow. She'd have to take Avery's classes this fall, he told her.

"Oh, of *course*," she'd agreed, theatrical palm to her chest, ever the drama. "It'll all be in her *hon*or. We'll do tragic deaths—*Bohème*, maybe. Or *Tosca*."

He hated how she talked, he thought while changing lanes again. Like everything was theater, like she was the star.

With her finally out of the picture, he'd used his cell to leave a terse "Contact me" message for Trey Welliver. The know-it-all cops—"real cops," he said out loud—had not been savvy enough to ask who'd been behind the camera for the party video. Now he could tell Trey that the shit was about to hit, maybe get ahead of the story.

The pretzel of Logan Airport exits appeared, and Edward, almost not speeding, tried to decipher the constantly changing signs and get to the correct terminal, wondering how he could save his reputation.

The damn video put the whole thing at stake. Certainly, if it got out, if the media latched onto it, it'd go viral in a sickening instant. College kids drinking—*drunk*—and semi-carousing with their now-dead professor was not the content you wanted in the headlines. That, though, he could possibly handle. Address, diffuse, dismiss. Let schools without sin cast the first stone, he'd say. And point to Adams Bay's stellar record of conduct.

Trey Welliver was never shown, though anyone who'd been there could place him—with that whiny Isabel girl—at the party. That he could handle.

Edward wasn't shown either. But there was the land mine. The students could simply *reveal* he'd been there. As well as how "friendly" he and Avery were. *That* would not be so easy to address or dismiss.

He pressed the metal button at the parking lot entrance gate, waited as a striped barrier arm lifted to let him in.

But hell. They were kids. *Drunken* kids. Maybe that was an ironic plus. Who'd believe them?

He trolled for a parking place, arguing with himself. Brinn, for one, would believe them. And that would be plenty. That nugget of toxicity could not be glossed over, erased, redeemed, or Band-Aided. If his relationship went public, that would be disaster. Disaster in every way.

He found a spot, noted the letter and number. Luckily no one could hear his thoughts, he realized. Someone would certainly wonder why he hadn't been grieving Avery's death, and focusing on how the hell she died. But reality was, she was dead, he hadn't killed her, and now it was his own life he needed to protect.

WILLOW GALT

Stop, she ordered her frantic brain. *You're losing it, Willow.* She used every cell of her resolve to pull it together.

She huddled in the chair by the window, feet tucked underneath her and arms wrapped around herself. She'd paid in cash, gotten the room key to this no-brand hotel, some random place the cabdriver had brought her. Locked the door behind her. And tried to figure out what to do.

One thing for sure. She had to keep Tom out of it.

She closed her eyes, wishing she could sleep. Forever, maybe. But all she could think about was that man she'd bumped into this afternoon on the sidewalk in Kenmore Square. It was no accident he was there. Of that she was certain.

He'd been waiting for her, again, as she left Java Jim's. *Waiting* for her. Why else would he have been there?

She'd run from him, not even glancing behind her. Leaped into a cab. I must look like a crazy person, she'd thought. I need to call Tom.

She'd seen that man *before*. She had. But where? And in which of her lives? As actress Daniella Ladd? Or as housewife Willow Galt?

She'd closed her eyes in the back of the cab, in fear and fatigue and terror, and tried to remember. She'd seen him. Recently. Where? She'd replayed her day.

Putting the scrapbook in her tote bag, leaving with Tom, crossing the street to the library, inside the library, the shopping, the tea, and then busy Kenmore Square, crossing the street to the—*Wait!*

Yes. On the way to the library. At the zebra-striped crosswalk. He'd gestured her to go first, pretending not to give her the eye. She'd ignored him then, because she was used to being looked at, even as Willow, and besides, she'd been on a mission. But maybe it wasn't random that he was there. Maybe he'd been sent by Roger Hayden. Sent to follow her.

Later she'd bumped into him—*or him into her?*—outside Java Jim's. And then she'd seen him again five minutes later. *He'd asked where she was headed.*

They knew who she was. They knew who Tom was. And they'd never leave them alone.

The killer had made a horrifying error. Certainly—more than certainly—the victim was meant to be her, Willow. Maybe to punish Tom for his whistle-blowing? So that meant *she*—inadvertently, but just as certainly as if she had done it herself—had caused the death of Avery Morgan.

She'd asked Olive, flat out—no need to hide her fears, "Do you think they killed Avery by *mistake*? Thinking it was me?"

Willow would never forget that pause, that moment when her handler clearly considered it.

"I don't . . . think so," she'd replied.

"Is Roger Hayden still in custody?" Willow had asked that, too. "Or did he tell all to the US Attorney? Like we did?"

What if he was in witness protection, too? If he was, she'd never recognize him!

Her mind flew back to the man she'd seen three times today. Could that have been *Roger*? No, she assured herself. No way. The man was taller, older, broader. She'd gotten a good look at him, though, and if she ever saw him again, she'd know.

She burrowed down into the pillows of the chair. Neon glowed outside, the hotel sign making hot slashes on her bare legs. Olive had bought plane tickets for her, but Willow was hiding instead of flying. She couldn't just run away. Couldn't leave Tom.

If she told him about this? He'd say she was silly, and ignore her warning. Then, soon, it would be too late, and it wouldn't matter that she was right. Because they'd both be dead.

Because of her, their new life was ruined. They'd arrived here scarcely three months ago, to start their new life. He'd become Tom and she Willow and so they forever would be. Now forever was over. She'd have Olive contact him, and they'd have to start again—*again*. All because she'd called the police when Avery drowned.

But what else could she do?

She slid the anti-anxiety meds from her pocket. Looked at them, two pale yellow dots raised on her open palm. She tossed them into her mouth, swallowed a shoot of water from her plastic bottle. Maybe another one? Yes. She swallowed again. She still had time before Tom would worry about her. She would relax, maybe nap. And then she, somehow, would figure out what to do.

She closed her eyes. And thought of something else.

A sound escaped her throat, a tiny note of fear. Her eyes flew open.

Maybe Roger Hayden wasn't the problem.

Maybe Tom was not in danger.

Maybe Avery's killer had hit the *correct* target. But noticed Willow watching, witnessing through her bedroom window. And realized she'd seen. Whatever she'd seen.

What if the man in the crosswalk, the one outside the library, was someone Avery's killer sent to shut her up?

That had to be true. That's what made sense.

Which meant her new identity was no protection.

The one in danger was Willow Galt.

33

JAKE BROGAN

"Getting confirmation now." DeLuca was reading from the screen of his cell phone as Jake steered around the last corner, almost on two wheels. They'd made it up Huntington, past the Pru, past the projects, through the South End in record time. "Female, Caucasian, mid-forties. Cause of death, unknown. Time of death—crap."

"What?" Jake said. It was pushing 7:30 now, but still almost daylight in Boston's waning summer. Violet Sholto was dead. A cleaning person, some maid, according to dispatch, called to report the body. The maid was still there, living room, dispatch warned them, freaking out. Next of kin, husband Clooney Sholto, out of town somewhere. But why hadn't Grady told them about this? Maybe their informant hadn't known. Possible.

"They don't know time of death either," D said. "ME's on the way."

"How nice for you," Jake said. "Give you two something to talk about."

"We don't talk much," DeLuca said, leering. "She's too busy being—" He pointed. "There it is. That house. Guess how I know."

A ribbon of yellow crime scene tape already stretched across the manicured front lawn, draped over a row of carefully sculpted shrubs, drawn taut across the flagstone walkway and attached to a white-painted lamppost. A uniformed cop stood sentry next to one of the fluted—and too-big—white columns bracketing the broad front porch.

Not one person on the street. No onlookers. No curious neighbors. Out of respect? Or fear? No press. Matter of time, though.

Jake banged the cruiser up onto the sidewalk, flipping off the siren as he jounced the front wheels over the curb. He and DeLuca had their doors open almost before the engine stopped. Boston's Jamaica Plain neighborhood—JP, they called it—had a surprise around every corner. A block away was the Caribbean quarter, a strip of exotic shops and restaurants that the neighborhood's other residents, hip lawyers and do-gooders, had recently discovered. Some of JP became a gentrifying haven for millennials. Other parts were enclaves of longtime locals who barricaded shoveled-out parking spaces every winter with laundry bins and folding chairs, who ordered "coffee regular" from Dunkin's, and who hoped their sons would be cops and their daughters married. One sliver on the west edge was the territory of Clooney Sholto and family.

On paper, apparently not believing in cliché, the Sholtos ran a plumbing supply company. Every cop knew what the Sholtos really did. Stopping them, though, was a question of making a case against them. So far, the cops, as well as the administrations of two separate district attorneys, had failed. If Violet Sholto was the dead body discovered on the second floor, Jake would not be surprised if it was murder. With any number of possible suspects and motives.

Retaliation? Revenge? A rival-gang thing? Maybe her past. Every cop understood the Sholto-O'Baron family rivalry still seethed, even with the supposedly peacemaking marriage. Anything was possible. If Sholto and his pals decided to fight back, eye for an eye, against whoever killed Clooney's dearly departed wife, Boston would have a problem on its hands. Or could be Clooney killed her himself. Or she might be dead of natural causes, in which case they could all go home. They'd figure it out.

But why hadn't Grady called them?

"Fancy schmancy." DeLuca eyed the Sholto home as they neared the door.

"Lotsa money in plumbing," Jake said. He had a thought. Stopped, turned to DeLuca. "She didn't drown, though, did she?"

JANE RYLAND

The immutable laws of the universe were changing. That was the only explanation. This day seemed as if it would have way more than twenty-four hours. Jane felt like she was dragging herself along Beacon Street to their new destination. She and Fiola had wrapped up their meeting with the SAFE women—*that* was a success, at least—and plans were in the works for tomorrow's party. Well and good. And worthwhile. But still, she'd longed to go home, see Jake, and participate in any accompanying etceteras.

"So near and yet so far," she muttered.

"Huh?" Fiola was checking addresses on brownstones. "Fab. Right across the street," she said. "This'll be great. I cannot believe Tosca called you, that she actually wants to talk—*right now,* yet."

"Yeah." Jane had to admit she was intrigued. "Wonder what happened."

"Who cares?" Fiola pushed 1584, a tiny black button in the center row of a massive silver-louvered array of intercom connections. The heavy glass and metal door clicked, its heavy steel lock vibrating and buzzing.

Jane had already pulled the door open. "It wasn't locked," Jane said. "At least we're announced."

If Jane had tried to imagine Tosca—and she guessed she had as they rode a gray-walled elevator up fifteen floors—she would have been an eccentric misfit, vulnerable and lost. Or an unsophisticated, small-town girl—Jane laughed at the cliché, because she herself had grown up in semirural Illinois—plopped fish-out-of-water into the urban bustle of metropolitan Boston.

But real-life Tosca, meeting them at her apartment's front door, was a rock star. Maybe a nascent diva, Jane thought, scouting the opera post-

ers on the wall. Shorter than Jane. Petite, dark, with elegant cheekbones. Somehow a presence, even in a black tank top and cutoffs. What Jane *had* predicted correctly was the sorrow and suspicion in her eyes, the dark circles, her pale legs and arms, the silence of this little apartment.

A goldfish, just one, swam circles in a bowl. Window to the balcony, open, striped curtains barely moving in the evening breeze. *Fall is on the way,* the atmosphere was saying. Change.

"Thanks for coming," Tosca said. "I don't like to . . . go outside."

"Oh, no problem. We were pleased to get your call," Jane said. She "didn't like" to go outside?

"We were already here, in the neighborhood, luckily," Fiola said, "so it was easy to—"

"Because of what happened?" Tosca interrupted, then gestured them into the room, waved them to the couch. "Sorry," she said, picking up some books, closing and stacking them. "It's usually only me. But the death. In The Reserve. It's all over Facebook. About Avery. Is that why you were here? Covering that or something?"

"Is there any news about it?" Jane didn't need to tell Tosca why they were nearby. And seeing her now, Jane knew Tosca hadn't been at the SAFE meeting.

The girl perched on the edge of a spindly side chair, wrapped one leg around the other, crossed her arms. Making herself as small as she could. "Well, no. I mean, yes, they're saying it's Avery Morgan, I mean, Professor Morgan, and I—" She paused, scratched one bare forearm so hard Jane could see red welts. She stopped, looked at the red, blew out a breath. "Sorry. It's upsetting. No one is safe, though. No one, not ever. Not anywhere."

Jane and Fee exchanged glances. If this girl—a potential diva maybe, but emotionally raw—knew something about the death, they couldn't ignore it simply because it wasn't "their" story. Every story was their story. They were journalists. According to the six o'clock news Jane read online, the school wasn't confirming anything or giving a statement yet. But this girl was corroborating for Jane what Jake had told her: The victim's name was Avery Morgan. *Professor* Morgan.

"I'm so sorry for your—the loss," Jane began. This was a tough one. Tosca had called them about their campus assault story, but still. "Did you know her?"

"Of course!" Tosca's eyes, deepest brown, flew open. She un-pretzeled herself, leaned forward. "We all knew her. I'm a theater major." She waved at the colorful opera posters. "Opera, you know? And Professor Morgan had rehearsals at her home and . . ."

Her voice trailed off, and she stared at the icy blue wall across from her, as if remembering. A tear welled in one eye, and she brushed it away, still looking at the wall. "Little shows, and practices, by the pool. We'd all sing, and—and it was in that very pool where she was . . ."

"She drowned?" Fiola almost whispered.

Jane shifted on the couch. The cause-of-death info hadn't been released. This was potentially a big deal. A possible homicide. And they were TV, and TV needed pictures. If this girl had a photo of the victim, that'd be newscast gold. Jane tried to evaluate the always-difficult news-need versus personal-intrusion calculus.

All Tosca could do was say no. And throw them out. And never speak to them again. And their documentary would be ruined. And Jane would be out of a job again. But maybe not.

"Ah, um, Tosca?" Jane said. "I was wondering . . ."

34

ISABEL RUSSO

Jane was nice, Isabel thought. With a nice voice, Isabel always noticed that. And a thoughtful manner, kind of welcoming, like a friend. Not like that other one, the bossy one, acting like a second-rate alto who always wanted center stage. Jane was clearly, like, sincere. Somehow you could tell. And successful, and engaged in her profession. Isabel felt it, the connection, soon as the two older women entered her apartment.

After that scary phone call with the *Tosca* music, Isabel had first decided not to say another word. Not about anything. But then, she'd regrouped. First of all, it was probably a dumb coincidence. Who knew what they used for "hold music" these days.

"My whole life is not a melodrama, Fish." She had said that out loud. "Why am I making it one?" She wouldn't mention the mysterious call to Jane and Fiola, because really, what could anyone do? So she'd screwed her courage to the sticking point, like they said in drama class. And, with her newfound resolve, she wasn't waiting until tomorrow to call. Still, she was surprised these women had been able to come so instantly. Maybe it was fate, or whatever controlled the universe.

"O Fortuna," she'd sung the portentous notes of the Orff, holding out her arms dramatically, head high. She missed performing, so much. But it was too—she blew out a breath. One step at a time.

She didn't want Jane and Fiola to be here at the same time as Grady, so she'd stalled her dinner for a while. Grady might not be the delivery person tonight, anyway. She could never predict. *O Fortuna.*

Now Jane was asking her something. About Professor Morgan. Isabel stared at the wall, envisioning the last time she'd seen her professor.

"Yes? Wondering what?" She blinked away the memory and turned to Jane. She loved Jane's hair, the way it naturally curled under, wondered if that chestnutty color was real. Good makeup, too, not too stagy or TV. When was the last time she'd entertained at her apartment? Not that this was "entertaining." This was revenge. Or . . . justice.

"By any chance," Jane said, "do you have any pictures of Professor Morgan? I mean, there's probably one on the website, we haven't looked, but now that we're here . . . maybe a video?"

Isabel tried to read the expressions on Jane's and Fiola's faces. Video? Did they know? *Jane didn't know. She couldn't know.* They were reporters. Reporters always asked for photos and video.

"I'm sorry, Tosca." Jane smiled. At the nickname, Isabel guessed. Or maybe mistaking her hesitancy for reluctance. Or criticism.

"Part of the job, unfortunately, to ask," Jane went on. "If you don't have any photos or videos, you don't. It's fine."

"Let me think," Isabel said. Stalling. If they wanted to see only Avery, they wouldn't have to watch the whole thing, of course. She'd downloaded the clip from YouTube the day after the party, thank goodness, because it wasn't online anymore. Amazing that he'd posted it in the first place! She'd figured—hoped!—the police would want it at some point, because even though it wasn't exactly *evidence,* it was certainly proof. Of, of . . . lots of stuff. Should she show it?

Maybe. Because more important, Jane couldn't possibly know about her "Someday" file. And she never would. The video had once been on YouTube, Isabel reminded herself. Maybe they could retrieve it anyway. Jane was so nice, and seemed like she was really trying to help her.

"There's kind of a video," Isabel began. And from Jane's expression, Fiola's, too, she knew this was a good thing. Maybe if she could help them, they could help her. Somehow.

"I, um, haven't really looked at it," she said. "It was, like, in May."

"*Kind* of a video?" Fiola said. "Can we see it?"

"Great," Jane said. She gave her producer a funny look, then reached out, spreading her palms as if to smooth out wrinkles in the air. "Whatever, okay? No pressure. But would you mind showing it to us? Forgive me."

For what? Isabel thought. But kept silent.

"Because, you know, we're TV." Jane looked apologetic, tilting her head as if she wasn't quite sure she should say this. "And if there are no pictures, there's no television. We could alter it however you want, blur faces. Not say where it came from, not ever, since absolutely everything between us is confidential. In every way, until you say it isn't."

That was an easy one.

"I'll never say it isn't," Isabel said.

"Done," Jane said. "It'll always be confidential, one hundred percent. So, the video?"

Isabel had to decide. Her apartment was so silent, she could almost hear Fish swimming through the ferns, layered with the sound of the three women breathing, and all the traffic below filtering through her open balcony window. *Yes.* Show it. It existed, and pretending it didn't was like hiding her head in the sand.

"It was a fun event, kind of a rehearsal," Isabel began. "We were just practicing for another show we were putting together. We did one in April, and . . ."

"Okay, terrific." Jane was nodding, looking appreciative. Isabel tried to remember exactly what was on the video. Probably, maybe, she shouldn't have mentioned it until she'd looked at it again, but now Jane and Fiola were here, and being so nice . . . *She kept saying the word "nice"—she had to get out more!* Talking to real people. It was such a relief.

"I'll get it for you." She couldn't very well take it back now, or make up some excuse about how she couldn't find it. It took two seconds to boot her laptop, bring up the file, click it open. "I haven't watched it for . . . a while," she said. "But I know Professor Morgan is on it."

She almost burst into tears as she saw it, hadn't expected that gut-chilling reaction, hadn't known *what* to expect, really. That soft May night, lanterns twinkling in the leafy trees, yellow and red plastic cups, and everyone in shorts and T-shirts, long floaty skirts. A little night music, Isabel thought, as she watched the people she used to know laughing and chatting.

"That's Avery Morgan," she said, pointing. Professor Morgan was smiling, talking to someone Isabel couldn't see. She narrowed her eyes. That weasel Tarrant, the creep, keeping off camera. He'd acted like he owned the place, and owned Avery, though he probably thought he was being discreet. You had to be a better actor than that to fool Isabel.

"So thin," Fiola said. "Pretty, like a movie star."

"She came from Hollywood, did something in films." Isabel knew this from class and Google. "Yes, she is. Was." Hard to believe she was gone, she commanded the screen so completely. Life changed so quickly, so irrevocably. Haunting, now, to see the past captured: the sounds and the gaiety, the twinkling lights and the carefree faces. No one knew that so many lives were about to change.

"Who took the video?" Jane asked, eyes still on the screen.

"Oh, I—don't remember." A lie, a big one, but there she would not go.

"Uh-huh," Jane said. Seemed to believe her.

The students began to line up. Neesha, and Claire. She missed them, so much. The kick line started. She must have been up in the bathroom when it began.

Avery Morgan stood, her hair thrown back, plastic cup in hand. Tarrant was never shown in the video, Isabel noticed. Weasel.

"Over here!" Avery-on-tape called out. "Isabel!"

Every cell in Isabel's body froze. The hair on the back of her neck prickled. Her heart sank to her toes. She'd forgotten this part. And there was no way, now, to prevent it. If she reached out and bashed the mouse, making it stop? What good would that do? It was too late.

"Isabel!" Avery Morgan was waving. At her. Now she remembered that, remembered it all. There she was, looking happy and free and—Avery had flung one arm around her. Kissed her on both cheeks, like she always did. They both turned, waving at the camera, Isabel picking up her red cup, toasting the night.

It made her sick now, to see it.

Jane reached over, clicked the mouse. The scene froze, an unmistakable and irrefutable tableau. "Should I—we—pretend we didn't hear that, Tosca?" Jane whispered, touching, briefly, a gentle hand to Isabel's shoulder. "It's okay, you know. You can trust me. Us."

See? She knew Jane was good, knew she would protect her. They were in it together. One hundred percent, Jane had said. The three of them stood there, bearing the weight of their new knowledge, Fiola looking at the computer screen, Jane looking at Isabel.

"Yes. No," Isabel said. "Yes."

JANE RYLAND

"Yes." Tosca said it again.

This was astonishing. Why had the girl shown that video if it revealed her real name? She'd told Jane and Fee she hadn't watched it for a while. Why not, if it was such a treasured memory? But then, these days, that was typical, standard, everyone took photos of their every move. How many photos were in Jane's phone right now, snapped and then never looked at again? People documented everything these days, but that didn't mean they ever referred to any of it again. So, yeah, believable.

"That's me," Tosca was saying. She was looking at the floor, or at her bare feet, or at the woven sisal rug. "I'm Isabel. Isabel Russo. A senior. I graduate next year. I guess you'd find out eventually. Not that it actually matters, right? Because you'll never use it, or tell anyone."

Fiola extended her hand to shake Isabel's. "You're a rock star, Isabel," Fiola said. "We appreciate this."

Isabel took her hand, silent. Then nodded, as if making a decision. "Thank you," she said. "If I can help even one person, it matters."

"Exactly," Fiola said. She glanced at Jane. "I understand."

"Thank you, um, Isabel," Jane said. "And of course. One hundred percent confidential."

Jane watched as Tosc—*Isabel.* It'd be hard to think of her as that right away—clicked the mouse again, and the video resumed. Dancing, now, a kick line of smiles and enthusiasm. Jane recognized the summer's top video, re-created, gesture for gesture, in this Boston backyard. The hostess—teacher, professor, mentor—was now dead. And one of the students in it, smiling and singing for the camera, was now a victim of sexual assault and afraid to give her real name. *Life,* Jane thought.

The camera panned across the dancers. Avery Morgan, all in white, waved at the lens. *So happy,* Jane thought. *Life is so short.*

In the background, someone else entered the shot. A young man, clearly the delivery guy. Three pizza boxes, a brown paper bag balanced on top.

"Oh," Isabel said. Jane felt her energy change.

"What?" Jane asked. Isabel had put her fingers to her mouth. She hadn't taken her eyes off the screen.

"Nothing," Isabel replied. "Nothing."

"Pizza," Fiola said.

"Yeah. Beer and pizza."

Pizza. Which reminded Jane she was starving, which reminded her of dinner, which reminded her of Jake.

Jake. Who was working on Avery Morgan's possible murder. The video continued for a few more moments, faces Jane didn't recognize, probably would never see again. But what would Jake see? A video full of possible suspects, or at least people who knew the victim. Clearly he'd want to watch it—it might even help him solve the case. Could she tell him about it? Somehow? He could have found it on his own.

And then she had another thought. Why would Isabel keep it?

"Isabel," Jane began. She had to ask, even though it was iffy, and problematic, and every other thing that made journalism a constant battle. Campus sexual assault, insidious and pervasive, the unspoken but shared lifelong trauma of so many young women. A crime that, unlike many of the punishable-by-twenty-years-in-prison rapes that occurred off campus, was too often covered up, papered over, dealt with by silence and fear.

Another difference made it more terrifying. Often, so often, the women knew their attackers. Had to go to class with them, see them in the hallways, watch them laugh with other people. It was a crime where the criminal was known.

Where the criminal was free. Like nothing ever happened.

But Isabel "didn't like" to go outside.

Jane took a deep breath, trying to balance propriety and curiosity and urgency and compassion. "Isabel? Is *he* . . . in this video? Was this the night . . . it happened?"

35

JAKE BROGAN

"Two dead women? In suburban homes?" Jake frowned as they approached the Sholtos' house, thinking of Avery Morgan. "What if Violet Sholto drowned, too?"

"Oh, good one. You're thinking suburban serial drowner?" D rapped his knuckles on the door, an ostentatious slab of dark green with a roaring lion on the knocker. "Alert the media."

"Just being prepared for all eventualities." *Alert the media.* DeLuca's shorthand to remind Jake he was aware of Jane. Good thing they were going public soon. D's needling was getting old.

D knocked again.

This time, Jake heard muffled footsteps from inside. He did a quick scan, corner to corner, wondering if the Sholto place was wired with surveillance cameras. If it was—and if they worked—that'd help. Hadn't helped Avery Morgan, though. The door opened.

"Jake. D." T'shombe Pereira cocked his head back toward the interior. All the lights were on, a long hallway stretched behind him. An ostentatiously elaborate chandelier glowed above, too big even for this gaudy entryway.

"This is *the* Sholto, right?" Jake had to confirm.

"Yup. King of plumbing. And better get in here," Pereira said.

In thirty seconds they were inside the world of Clooney and Violet Sholto, a knickknack-filled chaos of stuff, too much leather furniture, too many chairs, too many paintings and vases and flowers. On a lace-pillowed expanse of navy-blue plush sat a tiny woman in black pants and black blouse, red-eyed and trembling, a white apron, smeared with red, still tied around her waist. Officer Something—Winnick—sat next to her on the couch, half-babysitter, half-cop.

"This is Rissa Murphy," Winnick said. "Housekeeper. She found her employer, Mrs. Violet Sholto, in a bathtub full of water."

Jake glanced at D, eyebrow raised. *Ha.*

"Why would she kill herself?" The weepy young woman looked up at Jake and D with beseeching eyes, whispering. "She had everything."

"I am so sorry for your loss," Jake began. "Officer Winnick? Could you get Ms. Murphy something to drink?"

Taking the officer's place on the couch, Jake turned to Rissa Murphy, introduced himself. He saw her knuckles whiten as she clenched her hands in her lap. She'd crossed her legs, tucking one black canvas shoe behind an ankle.

"Miss Murphy. I know you're upset."

"What will happen to her? Why would she do this?"

"Ma'am? Miss? 'Why would she do this?' Are you saying you think it was suicide?"

The woman looked at her apron, the red smears, pulled it away from herself with two fingers. "Her . . . she . . . upstairs." Her voice was barely audible. She pointed to a curving carpeted stairway, the one they'd passed to enter the living room. Pereira had stationed himself at the bottom step. "I have Sunday and Monday off, so—"

"I'll go up," D said.

"Be there in a few," Jake said. He turned to the woman again. "I see. I need to ask. Where's Mr. Sholto?"

"New York." The woman clapped her hands over her mouth, her eyes widening. "Oh. How will I tell him?"

"We'll take care of that," Jake said. "And the medical examiner is on the way, and she'll be able to help us with the—other things. But, miss? Mr. Sholto. Do you know where to find him? How long has he been gone?"

"In New York. Since Friday. Last Friday," the housekeeper said. She accepted a tall glass of water from Winnick, took a sip. "I haven't seen him since then."

"And Mrs. Sholto was alone?"

"I—yes. I mean, I have Sunday and Monday off. Tuesday I do shopping, and so I didn't get here until, uh, three, and then I do the kitchen, and I don't see Mrs. Sholto, but maybe she's not home, she goes—I don't know. Luncheons, things like that. So then I do the kitchen, like I said, and I go upstairs, and, and and . . ."

Jake wrote it all down as Winnick hovered. Victim VS is suburban wife, shopping, luncheons. Phone calls. Mother, Nuala O'Baron, age 73, comes to visit. Sometimes victim goes to her. VS enemies, none. VS drug use, none.

Rissa Murphy had looked baffled at the very questions.

"Money problems?"

Rissa waved her hand, encompassing the possession-filled room. "No," she whispered. "Not that I know."

"Lots of money in plumbing, I guess," Jake said, keeping a straight face. "So did Mr. Sholto call over the weekend? Do you have a number for him?"

"No," Rissa said. "I only come here. I don't—anything else."

"Jake?" DeLuca's voice from upstairs. "You almost ready?"

"Thank you, Miss Murphy," Jake said. "Can you stay here briefly, please? Officer Winnick needs to get your contact information."

Crime Scene was on the way, but Jake, touching nothing, climbed the ruby-carpeted stairway and followed the lights, two left turns, to a floral explosion of a bathroom. Wallpapered with violets in every shade of purple and trimmed with a border of green leafy vines, it was the size of Jake's entire college dorm room. Air-conditioning blasted. Mirrors covered the left wall, and on the right sat a lavender-tufted vanity, magnifying mirror surrounded by pink-tinted movie-star lights. Not a bathroom that was shared with a man. It had probably once smelled of perfume. Not anymore.

"See what you get from this," D said. "Doesn't look like a mob hit to me, but who knows. I'll head downstairs. She was an 'actress,' right?"

"Not anymore," Jake murmured as D left.

He snapped cell phone photos of Violet Sholto's final resting place, an oversized enamel bathtub with gold-clawed feet. Her head lay against the flat back at one end, her lavender-painted toes just visible under the gold fixtures at the other. Her arms could not be seen beneath the grim, dark-colored water, a translucent shroud that reached to the victim's chin. Strands of matted dark hair made jagged lines on her vacantly expressionless face.

Jake tried not to look in the mirrors, each of which reflected the finality of death. She'd obviously been obsessed with beauty. In the end, it didn't matter.

A dank pyramid of reddened towels, plopped on the floor, leaked lines of red rivulets onto the now-pink grout between the white tiles. Had someone tried to stop the bleeding? Or clean it up? Or both?

Suicide? Or murder?

When Medical Examiner Kat McMahan arrived—at 8:42, Jake noted—he managed to refrain from making any cracks about her clandestine relationship with D. They said their goodbyes, leaving the two officers and Kat at the scene.

"Kat will give us the scoop, soon as she knows," D said as he got back into the cruiser. "Nothing more for us here—no break-in, no nothing. Someone she knew. Or someone very skilled."

"Like Avery Morgan." Jake cranked the ignition.

"Like half the murders in Boston, conspiracy boy," D said. "There's no frigging connection between Violet Sholto and Avery Morgan."

"Kidding me?" Jake said. They backed out onto Mishawum Street, the lights in neighborhood windows beginning to bloom behind gauzy curtains. "Of course there is."

ISABEL RUSSO

So that was totally the question she'd hoped Jane wouldn't ask, and now she had.

Was that the night it happened?

Yes, it was, she acknowledged to herself.

Was "he" in the video?

Yes, he was. Sort of. She'd saved the file as proof that he'd been there, and that she'd been there. Like a trusting, naive, stupid person, a person who thought the world was interested in honor and justice. She stood, turned away from her visitors, faced the kitchen. The video was playing again, she could hear the muffled music behind her. Jane and Fiola must be watching, but she couldn't face another second. *The memory of that night . . .*

Was it her fault? She'd flirted with him, that was the thing. Laughed, and shared class notes, back when her life was fun and she was a student and on her own. He'd even come to their little opera night—she saw him applauding after she sang one of her favorite arias, *"Vissi d'arte."* Oh!

"I'm so sorry." Jane came up beside her. "I didn't mean to upset you."

Isabel could see that Jane was worried, saw her exchange glances with Fiola, knew she'd failed, miserably, at keeping her secret. But Jane and Fiola didn't know everything, not even from that video, especially not from the video. If she could only keep it together, she'd be fine.

But *"Vissi."* She'd forgotten about that little opera night, when she'd performed the beautiful aria from *Tosca.* When she'd *been* Tosca. Now she needed some time to think.

"Could you"—she spoke in a whisper, gesturing toward the kitchen sink—"get me a little water?"

Jane and Fiola fussed in a cabinet. Glasses clinked.

Isabel needed to regroup. The music on that creepy phone call, the aria from the second act of *Tosca.* The moment Tosca understands she has no hope. *He'd* heard her sing it. She'd told him the story! That's why he'd chosen that music on his call, that was *why*! Was it a threat? Why?

Her brain struggled to untangle it all. Maybe the call meant something good was happening? Hard to believe, but maybe? Maybe the authorities were looking into her complaint, what she'd told Edward Tarrant? And now, finally finally finally, the school was catching up with Trey?

Oh. She'd said his name. To herself, but still. She never would again.

But maybe that's why he'd called? To warn her not to say anything? Not to testify against him? Should she tell Tarrant? Yes, yes, definitely she should. She'd report it instantly.

She stood, feeling electric, feeling powerful, feeling . . . in control. *My turn,* she thought.

"Here you go." Jane handed her a green glass, wrapped in a strip of paper towel. "I didn't want to look through your drawers for a napkin."

Isabel took a grateful sip. "Thanks," she said. She put the glass on the kitchen table, slowly, deliberately, because as soon as that was done, she'd have to say something. Either way, her life would change. She looked at Fish for guidance, for advice. But Fish just continued swimming his circles.

"So, yes," Isabel had to begin. "Yes. That was the night. And yes, he was there." She cleared her throat. "And yes, I'll tell you about him and the video. If you swear to keep it secret."

She watched Jane and Fiola process this, almost as if she could see the gears in their brains at work. They had to be thinking they were about to be told the name of a criminal. And being asked not to talk about the crime. Could a reporter, even one who seemed sympathetic and reliable, agree to do that?

Isabel got up and closed the laptop screen. If they wouldn't keep it secret, or couldn't, she wouldn't tell them. Easy enough.

"Isabel," Jane said. "And I think Fiola will agree with me. I—we—don't want to know his name. It puts us in an impossible position."

Fiola nodded. "Jane's right. We don't want to be called to testify in court, we don't want to be asked to give evidence to the police. If you tell us, all it does is make things more complicated."

"So . . ." Isabel tried to understand this.

"The power of the truth," Fiola went on. "That's what our documentary is about. Your *particular* case, what happens with it, that remains in *your* hands."

"We'd love to go after him, track him down, look up his records—of

course we would." Jane went back to the couch, motioned Isabel to follow. "But we can't name him simply because you say so. We'd need to get
his side of the story."

"But . . ." Isabel frowned. *His* side? There was no other side.

"There's always another side," Jane said, as if reading her thoughts.
"And as journalists, Fiola and I need to explore them. But we can't initiate
an investigation at Adams Bay. That has to be done by you. If we reported it
to Edward Tarrant, or whoever, he'd—"

"He'd throw us out." Fiola sat in the side chair.

"I told him already," Isabel said.

"You did?" Fiola looked at Jane.

"And told him your attacker's name?" Jane asked.

"Yes," Isabel said. But now her new idea was weaving through her
consciousness, taking hold. Maybe she *had* misjudged. Maybe there was
an investigation, had been all along, and she just didn't know about it.
How could they *not* investigate? She'd asked them to. Maybe soon, they'd
come to her, and she'd tell what she knew—as much as she knew, which
wasn't everything, but maybe it was enough, and then it would be over.

Yes, she had her "Someday" file. And someday, she could use it.
Maybe. But maybe she wouldn't have to.

She turned to Jane. "Yes, I told him. And so far, nothing's happened.
But maybe these things take time."

"Possible." Jane seemed to agree.

"So maybe I won't say anything." Much safer, Isabel decided. Go by
the book. Wait for Tarrant. Don't make waves. She knew these two would
be disappointed, but she had to do what was best for her. For her*self*. For
her brand-new in-control self. "I'm so sorry. But I think I'll wait for the
investigation."

Fiola stood, looking unhappy. "But you already—"

"You know what? Fiola, sorry to interrupt," Jane said. "But I just had
a thought. Isabel? If you could go back to that night, would you do anything differently? Or, knowing what you know now, would you have any
advice for other young women?"

"That's what our doc is about, exactly," Fiola said. "Not about the investigation of *your* case, but allowing you to help other people. Are you interested in that?"

Was she? All her newfound resolve deflated, reversed, and changed direction. Could she use her power for good? If she could help someone else, even one person, would that make up for her horrible horrible imprisonment in this apartment, all those days, all those crossed-off days on her calendar . . . might they mean something if she spoke up? But then her story would be out there.

"But wouldn't it be out of my control, then?" Control, Isabel realized, was what had kept her sane all these months. Inside, where she knew what was where and what would happen. She could control *herself,* and where she went and what she said.

"Control?" Jane had a funny look on her face, like she was considering something.

"Yes. That's why I don't . . . like to go outside. To keep control. And even if I'm in silhouette, my story will be out there. Then I'm not in control of it anymore."

"I have an idea," Jane said. "Of what you might do to keep control. You have to be brave, Isabel. But you *are* brave. Or we wouldn't be sitting here."

36

JANE RYLAND

Jane opened her condo's front door as Jake's key clicked through the dead bolt. Watch-cat Coda had padded into the foyer before Jane heard anything, sensing the arrival of someone who wasn't completely enthusiastic about her species.

Jane had followed, eager to give Jake the full view of her new ensemble. More of a camisole and sweatpants girl, Jane could never quite relate to dressing up in a lacy something to entice a guy. It seemed so unspontaneous. "Lingerie" was a word from the fifties, and clothing hyped as "seductive" always turned out to be uncomfortable. Or cold. But this was going to be hilarious.

"What do you think? How do I look?" Jane posed, cover-girl hand on hip, attempting to convey wide-eyed innocence. Which lasted about half a second.

Jake stood, slack-jawed, in the open doorway. Then burst out laughing. Coda tried to make a run for it, but he scooped her up, not taking his eyes off Jane. And continued to laugh.

"Laughter? *Laughter?*" she pretend-criticized. She adored his laugh—so carefree, his eyes crinkling. After this long, ridiculous day, his dear face was such a treat, and she couldn't wait to kick back with him. Forget everything. He always made it easy. "That's all you got? Laughter?"

"No, no, you always look great." Jake leaned in, kissed her on the cheek, then stood back, arm's length, giving her a head-to-toe once-over.

He frowned. "Um. It's . . . kind of a new look for you. I'm not used to all the . . . legs."

"Do I look like a college girl?" Jane twirled, then paused so he could get the full view from the back. Facing him again, she extended one pointed toe. "See? Really short skirt, little boots, tank top?"

Silence.

Now it was Jane's turn to laugh.

"I wish you could see your face, poor thing." Jane stood like herself again. "But seriously. It's a disguise. A college-girl disguise. Okay, I know, I'm thirty-four. But like, in the dark? And maybe I went back to school, after I toured Europe?"

"Long trip," Jake said. "But, sure. No question. It's certainly possible, honey. Can I come in? I got you a cat."

He held out the writhing Coda and closed the door behind them, the cat skittering away down the hall. After a while they untangled from a proper greeting, Jane's knees as always going to jelly and the cares and stresses of the day disappearing, then stayed arm in arm as they headed for the kitchen. She needed to tell him about her court appearance, the non-identification, then thinking she was off the hook, then being told she wasn't.

First things first. Food.

"The usual?" she asked. "Have you had dinner? I haven't—which is a situation, food-wise. We could call Gormay?" Which reminded her of court again, so maybe not. "Unless you're up for peanut butter toast with your beer."

"Perfect," Jake said. "Goes with wine, too. Want some? You okay with PB toast?"

"Sure. You know I love to cook." She did, actually, only she never had time. Jane took out bread, made sure it wasn't green. Jake's head was in the fridge, his voice muffled.

"Want to tell me about that outfit? Being a trained professional, I have cleverly determined that you're not trying to seduce me. That having been well accomplished." He poured her Shiraz, twisted open his IPA.

"*I* seduced *you*?" She turned, pointing the peanut butter knife at him. "I don't think so, buster. I seem to clearly remember—"

"Whatever," he interrupted. "So—the skirt? The legs?"

"It's *such* a good idea," she began. She pushed down the toaster thing, turned the dial to "medium," and continued, "For our story. Fee and I interviewed this Adams Bay girl—she's a senior, actually, so a woman. Anyway, it's complicated. I'll tell you the whole thing someday."

The toast popped up. Jane checked it, pushed it down again.

"I hate toasters. They never toast. So. The student. We're going with her, and some other Adams Bay women, to a college party. Tomorrow night. Great, huh? I'm wearing this so I don't stick out like a . . . well, whatever. Maybe I'll work on it a little."

Jake made a sound.

"What?"

"Nothing. You were saying. About not sticking out."

"You're just freaked out about being with such a hot younger woman." She gave a little wiggle, but Jake simply laughed again.

"Fine. Maybe I'll wear glasses or something. A-ny-way. It's in a public place, not like a sorority house, so I'll take a little Quik-Shot, hide it in my purse. Fiola, too. We'll get authentic atmosphere. The talking, the drinking, the hookups." Jane took a sip of her wine. "Yum. Thank you."

"And the drugs, no doubt." Jake had stopped laughing, and was twisting his beer bottle on the kitchen counter. "At Adams Bay."

The toast popped up again.

"Come *on*," Jane said. But she wasn't really annoyed at the toast. She should never have told Jake, not until this was a fait accompli. He was always unhappy when she went undercover. Nervous. He'd been trained to do it, he always argued, she hadn't. Now, from the look on his face, he was obviously about to try to talk her out of it.

"Honey? Listen, okay? We don't know what's going on at Adams Bay. The death in The Reserve." He stopped. Pursed his lips.

She loved his lips.

"You trying to remember how much you've told me?" She pulled up a wicker stool, sat, then scooted her bare knees up to his. "Better get used to it, bub. To make this easier, it was last night. You said the victim's name, Avery Morgan. And I also know she's a—was a—visiting professor, found in her swimming pool." She didn't have to tell him how she knew that part.

"I'm not even gonna ask," he said, draining the last of the beer. "But say that's right. Now you're going to put yourself in the middle of who-knows-what over there?"

Jane shook her head, quickly retrieved the browned toast between two fingers, put it on a blue-rimmed plate, and pushed down two more pieces, sucking her forefinger to prevent the burn. He was being protective of her, and she shouldn't dismiss his concern. Even though she felt like it. This clinched it. No way would she tell him about the "SAY NO MORE" note. He'd go ballistic. For no reason. Well, probably for no reason.

"Hon?" She looked him in the eyes to prove she was open to him. "You truly think there's any danger? I honestly don't. I mean, there's dozens of murders a year in Boston. It doesn't keep us all hiding inside. And I'm perfectly capable of—"

A knock on the door. They both turned, surprised. How'd someone get into the building without buzzing?

"Expecting someone?" Jake asked.

"Nope," she said. The toast popped again, but Jane headed for the door, Jake right behind her. She felt more secure, she had to admit, not being here alone. The residual unease from this afternoon's hearing still clung to her—even the stupid note, she had to admit—coloring everything in worrisome emotional gray. I need food and sleep, she thought. And Jake.

She peered through the peephole, Coda hovering at her feet, and Jake, now carrying the peanut butter jar, at her shoulder.

"Hey, Neen," she said, opening the door.

The building super, in her usual yoga pants and toting year-old baby Sam tucked into a Snugli, held out a sheaf of papers.

"Brought your mail," Neena said. "From the box and the lobby table. And floor. You always forget it, and somehow Sam goes to sleep better if I walk up and down the stairs."

"Seems like that ought to make *you* tired, not him," Jake said. He scooped up the escaping Coda again. "Hey, Neena. Want a cat?"

"Thanks, Neen, come in," Jane said. "It's always junk and *The New Yorker,* so getting the mail only makes me feel guilty about all that paper."

Jane tossed the newly arrived stuff on the dining room table with the rest of her piles.

"That table's an archeological dig," Jake said.

"Happy to have you clean it up," Jane said. "Feel free."

"So: Halloween, I'm guessing?" Neena bounced baby Sam as she examined Jane's outfit. "It's two months away. Are you going as Sorority Barbie?"

"See?" Jane said, pointing to Jake. "It works. I look like college."

Neena eyed Jake. Then took a step backward, dramatically shielding baby Sam's eyes. "Or—are you two role-playing? Yeesh, sorry. Yeah, I see the peanut butter."

"Good idea," Jake said. "Jane'll be the schoolgirl, I'll be G.I. Joe."

"No, come on, it's for work," Jane said. "Really."

"I'll leave you guys alone." Neena opened the door. "To 'work.' "

"Bye, Neena," Jane said, giving baby Sam a quick kiss. It was pretty funny, she thought, playing the student and the macho guy roles. But then again, was it?

She turned to Jake, clearing her thoughts as they went back to the kitchen. The place smelled like beer and toast and peanut butter, which, right now, was comforting and safe and divine. She was happy, and lucky, and she shouldn't forget that.

Jake had twisted open another beer—two was his limit on school nights—and tossed the cap into the wastebasket.

"Where were we?" she asked. "Oh, yeah, so, seriously. I'll be fine. We're going in a group."

Jane slathered peanut butter on a now-lukewarm piece of toast, the overcooked edges crumbling. She hated toasters. "And listen. The college girls? They've got a—"

Wait. Should she tell Jake about the creep list? Maybe not.

"They've got a group of women who go places together," she papered over the end of her sentence. "Watch out for each other. I'll be with them. Really, it'll be fine." She broke her toast in half, took a test bite.

Jake kept his whole and ate it in three chomps.

"I'll say my name is June." She paused, took a sip of wine. "Hi!" she said, as perky as she could manage with a mouthful of peanut butter. "I'm . . . June. June Runion from—"

"Don't stay out too late, *June*." Jake stood, wrapped one arm over her shoulders. "I think you'll have 'homework' waiting for you here."

"I love homework, G.I. Joe," she purred, tucking herself into the curve of his arm. "And you'll be here when I get back tomorrow night, right?"

She felt his body tense, felt his breathing change. She'd known him for what, just over a year? She'd made peace with his imperious mother, played tennis with his father, shared her hopes and fears and loves with his Gramma Brogan. She knew how he twitched when he was dreaming, recognized the faraway expression that meant he was mentally working a case. And right now, she could tell from his layered silence that something was up.

"Jake?" She was almost afraid to move, but she did, turning to face him. He smelled of peanut butter. She must, too.

"Yeah." Jake closed his eyes briefly, and when he opened them, the twinkle was gone. "Situation. I might have to go out of town."

37

EDWARD TARRANT

Almost fricking midnight. Edward Tarrant tried to look welcoming, tried to look loving, tried to look like the affectionate husband of a weary-but-devoted spouse and the son-in-law of a conscientious college president who'd cut their vacation short to handle an emergency. Not only had said relatives' flight been ridiculously late, but they'd clearly been the last to deplane. His ass hurt from the plastic airport seats. If he never saw another cup of coffee again it'd be too soon, and he'd gotten fifty thousand texts from Sasha Vogelby.

We need to talk, she'd written. And then: *When can we talk?*

Who the hell would text someone at this time of night?

Another text pinged. *Are you ignoring me? Do not ignore me!* With an exclamation mark, like a schoolgirl.

Certainly he was ignoring her. And her badgering texts. He'd call her—no, show up at her office so he could read her face—tomorrow. He didn't give a shit what she wanted. Only the attention-hungry Sasha Vogelby could use someone else's death—unconnected to her, and none of her business—to grab the spotlight for herself.

The good news? She'd leave him the hell alone as soon as Brinn was back in town. More good news: no cops had called him. And no reporters. The eleven o'clock TV shows, headlined and bursting with stories about a Red Sox win, had come and gone without a mention of Avery Morgan. He'd watched it all from the corner stool of the Take-Off Bar, having bribed the bartender with a five to turn up the volume.

He narrowed his eyes, seeing two familiar shapes, each pulling a black roller bag, coming toward him on the carpeted concourse. All the other gates were deserted now, Logan Airport's Terminal C echoing with late-night emptiness.

"Darling!" Brinn called out, waving an arm, as if there was some way he wouldn't have seen her. She'd turned to her father, pointing toward Edward like she'd won the lottery by spotting her own husband. *Brinn.* Her hair cropped and carefully silver, in her predictable travel outfit of little black sleeveless dress, flats, a scarf looped around her neck.

Reg Buchholz, equally predictable in his gold-buttoned blazer, wrinkle-free even after a transatlantic flight, raised a palm in greeting.

In the brief time it took them to reach him, Edward reminded himself of all he had to accomplish. These two, wife and father-in-law college president, should be handled as allies. He needed to remember that.

"I'm so sorry." He turned on a smile as they drew closer. "I had no idea you were coming back so quickly."

"What the hell did you think I would do?" Buchholz wheeled his bag to heel as if it were an obedient dog. "A death, and possible homicide?"

"Hello, darling," Brinn interjected. A hint of Beacon Hill lingered in her voice: *dah-ling.*

She kissed him once on each cheek, as if she were still in Paris. He felt his skin flinch as her lips touched his, hoped she didn't notice.

"Welcome home," Tarrant said, gesturing toward the exit. "The car's out there. I take it your flight was—"

"And, Daddy." Brinn hadn't stopped talking. She spun her black bag toward Edward, relinquishing control of the wheelie while she turned to her father, talking over her shoulder as they walked out the glass doors and entered the parking garage. "No need to discuss all that here in public. We'll get in the car, we'll drive home, we'll . . . I don't know. It's six A.M. Paris time. I'm exhausted."

"There's no time for *me* to be exhausted," Buchholz said. He'd left his bag on the pavement, apparently for Edward-the-lackey to deal with. "We have a possible murder to solve."

Edward let go of both suitcases to click open the car doors for them, ever so considerate, then loaded their bags. He slammed the trunk. A "murder" to "solve"? *Hell no. That's not our job.*

They drove to the airport exit in silence. The elevated highway revealed the lights of the surprisingly modest downtown Boston skyline glowing in the distance before the car descended into the gloomy darkness of the Sumner Tunnel. Edward was always aware of the depths of Boston Harbor above and around them, a few feet of luck and complicated engineering protecting travelers from drowning in the unimaginably crushing weight. He always wanted to drive faster through here.

"Is someone texting you? Your phone keeps pinging." Brinn's voice from the backseat. He'd gotten lazy in her absence, kept his ringer on.

"It's nothing," he said, clicking it to "vibrate." Damn Sasha. It was almost one in the morning.

"Any calls from the media? What did you tell them? Do the police think there's a danger to the students?" Buchholz fired one question after another at him across the front seat's center console as they continued through the tunnel, annoyingly crowded for this time of night. "I assume not, or you'd have certainly conveyed that to me, correct? Do we have a plan? Am I holding a campus-wide meeting? Or making a statement? Is it written? I'll need to see that before . . ."

Tarrant tuned out Buchholz's high-handed interrogation. Preposterous. Obviously he'd handled it. Obviously there was a plan. That's why he had this job.

By the time the lights of Boston reappeared on the other side of the tunnel, Tarrant had finalized that plan. His first priority was making sure Brinn Buchholz Tarrant never suspected her husband's liaison with Avery Morgan. Even dead, that woman could ruin his life.

WEDNESDAY

38

JAKE BROGAN

Too early. *Too early.* Jake plastered a pillow over his face, trying to drown out the sound of Jane's alarm clock by pretending he was still asleep. He failed. Threw the pillow to the floor. Six o'clock.

Jane turned away from him, the flowered sheet falling from her bare back as she stretched out to slam the "snooze" button. She always hit "snooze." He was more of a "turn it off, hop out of bed" kind of guy. Though somehow, not when he was with her.

"Nine lovely snooze minutes," Jane announced. She rolled onto her back, propped one ankle on her knee, and linked her hands behind her head, reclining on her three pillows. Talked to the ceiling. "What shall we ever do?'

Jake tossed the sheet back over her, watched it settle into curves and hollows.

She yanked it from her face, leaving it pulled neck-high as she turned to him. "Chicken."

"I have to work," he explained. "You're too tempting, lying there like that."

"You might as well be on your way to California already," Jane said. "Such a Boy Scout. But fine. I can face reality. I'll take you to the airport—how about that for true love? When's your plane?"

"Beyond the call of duty," Jake said. "I'll get D to drop me off."

He pulled her closer, curling her into the curve of his shoulder. "If I have to go, and that's still an if, I'll only be gone maybe two days. I've got to track down Avery Morgan's family out there, if I can, her landlord, her employers. Can you keep yourself out of trouble until I get back?"

"No," Jane said. "And it'll be on your head."

She extricated herself, turned to face him, up on one elbow, head propped on her palm. A lock of hair dropped over one eye and she brushed it back. She had on Gramma's ring, he saw.

"You don't think someone from around here killed her?" Jane asked. "That's pretty interesting, copper. I mean, if not a, I don't know, maniac serial killer, then boyfriend, girlfriend, lover? Crazed grade-hungry student? Why would you go all the way to California?"

"You sound like D," Jake said. It was possible they were right, and this was a goose chase. And the supe was not happy about the airfare. But even with only the bare bones the US Attorney's Office had told him, clearly something was going on. How much could he tell Jane? Did it matter? When in doubt, say nothing. Always a good plan. "She has connections out there. From where she used to work."

"Like what?" Jane asked.

" 'Like what?' " Jake mimicked. Like she might have been in witness protection, he didn't say. "We're not sure. But it's always best to check it out in person. You see things, hear things. Get impressions. Stuff you can't get on the phone, or the Net."

"Ha!" Jane sat up and pointed at him as the sheet fell away again. She yanked it back up. "Which is exactly why going undercover to the party is the only way to get the scoop on what happens at Adams Bay. Like I said. *Ha.*"

Before he could protest, the snooze alarm went off, an insistent three-note ping. Then another sound: Jake's cell phone, set to vibrate, buzzing across the nightstand. And then another sound: Jane's phone, buzzing across the nightstand on her side. Coda leaped up, pounced onto Jake's stomach.

"And the gang's all here," he said. Both phones continued to buzz. "Guess we're getting up."

"Jane Ryland," she said into her phone.

"Brogan," he said into his. Coda, displeased, jumped down and bolted away.

"You're kidding me," Jane said.

"He's what?" Jake said.

JANE RYLAND

Fine. If Jake didn't want to tell her what "He's what?" meant? Fine. Jane had enough on her mind as she scrambled down the stairway, in bare feet and terry-cloth bathrobe, to retrieve the morning *Register*. Not on her front stoop? *Again?* No, wait. She'd canceled it a few months ago, in protest, after she'd proved some of the stories in it were not exactly true.

She paused, assessing whether she could dart next door, steal one of her neighbors' and peek at the Metro section, but it looked like everyone had gotten up earlier than she had. Or maybe they'd canceled their subscriptions, too. Serve the paper right. She ran back up the three flights, hoping Jake was still in the shower. That'd give her enough time to check the *Register*'s online edition, hope it had the same photo.

She slammed into her desk chair, clicked onto the Internet. Scrolled through as fast as she could. It'd be interesting, beyond interesting, to see if what Fiola had just called about was true. Fee had only glimpsed the driver of the hit-and-run car on O'Brien Highway, not seen him clearly as Jane had, but Jane had sure described him to her enough times. The *Register*'s website appeared on the screen.

Nothing. The story was there, sure, but no photo like the one Fee described. She needed the real paper-paper.

"Hey, honey." Jake appeared at the door of her office, fully dressed, drying his hair on a white towel, spattering wet spots on the shoulders of his black T-shirt. "I gotta go. I'll call you, soon as I know anything, okay?"

Should she tell him what Fiola said?

Instead she asked, "Are you working on the Violet Sholto, um, possible homicide?"

He stopped drying his hair, held the towel beside his ear. "Huh? Why?"

"You're such fun to talk to." She shrugged. "Just wondering," she lied.

But then, come to think about it, why not? She went at it another way. "Two affluent-ish women, dead in their affluent-ish homes, all I'm thinking. It's kind of suspicious. Don't you think? Or is Violet Sholto not suspicious? The darn online paper doesn't really have much info."

"Neither do we." Jake went back to drying his hair.

"Was it the husband?" Jane asked. "It's always the husband."

"Not this time," Jake said. "And now I have officially said too much. You're not covering that story, are you? Why do you care?"

"Nope. I mean, I don't. Care," Jane said. He'd never believe that. "I mean, I do care. Two women murdered? *If* they were murdered. I mean, what if what's-his-name, Clooney Sholto, killed his wife? And Avery Morgan, too? What can I tell you, I can't turn off my reporter brain."

"I never want you to turn off," Jake said. "Maybe you should close that bathrobe."

"Why, is it distracting you?" Jane stood, grabbed his towel, dangled it in front of herself, teasing.

She saw the look on his face. Well, truth be told, she wanted to go to work, too. See the photo Fiola was talking about. She was only teasing him about the distraction thing, but she did hate it when he went out of town. It didn't happen much, but his long-distance absence felt different from his merely being at his house across town.

"Okay, duty calls," she said, relinquishing the towel. "I get it. Your mind's elsewhere. I have failed, miserably, as a woman."

"You have never failed," Jake said. "At anything. But you're right. I have to go. I'll let you know whenever."

She stood, tucked her arm through the crook of his as they walked to her front door. Jake turned her toward him. She felt the weight and the

pressure of his hands on her shoulders. That citrus fragrance, and tooth-paste. She thought about last night, and the nights to come.

"You sure you don't want to do some more 'peanut butter'?" she asked. "Ha. PB and Jane. Get it? That's my last bit of ammo."

"I love you," he told her. "And you have to be careful."

An hour later, his words echoed in her brain as she saw the photo in the newspaper Fiola was holding. Jane had showered and made it to her office at Channel 2 in record time, feeding Coda, forgoing makeup, and yanking her hair into a scrabbly ponytail. She would come home later to change for tonight's party.

"I'm an idiot," she said, eyes on the newspaper. "I could have had you take a cell photo of this and send it to me."

"Yeah," Fiola said. "Neither of us was thinking straight, I guess. But now you're here, and there it is, and it's easier to see in real life. Am I right, or am I right?"

The entire Metro front had been the Red Sox and their blowout win over the Yankees. A misguided headline writer had come up with "Sox Rox." Inside, a short paragraph in Newsbriefs mentioned Avery Morgan, how the police were still searching for suspects, how school administrators were not yet making a statement, how they'd assured summer students there was no campus threat. No classes had been canceled. A memorial was in the works.

Then, page three, the headline. "Wife of Local Figure Found Dead." And the subhead: "Sources Say Victim Found in Bathtub."

"In water, like Avery Morgan," Fiola was saying.

Jane was mesmerized by the black-and-white wedding photograph of Violet O'Baron. "File photo," the caption said. Dated ten years ago, an obviously posed and more obviously airbrushed portrait. The bride in puffy white sleeves and elaborate veil. The groom wearing a dark suit and grim expression.

"See?" Fiola pointed at the photo. "I mean, how would you describe that guy?"

Only one way, Jane knew. "Middle-aged, Caucasian, widow's peak, grayish hair, pointy cheekbones, thin lips, clean-shaven."

"Thought so," Fiola said. "Sit-chu-ay-shun. I mean, I could be wrong but—"

She took the paper from Jane, rattling the page, folding it so only the photo showed. "Who the hell is Clooney Sholto? The article is totally weasel-worded. 'Local figure.' 'Plumbing company.' That's shorthand for 'bad guy' if I ever heard it. But if he's so 'local figure,' why didn't you recognize him?"

"I only got to Boston three years ago." Jane stared at the photograph and lowered herself into her office chair. Could she be wrong? The photo was ten years old and retouched.

"I mean, I've heard of Clooney Sholto," Jane went on. "He's somewhat of a gangster. Funny word, but yeah. Old-school. Never in public. Never leaves Boston, apparently. And I don't think he's ever been arrested. So I've heard of him, sure. But I never saw him. I mean, why would I?"

"So you agree? You think this is him?" Fiola handed her the paper, then faced her, hands on hips.

"I have to say . . ." Jane paused. This was only Fee. She could always change her mind. "Yeah, I think it is."

"I knew it," Fiola said. "So now what?" She brandished the paper at Jane, like a prosecutor presenting indisputable evidence to an indecisive witness. "You gonna tell McCusker you found the hit-and-run driver?"

39

JAKE BROGAN

"So. We've gotta go to the hospital," DeLuca continued, as Jake risked the coffee-colored muck from the squad room pot. "Find out what happened."

Jake added more sugar. Maybe that would help. "Negative. No way we're doing that."

He sipped, winced. D sucked at making coffee, but it was better than nothing. The phones were silent, as they usually were this time of morning. But it meant no one else was dead. For now.

"Listen. Two cops? Even *one* of us?" Jake envisioned the disaster. "Even in plain clothes? Walking into Boston City Hospital to see Grady Houlihan? That's a death warrant for him right there."

"How'd you learn it was him in the Melnea Cass accident, anyway? Where he was?"

"I called him last night." Jake stirred in some fake creamer. "To give him grief about not telling us about Violet Sholto. He didn't answer."

He dismissed the plate of yesterday's doughnuts and bagels, an unappetizing display of leftover carbs. "A good thing, turns out. Otherwise, who knows how long it would have taken them to get his ID. The nurse who returned my call this morning said they'd checked for contacts on his phone, but there weren't any."

"Smart boy," D said.

"That's what we pay him for. To be smart."

"Not enough, apparently, Harvard. Else he would've given us a bell about Violet Sholto."

"Possibly." Jake abandoned his coffee and tossed the cup, eager to get on with the day. Should they head to Boston City Hospital, wait for Grady's sedation to wear off? Or canvass the Sholto neighborhood? Or Avery Morgan's? Or visit Edward Tarrant? Somehow it was Willow Galt who most intrigued Jake. That woman was not telling everything she knew.

Definitely—a visit to the Galts. Grady would recover, according to the nurse. So maybe, no rush. But what if he was in danger?

Damn. Were he and D the only fricking cops in Boston? The mayor, hoping for reelection this fall, had promised more troops. But the election was three months away. That left Jake and D with two cases to solve. And an informant at risk.

Jake's plane for L.A. departed at three. Question was: Would he be on it?

D approached, a telltale powdered-sugar trail on his black T-shirt.

"You're gonna kill yourself, eating like that," Jake said.

D took another bite. "What's your take on this? One way or the other, we should send a guy to keep watch on the kid. He might be Violet Sholto's killer, right? Or that killer's next victim."

"Exactly." Jake pointed a forefinger. "Plus, like I told you last night, Grady's the link between Violet Sholto and Avery Morgan. Tarrant's video proves he was at Morgan's house. Maybe he can give us something about that night. Names."

"Drugs, even," D said. "Maybe that's why he was really there?"

"And Grady's obviously connected with the Sholtos," Jake went on, almost thinking out loud. "So whatever Grady knows, or did, that's gotta be why someone smashed his Gormay truck on Melnea Cass last night. They followed him, tailed him, and wham. Talk about sending a message. Couldn't have been clearer if they'd spray-painted 'Shut up' on the side of his van."

"You think Grady might've killed them *both*? Avery Morgan and Violet Sholto?"

Jake nodded. Then shook his head.

"I take that as a maybe," D said.

"Seems too . . . out there." Jake thought about it, the millionth time. "I mean, does Grady seem like a murderer? Why would he kill them?"

"Short answer? Money." DeLuca raised his coffee cup, toasting. His phone buzzed in his pocket. "Or an assignment. What if Sholto was making him prove his allegiance? Whatever. Or maybe he killed for love. Or, I don't know. By mistake."

Jake shook his head, dismissing. "I don't see it. Dozens of murders a year in Boston, so maybe there's no connection. Or someone else might have been connected with them both. Or maybe Avery Morgan wasn't murder."

"Huh." DeLuca was reading his phone screen. "Lookit this, bro. Someone sure murdered Violet Sholto. Here's a text from—well, the Medical Examiner's Office, shall we say. Confirming it."

Jake toasted D this time. Kat McMahan often released her findings to them in advance, so often that they now took it for granted. "Always nice to have an 'in' with the ME," he said.

" 'In' the ME is right," D said. "Often as I can."

"Grow up, D," Jake said.

"Why now?" D was texting as he talked, somehow able to leer and type at the same time.

"You were saying?" Jake had to change the subject from the TMI on D's love life. "Violet Sholto's cause of death, Kat says . . . what?"

"Suffocated," D said. "The wrist slashes were inflicted postmortem. Kat says whoever killed her did a good job trying to hide it. You saw the prelim e-mail from crime scene—bathroom's clean, no unknown prints, no anything."

"Someone knew what they were doing. Cleaning-wise, too," Jake said. "Not the housekeeper, though, certainly."

"Husband?"

"Out of town," Jake said.

"Says the housekeeper."

The movie of the crime spooled out in Jake's imagination, as it often did when he was investigating. Part of a detective's job was imagining the setup, the motivation, the actual performance of the crime. Could it work? Was it feasible? Who would have to be where, and why? The movie of the crime allowed him to envision reality. Whether it would have been too dark to see, if a victim might have tried to defend himself, how the murderer got in, whether a neighbor would have heard a commotion. Where there'd be fingerprints or DNA or trace evidence. Whether a cover-up could be successful.

He envisioned the Sholto home. Envisioned Grady, trusted under-ling, arriving at the front door. The housekeeper—he checked his notes. Rissa Murphy—lets him in. He tells her—

"Hellooo?" D said. "Earth to Jake. Where did you just go?"

"About the housekeeper. And Grady. Maybe you're right."

"Imagine that," D said.

"Listen." Jake ignored him. "Sholto orders Grady to kill his wife. He does. He scrams. The housekeeper cleans it up. Everyone shuts up. I mean, it's the Sholtos. That's what they do. And Sholto himself's got the perfect alibi. He's outta town. And ain't no one gonna say otherwise."

"And we're screwed." D put his empty coffee mug on a stack of files. Brushed cruller crumbs from his chest. "Should we go have a chat with Grady? Being an informant won't get you out of jail free if you kill someone."

"Gotta hand it to Sholto." Jake shoved his notebook into a back pocket. Patted for his car keys. "I know it's not exactly logical, but it's sort of proof he did it. If he's out of town, it proves he must be guilty, because he never goes out of town. He's like . . . travel-phobic. So this proves he'd do anything for an alibi, anything to disconnect himself from this. Which means he's connected."

"You're nuts," D said. "Proving a double negative. Tell *that* to a judge."

"Listen. What if Grady kills Violet Sholto on, say, Monday morning. For some as-yet-undetermined reason. Then kills Avery Morgan—who he also clearly knew, and also knew where she lived. On Monday day. Again, for now, reason unknown." Jake shook his head. He hadn't even convinced himself. "Okay, maybe, more likely I guess, what if Grady *knows* who did it? Because then Monday night he gets nailed in a hit-and-run. So either way, it could be—"

"Retaliation. Or a cover-up. Or silencing him." D filled in the blanks. "A message. Either way."

"I've got about five hours before my flight. If I go. Hospital?" Jake asked. "Take our chances?"

"Grady shoulda kept his mouth shut," D said.

"Let's hope he can talk now. When we get there, I mean." Jake's intercom buzzed, an insistent burr across the deserted squad room. He punched the "talk" button. "Brogan," he said.

"Detective Brogan?" Ming-Na's voice was carefully formal. The receptionist was using her "announcing a visitor" voice.

"Yes?" Jake turned to D. Held up his watch. Mouthed *All we need.*

"It's a Mr. Tom Galt," Ming-Na said. "He says he needs to tell you his wife is missing. He says you'll know who she is."

40

EDWARD TARRANT

"I know about you and Avery Morgan."

Edward Tarrant pushed himself to stand, palms flat on his desk, using those ten seconds to formulate his reaction. Laughter? Dismissal? Anger? He hated the smirk on Sasha Vogelby's face, hated how her hair went behind her ears, hated her veiny hands and theatrical makeup. And now she was accusing him. Was this a trap? A trick? Or true?

"Excuse me?" Edward tried to calm his rising apprehension, tried to make sure his face was a mask of confusion. "Avery Morgan—what?"

"I see your wife is back in town now, and her father." The woman, un-invited, pulled one of his visitors' chairs closer, making parallel gouges in his carpet, and propped her elbows on his desk, lacing her hands in front of her chin. "No *won*der you look tired. Stress is so exh*austing*. Isn't it?"

"Stress?" The less he said the better, Edward decided. Let this woman show her hand.

"Very cagey of you to use 'privacy' as the reason for withholding student names from the police." She winked at him, as if they shared some secret. "Very plausible, and even honorable. But you and I both know the real reason you don't want those officers to know the realities of that videotape. I may not have been invited to that party—"

"It wasn't a par—"

"Edward? It's me here. I don't need your sanctimony. And trust me, it won't be effective. But, though you certainly don't deserve it"—she smiled, raised one eyebrow—"you should know I'm here to help."

He opened his mouth, about to repeat, "Help?" Then thought better of it. He waited, took a sip from his coffee cup. Damned if he was going to offer this woman any.

"Yes, help," she went on. "Because even if I wasn't invited to Avery's little soiree, I know who was. And I have seen that video. Honestly, just between us? The person who took it forwarded me the file. So charming of dear Trey. He was so proud of their performance and wanted me to see the whole thing."

Tarrant tried to calculate the nightmare-level damage. Damn Trey. Not only would the video give police, the press, and the college community here and every damn where else indisputable evidence that he and Avery Morgan had known of—and condoned—underage drinking, a transgression so egregious he'd never work again, it was also corroboration of a relationship. Because of what Tarrant had not said.

Sasha was shaking her head, looking at the floor briefly in exaggerated concern. "And certainly when the police discover—and they will—not only who shot it, but who else was present? They'll certainly wonder *why* you didn't *tell* them you were there. Won't they?"

Tarrant had to stop this. Stop her. "That doesn't matter."

"It doesn't?" Sasha twisted a strand of hair around her forefinger, as if contemplating. "I think it does. It does matter. Because you—clearly, actively, purposely—kept information from the police. And that makes you, dear Edward, suspect number one."

It did. It did. That's what had been haunting Edward ever since he'd shown the cops that video. He hadn't killed Avery, didn't know who did, had no idea about any of it. But if it came out that he'd attended the party, if any student testified—testified!—about his actions, he'd have to resign. Simply and completely. Brinn would go ballistic.

"Ridiculous," he said.

"As my students so often say"—Sasha cocked her head, affected a student-like attitude—"*You wish.*"

"I—"

"And." She interrupted with a raised-hand stop sign. "Whether you are guilty of murder or not"—she touched her pink-painted nails to her chest in feigned despair—"your life will never be the same after the media, and the parents, and the students you've 'counseled' begin to put together the pieces of the life you've been leading."

She actually batted her eyelashes at him. The blood was draining from his brain, it must be, he felt his face go white, then flush, the fear and potential for personal and professional disaster paralyzing his ability to comprehend. What the hell did she want from him?

"However," she said. "I have a plan. For both of us."

JANE RYLAND

Was this making a deal with the devil? Too late now, Jane thought.

Before she'd called McCusker about the newspaper's wedding photo of Clooney Sholto, Jane consulted with Marsh Tyson, hoping for some reprieve, some way to avoid it. Instead, the news director had sent her here to the DA's office without a moment of hesitation. Not a whit of concern about crossing the journalistic line between *reporting* the story and *being* the story. Could she bring a lawyer? No, Tyson had said. Just go.

So here she was. Down the rabbit hole. Alone.

With Frank McCusker standing, arms crossed, in the back corner of his office, the district attorney's sketch artist, Beverly Wolov, sat at his desk, her sketchpad open. ready to create the portrait of the hit-and-run driver from Jane's description.

"For this to be allowed in evidence, it's gotta be from your recollection," the DA told her. "I'm somewhat concerned you saw that photo in the paper, to be honest. It's ten years old, but some defense attorney could argue it colored your memory. So put it out of your head. Simply describe the person you saw driving the car. Bev's our best artist."

"White, male, middle-aged. Pointy chin," Jane said.

"Okay. Now what's the next unique characteristic you remember?" artist Wolov asked.

"Widow's peak."

The room was so silent Jane could hear Wolov's pencil move across the thick paper on her spiral-bound pad. Jane had expected some computer-generated process, images popping up on screen, but Wolov had explained that sometimes witnesses thought the computer faces looked unnatural.

"Pencil works best." She adjusted her tortoiseshell glasses. "Nose?"

"Pointy," Jane said.

"Cheekbones?" Wolov tucked her pencil into her blond chignon, then opened another spiral-bound notebook, this one full of numbered playing-card-sized mug shots. She opened to the page headlined "Cheekbones," held it up so Jane could select.

"Pointy." Jane studied each photo. "Like picture number four."

After fifteen minutes of pointing and choosing and Wolov's confident pencil strokes in response, the artist held up a sketch. Pink shards from her eraser sprinkled her navy uniform. Her left forefinger was smudged from shadowing the hollows of the portrait's cheeks.

"Like this?" she asked.

"Exactly." The artist had captured the driver perfectly, so much so that Jane's stomach clenched in recognition. If the hit-and-run driver was Clooney Sholto, bad guy and thug, this was not a good thing.

"Thanks, Beverly, we'll be in touch. So, Jane." McCusker pulled out his desk chair and sat, leaning toward her, as the door closed behind the artist. She'd left the sketch, signed and dated, on his desk. "Can we get you some water?"

Get me water? Jane thought. *You can get me the heck out of here, is what you can get.*

"Thanks, Frank. Listen, no, I just want to know what happens now. I mean, if this guy . . ." She paused, tried to deconstruct how she'd become a potential victim. She'd seen a stupid fender bender, a nothing, and she'd reported it to the cops like any good citizen. "So are you going to arrest him? Or what?"

"Off the record?" McCusker asked.

"'Off the record'? 'Off the record'?" Jane heard her voice go up an octave, couldn't decide whether to laugh or burst into tears. This whole thing was beyond out of control. She stood, pointing at him. "Frank? I am standing here, in your office, having just described to you, in contradiction of everything I hold dear, a person I saw in a fender bender. It's your turn, Frank, your turn now. What the heck is going on?"

The hum of the air conditioner seemed to grow louder in McCusker's silence.

"I don't have to testify," Jane went on. "My station will fight it, up one side and down the other." She hoped that was true. "You've as much as told me the guy I saw was Clooney Sholto. And all that entails. So you arrest him for a hit-and-run? Or wait—don't? Is he above the law? Is that what this is?" She'd just come up with that plot twist, but it was an interesting thought. Was McCusker protecting Sholto?

McCusker started shaking his head before Jane finished her sentence. "Jane, understand this. We want Clooney Sholto more than I can tell you. In fact, turns out the kid who confessed to the thing, one Rourke Devane, is a little-fish Sholto operative, one of many he's got in the neighborhood. And apparently sent to be the sacrificial lamb. Making his bones, you know? But there's more to this."

"Like what?" Jane demanded. She sat down again, to establish that she wasn't leaving until he told her.

"Here's the plan," McCusker went on. "And it's one hundred percent off the record. We're gonna unleash the red tape. We're gonna tell Devane's lawyers—who are certainly bankrolled by Sholto—that we're postponing the hit-and-run case for lack of evidence. We can't charge Devane, we'll say, because you didn't point him out in court."

"Because he wasn't the driver!"

"We know that," McCusker said, reassuring her. "It's all about stalling. We let the lawyers think we believe this Rourke Devane is guilty, but we're being forced to cut him a break. Because, possibly, you were mistaken. And the best part—for you at least—we'll make it look like you stopped cooperating. Right? And you'll be safe."

"Safe?" If McCusker had to worry about whether she was safe, that's exactly what she wasn't. "How about that SAY NO MORE letter I showed you?"

"Listen, Jane. They won't want to hurt you," McCusker said. "They'll only want you to keep quiet. And now they'll think you've followed their directions. If, indeed, that letter was their 'directions.' So we'll keep mum, not say a word outside of our team, use this time to make our case. Once we have Sholto safely in custody, you can safely testify you saw him. But by that time, we'll have him. Dead to rights."

"All this for a fender bender?" That didn't make sense.

"For murder," McCusker said. "Sholto's told NYPD he was in Manhattan Monday morning when his wife was killed. In New York."

Oh no, Jane thought. She realized instantly what McCusker was about to say.

"But, Jane?" McCusker's forehead furrowed, his eyes saddened in a half-apology. "There's no escaping this. You're the proof he *wasn't* in New York. Because you—a very reliable witness—you saw him in Boston."

41

JAKE BROGAN

Oh, right, Jake thought, listening to the disheveled man fidgeting in the high-backed chair in the victim room. "Victim room," because the upholstered furniture and potted plants made questioning of crime victims or witnesses less intimidating than if they had to sit in the bleakly concrete and metal interrogation rooms down the hall.

Sometimes, though, Jake used these rooms for other purposes. A visitor with a dubious story might be lulled into relaxed and chatty complacency if the furniture was comfortable enough and the coffee hot. And "a dubious story" was exactly what Jake was hearing. First Avery Morgan drowns, the circumstances still under investigation. A 911 call, certainly from the Galt residence, reports the crime. And now Tom Galt says his wife is "missing"? *Right.* Jake's "no coincidence" meter was pinging off the charts.

"Detective Brogan, it's not too soon for you to look for her, is it?" Galt had raked his hand through his gray hair so many times, Jake could still see the furrows. "I mean, on TV they always say you have to wait twenty-four hours."

"This isn't TV. This is real life," DeLuca said.

Jake shot him a shut-up glance.

"Sir," DeLuca added.

"We can use our judgment in these cases," Jake assured Galt. "Let me ask you this: Do you think your wife's disappearance had anything to do with what happened to Avery Morgan?"

"Did you *know* Avery Morgan?" D asked.

Why was D so cranky? It threw off their rhythm, and it was time-sucking enough that Galt's arrival had derailed their visit to Grady Houlihan.

"Detective, can you give a call to the hospitals?" Jake said. "And the usual other checks?"

"You da man," D said. "Back in two."

D. When this was over, they'd need to have a talk, Jake thought. But first, Tom Galt.

"We were talking about Avery Morgan," Jake said.

"What does Avery Morgan have to do with this? We're talking about my *wife.*" Galt frowned, eyeing Jake as if he didn't understand English. "Last I saw Willow was yesterday morning. She said she was going for a walk, but she—she's still gone. She didn't call. She didn't take anything, not that I can see. I got home late, but—"

"So nothing untoward at your home, no signs of a struggle, anything like that?" Jake could check for himself if the time came.

"No, no, nothing," Galt said.

"Exactly like the situation at Avery Morgan's house," Jake said.

"Well, possibly. I mean, I have no idea," Galt looked confused, Jake's precise goal. "But now you're worrying me even more. What does that have to do with Willow? Is there some killer on the loose? Someone who may have murdered both of them? Just tell me!"

Jake scratched the back of his neck, gave himself some time to think. "Mr. Galt? Sit back down, okay? You know, after we talked to you and your wife Monday night, I did some checking on you."

Galt paled, fussed with the rolled-up sleeve of his light blue shirt. Didn't meet Jake's eyes. "Checking?"

"Yeah," Jake said, keeping his voice pleasant. "You and your wife Willow. Funny thing. What I've seen so far, you pretty much don't exist."

"Don't exist?"

"You keep repeating what I say, Mr. Galt," Jake said. "But yes, these days, it's SOP to follow up on witnesses, see if there's anything in their history or information that might be relevant. But in your case, and your wife Willow's, it's not a question of *relevant* information. It's a question—"

Jake stopped as his cell phone rang. "Brogan." He listened as D reported what he'd learned. Nodded a few times, and glanced at Tom Galt, who was watching him, obviously straining to hear. What D said confirmed another connection between Willow Galt and Avery Morgan. "Thanks, D."

"Did they find her?" Galt asked.

Jake took longer than necessary to stash his phone. He wasn't ready to answer that.

"So, Mr. Galt," he said. "We checked the airlines. Your wife apparently had a ticket to Long Beach, California, on a plane that arrived there last night."

"So do you know where she is? She's okay?" Galt looked at his watch, then at the ceiling, then at Jake. "She's in California?"

"Any idea why she would go to Long Beach?" Jake was trying to understand this latest development himself. Galt seemed genuinely surprised to hear Willow was in California. Maybe because he knew she wasn't there.

Jake pushed the black intercom button, the one that summoned reinforcements. He needed his partner here for this next move. The wooden door clicked open, D holding a new cup of coffee. Clicked closed behind him.

"Our friend is still asleep," D said.

"Understood," Jake said. Grady could wait. "Detective? Mr. Galt here is asking whether his wife is in California. But I was just about to explain what else you learned."

"Ah." D lifted his cup, giving Jake the floor.

"So, Mr. Galt?" Jake continued. "I guess the answer is no, we haven't found your wife. Because according to the airline, she never made that flight. So that leaves me asking you—is there something you're not telling us? Like where she really is?"

The silence became a thickness in the air, all exchanged glances and

42

JANE RYLAND

Life was good.

Jane examined her new self in the medicine cabinet mirror and burst out laughing. Coda, sitting on the closed toilet seat, jumped into the still-damp bathroom sink, her newest attention-getting ploy. Cat was crazy, and now, possibly, confused. Jane was no longer recognizable. With out-of-style horned-rim glasses (her own, backups to her contacts), her hair in a ponytail, no makeup, short-ish skirt and Adams Bay baseball cap, Jane looked like . . . well, she didn't know. Not Sorority Barbie, since that attempt had been pretty much a disaster. But also not like a thirty-something reporter. She hoped.

But life was good, because the party at the Spotted Owl was on. Jane and Fee were all set to attend, and Isabel/Tosca, brave girl, had finally decided to go with them. "I'll be fine," she'd insisted. Jane wasn't sure, but there was nothing to do but see.

They'd meet Elaine and her SAFE crew at the bar around eight. Jane could introduce Isabel to Elaine, and make a potentially life-changing connection.

This afternoon she and Fiola had worked on their documentary. The DA's office did not call her. No Sholto creeps showed up. And, pièce de résistance, something had happened in police world that meant Jake didn't have to go to California.

He'd texted her "developments" and "looking for someone" and "be careful" and "love." And deliciously, "See you tonight." She'd leave this lifted eyebrows. Interrupted by the triple *bing-bong* chimes of Jake's cell phone.

Only nine in the morning. Already this day was about to crush him.

"Brogan." He tried to keep the annoyance from his voice. Failed. But Shom Pereira didn't even say hello. Jake listened as the officer spilled the news, his mood changing, annoyance evaporating with every word. About. Frigging. Time.

This news didn't make Tom Galt not guilty of killing his wife, if indeed she'd been killed. That investigation was still open. But maybe Galt hadn't killed Avery Morgan. Because according to Shom, that case was about to be closed.

"One moment," he said to Galt, signaling with a finger. "Something's come up, and we've got to go. But we'll have an officer take your statement, sir. We'll do all we can to find your wife. So go home. Don't worry. Call us if you hear anything. And we'll be in touch." He motioned DeLuca into the hall. Safely away from Galt, he held up the phone in triumph.

"T'shombe Pereira says we've got a semi-anonymous tip about Avery Morgan," Jake said. "It says the killer is a kid. Well, a student. Who the tipster says had a big crush on her. And listen to this. He's got a record of sexual problems. Inappropriate behavior. Documented in his school records. It's all there, the tipster says. And remember Tarrant's video?"

"He in it?" DeLuca asked.

"He shot it," Jake said. "Kid's name is Trey Welliver."

"You ready?" D said.

"Let's go find him," Jake said.

outfit on, just to torment him. So, yeah, life was good, and possibly about to get better.

She gave Coda a pat and a goodbye cat treat, then checked herself one last time in the entryway mirror. Trusty little Quik-Shot camera in her purse, the lens centered in a cut-out hole and hidden by a scarf. When she moved the scarf, the lens would be uncovered and she could shoot video without anyone knowing. Fiola had a camera of her own, so between them they'd nail it.

"Party time," she said out loud. And closed the door behind her.

ISABEL RUSSO

The first steps wouldn't be the hardest. It was the steps after that. Isabel opened her front door, and stood there, silent, feet on the thin metal threshold. She'd ventured out this far before, so in some ways this was still comfortable. But this time, she'd get in the elevator. Ride down fifteen floors, and go outside. She had not been outside the building since May. May twenty-first to be exact.

She calculated the time, persuading herself. It had been sixty days. Or so. People were, like, in the hospital for sixty days, and they came out fine. Astronauts. Explorers. Missionaries. She had *decided* to stay in. She could *decide* to come out. It was all about power and determination. And she had both.

Isabel closed her eyes with the weight of it, standing in the hall, wearing her jeans and a little pale pink silk top. Her hair had turned out fine—she hadn't lost the touch. The matching pale lipstick worked. For one fleeting moment, forgetting, she'd been pleased with her mirror image. On the outside, she was simply another college face in the crowd.

On the inside, though, she felt something she couldn't even name, more fragile than a butterfly wing, more delicate than a single silk thread, more tentative than a hummingbird. She was about to go out into the world. If she didn't do it right now right now *right now,* she'd retreat into her little apartment and never come out.

"Showtime," she said aloud, though the hallway was empty. Maybe she could pretend it was a performance. Yes. She could do that. She whirled, as if on cue, slammed her door closed, locked it, ran down to the elevator and punched the button, stepped into the elevator with eyes tight shut, and opened them only when she heard the swish of the closing doors.

Her stomach lurched as the elevator took her down, fifteen floors. She clutched the brass railing and watched the glowing numbers carrying her to a new life, maybe the rest of her life. Maybe that would include helping people, other girls like her. Same as Fiola and Jane were doing. Maybe this was her mission, the reason bad things—one bad thing—had happened.

This would be the end of her silence. The door opened, sending her into the soft twilight and the sound track of real life. Outside.

The sound of birds. Their fluttering trill, grace notes in the leaves of the scattered trees dappling the sidewalk with the last of the sunlight. *Outside.* So intensely colored, so full of the music of the evening she almost cried. Inside had been good enough—it had, until she'd opened this door. She reveled in the sunset coloring her face, felt the breeze riffle the ends of her hair, smelled the exhaust and the perfume and the dust. The sidewalk pavement was sunbaked and solid under her ballet flats. The clouds stretched across the darkening sky, tinged pink and purple, fuchsia and hyacinth. She'd almost forgotten how big it was, the ceiling of the sky so endless, so gorgeously, touchingly infinite. She'd felt safe inside, safe and gray and colorless. Now the spectrum of the world poured back onto her, into her, so profoundly beautiful and compelling she almost forgot what she was doing.

"Isabel?"

She pivoted, the voice yanking her back to reality. Jane. And Fiola, too. Standing side by side on the pavement. Waiting for her.

"Hey," Isabel said. "You two look . . ." She tried to choose a word. If their pretend-hip outfits were attempts to fit in as college girls, they were not totally effective. But whatever. ". . . different."

"Well, *you* look wonderful," Jane said. She tucked her arm through the crook of Isabel's elbow.

The warmth of Jane's skin skimmed Isabel's bare arm, the scent of Jane's clean citrusy fragrance exotic and intoxicating. Isabel wondered when she'd last touched another person.

"You okay?" Jane asked.

"She's fine," Fiola said. She tucked her arm through Isabel's other elbow. "We've got cameras, we've got batteries, we're on a mission. Ready?"

"*Vincerò*," Isabel whispered.

The music in her head played even louder than the insistent hip-hop blasting from inside the bar. *Vincerò.* She almost sang the triumphant aria out loud as Jane pulled open the black-lacquered door to the shadowy ambience of the Spotted Owl, letting Isabel go inside first. She took that step, the first step, she knew, of her return to the real Isabel, and the recognition, the *regaining,* of her power. *Vincerò. I will win.*

Music surrounded her, and the fragrances. She remembered them with a rush of longing—yeasty beer and salted peanuts, popcorn, and a hint of weed. The last of the twilight disappeared behind the closing door as the three women joined the chaos of bodies and laughter and chatter of other people. One room, then into another, each filled with people with hopes and desires. With futures. Like hers.

She felt the muscles of her back stiffen, her shoulders square, her chin lift. She would tell everything, no matter who didn't want her to. Who was Edward Tarrant to tell her how to live her life? To dictate what was "good" for her? *"Prudent?"* She'd done nothing wrong. And what she could never reconcile—Tarrant knew about Trey Welliver. What he'd done. So why had nothing happened to Trey? Again, though, maybe there was something she didn't know.

But now was now, and now was new, and in this new life, Isabel would prevail.

"Isabel?" Jane was saying something, close to her ear. "You still okay?"

"Sure," Isabel said. And she was, she really was.

JAKE BROGAN

"We're gonna look like somebody's parents in there." Jake, dubious, pretended not to be stalling as he and D paused on the Hemenway Street sidewalk in front of the black wooden door of the Spotted Owl. If the elusive Trey Welliver was inside, as his stubbornly unhelpful pals had finally suggested, it would be best if they could bring him out quietly, no fuss, no attracting attention. But even in plain clothes, he and D were obvious intruders, would never be able to pass as college kids. Not that they were trying to. He smiled, thinking of Jane, wherever she was, and her silly getup. He'd tease her about it later tonight.

One Theodore Winston Welliver III, white male, age twenty-one, of Darien, Connecticut, was now in their sights for the murder of Avery Morgan. One phone call to the begrudgingly cooperative Tarrant had confirmed Welliver was a student of Morgan's. Took that video of the party. Had certainly been at the Morgan House before the night of the video.

"He seemed smitten with her," Tarrant had told them. "And come to think about it, he's the one who informed me about Avery's death. When I asked how he knew, he was . . . evasive, I suppose is the word."

"Why didn't you mention that before?" Jake and D had exchanged annoyed looks across the squawking Bluetooth speaker in their cruiser.

"As I told you, privacy," Tarrant had said. "But since you already knew the name, it seemed acceptable. And as you said, he's not a juvenile."

"Our source says Mr. Welliver has a history of 'sexual misconduct' on campus," Jake said, deciding to push Tarrant. See what else he would give up.

"All I can tell you, that's under investigation," Tarrant said.

"What would *he* say if we asked him about it?" Jake rolled his eyes. This guy was a piece of work. But at least he was talking now.

"I couldn't possibly predict," Tarrant said. "Although I'd be quite interested to know. He's an adult. He makes his own decisions."

Jake hoped "his own decisions" would not include asking for a lawyer. Not until they got some information. Armed with a yearbook photo from the *Adams Bay Eagle,* they were about to make the next move in what Jake now more than suspected was the murder of Avery Morgan. Grady Houlihan, recovering at Boston City Hospital, might still be part of the equation, but that was for later.

Trey Welliver. The first person to know about the murder. An alleged sexual offender, so said the tipster. Smitten with the victim. Familiar with her house. Bye-bye, Trey. If it wasn't enough for a warrant—which would be absurd—it was certainly enough for a little chat. If not a big chat.

"You think we'll look like somebody's *parents*?" D tossed his empty coffee cup into a trash receptacle on the sidewalk outside the bar. "More like grandparents. But, hey. If they make us as cops, they make us. Maybe it'll scare the crap out of them. Serve 'em right."

Jake reached for the door. "Let's do it as planned and hope he comes quietly," he said. "No reason to ruin the party for everyone else."

43

JANE RYLAND

"There they are." Jane raised her hand, signaling Elaine across the student-crammed hubbub, glimpsing her face through the blur of beer bottles and clinking glasses, girls in skintight denim and even tighter tank tops, gyrating shoulders and echoing laughter. She saw the SAFE organizer blink, once, looking puzzled. Elaine finally broke into laughter, head back, when she recognized Jane, and pointed toward a back room, gesturing them to follow, still laughing. *Fine*, Jane thought. You'll be old someday, too.

"Man," Jane began. "Did we dance like that? Dress like that?" Jane shook her head, feeling the inexorable creep of impending fogeyness. "I sure hope this isn't the way *we* looked in college."

Fiola did not respond.

"Fee? You with me here? What's up?"

"Nothing." Fiola waved her off. "Memories."

"Tell me about it," Jane said. Then she stopped, put her hand on Fee's arm. "Oh."

"Yeah. Sometimes it—" Her producer took a deep breath, let it out. Adjusted the Levi's jacket over her boho midi dress. "That's why I didn't bring it up. You have to just let me be. Let me work."

Jane locked eyes with her. Making sure.

"Thanks, though," Fiola said, her voice low. "Tonight's not about me, okay?" Then, as Isabel turned back to them, she changed her expression. "Hey, sister. You two ready?"

"Ready," Isabel said.

"Sure," Jane said. "Let's work the room. See who and what we can find. And come on, Isabel, there's someone we want you to meet."

The music surrounded them as they headed through the partying throng, Jane arm in arm again with Isabel, Fiola leading them toward the posse of SAFE women stationed beyond an archway in the club's inner room. Pin spots twinkled on the zinc-topped bar, and the floor-to-ceiling mirror multiplied the array of glasses and multicolored liquor bottles lining the glass-shelved wall. Laughter, bare skin, dangly earrings, and exaggerated gestures, everyone vulturing for position at a long line of bar stools. In each person's hand, and lined up along the bar, a stubby highball goblet, or a snifter with an orange straw, or a long-stemmed martini glass, drinks green and pink or colorless with a twist, nursed, sometimes ignored, always accessible.

It would be so easy, Jane realized, her unseen camera rolling, to drop something in one of those drinks. She wondered if that's what Fee was remembering. Or Isabel.

The sound system's incessant bass rumbled the wooden floor, and the exuberant bounce of the dancers kept the three women dodging and weaving their way ahead. It had been barely twilight outside. But here, with the flashing colored lights and shifting reflections and windowless walls, there was no time but now.

Jane pulled Isabel closer as they continued through the crush. "How're you doing?" Jane asked, trying to connect over the music. "We don't have to stay too late, okay? I'm here, long as you need me."

"I'm fine," Isabel murmured. Jane saw her scanning the room as they walked, eyes darting back and forth, nervous as a sparrow. "I just haven't seen these people in a while. And I keep worrying that—"

"Hey, Jane. Hey, Fee." Elaine, perched on a bar stool in jeans and black T-shirt, called out to them from a few yards away. Elaine then slid from her seat, acknowledging Isabel with an outreached hand as they approached. "I'm Elaine."

ISABEL RUSSO

"Isabel," she said. She shook the woman's hand, trying to calm her racing heart. Was Elaine her lifeline? Or maybe she herself was the lifeline. Or maybe it was just a party, and she was merely a student. She tried to let the music take her away, as music always did, tried to become part of the real world again.

"Glad you came," Elaine was saying. "Here, take my stool. And there're some people here you should meet, if you're interested. Okay?"

"Thanks," Isabel said. What was she supposed to do? She knew Elaine's "people" were other victims, Jane had explained that, but—

She turned, needing Jane. But all at once the colors of the room changed. The music turned to white noise. And the floor shifted, shifted, and it wasn't from the music and it wasn't from the lights, it was—it was him. Standing under the archway.

A room away, a hundred people between them, and she saw only a sliver of his smile, then a sliver of his shoulder, and then the top of that sandy hair, he was always a little taller, and a little bigger and—but it didn't matter, she didn't need to see any more, there he was, he was here and she was here, and she'd seen him, exactly as she had tried to stop herself from imagining, the worst possible thing, the *worst*, and she had to sit, no, she had to run, she had to get out of here, get OUT—

JAKE BROGAN

"Holy shit," Jake said.

"Yeah," D said.

They stood just inside the front door of the Spotted Owl, instantly deafened and sent into sensory overload. They'd entered, unquestioned, past the slacker so-called bouncer at the entrance. Now Jake couldn't resist calculating the occupancy rate in this multi-roomed crush of college students.

"Fire code," Jake said.

"Big time," D answered.

"Underage drinking." Jake sniffed. "And dope."

DeLuca eyed the crowd, assessing. "Indecent exposure, too. Some-body oughta call the cops."

"Want to see the photo one more time?" Jake took out the picture they'd copied from the yearbook, unfolded it, compared faces. "I don't see him out there now, do you? There's a back room, though."

"Don't see him," D said.

They stood, keeping to the door's lee shadow, assessing and dismiss-ing one face after another. "You think those kids meant he was already here, or on the way here, or coming here later?"

"Who knows," D replied. "Nobody's paying attention to us, anyway, so we can stand here, stake it out, see what we see. Listen to this great so-called music. Maybe get a beer, so we don't look outta place. Even have some popcorn."

"Right," Jake said. He'd love a beer, but duty was duty. "Speaking of popcorn. What's up with the dog?"

"Bureaucrats," D said, making it sound like an obscenity. "Animal Control made us sign some kind of foster bullshit, paperwork, so we shall see. But you know Kat. She's all like, *Oh, poor doggy.* She changed its name to Rocco—dumb dog already answers to it. I'd have dumped the yapper."

Jake took his eyes off the crowd just long enough to sneer at his partner. "Liar," he said.

"As some have often noted," D said. "Usually they're assholes, though."

"D," Jake said.

"I didn't call *you* an asshole," D said. "I was merely—"

"Nine o'clock." Jake clocked his chin to the left. "Couple of feet from the archway to the back. By the Sam Adams sign."

D narrowed his eyes. "Ah . . ."

"Oh, yeah," Jake said. "Gotcha."

44

JANE RYLAND

"Isabel?" Jane felt the girl's body stiffen, watched her sink onto the bar stool Elaine offered, then stand again.

Her eyes had widened, then closed, and now she stood, a statue, hands at her sides. Jane watched them curl into fists, then open, as if choosing an emotion, anger or fear. Fee had disappeared, maybe gone to the bathroom, maybe off getting more pictures.

"Isabel?" Elaine was saying, greeting some new arrivals. "I want you to meet Man—"

"I have to leave," Isabel whispered to the space in front of her. Her fingers found Jane's arm, clutched it. "Right now."

"Sure," Jane said. But this was a situation. A tough one. They'd come here to get video. Jane and Fiola were working journalists, shooting their documentary. They needed to be here. But Jane had promised Isabel she'd stick with her—and with that one vow had probably stepped over the reporter line.

Where the heck was Fee? Elaine turned to welcome some other women, apparently unaware of Isabel's apparent distress.

"But, Isabel? Can you tell me why? Maybe that'll help?" Jane signaled the bartender, a ponytailed blonde in a black apron. "Can you get my friend some water?"

As Isabel stayed silent, Jane took the opportunity—hoping it wasn't the last—to angle her camera into the room. She panned it, left to right and then back again, then zoomed in for close-ups of the drink-lined bar.

They'd blur faces, and add special effects to hide the club's identity. The footage would illustrate the packed-together bodies, the free-flowing alcohol, and the disturbing impossibility of knowing who might put something in a drink, or exchange one for another. The crowd ballooned, changing shape with the rhythm of the music and the surging current of the new arrivals.

"Isabel?" The water arrived, iced and lemoned in a highball glass wrapped in a black napkin. "Are you okay?"

The girl took it, but clutched the glass, without drinking. She stared toward the entrance to the back room, a lofty archway separating where they stood from the main bar area. Following her gaze, Jane could see nothing untoward—

Jake? Jane, startled, tried to regroup. Stood tall as she could, peering over tops of heads. Jake? In the Spotted Owl? Why? She definitely had not told him the party was here. Definitely. Not. Had he followed her? Last night he'd warned her, as always, against going undercover, and she'd reassured him, as always, that she'd be fine. But if he thought she needed to be supervised, or monitored, that was . . . well, it was silly. Was she overreacting? Maybe it showed he loved her, and he was concerned about her? He was in her life. Maybe she needed to embrace that.

But wait. There was DeLuca, too. And they were moving from the entrance of the Spotted Owl toward her. Coming her way? *This ought to be interesting.* She felt a mischievous smile. How would she handle these two?

She'd almost forgotten her mission. "Isabel?"

"Hang on," Isabel said.

Jane tucked herself behind Isabel's stool, camera lens still pointing toward the dance floor, watching Jake and D make their way.

They stopped, one of them on each side of a young man, sandy-haired and flannel-shirted, tall, with confident shoulders. Looked like a student, holding a beer bottle. Jake seemed to ask the kid a question. Funny, seeing it from this angle. Reading Jake's body language and stance, she decided that this was not a personal encounter. Though Jake and D were both smiling, pleasant expressions on their faces, Jane could tell something *un*pleasant was under way.

A new song blasted through the enormous ceiling-mounted speakers, throbbing, and as the crowd parted, a random moment allowed Jane's camera a clear view of the three men. The student-guy was nodding, at first apparently agreeing, then he frowned and retreated, but Jake and D did not move from his side. Whatever was happening, Jane had it on camera.

The three of them turned, Jake's arm over the kid's back. Beer bottle still in the student's hand, they walked toward the exit. Three buddies, to any other observer. Jane suspected otherwise.

And out the front door. Okay, *bizarre*. Jake and DeLuca hadn't looked for her, since they easily could have found her, so their visit to the party wasn't about her. She'd find out more tonight. Maybe even taunt Jake with her video, since it proved how very proficient she was at going under-cover. So skilled he hadn't even noticed her. Maybe she'd ask where he was first, just to see if he told the truth.

Were they always telling the truth to each other, though? She hadn't told him about the "SAY NO MORE" note—though why should she have? It would have just worried him, made him even more overprotective. She hadn't told Jake the truth about her recognizing Clooney Sholto, either, because McCusker had sworn her to secrecy. So much for their deal about sharing their lives.

She felt Isabel let out a sigh. Turned as the girl took a sip of water.

"I'm okay now," she said. "He's gone."

" 'He'?" Jane said.

JAKE BROGAN

Any minute now, the kid could ask for a lawyer, and this questioning session would all be over. But Theodore Winston Welliver, age twenty-one, was an adult. He could make his own decisions, and, given the rolling papers and lighter Jake had noted but left unmentioned, maybe "lawyer" wasn't tops in this kid's vocabulary. What Jake and D were trying to figure out right now, in the unthreatening ambience of the "victim room," was whether that semi-anonymous tip T'shombe Pereira had forwarded contained any level of veracity. If it did, Welliver was toast.

The ever-generous Boston Police Department had provided Mr. Welliver with a Pepsi and a bag of Doritos, though Trey, as he was called, clearly would have preferred a blunt, or something even more illegal. Not the brightest bulb on the planet. Which, sadly, might serve the path to justice. With one wrong word in the next half hour or so, Trey Welliver, student, could become Trey Welliver, murder suspect. All they needed was one glittering gem of probable cause.

"So you knew Avery Morgan, you'd been to her home," Jake reiterated, as if simply reminding himself.

"She was cool." Trey took a slug of Pepsi. "You know, hip. She'd have students over for rehearsals, stuff like that. She had that little dog, went everywhere with her."

"Right," D said. He checked a pinging text, held up his phone screen to Jake. "Detective? Willow's 'okay,' so says the man. He's at home, waiting for her, says 'never mind.'"

"Kidding me?" Jake said. Never mind "never mind." Jake was not done with the mercurial Mr. Galt. The good news—with no California mission and no missing suburban wife, he'd see Jane tonight. Eventually. It was already after ten.

"Good-looking, too," D was prompting Trey. "Ms. Morgan, I mean, not the dog."

Trey shrugged. "I guess so. Sure. Yeah."

"Is there anyone you think we should talk to about what happened?" Jake tried to keep this low-key. Didn't want to scare the guy, and no way to gauge yet what might spook him into calling a halt to the inquiry. "As we explained, we're attempting to get a picture of what her professional life was like, as well as her personal life. Any—you know—special friends? Boyfriends? Girlfriends?"

"Um." Trey looked at the ceiling, maybe searching for heavenly intervention. "Huh-uh. Not really."

Not really. One of Jake's favorite answers. "Not really" generally meant exactly the opposite. "Not really" meant "Really, but I don't want to tell you."

Jake patted for his spiral notebook and pretended to consult it, though he knew exactly what Edward Tarrant had told him. "So, just making a time line here, how did you first find out about Avery Morgan's death? If you remember."

"Uh, I was riding my bike over there. The Reserve. *They* get the streets paved, it's not like regular Boston. And I saw the cop car."

"I see." Jake nodded. "And someone told you there was a murder?" Unlikely.

Trey considered this, like a test question he hadn't studied for. "Yeah. A cop kind of told me. I mean, he was calling for backup. And he was wet. She had a pool, you know. Two plus two."

The new math. Which also added up to Trey's being at the scene of the potential crime. Though not what time he'd arrived. Maybe it was Trey who told that reporter? "Okay then. Did you tell anyone else about it?"

"Anyone at all," D said.

"Um." Trey picked up the soda can, rattled it. "Is there more Pepsi?"

"How about this. Do you remember where you were earlier that afternoon? Anyone with you? Wherever you were?"

"Um." Trey rattled the can again, looked like he was contemplating crushing it. "Not really."

"Do you remember telling Edward Tarrant?" Jake asked. "The dean at Adams Bay?"

"Edward Tarrant?"

"So, why would you go to Tarrant about it, Trey?" Jake put on an intrigued-but-confused face. "Do you have a relationship with him? What kind?"

"Re—"

"—lationship," D said.

"Or with Ms. Morgan?" Jake asked.

"Tarrant?" Trey said.

"You shot the video at that pool party in May, right?" DeLuca said. "It was clear how she looked at you, waving at the camera."

"She? May?" Trey asked. "Hang the frick on. You mean . . ."

Jake waited, signaled to D to do the same. D pulled up a folding chair and sat, silent, watching. The kid seemed edgy now, or worried, even angry, fidgeting with his Doritos bag, stabbing out the crumbs with a forefinger. Edgy was good. Worry was often the precursor to confession, or affirmation, or revelation. Anger was often the precursor to truth.

"Did that asshole rat me out? Shit. Yes, I played the opera music to her. It was just on the phone, for crap sake. In *case* she was about to talk. All those girls, going around making a big deal about 'just say no' and shit." Trey's face went red. "Geez. Tarrant. Freaking guy knows everything."

He stood, a wounded bull, and his motion knocked over his empty Pepsi can. It fell off the conference table and onto the floor, rolled to the closed door, and teetered to a halt. They all stared at it. "*A*sshole. He freaking ratted me *out.*"

D stood, as if to pick up the can. Bent over. Looked at it. Stopped. "Uh, Jake?" he said.

"Stand by, okay?" Jake said. Whatever D wanted could wait one second. He turned to the kid, facing him dead on. He was clearly in full-out talk mode now, and Jake could not wait to hear what he was about to say.

"Ratted you out?" Jake repeated. Let him talk, whatever this kid was saying.

"Hell, yes." The kid extended his middle finger, apparently at the universe. "He promised he wouldn't, the asshole. Promised my dad. That was our deal. I'm gonna—"

Trey stopped, breathing hard, narrowing his eyes, as if the effort of thinking was overpowering, as if trying to come up with the worst possible threat.

"Ha," he said. "I'm gonna tell my parents."

"Jake?" D again.

Jake, annoyed, whirled to face him, but D wasn't there.

D was down. On the floor. Collapsed, one arm under him, motionless on the thin grimy carpet.

45

ISABEL RUSSO

Her apartment door closed behind her, and Isabel paused, smiling, home again, but no longer a prisoner. She'd been outside. She'd done it. She'd broken the spell. Like some Rapunzel fairy-tale princess. She could think that to herself, silly but true.

"True, Fish," she said, tapping just the right amount of fish flakes into his bowl. "Good night, swim tight." It *was* a good night. She couldn't remember the last time she was up this late.

Now she had plans, she had a future. She'd go to class even. Tomorrow, or the day after that for sure. Tomorrow afternoon was coffee with Elaine and the group. Last night they'd bonded over Edward Tarrant, and his perverse tactics to keep families silent. What Tarrant didn't know: Manderley, awesome girl, had listened to every phone call. And kept notes. That disgusting man was about to get a visit he'd not soon forget. Plus, they'd told her they'd compiled what they called a "creep list." Awesome, and Isabel couldn't wait to add one certain name to it. Unless, perhaps, it was already there.

And then Jane and Fiola were coming to do the first shooting of her interview. All good. She'd be in silhouette, but it was what she said that mattered, and nothing could stop her from saying it now. Not the vile Trey, not the hideous Tarrant, not her timid and unsupportive mother, not anyone. *Vincerò.*

She went to the window, pulled back her striped curtains—they were so pretty, everything was pretty—and stepped out onto her balcony. The night, bejeweled with the lights of the square, twinkling stars, flashing neon, the flare of headlights and even the traffic signals, all at once, all green. All green.

The colors below had never been so vibrant. It was as if the world were in color again, as if someone had flipped a switch—Jane?—and given Isabel her life back.

She wrapped her fingers around the spindly iron railing, replaying the evening. She'd seen him, Trey, coming into the Spotted Owl. Before he went away with whoever those guys were. She'd relived it, what happened in May: the revulsion, the dread, the incomprehensively unnerving gaps of memory. Her brain was clear right up to . . . when? Reality only pounced on her afterward, when she'd awakened, tangled in sheets, naked, sticky, alone.

She'd told Tarrant back then. The whole thing. He'd as much as ordered her to keep quiet. Convinced her mother, too, not to say a word. It was about her reputation, Tarrant had insisted. Her future. Her mother had believed it, had even been grateful! But not her, not anymore. What she'd learned last night? She wasn't the only one. Talk about a creep.

She'd entered tonight in her "Someday" file. She was keeping track of Trey. Oh, yes. Maybe someday she wouldn't have to.

She closed her eyes briefly, making a wish, as she leaned forward on the balcony rail, pushing all bad thoughts away. She looked down, over the edge, onto the street fifteen stories below.

WILLOW GALT

Willow had blinked at the darkness, struggled to come out of the drug-induced fog. She was . . . in that hotel, right, and it was . . . She had tried to stand, then fell back on the chair, swimming through the uncertainty and searching for bearings. The crosswalk. The man. The sidewalk. The man. Java Jim's. The man.

Ten-seventeen, the time displayed in white electronic lights on the hotel's nightstand clock. She'd slept for all that time? Maybe. She'd taken another pill. Or two. "For better or for worse," she and Tom had made that vow, but she'd let her paranoia and panic erase it. After ten at night? He'd be frantic. It was time for the panic to be over.

Whatever she'd seen—and she'd seen, she had, she could not erase that memory, more like half a memory, but still indelibly drawn— whatever she'd seen, whatever she'd witnessed, she'd have to tell. She'd dialed her cell phone, fearing Tom's reaction, eager for his reaction, knowing his love for her would outweigh his anger. He'd be angry, yes, but only because he loved her. *I am Tom and you are Willow.*

No answer. Should she leave a message? "I'm okay," she'd whispered. "I'm coming home." Where was Tom? What if that man had already—

Without thinking, without planning, panic taking over again, she'd flown down the fire stairs, out through the lobby, into the urban darkness, neon, and headlights. The hotel's front door was deserted. The street sign at the corner said Boylston and Clarendon. Cab. She needed a cab.

And one arrived, because it was meant to be and soon she was home and that's why she stood here, in her own entryway of their own house, safe, she hoped, in The Reserve.

She paused, listening. Tom might be upstairs, asleep.

She checked her phone again. But of course no one had called her— this was her prepaid, the one she'd used to contact Olive, and later to tell her never mind. And probably why Tom hadn't answered. The number would show up as "unknown." They were trained never to answer unknown calls.

She tiptoed up the stairs, light still off, hating to awaken Tom, listening through the darkness for his breathing, or the rustle of sheets, or some sound reassuring her she'd done the right thing. Had he heard her message?

Tom would take care of her. They were in this together.

Down the hall, the bedroom light flipped on.

Her heart filled. He must have known it was her. He was there.

"Willow?"

She couldn't find the voice to answer. She dropped her bag onto the floor, had to get there more quickly, threw herself down the hall and around the corner until she was facing him.

Tom was standing by the side of the bed. Fully dressed.

Pointing a gun at her.

"No!" She screamed it, her throat closing her mind exploding her world ending—and she steeled herself for what was to come, the pain and the answers, that the reality of life wasn't always what you expected. "No!"

"No, no, Willow, Willow." Tom was holding her, and the gun was on the floor, and she was in his arms. "It's all right. It's all right. I got your message—where *were* you?—and Olive's, too. About what happened. But I didn't know it was you on the stairs. When you didn't answer, I thought it was—"

The man. She almost said it out loud.

But she was crying then, full out, the day and the night and the fear and telling the secret of what she'd seen.

46

JANE RYLAND

Jane pulled her car out of the parking lot behind her condo again, muttering. Some moron had parked in her space. Now, just after midnight, she would have to risk a ticket by parking on the street.

She was too darn nice, she berated herself. She should call, get the car towed, and reclaim the space she paid way too much for. She drove up Corey Road, top down, searching for a spot. The drapey silver maples rustled in the August night. Blue lights of flickering televisions glowed from the windows of her neighbors' brownstones and an occasional horn bleeped from Beacon Street a block away. Parking was a pain, but she was still floating from the night's success.

Great pictures. She'd already rewound the video and seen the club, the music, the drinks, the bar, the whole up-too-close-and-personal atmosphere. Isabel, after whatever emotional bump in the road she'd encountered, seemed to regroup, and went off with Elaine and her pals, assuring Jane and Fee she'd be fine. Plus, Jane had a pretty darn great shot of Jake and D and that guy they'd corralled. Maybe Jake was already here, upstairs, with a glass of wine for her. And plans.

Head on a swivel, she drove all the way up to Winthrop—*nothing*—then pulled into a driveway to make a U-turn. Every spotlight on the exterior of the house flashed on, blasting her with light. Motion detectors. *Sorry, sorry, I'm leaving,* Jane thought, and backed into the street to try again.

Bingo. Not half a block away from her building, a spot. She gunned her Audi—not that there was anyone else vying for the space at this hour—raced ahead, and snagged it. Checking the rearview, she parallel-parked in one try.

Put up the top, she reminded herself. She checked the rearview again, and laughed. She still didn't look like herself, in the ball cap and ponytail. Her dumb glasses. The convertible top *whomped* into place, and she clicked the latches, grabbed her bag, opened the car door.

Paused.

The street was deserted, cars lining each side, streetlights creating a string of orange pools alternating with shadows. Up the street, the motion sensor lights flipped off, deepening the darkness.

She took out her cell phone. Clicked it on. Slammed the car door closed and locked it. An ambulance screamed up Beacon Street, flaring the side street with a sudden bath of red light, its wail fading as it headed toward Kenmore.

She snapped her head around, noticing another change in the darkness. A light inside a parked car. Down the street, a blue or black car. She fingered her cell phone as she walked. Three floors up, her windows were still in semi-gloom, only the fool-the-burglar light she always left on glowing protectively. Jake wasn't there.

"Get a grip, sister," she whispered. Trying to laugh at herself, she trotted toward her building, feeling the ponytail jouncing, the short skirt still strange. She made it up the front steps, and hearing the front door lock securely behind her, grabbed her mail, some of it on the floor as always, and took the stairs to her apartment two at a time.

All good, all good. Coda greeted her at the door. No Jake. She flipped on the lights—nothing, no intruders, no sense that anyone had been here. Not that anyone would have been.

She stashed the phone, dumped her tote bag, hefted her newest stack of bills and magazines and added them to the dining room table pile with the ones Neena had delivered the night before. She'd look at all of it tomorrow.

Well, maybe just a quick look now. Bill, bill, circular—and then, in Neena's pile . . .

A plain white envelope.

White, sealed. No stamp. Addressed to her. She turned it over. No return address.

She slid a fingernail under the right corner, peeled it away, ripped it open, Coda curling around her ankle.

"I don't like this, cat," she said.

She unfolded the single piece of white paper.

Black ink. Three words. Block letters.

SAY NO MORE.

47

JAKE BROGAN

"D? Can you hear me?" Jake knelt beside his partner, felt for the carotid pulse. Weak. D's face had gone gray, green, sweat coursing down one cheek, his skin clammy, hot and cold at the same time. Eyes closed. Breathing? Barely.

"What's happening?" Trey Welliver cringed in his chair, as if something he did had triggered this.

"Use that black phone on the table," Jake ordered Trey. "Push zero. Say 'Interview room C, we have an officer down.' Got it? 'Officer down, room C.' Now. Now. *Now.*"

With his own heart slamming against his ribs, willing his hands to work and his brain to function, Jake rolled D—*D!*—onto his back, opened his collar, loosened his belt, watching his friend and partner changing into a wraith, a ghost, a . . . Jake thought of all D's cryptic phone calls, that surreptitious texting.

"You okay, D?" he whispered. "Stay with me here, bud." He heard Trey on the phone, saying what Jake had told him to, already heard footsteps in the corridor hall thudding toward the room.

Aspirin. I need to give him an aspirin. He patted the pockets of D's jeans, felt a lump. Pulled out a flat pad of folded tissue, opened it. Aspirin. He put one under D's tongue, wondering if this was a myth or if it would really help.

CPR. *Do it.* He cleared D's airway, adjusted his head, and started pumping his chest. The door slammed open and three uniforms pointed their weapons at Trey.

"Hands in the air!" one yelled. "Freeze!"

"No!" Trey yelled.

"No!" Jake yelled, too, realizing what this must look like. "He's not a shooter! It's D. I think he's having a heart attack."

How many bodies—*people*—had Jake seen, lifted onto stretchers, strapped in by medics? How many oxygen masks and chest compressions? It was all part of the deal, part of his day, part of what he'd signed up for. But this—was D.

The medical team flooded into the room, moving Jake aside to begin the swift efficiency of their lifesaving dance.

"Thanks, Jake, we got this now," one EMT said.

During emergencies, Jake's mind always worked triple-time, torqued up, the pressure and the speed and the uncertainty, the need for instant decision-making all part of his skill and training. But this was D. This was different. This was the other side of the equation. And Jake was full-blown angry now. The medics were pushing him out of this, all by the book—this wasn't *his* job, he understood that—but he had to go to the hospital, go with D, and they were saying no.

"Why the hell not?" He grabbed a medic by the arm, demanding. "He's my partner, for crap sake."

"You're interrogating a suspect, Jake. You can't just leave him," she said. "And we can't wait for your backup. Sorry, Jake. We've got DeLuca, okay? Got him. Rely on it."

Forget that. He'd go to the damn hospital on his own, haunt the place if he had to. They were partners. EMTs were already powering D away, racing down the hall on the rumble of metal wheels.

"Uh, sir?"

Trey. Right, Trey. Standing there, looking annoyed, or bored, or confused. Trey, the polar opposite of DeLuca. Young, strong, wealthy, privileged, with the rest of his life ahead of him. And a criminal.

Tell his parents? Jake remembered the kid's imbecilic threat. He'd better tell his parents to get a lawyer. A fricking good one.

"Theodore Welliver." Jake spat the words, furious with the whole ridiculous unfair world, a world where happy endings were rare, a world that was unreliable and could take away a colleague—a brother—before you knew what happened.

He had one more thing to do, damn it, before he raced to the hospital.

"Yeah?" the kid said. "So can I go?"

Jake focused on him. He should clear this with the DA, of course. Jake knew the protocol. But screw protocol.

"Theodore Welliver? You are under arrest for the murder of Avery Morgan. You have the right to remain silent. . . ."

THURSDAY

48

JANE RYLAND

Jake. It had to be Jake. Jane almost fell out of bed, grabbing the phone. Six A.M. The emptiness of the space beside her had kept her touching only the edge of sleep all night, every sound she heard or imagined she heard startling her hyper-awake, hearing the rattle of his key in the door, willing it, waiting, disappointed. And that second note. Another three-word note. She needed to tell Jake. And McCusker. But what could either of them do?

"Hello?" She willed herself into clarity, propped on her elbow. No answer. No answer? *The note. The blue-or-black car with the light on.*

Coda slept, oblivious, in her spot by Jane's left foot. Where was Jake? If he weren't a cop, she'd be worried. She was worried anyway. She touched Gramma Brogan's diamond, hoping it'd telegraph, somehow, if something was wrong. Jake had to be fine. But where was he? She'd texted, but he hadn't answered.

"Hello?" Silence. A million horribles slithered through her mind. "Hello?" And then the phone connection clicked into life.

"I thought you were the one with the cop shop source, sister."

Fiola. Not Jake. Not a bad guy. But cop shop?

"What's wrong?" Now Jane's heart actually leaped, she felt it, and her hand flew to her chest to hold it in place. Coda blinked, resettled herself. "Is something wrong?"

"Well, 'wrong' depends on who you are."

Jane heard the tone in Fee's voice, wry and amused.

"Your friend Detective Jake Brogan—"

"Fee." Jane had to interrupt, fear twisting her voice. "What about him?"

"—made an arrest for the Avery Morgan murder. Last night. So say *my* sources." Fee was clearly proud of herself.

"He did? Last night?" Jane stood, went to the window overlooking the courtyard. If she twisted the right way, she could see a sliver of street. The blue-or-black car was gone.

"It's not public yet," Fee went on. "So we can't use it. Yet. But apparently it's all teacher-student intrigue, secret assignations, unrequited lust, and jealousy. He killed her Monday afternoon between two and four, so says the source. Got to love it."

"Who'd Jake arrest? When? Where? Why?"

"You forgot 'how many,' Miss Journalism School," Fee said. "And the answer to that is 'one.' One kid, a senior, guy named Theodore Welliver. They call him Trey."

A kid. A college kid. Jane knew where Jake had been earlier that night—the Spotted Owl. And she'd seen him and DeLuca with a "kid." Jake was probably still processing the guy. He couldn't have texted her about it—that would have been way out of bounds. Though he had texted "developments."

Could she have videotaped the actual arrest? She knew exactly how to find out.

"Photo?" Jane asked.

"Looking," Fee said.

"Because, Fee? Last night at the Spotted Owl, did you see . . ." No, Fee *hadn't* seen Jake, Jane realized. Because first of all, Fee had been in the bathroom, and besides, she'd never met Jake.

And Jane hadn't *told* Fee about seeing Jake, because she might assume Jane had divulged where they'd be. Which she hadn't, though no one would believe that. Another example of why the cop/reporter relationship was dangerous.

It took Jane thirty seconds to get rid of Fee—ignoring the producer's efforts to get more deets but promising to come in to the station—so she could call Isabel. Yes, it was too early. No, that wouldn't stop her.

She could hear Isabel breathing on the other end of the line as Jane told her all she knew. Which was not much except for the kid's name.

"So?" Jane wrapped up. This was a story, a big one. This was where breaking news kicked in, no matter what other assignments a reporter had. Jane had to tap any source she could. "Whatever you say is confidential. But do you know him? Anything about him?"

Silence.

"Isabel?"

"Can you come over?" Isabel said.

Great. "Sure. Like, now? Is it too early?" Jane yanked off her T-shirt as she juggled the phone and headed toward the shower, trying to move as quickly as possible. She'd decided to tell McCusker about the new note. But this came first.

"It's fine," Isabel said. "See you soon."

"I'll hop in the shower," Jane went on, undressing as she went, "throw on jeans, and come over, a-sap. Thirty minutes. But, so, you know him? This—"

She stopped, naked now, in the middle of the still-dark hallway, Coda's cold nose nudging her ankle. "Isabel?"

Dial tone. Had Isabel hung up? Maybe she'd thought the conversation was over.

It took less than thirty to get to her apartment. The glass front door to Isabel's building was unlocked, as it had been the other time Jane was there. In the dingy marble lobby, its walls covered with taped-up notices for guitar lessons and tutoring and lost laptops, Jane jabbed the elevator button, impatient. No creepy Sholto guys, or any guys, had been skulking around her condo, and there was no parking ticket on the car she'd left illegally on-street all night. No way was she going back outside last night, not after getting that note.

Had someone waited for her, but been confused by her disguise? She

should have called Jake about it, but she'd expected him home any minute. Then fallen asleep. Kind of asleep.

The elevator doors opened. Two texting girls in cutoffs came out, ignoring Jane. In a minute she was at fifteen, at Isabel's door. Which was open. Less than an inch. But open.

"Isabel?" Jane stepped inside, one step, easing the door open across the pile of the pale blue carpet.

"Isabel?" she called out, her curiosity edged with a wisp of uncertainty. "You okay?"

"No." Isabel's voice, from deep inside. "I'm not."

49

JAKE BROGAN

What if he had been in California? And all this had happened? Jake couldn't face another cup of coffee, but this time of night—morning—and in this situation, waiting helplessly in Boston City Hospital, what else was he gonna drink? He'd had zero sleep. But he wasn't dead.

And neither was DeLuca. *Yet,* he couldn't stop himself from thinking. Though that reality was inconceivable. An array of white-coated doctors had shown up, grim-faced and talking jargon, but Jake decided he could translate their doctorese into cautious optimism. Emphasis on "cautious," Jake realized, and wondered again whether he might have done anything more. Better. Lifesaving.

"You did all you could," the receiving ER doc had assured him. DeLuca's cell produced a raft of texts from doctors, and from Kat, urging him to take it easy, cut back, slow down. That's what his partner had been hiding. Jake had called Kat, woke her up, tried to break the news without terrifying her. She, privilege of a doctor, was already in D's room.

Jake zipped his jacket up, then down. He smiled, even now, remembering how Jane always teased him about his nervous habit. He'd call her, too, soon as it was halfway appropriate. She slept with the phone by her bed, like he did, so she'd awaken if he texted. For now, six A.M.? Let her sleep.

Down the hall Grady dozed, groggy but coming out of his drugged haze. With Trey Welliver under arrest, Grady was no longer even a marginal suspect in the Morgan murder. As for his connection to Violet Sholto's death, that verdict was still out.

Had Grady gone back, over to the dark side? And if so—Jake tried to replay their supposedly private conversations—when?

He settled himself onto the hospital's ratty waiting-area sofa, a battered careworn thing probably from the fifties. A hardscrabble urgent care facility like Boston City couldn't afford even an attempt at luxury, let alone comfort. Most who came here—patients and families and cops and lawyers—were connected to violence in some way. The shootings and stabbings, overdoses and freak-outs, all the blights of a big city, all the casualties arrived here at Boston City, where beleaguered medics tried their best to bandage and stanch, knowing a disquieting number of patients were wearing handcuffs along with their hospital ID bracelets, and many had police guards sitting vigil along with their relatives.

They'd brought DeLuca here because it was closest.

Jake stared at the putrid green wall, in limbo, in purgatory, life on hold. His partner, with tubes and oxygen mask and attentive nurse, hovered on the edge of consciousness.

Heart attack. The scourge of a cop's existence, the officers who fought a daily battle against relentless pressure and stomach-twisting stress and long hours and fast food and caffeine and sugar and too often, like DeLuca, went down in defeat in middle age, not from a gun or some asshole bad guy, but from shitty diet and bad luck.

Footsteps. A white coat. Jake's own heart lurched. But the doctor gave him a wan smile and walked on.

Trey Welliver. Jake had sure been on the wrong track about that one. Good thing he'd left a message for that Treasury agent Olive Brennis in California, canceling his trip. Bad thing he'd told her he thought her informant was dead. He'd been cryptic about it, because who knew who listened to Brennis's messages? But with lovesick—or drugged-up—student Trey Welliver the killer, whether Avery Morgan was an informant had nothing to do with that case.

Random beeps echoed along the tile-walled corridor, some kind of mechanical hiss, and that sinister hospital silence. Avery Morgan had drowned three days ago, her death an open question, with no witnesses, no motives, no slam-dunk clues. Funny how murder investigations worked. The roller coaster first progressing gradually up the hill, agonizingly, tick by tick, before finally, as all the puzzle pieces of the crime slammed into place, blasting downhill to the solution and arrest.

He and D had gotten their man. As they always did. But instead of celebrating a victory for justice, here he sat, alone, exhausted, and worried as hell.

ISABEL RUSSO

Too much information. Isabel understood that phrase now. She stood, framed in her balcony window, clutching her phone and staring at the awakening street below. An irresistible force meeting an immovable object, her mother used to say. Isabel never understood that, not until this very moment, as she struggled to process an avalanche of impossible, unthinkable facts. Fifteen stories below, commuters straggled into Kenmore Station, and a few cars made illegal left turns. She didn't use her binoculars. Not today. Because Trey wasn't down there. He was in custody. Jane's voice, and her news, echoed in her brain. Which now was about to explode.

The first piece of information had come last night after she'd asked Elaine one critical question. "Confidential," she demanded. Made her promise.

"Sure," Elaine said.

"Is a Theodore Welliver on your creep list?" Isabel didn't tell her why.

"Oh, yeah," Elaine said.

So that was good. Good in a perverse way.

Then, this morning, Jane called, first with her questions, then word of the arrest. Isabel rejoiced, the only appropriate word, because finally Trey Welliver would get what was coming to him, and she'd be free and he'd pay and pay and pay. "Creep list" wasn't the half of it, she thought, planning to open her window and blast triumphant music from her speakers, *Vincerò,* and *O Fortuna,* and thank the universe for karma and comeuppance and revenge and freedom.

Then Isabel asked Jane *when* Professor Morgan was killed.

She'd burst into tears at the answer.

Because Trey was guilty, he was guilty in the deepest essence of the word, he'd ruined—no, *almost* ruined—her life, and she'd spent since May, since May twenty-first to be exact, plotting and wishing and scheming and stalking and dreaming, dreaming of the day *his* life would be ruined, and not just *almost* ruined, and now her dreams had come true.

Trey would be convicted, go to prison, and rot in hell.

And she would be free.

All she had to do was keep quiet.

"Isabel?"

She heard a voice from the doorway. Jane's.

"Are you okay?"

50

JANE RYLAND

Jane thought of the fictional Tosca. Thought of this fifteenth-floor apartment, its balcony, and the sorrowing and fearful girl who had imprisoned herself here. How whatever happened to Isabel—and Jane still didn't exactly know what it was—had almost killed her, sure as a fifteen-story fall.

"Isabel?" Jane heard the apprehension in her own voice. The girl answered her, with that plaintive "no," so she was not dead. And as long as she wasn't, this story wasn't over.

Jane eased open the front door and steeled herself for whatever was to come.

Isabel sat at the kitchen table, the goldfish swimming circles in its bowl beside her.

Jane stopped, planted, not knowing what to say.

"You promised whatever I tell you is confidential, right?" Isabel stood, turning her open laptop toward Jane.

Whatever Isabel was about to show her—and it had to be the identity of her rapist—Jane could not let herself see. No one was jumping off balconies, though. Good.

"I don't want to know who raped you." Jane paused as the pieces of a potential puzzle picture clicked into place. Only one chair was near the kitchen table, Isabel's, so Jane stayed put, relieved the computer screen was too far away to read. "I believe you. But I don't want to know."

"But I asked you—"

"Yes, definitely. Confidential." Jane tried to untangle her responsibilities, and it seemed as if justice was the only one. But justice for who? Jane knew what could happen if you kept your word and kept silent. Next life she would choose an easier career. Like rocket scientist.

"When was Professor Morgan killed?" Isabel asked. Her transformation last night into a hip and attractive college woman had vanished. Now her hair went spiky and wild, a tiny white T-shirt pulled tight over her narrow shoulders, eyes smoky, with exhaustion, maybe. Her dark circles were back. "I know I asked you before. But are you sure? Exactly sure?"

"Well, our sources say between two and four. In the afternoon. Yes, I'm sure as anyone can be."

"Monday."

"Monday."

"And they think Trey . . ." Isabel swallowed, hard.

Jane could tell she was deciding.

"Trey Welliver killed her then?"

"Yes," Jane said. "He's in custody. Charged."

"He was on the creep list, you know," Isabel said.

Jane didn't. "Huh."

"And we're all going to see Dean Tarrant today," Isabel said. "The SAFEs. About it all. They're going to call me when we get an appointment. That'll probably be soon."

"Okay," Jane said, simply listening. "Sure." As long as Isabel kept talking, she wasn't jumping off a balcony. So hurray, Jane wouldn't have to talk her off the ledge. Literally, at least. The computer screen popped to black.

Jane perched on the arm of the couch, balancing on one pointed toe. "What are you trying to say, Isabel? It's just me and you, you know that."

Isabel turned her back, walked to the window, facing outside. *Oh, no. Not the window.* Jane hurried to her side.

"Isabel?"

"Tarrant's office is just over there." Isabel pointed. "You can see his window. He's on sixteen."

Jane narrowed her eyes. "Okay."

"I always look out from here, you know?" Isabel's voice softened. "Seeing the world. It's my way of connecting. Staying real, and human, and like, part of it."

"You can't really see much, though, up here," Jane said. "Except colors and pavement and cars. Pedestrians, I guess, but not really . . . faces."

"That's why I have these," Isabel said. Jane turned from the view. Isabel was holding chunky black binoculars to her face. She handed them to Jane. "Now look."

Jane adjusted the focus wheel as she held the glasses to her eyes. She took a step backward, almost thrown off balance as the world leaped into hard-edged clarity. Office windows precisely visible, some revealing shadowy figures moving behind them. Jane twisted the focus again, riveted. She could read logos on cars, see each cobblestone on one sidewalk path. See people's faces, even tell who was smiling, almost hear them talking. A pigeon bobbed on a patch of grass, battling with another over scraps in a Dunkin's wrapper. The lenses were so powerful Jane saw the bird's individual feathers. She wheeled the lenses toward Tarrant's office, curious. But she could make out only a snippet of curtain, a fraction of a window. Where was Isabel going with this?

Jane handed the binoculars back. "Okay," she said. Her phone pinged, a text. At this hour? *Jake. It must be.* "'Scuse me," she said. She grabbed her phone, checked it. Kat? Why would the medical examiner be texting her? She read the message, and her eyes began filling with tears.

"Jane?"

Jane's knees were not working. Nor was her brain. But there was nothing she could do, nothing, and right here right now could not be avoided. Poor D. Poor Kat. Poor Jake.

"Jane?" Isabel persisted. "Look again. You see Colonial Hall, right? Tarrant's building? Then the coffee shop, Java Jim's. On the other side is Endicott Library. See?"

Where Jane and Fee had met with SAFE. "Yes," Jane said.

She tried to focus, tried to be patient. Isabel had asked her to come over, and at seven in the morning, it wasn't for chitchat. Jane longed to race to the hospital, but first she had to hear this. Nothing she could do there, anyway. Nothing but be with her Jake.

"So, Jane," Isabel was saying. The rising sun glinted through a little crystal suspended on an almost-invisible wire, rainbowing the girl's face. "Thing is. I watch out the window all the time. But I am not simply . . . looking. I watch for the man who raped me. And I see him. All the time. And I keep track. Where he is. How long he stays."

Jane scratched the side of her nose, watching the shifting prism of colors.

"Why?" was all she could think of to ask. *Poor D.*

"To stay alive," Isabel said. "To have . . . power, I guess. Because he would hate it, and I hate him, and it makes me feel like God."

If Jane could have heard the fish swimming, she wouldn't have been surprised.

"I know you don't want to hear it." Isabel's voice grew stronger, each word with an edge. "But the man who raped me is Trey Welliver."

"Isa—" Jane's mouth opened, her brain trying to catch up, but failing. "You—"

"Look at this calendar," Isabel interrupted. "See the red dots? And notations? I know where he was, exactly, between two and four on Monday. In fact, the entire time between one and five. At the library, and Java Jim's. Trey Welliver could *not* have been at Avery Morgan's house."

"You're saying . . ." Jane's brain went to warp speed. She had to tell Jake. The boundaries of their jobs didn't matter. Not in a situation like this. ". . . they arrested an innocent man."

"No question," Isabel said. "I saw everything."

51

JAKE BROGAN

Jake's cell phone buzzed in his pocket, an insistent burr that might have awakened him, might have, except he certainly wasn't asleep, would not have fallen asleep.

He blinked, trying to ground himself in time and place. Hospital. *DeLuca.* He needed to call Jane. His eyes flared open, and he scanned the corridor to the left, the right, and then left again.

What?

He stood, inch by inch, understanding this wasn't a dream. His mind, groggy and exhausted, struggled to make sense of it. Hospital bells pinged. An unintelligible voice squawked over the PA system, then stopped.

"Hello, Detective Brogan," Jane was saying. Ten steps away now, holding her cell. And not alone. His cop's brain catalogued the woman with her. White female, approx. 20, dark hair. Who? Why?

"Hello, Ms. Ryland." Jake, taking Jane's cue, played along with using their public personas. His phone stopped buzzing as she put hers away. He understood why she was here, but who was with her?

"How's Detective DeLuca?" Jane asked.

He could see her eyes narrow, read the sorrow in them, understood that Jane—*he adored her*—was trying to transmit her concern.

"Hanging in. Last I heard. They just took him upstairs, some specialist." Jake cleared his throat. "Did you . . . hear about it from the medical examiner?"

Jane nodded. "Half an hour ago."

"I didn't want to wake—"

"It's okay," Jane said.

This was impossible, an impossible situation. He wanted to throw his arms around Jane, break into tears, have her comfort him—damn it, it was D. Now he had to pretend, because of whoever this girl was, that he hardly knew her.

"Um, Ja—Detective Brogan?" Jane was saying. "I apologize for doing this now. Forgive me, but it's important. Is it true you arrested Trey Welliver in the Avery Morgan case?"

"Why?" *Welliver?* Had the kid's parents called the television station? Or had his lawyer blown the whistle? Could people never shut up?

"I know." Jane looked apologetic, waved her hand toward the hospital ward. "The ME told me the whole thing, and I am so, so sorry. But this is—" She turned to the girl.

"Yes," the girl whispered. Looked like she was about to cry. "I'll tell him."

What the hell?

"This is Isabel Russo," Jane said, putting her arm across the young woman's shoulders. "She goes to Adams Bay. She's an acquaintance of Trey Welliver. And at the time you think Avery Morgan was killed at her home . . . well, she knows Trey Welliver could not have been there."

A wail of a siren ripped through the silence. A blast of sounds, a chaos of noise, more sirens, and a battery of claxons. Jake's phone buzzed in his pocket, red lights flashed in the hallway. Footsteps, running, white coats.

"Code red code red code red," an automated voice blasted through the tinny speakers. "One two three," the robo-voice announced. "One two three."

Jake drew his Glock. One two three. Code for active shooter.

"Get down," Jake commanded. "Under that bench, both of you."

Two more white coats ran by. Direction of D's room. Doors slammed down the corridor like gunshots. "No. Into that closet." He slammed the flat metal plate that opened the solid-looking metal door. "Do not come out till I tell you."

He saw the look in Jane's eyes, read it, chilled, but there was nothing else to do or say.

"Shut that door!" He slammed his body at it, closed them inside. He could just make out Jane's face through a rectangular sliver of wire-meshed window. "Stay *down!*"

52

WILLOW GALT

"Maybe it's good that they're not calling you back," Willow said.

From her seat at their kitchen table, Tom across from her, Willow could see the tiny path where Avery had pushed through the bushes on that first day. Poor Avery. "Maybe the police have solved it. Without us."

Willow hoped against hope this was true. After Olive's phone call earlier this morning, Tom had changed his mind about keeping things secret. They'd decided, together, that they'd face the world, or at least the police, together. And the consequences. Even if they had to start another new life. Secretly she also hoped that if she spoke up, if she told the truth and made the world right, the universe would forgive her. Leave her alone. Leave *them* alone.

"We'll wait," Tom said. "It's only seven-thirty in the morning. Maybe it's not their shift. Maybe they don't care. They're cops, after all."

Willow watched the steam curling from her white mug of coffee, felt Tom's leg touch hers under the checked tablecloth. Morning was special in The Reserve, with a gently filtered light. Maybe the peace and solitude they'd longed for would follow. Tom had said the right thing, done the honorable thing, in California, told the feds about the financial house of cards at Untitled constructed by the embezzling Roger Hayden. They'd been moved three thousand miles in witness protection because of it.

Now it was her turn. She had witnessed Avery Morgan's murder—she guessed you could call it "murder." She would say the right thing, too. If she had to.

And if she needed proof that the world was a calculus of irony? Last night their handler, Olive Brennis, had called Tom, telling him Detective Brogan had left her a message saying her informant was dead. Until Willow called her, Olive—and briefly, Tom—had assumed the detective meant Willow.

Olive had called the Galts again, half an hour ago, having followed up on the detective's call. "I get it now," Olive had said. "Brogan probably meant *Avery Morgan,* can you believe it? Because of her Untitled connection, apparently he thought *she* was the informant. Close," she'd scoffed, "but no cigar."

The feds were now calculating how much they could say to set Brogan straight.

"Tom," she began.

"Willow," he said at the same time, and that's because they loved each other, and why the world would work.

"When I thought about you being dead," Tom went on, stirring his coffee, "I understood how much I loved you, what you gave up for me. For us. And no matter what happened in the past, I knew you'd forgive me. But part of me worried. That you wouldn't."

"There's nothing to worry about." Willow felt her heart melt. She loved him, too, and there was nothing he could say or do that would ever change that.

"Here's the thing. I knew Avery, in California. Uh, pretty well. Before you came," Tom said. "She was a freelancer at Untitled. But she probably didn't tell you that, right, as Willow? It was like working at Enron, or some disgraced corporation—everyone touched by it tried to erase it from their past. When you told me her name . . . well, I didn't want to tell you. But when she was drowned . . ." He pressed his lips together, closed his eyes briefly.

"Roger Hayden," Willow whispered. "I *told* you, from the beginning. . . ."

Tom nodded. "I know. I know. I started thinking, though. He's the only person who could know that she was here and we were here. And God knows what he might have said or concocted or lied about. I mean, you and I had been here for a month before she arrived. What if there was more to it? Maybe Hayden had arranged it. Then *sent* Avery himself! To threaten us! And when he ratted us out, the police would put two and two together and might blame *me* for Avery's death, figure that I was trying to keep her quiet."

Willow frowned, remembering. It couldn't have been Tom she'd seen at the pool that morning. "But—"

"Let me finish. That's why I never wanted to 'meet' Avery. What if she recognized me? You insisted you hadn't seen anyone at the pool, so you couldn't say it *wasn't* me. I'd been walking on the Common, so I had no great alibi. Once the police suspected me, questioned me, our life would be over. For real, this time. Last night Olive told me you were running, and part of me was . . . relieved. But I had to go to the police, because what if they discovered you were missing? And I hadn't reported it? When you finally came home last night, I truly believed you were Hayden. I was ready for *him*."

Tom, her dear strong Tom, was more paranoid than she was—and *she'd* ridiculously decided the crosswalk man was a blue-blazered assassin. She almost laughed, but nothing was funny. Tom was in anguish. Exactly as she had been. "But you didn't do it! They'd never have convicted you."

"Of course I didn't. But convict an innocent man? It's happened. Way too often."

Willow saw her husband sigh, then he stood, putting his hands on her bare shoulders. "I was terrified," he said. "That's why I didn't want you to say anything. If you had told me the truth, from the beginning, about what you saw, we could have—"

"But I couldn't! I was worried about you!" She leaned into his soft, strong chest, her words muffled in his still-pristine new white T-shirt. "What would happen if I told, and they found out who we were?"

53

EDWARD TARRANT

Eight-thirty now, Adams Bay would be coming to life. Certainly the press would arrive on news of Trey, and the spinning that came so naturally to Edward Tarrant would be under way. He'd manage, with eloquent sorrow and oh-so-deeply-felt regret. Avery's murder was "solved," thanks to Sasha's quick thinking, and as she'd explained, in the after-hours conversation that bound her to him forever, it wasn't really murder.

So now there was nothing but smooth sailing ahead. Trey was out of the picture one way or the other, Brinn would never know about Avery, he and Sasha were protected by mutually assured destruction, and all was right with the world.

What Sasha Vogelby wanted with him—some "future"—that was yet to wrangle. But he could keep her quiet, too. No matter what he had to do.

Edward swirled the last of the amber oolong in the delicate china cup, the scrolled handle almost too small for his hands, but he used it almost as a tribute. Part of a gift from a grateful family, a *bequest,* given in gratitude for his compassionate advice about the delicate situation in which their daughter had entangled herself. It had come with a check, made out to "Cash." Which it soon had become. Off the books.

"You make your own bed," Edward said out loud, to no one, taking the last exotic sip, the comforting morning silence of his office, his second home, surrounding him. He'd come in early, putting off the clingy and questioning Brinn, pleading the complicated "firefighting" that was certain to come. Those cops, reliably morons, had arrested Trey Welliver. Had to

"I was worried about *you*," Tom said. "If they accuse couldn't prove it wasn't me, what would happen to you, and—

"Shhhh," Willow whispered. The scrapbook was safely h still accessible to them, just like their pasts. "We'll tell the trut on with our lives, and never keep anything from each other aga admit, Sasha's idea was delightfully clever. Trey was guilty of rape, of that Tarrant was certain—the idiot boy had bragged about it. If Tarrant had turned him over to authorities for *that* last May, his punishment would not have been much less harsh than it would be now. Trey was guilty, so who cared guilty of precisely what?

He heard the door to the outer office open. Must be Manderley, here early for once. She'd be gone when the fall semester started next week, and he'd hardly miss her. She probably would want a recommendation. Pretty enough girl, but no commitment. No spark. *Pity.*

His intercom buzzed. "Mr. Tarrant?"

Who else would it have been? "Yes?"

"May I speak with you, briefly?"

"Come," he said. The recommendation, no doubt.

Edward stood, went to his casement window, the double tall panes sliding open to the summer morning. He let the air conditioner continue to hum, a waste, he supposed, but the school could afford it, and there was nothing like the glorious hubbub of Kenmore Square waking up, the sunshine on his face, this window, higher than some of the treetops, the scurrying colors of the pedestrians below.

The office door opened. Manderley. And—he narrowed his eyes—another student, a girl. And another one. Elaine something, maybe.

"Mr. Tarrant," Manderley began.

"Ah. Do you all have an appointment?" Tarrant was certain they didn't. There were, what, four of them now? Girls, Manderley fronting a trio of others, Elaine, that was right, then a skinny black girl in a Yale sweatshirt, and a wacko with pink hair. He remembered her now, too, Rochelle, or Michelle. Rochelle.

"We don't exactly," Manderley was saying. She'd stepped into his office, the others following her, and they stood, in a row, facing him.

What was this?

"Do you remember me?" *Rochelle.*

She better not have decided to go public with her "case," he thought. Her parents had been particularly kind.

"To what do I owe the—"

"I said—do you remember me?"

"Or me?" This one was Elaine, he was fairly certain.

"Please take a seat," Tarrant said, stalling. If he went behind his desk it would give him more of the power position, but it didn't seem appropriate to move. It might seem weak, as if he were barricading himself from them. An edge of floor-length linen curtain caught in a sudden breeze, nudged him, and he stepped away from the window.

"You're . . ." He tried to look sheepish. Held out his hands, so apologetic. "Forgive me, so many students want—"

"We've come to chat with you," Manderley actually interrupted him. "About what you're doing to us."

"To the women who relied on you. Who trusted you."

"We came to you." *Elaine. Right.* "When we were raped."

He gasped at the word. It sounded so harsh.

"Raped," Yale sweatshirt repeated. "I was eighteen years old. I will never, ever, ever be the same. And you—"

"Covered it the hell up." Rochelle again.

"And we are going to tell." Manderley took a step closer to him, and he backed up a bit, had to. His phone was on his desk, but no need to call security, what could these silly girls do? Let them talk it out. He could handle it.

"Moreover, we know about the others." Manderley pulled out a notebook, flipped it open. "I listened to every one of your phone conversations this summer. Every one," she said. "And Sarah—you remember Sarah? Your last semester's assistant. She listened, too. Starting in May. When Trey Welliver bragged to you what he'd done to poor Isabel Russo. We know *she* told you, too. But what did you do? Nothing. Nothing. Nothing."

"Listened to my conversations?" Edward tried to process this, remember what he'd said. And to whom. Although he knew full well, knew every parent and every student, every word. Every result. Not only assaults, but how many harassments, drug deals, illicit pill sales, shopliftings, and dorm thefts had he smoothed over this year? Seven? Eight? More? Still. The *audacity.* "How dare you!"

With one swift motion, he'd done it: grabbed the notebook out of Manderley's hand and flung it, with one wide sweep of his arm, out the window. The girls pushed forward, watched the pages of the spiral notebook flap and flutter, sixteen stories down, to the sidewalk below.

"Thank you, Mr. Tarrant." Manderley had not moved. She stood, hands on hips, smiling.

Smiling?

"Because, Mr. Tarrant, that one action proves you are guilty, proves you are complicit, proves you—"

"Are the biggest asshole in the history of the planet," Elaine said.

"And, Mr. Tarrant," Manderley said. "First of all, that's not the real notebook. Don't you watch TV?"

Tarrant's guts were beginning to churn. His face . . . he could feel it reddening with a rush of blood and fear and the struggle to stay calm, stay in control. Fight this fire.

"Sit down, ladies." Tarrant gestured them to his chairs, his beautiful chairs, and wondered how this would all end. He'd handled more difficult things. Maybe.

"Screw you," pink-haired Rochelle said. "You're going to come clean. You're going to call the police. You're going to tell them all you know. We are not victims. Our friends aren't either. Not anymore."

"Agreed," he said. Okay, this could work, he would manage this. It was a negotiation. He'd negotiate. He felt his muscles relax a bit. There was light at the end. They'd never want their stories to go public. He'd use that. Use their fear of having to tell their pitiful stories to the entire world, to reporters, in open court. Use their secret fears of being branded damaged goods. That's why his plan had worked in the first place. Such humiliation would be unbearable. "Please, have a seat, and we'll talk like civilized people. Talk about what's best for you."

The girls did not sit. Did not move.

"And to be clear, Mr. Tarrant." Manderley was not as pretty as he'd once thought. "I mean I have listened to *all* your phone calls. I know about Avery Morgan. What you did, the two of you. Where you were. Where your wife thought you were. Where your father-in-law thought you were."

"Tell the rest, Man," Yale said.

"And of course the . . ." Manderley gestured at the room, her motion taking in the rug, and the china, the books, his pen, his shoes. His sport coat carefully hanging on its molded mahogany rack. "The money. The gifts. From grateful parents."

"Like mine."

"Like mine."

"Like mine."

Each voice, a bullet.

"Does your father-in-law know about *that*?" Manderley asked. "He's our next visit, by the way."

"No," Tarrant said. "Stop. Don't do that."

"No? Stop?" Manderley laughed. "Oh, please."

"You mean it, don't you? Because when you say no, the other person is supposed to stop, *aren't* they?" Rochelle's smile was a sneer. "But sometimes, guess what. They fricking don't."

"Unless . . ." Elaine held up a cell phone, as if offering it to him to make a call. "Unless you can come up with a better solution."

These bitches. These little fucking bitches were not going to ruin his—no. It didn't matter. He could handle them. He could deal with this. They were teenagers. *Students.* He was the *dean* of goddamned students. And they'd better get out of his office.

"After that, we have an appointment with your wife." Manderley again. "Trey Welliver wasn't the only one taking photos at Professor Morgan's party."

"You little—" He took a step forward. He could take them all. His fists clenched. "If you don't—"

"Oh dear."

Manderley actually laughed. *Laughed at him!*

"More violence on campus." She turned to the others. "Interesting reaction, don't you think? Did you get that, Elaine?"

She held up her cell phone again. "Rolling and recording," Elaine said. "I got it all. When he told us 'No,' and 'Stop,' that was my favorite part. So far."

"Or maybe we should just call your wife from here?" Manderley said. "I have her private number. Should we do that?"

His head throbbed, and his arm throbbed, and maybe he was having a heart attack? But no such luck—it would have made everything so much easier—but no, he was enraged, and furious, and fuming, but alive, and backed against the wall. There was no way out. Brinn, and his father-in-law, and the humiliation, and the headlines, and the wrath of the entire . . .

He blinked, looking at the finally silent line of attacking girls, thinking about what they knew, and what they planned, and what was inevitable. But he could still fix it.

"Will you give me until this afternoon?" he said. "Say, three? And then . . . I'll be in touch."

The four exchanged glances. A raised eyebrow. A shrug.

"Whatever," Elaine said.

"Sure," Manderley said. "And, Mr. Tarrant? I have my video with me. And there are copies."

The door closed behind them.

Tarrant was alone. Alone.

He turned, and without a look back and without another word, his decision was made and done and there was no other way. He felt the brush of the filmy curtain and the grit of the wrought-iron balcony railing, looked down, down, down, and saw Manderley's spiral notebook, its pages flapped by the unseen hand of a curious breeze. He felt the humid morning air and the last of the summer sun, and height, and space, and a touch of wind.

54

JANE RYLAND

"It could be a false alarm." Jane kept her voice low. Out in the corridor, bells and alarms still clanged.

"One two three. One two three." The robo-voice broadcast repeated the meaningless words in its unnervingly neutral tone. "One two three."

Isabel crouched beside her in the narrow dark confines of what seemed a linen closet. The tiny room smelled of bleach and lemon soap. Folds of terry cloth and cotton pressed against Jane's bare arms. The lights were off, but the door wouldn't lock.

"One two three," was all she heard on the hospital's loudspeakers, some sort of code, obviously, but Jane had no idea what it meant. Certainly something not good—that she knew from Jake's drawn weapon and his barked command for the two of them to hide. She knew it, too, from the anguish on his face.

"Really, this stuff happens all the time," she lied. Might as well try to reassure Isabel. Poor thing. "I'm in news, you know? It's hardly ever anything."

"Can you see out?" Isabel whispered. "Is anyone there?"

Jane inched up, flattening herself against the pitted metal of the door until she could peer through the tiny window. She felt around inside her tote bag for her cell phone. If she couldn't see out, maybe someone on the outside could tell them what was going on. Plus, whatever the outcome, as a reporter she had to call the assignment desk. Let them know something was up at BCH. She tried to envision herself reporting the story, whatever it was, not someone else reporting her and Isabel as tragic victims of it.

But the sliver of glass in the door was frustratingly narrow. She thought she could see white coats racing by, but when she tried to follow the action, the blur of whatever it was continued out of range. She had an inch, that was all, and all she could see was nothing.

She blew out a breath, sank to the floor again. Hit speed dial. "Nothing," she said, as the phone rang on the other end. "We'll be fine, though, I'm sure." She smiled, trying to convince herself as well as Isabel. "Probably a mistake, or some sort of drill." She gestured in the almost-darkness. "And I have almonds in my purse. So we won't die."

As long as it's not anthrax or a bomb, or terrorists, she didn't say. The Channel 2 assignment desk phone was still ringing. Why didn't someone answer? The morning news was certainly on the air. But the desk coverage was notorious—the chatty desk assistants always went for coffee at the same time.

"Jane?" Isabel's voice fell even softer, barely audible.

"Hang on, I'm calling the station." Jane put a confident smile in her voice, all intrepid reporter. "They'll know more than we do."

"I guess," Isabel whispered.

"News 2." *At last.*

"It's Ryland. Jane. Who's this? You got anything going at BCH?" She draped one arm across Isabel's shoulder, both of them sitting on the floor, knees to chest, backs against a metal shelf of folded linens. Hot in here now, stifling, but the least of her worries.

"It's Wu, noon producer," the voice said. "Going on? Like what?"

Jane bullet-pointed the whole thing: alarm, code, running white coats, closet. Wu was a veteran, thank goodness. He'd figure it out. At least they'd know where she was. Fiola would freak, but she'd get over it.

"Wanna go live?" Wu asked. "You're breaking news, and exclusive. *Awesome.* We'll patch your call through to the control room, do the whole thing as a live news phoner."

Go live? From the closet? In the dark? With no information on an unknown incident that could turn out to be nothing? Hardly "awesome." But Jane heard the news-lust in Wu's voice. Welcome to local TV.

"Can you find out what's going on first?" Jane asked. "We—" She stopped. No need to mention she was with an Adams Bay student. "I can't see anything. I don't know anything. That wouldn't be much of a story. Right?"

"Don't hang up," Wu ordered. "I'll get Marsh. He'll decide. We got BCH PR on the line, and she's talking. We're sending a crew, but it's gonna take twenty to get there. Probably longer. If it's something, you're all we got. Hang on. Don't move."

"But—" *Don't move?* She shifted in a vain attempt to keep her already-prickling legs from falling asleep. *As if.*

"Jane?" Isabel's fingers encircled Jane's arm, clutching.

"It's okay," Jane said. "They know we're here. Detective Brogan knows, too. Cops on the way, press on the way, a metal door between us and the outside world. It's all good."

"Sending you a photo." Wu's voice in her ear.

"Of what?" Jane asked.

"Hostage situation, active shooter, so says hospital PR," Wu said. "And it's 'of who.' One guy. We're sending you a picture of the apparent shooter. And 'who' is exactly what we're trying to find out."

55

JAKE BROGAN

Shooter? Hostage? Jake had holstered his weapon, raced full speed down the deserted hospital corridor, caught up with two lumbering BCH rent-a-guards, flapped open his badge wallet. "I'm Jake Brogan, BPD," he raised his voice over the alarms. "Tell me."

The guards explained, pantomiming the two words—*"shooter,"* *"hostage"*—then jabbed their forefingers down the hall, where a line of closed doors could have concealed any number of bad guys. And victims. D'd be bummed to miss this. He was still up in some exam room. At least he was safe. From this.

"Hostage? Shooter?" Jake had said the words out loud, grabbing one black-uniformed arm, stopping them both. "How'd you find out? Who? Where? How many people? What's the plan?"

"Plan is, we go code black," the shorter one said. "Total containment. Doors all on lockdown. Nobody moves. We do nothing. We wait for the big guns. We called SWAT. Hostage Rescue Team. Everyone."

"How'd you find out?" Jake needed to strategize. Make a plan. He fingered his radio. HRT should have called him, back channel, looped him in. But they didn't know he was here. He felt like "We do nothing" was not the best idea.

"Guy was messing with a patient's IV, a nurse came in, caught him, he pulled a gun, she ran, bat out of hell, pushed the big red button. He slammed the door, they're inside. They've got security video of the bad guy entering the hospital, nurse ID'd the guy."

"And now? What room? Where's the cavalry?"

"En route," the tall guard said. "We're supposed to wait."

"One guy?" No reason for Jake to go be the hero. Except that was his job.

"Yeah, so says the nurse," Short said. He waved a .38 down the empty hall. All doors stayed shut. "Shouldn't we—"

"What room?" Problem was, the gunman and one hostage were trapped there. There was no way out for the bad guy. And that might trigger the worst possible situation. But there hadn't been a shot, and sometimes it was worse to make a move, to panic a situation into a crisis.

No way to know what was going on inside the room. No way to find out except to go look. If he called HQ, they'd tell him to wait for HRT. That was by-the-book for hostage sits. Where the hell were they? "What room?"

"Four-two-two," Tall said.

422? It took Jake's brain a fraction of a second to connect.

Grady.

Grady, who'd told Jake, three days ago, he was afraid of what Sholto's people would do to him. Since then Sholto's wife had been murdered, Grady'd been injured in a hit-and-run, and now a guy with a gun had the kid in his hospital room. What Grady feared had hit the fan, and it was Jake's fault. He should have protected him. But now he had a chance to make up for it.

"I'm going in," Jake said. He drew his Glock again. Grady. Damn it. "Back me up."

"But we're supposed to wait for HRT." Tall exchanged worried glances with his partner. "I'm not sure we should—"

"I'll take responsibility," Jake cut him off. No time to negotiate. "Stay quiet. And no shooting."

"But what if—?"

"Unless *I* shoot." Jake gestured, pointed the tip of his weapon down the hall. "I know the hostage. I'll do the talking. You in?"

JANE RYLAND

"You seeing it?" Wu asked. "That's from the surveillance vid the BCH PR flack just sent us."

"Yeah." Jane narrowed her eyes at the grainy blur on her tiny screen. She'd recognize the guy—sure, if he were made of sand. "Wu, seriously. This is a still photo from a video, right? Can you send me the whole thing instead? This is like a snapshot from Mars."

"Yeah, whatever," Wu said. "It's mostly so we have pictures to put on TV, more than just generic hospital exteriors. Plus, some viewer might recognize the guy."

"No way." She aimed the screen at Isabel. Maybe including the young woman in the process might distract her. "Look at this. Can you possibly see a face? I can't, that's for sure."

"Video coming to you now," Wu said. "Gonna take a sec to download."

The smell of bleach was about to suffocate her, but at least the danger was contained. Not a masked gang, not biological weapons, not whatever other disasters Jane's brain had concocted. Only one horrible guy, for some horrible reason, making everyone terrified. Terrorist, Jane thought. No matter what.

"They're sending me a video, Isabel," Jane explained. "Of the bad guy. The police certainly have it, too, and they know exactly where he is. So this is about to end. And we're fine. It's—"

"I know," Isabel said. "I can hear whoever you're talking to."

So much for trying to protect her, Jane thought. A message pinged on her phone. *Your video is ready.*

"Jane?" Wu's voice. "You'll voice-over that surveillance video, we'll roll it when we patch you in. But look at it first, so you know what to say on air. Let us know when you're ready. You got it?"

"Got it," Jane said. "But I have to hang up before I can watch it."

"Listen, we got the vic's name," Wu said. "PR went crazy because of

HIPAA, but heck, it's a hostage. We're not using it, okay? Till it's over. But we're tracking him down. Don't even say we have it, PR'll get nailed for telling us."

"Who is it?" Jane asked. She needed to see the video, but a name was a big get. The HIPAA privacy laws protecting hospital patients' identities were stringent. Amazing they'd revealed this.

"Grady McWhirter Houlihan," Wu said. "Welcome to Boston."

"Jane!" Isabel had shifted, was now on her knees. Even in the gloom, Jane could see the look on her face.

"What?" Jane had to see the video. If she were going live, she needed something to talk about. Isabel'd have to chill, just until Jane got off the air. A live shot from a linen closet with a shooter holding a hostage down the hall. Had to be a first.

"I might know him," Isabel said.

"Know who?" Had Isabel recognized the person in the grainy photo?

"Grady," Isabel said.

56

JAKE BROGAN

"Noonan? You copy?"

Tall's—Noonan's—hip-slung two-way radio squawked just as Jake was about to lead the two hospital guards toward room 422. To Grady, right now being held at gunpoint. Maybe. They had no idea what was happening. And the clock was ticking. Though that might be a good thing.

"You standing by?" the guard's radio asked.

"Ten-four," Noonan answered, looking at Jake, acknowledging his lie. "Me and Palmeri."

"There's video of the shooter," the radio voice went on. "We're trying for ID. Continue to stand by. HRT arrives in five. Over."

Jake's phone buzzed. Then, with a blast of static, his own radio clicked on. They had him.

"Detective Brogan, this is BPD dispatch. What's your location?"

His phone buzzed again.

"Detective Brogan?" dispatch persisted. "You copy?"

Crap. Noonan and his partner Palmeri fidgeted, their eyes darting toward 422, then back to the elevators.

"We should wait," Noonan said.

"Screw that." Palmeri lifted his weapon. "Brogan says we go."

"This is Brogan." Jake shook his head. *No way out of this.* Keyed his radio. "At BCH. I'm aware of the situation. I have a—" He looked at the two guards, unabashedly listening to everything he said. They could not find out Grady was an informant—it'd kill the kid's cover. "I have a known hostage. I'm going in."

Jake's phone rang again. *Kidding me?* "Are you contacting me by phone, too, dispatch?"

"Negative," dispatch said. "Supe says stand by. Do not move. Do not take action. HRT arriving in less than two."

"You're breaking up," Jake said. "Reception's no . . ." He paused, clicking the transmit button a few times. ". . . you anymore."

He clicked off his radio, and with that, accepted the inevitable consequences and the unavoidable repercussions of disobeying orders. So what. Grady, who he'd promised to protect, needed protection. Jake was the only one who could provide it.

"Let's—" he began, and then his phone rang again. Jane. She'd better not have left that closet.

He answered. Probably another terrible decision, his better judgment buried by responsibility. And guilt. *His* fault she was in this mess, too.

"You okay?" He needed to be sure.

"It's Grady," Jane was saying. "The hostage. *Your* Grady."

"I know," Jake said. "How the hell do *you* know?"

"From Isabel. And, Jake?"

He heard something in her voice. Hesitation. Fear? He had to hang up, but what if he never saw her again?

"I love you," he said.

"I know, and ditto. But listen, Jake?" she said.

The phone went static, crackled, went silent. The buzz of connection returned.

"Jane? What?"

"Jake? Did you hear me?" she said. "I know who the shooter is, too."

JANE RYLAND

Grady. Grady Houlihan. The confidential informant Jake had told her about, the one she'd warned him to be careful of. Bad enough he was the BCH hostage. But that wasn't even the whole story. What had churned her stomach even more . . . When the surveillance video had finally downloaded, Jane had recognized the intruder.

Baby face. The guy who'd confessed to the hit-and-run. The one McCusker linked to the Sholto crew. She'd promised not to discuss it, but Jake needed to know. She could not, under any circumstances, allow him to walk cluelessly into a life-and-death face-off with a member of the ruthless Sholto organization because of an agreement she made with the DA. This very moment proved exactly why lines should never be crossed.

Now she *had* to cross. Phoning a cop who was on the trail of a hostage-taker had been a ridiculous move, but her only other option was to open the closet door, go out, find him, somehow, and tell him in person.

Now she could hear the tension in his voice. *I love you,* he'd said. As if it might be the last time.

"The shooter is Rourke Devane, he's twenty-five, twenty-six or so," Jane went on. "A Sholto lackey."

"How do you know *that*?"

"Too long to explain," she said. "Trust me."

"Are you still in the closet? With that girl? Do not come out, Jane, either of you. This is about to go down."

"Yeah." She nudged Isabel, who Jane knew had heard it all, including "I love you" and "about to go down." She smiled at her—*We're in this together*—but the girl did not smile back. "We're safely here," she told Jake. "Behind closed door." No need to mention she was about to broadcast live.

"Do not move," Jake told her. And clicked off.

U all set? The text from Wu pinged on her phone. *We got a 2:30 commercial break, Marsh sez go after that. Anchor intros u, u take it. Open-ended. Calling u now.*

Jane, huddled in the dim bleach-stench of the closet, pictured what was about to happen. Thought about her live broadcast, from Jake's point of view. What if the TV was on in Grady's room? What if the shooter was watching? What if her live broadcast put Jake in danger? And Grady?

It was a jaw-droppingly bad idea.

She certainly couldn't report that cops were in the hallway, or that something was "about to go down." Might her broadcast make a terrible situation even worse? Her worlds were colliding. Was there any way to stop it?

Her phone rang.

It was her job to report breaking news. That's what kept local TV stations in business. It would warn people away from BCH, and allow those now cowering inside to have some inkling, however murky, of what was going on in their building. So yeah, there was value in what she'd been told to say. But that wasn't the whole story. Even for a reporter, sometimes it was better to say nothing.

The phone rang again.

"Ryland."

"Connecting you to control," Wu said. "Stand by. You're on in two."

57

JAKE BROGAN

Nothing to do but go.

Striding down the hospital's green-tiled corridor, Noonan and Palmeri behind him, Jake reset the event-timer in his head. Forty seconds away. Thirty.

What would they find behind the closed door of room 422, barely half a hallway in front of them? HRT was on the way. If those guys got here first, fine. But this thing—Grady at gunpoint?—had gone on long enough.

He turned, checking on his new colleagues. Noonan gave him a thumbs-up, Palmeri a nod. Both had guns drawn. Jake did, too.

Twenty seconds.

Had Grady Houlihan murdered Violet Sholto? Or could he finger the killer? Was that why a Sholto operative was in his room right now? Had they attempted to silence Grady with the Gormay hit-and-run—and when that failed, sent a shooter to make the hit?

It made sense, in the underworld's perverted brand of justice. But if that was the case, why was there no shooting?

Maybe something else was going on. Maybe once a rat, always a rat. Maybe Grady had turned on the cops. Had the nurse specified *which* man had the gun?

He softened his footsteps as he approached the hostage room door. Signaled to the others, *Quiet.* They nodded, hanging back. Like him, they were disobeying orders, and if the three of them blew this operation, it would be a career-ending disaster. Might be anyway. Insubordination. Disobeying orders. Frowned on.

Jake held up a palm as they reached the door. Cocked his head, finger to his lips, signaling the guards to stand by. He flattened himself against the pale green wall beside room 422, the raised numbers pressing into his back. Listened, hard as he could. Nothing. No voices. No TV. Not even the beeps of the monitors Jake knew had kept track of Grady's vitals.

What if the shooter needed no weapon other than pulling a plug? Or using a pillow? And that's why it was so quiet?

Still, Rourke Devane, if Jane had it right, must still be inside that room. With a gun. What would he do when Jake broke down the door? If Grady was dead, Jake would blast the hell out of the shooter if he had to.

If Grady was alive, and a murderer, screw him. But if he was alive, and was a hostage whose identity as an informant was a certain death sentence, then Jake needed to save him.

Screw him? Or save him?

Jake hit on a plan. Either way, he'd have his answers soon enough.

Door opened in. *Good.* Assess for the weak spot? *Under the doorknob.* He stepped back, planted his weight on his back foot. Ready to smash the door with his heel. Took a deep breath.

"Doors don't lock," Noonan whispered. "It's a hospital."

Shit. In one swift motion, Jake grabbed the doorknob, twisted, swept open the door. Felt Noonan and Palmeri right behind him. And finally, down the hall, the drumbeat of pounding footsteps.

Grady in the bed. Kid in the chair beside him. No gun. Why?

Jake hit his stance, arms stretched in a V, weapon pointed dead ahead.

"Nobody move," Jake ordered. The footsteps—now accompanied by clamoring voices, bellowing commands, and squawking radios—were right behind him.

Now or never.

"Grady Houlihan," Jake said, aiming. Then broke every rule in the book. "You're under arrest for the murder of Violet Sholto."

JANE RYLAND

"Thirty seconds," the director's voice cued her over the phone. Jane, still crouched in the darkness, both legs asleep and Isabel beside her, had considered pretending her phone's battery was dying, considered pretending they had a bad connection, considered simply hanging up and pretending to be baffled about whatever had happened to ruin the live shot.

But she couldn't do it.

"Sorry, Isabel," Jane said. "It'll be a good tale for you to tell later, won't it?" Might as well make the best of it for poor Isabel, who was here only because Jane had insisted—well, suggested—that the right thing to do was to tell Detective Brogan herself, in person, how she knew Trey Welliver was not a murderer. As a result, Isabel had wound up in a storage closet, fearing for her life. She'd have been better off staying in her little apartment. The young woman was right about one thing—the outside world could be a dangerous place.

"Twenty." In her ear.

"I'm on in twenty seconds," Jane whispered. "Keep quiet, okay? No need for anyone to know you're here."

"Okay, yeah. I can hear the guy on the phone," Isabel said.

There was no way out now, not one that wouldn't get Jane fired. She was a pro, and she'd been assigned to do a live report, exclusive, big-time breaking news, from her hiding place during a hostage standoff in a major metropolitan hospital. It was the stuff careers were made of.

Tears came to her eyes, like this was some sort of turning point, or precipice, but she couldn't decide which way to turn or whether to jump. She hoped with all her being that she wasn't putting Jake in more danger. She'd never look at television the same way again. It could be a joy, providing a platform for the good she and Fiola would do with their documentary, revealing the ugly truth about college crime and exposing a tragic campus-wide reality.

TV could also suck. Like it did right now.

"Ten."

The light changed. Air rushed in, and the door swung open. Black-uniformed men, she had no idea who, reached in, pulling her and Isabel to their feet.

"Get out now," one ordered. "We're HRT. Front door. Go."

Jane, unsteady on her cramping legs, stumbled to her almost-numb feet. Turned to Isabel, who cowered against the linen-stacked shelves, eyes wide.

"Jane!"

"They're okay," Jane reassured her. "Hostage Rescue. That's us, sister—we are out of here." She extended her hand, and Isabel grabbed it. "You did great," Jane said. "You're brave as they come." Then into the phone, "Wu? Anyone? We've got to—"

"Get off that phone!" one uniform ordered. "Now!"

"Jane?" In her ear.

"Situation, Wu," she said. "Gotta go. They're taking us out. I'll call you soon as I can."

"But—"

A buzz-cut hulk in black, Velcroed with radios and blocky gadgets, snatched her phone. Clicked it. "I said *now.*"

He handed the now-powered-off phone back to her, one insistent hand clamped around her upper arm, propelling her forward. Jane's toes almost dragged over the floor tiles as she and Isabel were hustled toward the main entrance.

"Is it over?" Jane had to know, had to ask. He *had* to tell her.

"Yes," the officer said. "Ma'am. You both okay?"

They were halfway there. She saw daylight, and the relief on Isabel's face, and the whirl of blue lights through the expanse of wide glass doors. Jane tried to imprint the whole terrifying episode: the sounds, the fear, the uncertainty. This would be a story she could tell on the air. Soon she'd know every detail. But she needed to hear one thing right now.

"Yeah, but is anyone else hurt?" The guy didn't know she was a reporter—*good,* maybe he'd give her the scoop without making her call some public relations department.

"No injuries," the officer said.

"Were any police involved?" Jane tried to sound neutral. "What about the suspect? And the hostage?"

"Two in custody," the officer said. "And that's all I'm gonna say, Miz Ryland."

The glass door wheezed shut behind them, leaving Jane and Isabel alive, and free, and savoring the morning sunlight and shockingly fresh air.

58

WILLOW GALT

She wasn't imagining this. She wasn't. She clutched Tom's arm, moved even closer to him on the couch. They'd arrived at police headquarters, been sent here to the third floor, told to ask for Detectives Brogan and DeLuca. The same two who'd come to their house, Willow remembered. The girl at the desk was nice enough, informed them Detective Brogan would return soon, and would they wait?

Of course they would. Willow tried reading one of the *People* magazines on the scuffed and battered coffee table, trying to make the time go by faster, but too many pages had been ripped out for the articles to make sense, and the tattered ones that remained threatened to escape the weakened staples at the slightest touch.

But it was fine. They could wait. The couch, lumpy and unforgiving, was the only place they could sit together.

"It will all work out," Tom had told her. "We'll take it together, one step at a time. And." He kissed her on the top of her head, the way he always did. "Avery would be proud of you."

"Of *us*." She was doing the right thing, she was sure of it.

It seemed like hours they'd sat there, and a silly clock on the wall, unplugged, was no help. But Tom's watch proved it had been only fifteen minutes.

The outer door opened. Her heart leaped. It had to be Brogan, and soon this would all be over.

But it wasn't Brogan. It was the crosswalk man. The blue-blazered sidewalk man. The one she'd decided this morning was no one. *Wrong.*

She grabbed Tom's arm, wondering if everything she'd feared, *everything,* was true, and he'd followed her—them—here!

"Tom," she whispered. "That man."

But she couldn't say anything more. Not with him right there! But why would a bad guy—a hit man? an assassin?—come to the police station? It seemed impossible. Dangerous. Ridiculous.

She hadn't told Tom about him. Why should she, it was too silly. Now, she realized, maybe it wasn't silly.

"What?" Tom asked.

But there was nothing she could say. Not without that man hearing. Did she have a pencil and paper in her handbag? Maybe she could write a note.

Willow burrowed herself closer to Tom. The man barely gave them a glance. Nothing could happen to her inside this police station, anyway. She was safe. And once Detective Brogan came back they'd be even safer. So strange—she'd once hoped Brogan would leave her alone. Now she couldn't wait to see him.

The man approached the receptionist. "I'm here to see Detective Brogan," he said.

She and Tom exchanged glances. Tom smiled, took her hand. "This is Brogan's office," he whispered. "Where else would a person come?"

"I'm Edward Tarrant," the man said. "I know he'll want to see me. Tell him it's about Avery Morgan."

Willow couldn't stifle her gasp. She saw the look on Tom's face. Still, agonizingly, she couldn't explain anything to him. But there it was, and she was right, totally right, and maybe the man had only pretended not to recognize her. Maybe it was a code, what he'd said to the receptionist. She could not bear it, and what if . . .

It was all she could do not to cry, to break down completely and cry.

EDWARD TARRANT

"Any minute now" was long gone.

Edward paced, impatient, calculating, revising. Assessing. A youngish couple, inappropriately intertwined in each other, sat on the supposedly-brown couch of the waiting room outside the police homicide offices. Edward could not bear to sit. The risk he was about to take, the tightrope he was about to walk, made staying still impossible.

"Tarrant the supplicant" was hardly his usual role. He was used to people coming to *him*, after all. But this was necessary. If he was going to extinguish this particularly dangerous fire, he needed to make a big move.

And now, according to the dismissive receptionist, he was on hold. She'd given him a mere pretense of interest, a terse "Detective Brogan will be back any minute now if you care to wait?" then returned to her crossword puzzle. Where the other one was, DeLuca, she insisted she didn't know.

He steeled his temper, knowing this would only work with patience and skill. Playing the right cards at the right time. And maybe—a smile crossed his face—Avery Morgan would thank him for it. It was justice, after all. And wasn't that what he was all about?

Ten steps across the seedy beige carpet, wall to wall, and ten back the other way. He eyed the peeling wallpaper, some fading stripe, the brown patches of stains under the half-empty water cooler. The battered magazines splayed on the too-small coffee table. The black-framed clock on the wall, its frayed power cord unplugged from the greasy outlet. Time had stopped. He didn't need some appliance to tell him that.

The best part, which he'd figured out last night—Brinn breathing next to him, her scrawny little body taking up more than its share of space in the bed—was that in reality, he'd done nothing wrong. In his role as student advisor, he used his best judgment, drawn from his experience, offered solutions and long-term benefits. That's all. If any parents or students had wanted to pursue their complaints, he'd agreed.

He'd blinked at the pale gray bedroom ceiling, approving of his argument. And there was proof he was right. Some parents had complained, and those cases—one supposed assault, and a drug deal, or two or three—had proceeded through the system. Not quickly, but proceeded. He could point to those. There was no cover-up, or any persuasion, or any quid pro quo, or any other distasteful word. There was process. Conversation. And decisions made in the best interests of all.

He had never, ever, asked for anything.

He was blameless in every way. Why he had let those girls browbeat him . . . He shook his head, understanding his inescapable vulnerability. Avery. Their dalliance. *Fine.* Affair. Now he'd never been more aware of Brinn's existence. Her power. Her anger. Her father. That was his Achilles' heel. But one obstacle at a time.

He'd tossed that idiotic spiral notebook into the trash. It was already covered with the shoeprints and filth of uncaring pedestrians. He could hardly bear to touch it, but he'd gone downstairs to get it, and looked at it only long enough to seethe at the pages. He'd fallen for it, the silliest trap imaginable, choked by his fear.

Still pacing, he was aware that the couple on the couch, the woman at least, was talking about him. Hopefully they hadn't recognized him, though on second thought what if they had? He was a fine, upstanding citizen, and about to make a deal to prove it.

As soon as Detective Brogan returned.

Any minute now.

59

JANE RYLAND

"Isabel?" Jane knew her next request was a lot to ask, and she wouldn't be surprised if the poor girl never went outside again. But right now, in the rear parking lot of Boston City Hospital, a major league story was unfolding. The HRT guy had ordered them to "vacate the premises."

No chance of that.

As she and Isabel had walked across the parking lot, Jane saw two police transport vans, idling, rear doors open. The bad guy was going to be brought out this way, that was clear. The hostage, too, maybe, if he was being taken away by the cops for questioning. The promised crew from Channel 2 had not shown up. Because of that, she needed Isabel's help.

"Do you have a cell phone?" Jane asked. They'd arrived at Jane's car, but this was no time to leave.

"Cell phone? Sure." Isabel dug into her little messenger bag, still strapped cross-body over her now-even-more-rumpled white T-shirt. "Are your batteries dead?"

"Nope. All good. But listen." Jane pointed across a row of parked cars. "Turn on your phone. Walk with me."

No one else in the lot. Empty cars. No cops by the vans. Back door to the hospital dead ahead.

"See that white BPD van? The one on the right? With the open back doors?"

"Yes, sure." Isabel was powering up her phone.

"You're now an official TV reporter," Jane said. "The minute anyone comes near that van, especially cops or HRTs with a person in handcuffs, I'm gonna roll my video. But I can't shoot two places at the same time. So if a second guy is brought out, handcuffs or not, you roll like crazy on that. Whatever it is. Just stay wide, nothing fancy. Take a deep breath, stay calm, make sure your camera is taping. In that case, I'll stay with the van on the left. You and I are gonna shoot the hell out of this."

Isabel smiled, a delighted grin that warmed Jane's heart. This girl was a superstar.

"Got it," Isabel said. *"Vincerò."*

"Exactly." Jane recognized the aria, Puccini's anthem to victory. *"Vincerò,* sister."

JAKE BROGAN

Room 422 was a shitshow. A circus. And crowded with more law enforcement guys than any one hospital room could handle.

Grady Houlihan, half drugged and half outraged, lay handcuffed to one iron side-railing of his narrow hospital bed. "I didn't kill anyone!" he yelled. "Come on, Ja—"

"You shut up," Jake yelled back, weapon still pointed.

HRT had handled Rourke Devane, one officer snapping the handcuffs, the other patting him down. They'd found ID, two blunts, and a .22 stashed in the kid's tube sock.

"What's this, buster?" one said.

Devane proclaimed, repeatedly, that he'd been there only to talk, that he hadn't been fooling with the IV and that the nurse was an "effing moron."

"Why'd you pull a gun?" Jake asked.

The kid's face glowed red, even his ears, as he blustered an answer. "I was only *showing* it to Grady. And she came in, scared the effing hell out of me, and I just turned and she saw it, and bolted before I could say a fricking word."

"That's not true." Grady's voice was a croak. "He threatened me with—"

"You. Shut up," Jake said.

"Next thing I know," Devane went on, "I'm like some crazy shooter, for chrissake. Trapped in this frickin' room with no way to—"

"You hit my effin' Gormay van, you asshole," Grady broke in. "I saw you in the rearview, you *ass*hole. I'm not going down for Violet Sholto. You know perfectly well that—"

"Not one more word, Houlihan," Jake ordered. "And you, Devane, if you're such a monument to innocence, why were you here in the first place?"

Grady's monitor, still safely plugged in, beeped once, then again. An alarm pinged, then stopped. The public address robo-voice in the hall had gone silent the minute HRT arrived. Suddenly, bizarrely, the room was still.

Jake, three HRTs, and the bedridden, handcuffed Grady waited for Rourke Devane to come up with an answer.

"I demand a lawyer," he said, pouting as only a guilty punk can do. "Call Randolph Hix. Call Molly Obele. I am not saying another word."

"Sholto's mouthpieces," Jake said. "Our pleasure."

Devane, the moron, with brusque assistance from the HRTs, turned his back on Jake and Grady, his feet almost dragging the ground as he was ushered out of 422. Now it was just the two of them. Jake, and his informant. Who, as far as the Sholto crew would hear and believe, was merely another lawbreaking creep, and under arrest for Violet Sholto's murder.

"Jake!" Grady whispered. "You're wrong, you're really freakin' wrong. He threatened to shoot me, but couldn't, you know, not after the damn nurse ratted him out and he knew you guys'd nail him. But he knows I saw Sholto in town when his wife was hit. Sholto even did it, maybe. Devane said he was just the messenger, making sure I shut up. But I would never—"

"I know." Jake reached for his key ring. "And now you're officially un-arrested. I'll have the handcuffs off in a sec."

"But—"

"Hang on, Grady." One twist, then another. With a click and a snap, the cuffs were off. Grady was safe for now. "Sorry for the bull, but I had to get that moron out of here without him finding out you and I were connected."

"But—" Grady still looked confused.

"You get well, dude." Grady had risked his life. For justice, sure. But for Jake. And Jake had almost failed him. "We'll get you protection. I promise."

60

JANE RYLAND

"Police sources tell us Rourke Devane is now in custody," Jane said into the studio camera lens, lights full up, floor director counting her down to the commercial break. *Three, two . . .*

"And we'll have more for you on this breaking story as details become available. For now, I'm Jane Ryland, News 2." She'd barely had a moment to comb her hair as she and Isabel had raced to Channel 2, Jane Bluetoothing info and instructions to Fiola as she drove. While Jane slapped on makeup, Fiola honchoed the video edit, banging out two usable minutes of Devane's unceremonious handcuffed exit from the hospital parking lot, semi-dragged by two bigger-than-life HRT guys in black. Devane had provided some extra TV juice by yelling "Call my lawyer" the entire way. Jane had rolled on every bit of it.

Isabel, apparently a news natural, had gotten video of Jane taking video.

"And we're clear." The floor director slashed a finger across her neck. "Great story, Ryland," she said. "Way to hustle."

Jane swiveled out of the anchor chair. It *had* been pretty great. Now that it was over. "Thanks," she said.

"So that was cool." Isabel stood, smiling, hovering behind her. "My video, on actual TV."

Isabel had watched Jane's live report from a nearby desk in the newsroom. "Hospital Hostage Showdown," Channel 2 had branded it. That victory allowed Jane to turn her harrowing morning into good copy, and the other stations would have to play catch-up. Always an antidote. Isabel seemed to be thriving on the same news adrenaline.

"You rocked it." Jane crumpled her notes, tossed the wad of paper toward a metal wastebasket. Made the shot. She would rework her script, type it into the prompter for the six o'clock show. Grabbing her tote bag from under a writer's desk, she checked her phone, perplexed. Nothing from Jake. Where was he?

"Seriously, Isabel," she said. "Thanks. Not everyone could have handled that. You okay, though?"

"Sure," Isabel said. "So what do you do next? Is there like, the next broadcast?"

"Let's go up to my office." Jane pointed to the metal stairway in front of them. "We need to call Ja—Detective Brogan. About Trey Welliver. Maybe it's even better if we go to the police station."

Jane watched Isabel's mood deflate, her eyes lower, as they started up the stairs.

"I guess." She stopped, one hand on the banister, turned to Jane. "I'd almost . . . forgotten."

"We're having quite the day," Jane said.

"Understatement of the century." A voice from the top of the stairs. Fiola.

"Hey, thanks, Fee," Jane said. They were an okay team. They'd make it work. Maybe even do bigger stories together. She and Isabel started up the stairs again. "Great job on the—"

"Frank McCusker's arrived to see you," Fiola cut her off, her voice telegraphing a message Jane couldn't quite catch. A dark silhouette, then another, appeared behind her, two shapes backlit by the fluorescent lights of the Special Projects corridor. "Marsh is up here, too."

The Assistant DA and the news director. Together?

Three minutes later, with Isabel and Fiola waiting in Jane's office, Jane faced McCusker across the oval newsroom conference table. Though the dialogue couldn't be heard, glass walls allowed everyone in the newsroom to watch whatever dramas unfolded. So much for privacy.

"So, Jane," McCusker said. "Detective Jake Brogan called my office, soon as they made the Devane arrest."

"Oh, so . . ." Jane felt her heart relax. Then tried to figure out how to phrase her question to get more details without seeming overly interested. Marsh knew of their relationship, but McCusker didn't. "He's okay? Detective Brogan? And the hostage?"

"Yeah." McCusker was frowning.

Marsh was frowning, too. Why was that? Was Jake not really okay?

"Jane?" Marsh asked. "Did you tell Brogan about Devane? Who he was? And how you knew?"

"I told you not to tell anyone." McCusker shot Marsh a look. "Could have blown our entire case."

Were they kidding? Jane's brain flared into overdrive. This was bull. The terror of the morning, the escape, the results, the exclusive, all circled the drain as the two men questioned her. About her *ethics*? Her *judgment*?

"There was a hostage situation." Jane kept her tone as courteous as she could. "I knew a police officer was in potential danger. I knew I had information that might help him. And you're suggesting I should have—that I shouldn't have—"

She stopped. She would not defend herself for making a perfectly rational, reasonable, not to mention correct decision. "I did not tell Detective Brogan *how* I knew who he was." Jane heard the sarcasm leaking into her voice. "I told him only *who* he was. Without explaining how I knew it."

She paused again in the silence, reining in her anger. Failed.

"There was hardly time for explaining, was there?" she went on. "What with potentially an entire hospital in danger?"

Marsh and the DA exchanged looks. Jerks. She should—*no*. She was not going to quit. They should apologize. They should reward her, actually. No one was going to order Jane to keep quiet when the man she loved—and hell, a whole hospital full of people—was under siege. Not even a news director could believe that would be the right thing to do.

"We'll discuss it later," Marsh finally said. "Maybe it'll be okay."

"But I do have some good news." McCusker's tone changed. "Your Rourke Devane turns out to be the weak link. Nobody likes the thought of prison, right? He told us Sholto ordered him to kill Grady by ramming that second Gormay van, figuring everyone would think someone was targeting *Gormay,* making Grady the unlucky, but random, victim. And—self-preserving paragon that he is—before his lawyers arrived and put legal duct tape over his mouth, Devane told us he also saw Clooney Sholto in *Boston* the day of his wife's murder. And the best part—he says he has evidence, something about a complicit housekeeper—he told us that Sholto himself killed Violet."

Jane blinked once, twice, then again. She heard the buzz of the lights, the hum of the air conditioner, the stubborn metal hinges of McCusker's chair creaking as he fidgeted. Rourke Devane had ratted out Clooney Sholto. So what Jane had witnessed on O'Brien Highway—the hit-and-run that had given the lie to a bad guy's alibi—now maybe it didn't matter?

Jane dug into her tote bag. Searching. The second "SAY NO MORE" note. Did she have it? She did. She stood, leaning across the table to hand the note and the envelope—now in a plastic sandwich bag—to Marsh and McCusker.

"It was in my lobby," she said. "At my *apartment.* This one also arrived the day of the hearing. But I didn't see it until last night."

The news director reached for it, but the DA took it, turned it over and back again.

"Another one, huh? It's not misspelled, so it wasn't from Devane," McCusker said, almost smiling. "But it's a nail in the coffin for someone, that's for sure. We'll make good use of it. Ten years in the state pen, law says, for witness intimidation." He slid the bagged note into the inside pocket of his suit jacket. Patted it. "Guess you weren't intimidated, Jane."

"But I'm not going to testify, I got that," she said. They wanted her to keep quiet? Darn right she would. "Marsh, right? *Forget* about it."

"Frank, we'll have to—" Marsh began.

"Understood." McCusker put up both palms, interrupting, accepting. "Bottom line? Doesn't matter what Jane saw. Sholto's being arrested even as we speak. Ratted out by his own bigmouthed lackey. And you, Jane? You don't have to say another word."

61

JAKE BROGAN

"So you had it wrong," Willow Galt was telling Jake. She sat in the big chair in the victim room, her husband standing protectively behind her.

Jake had the folding chair. And his notebook. Finally he was getting the whole story. Almost.

"Olive Brennis called me," Willow went on. "And that's why—"

"You can understand why we wouldn't say anything," her husband added.

Jake tried to process this. Thought of the hours of concern, the hours of uncertainty, the hours of police work that could have been used to a better purpose if this woman had simply told the truth from moment one. But if he had her pegged right, the word "simply" wasn't in her vocabulary.

She'd been on the verge of tears, every moment, as she sat in the same chair her husband had occupied when he, distraught, had reported her missing. Now he stood silent—almost—as she'd revealed what she'd seen but had decided not to tell until now.

You've got company, Ming-Na's text had pinged on Jake's phone when he arrived at HQ twenty minutes earlier. The receptionist, thank God, always tried to warn him if there were land mines awaiting him.

Jake had been trying to call Jane to find out how she was. What the hell had that girl with her been trying to tell him about Trey Welliver before their lives were interrupted?

Trey was still in custody, some hotshot lawyer apparently en route from Connecticut, and if Trey hadn't killed Avery Morgan, well, that would be a bridge to cross. But Jane hadn't answered his calls. He hadn't left a message, because who knew who might be listening or looking at her screen when she retrieved it—another dilemma in their ongoing charade. Maybe she was on the air? That made sense. Hard to decide which of their lives was crazier.

Jake had left Grady in the protective custody of Noonan and Palmeri until the cops could staff their own guy as sentinel. Jake had asked for T'shombe Pereira. He'd trust Shom to check on DeLuca, too, though Kat McMahan and a tiny white dog in a clandestine carrier stood sentry in that hospital room. Last update from the doctors was, "It's still in the balance" and "Detective DeLuca is doing the best we can hope for."

Which Jake tried to believe was promising.

Jake slammed the door of the cruiser and headed to the elevator. Texting Ming-Na as he walked. "Company? Who?"

"Galts" appeared on his screen. Ming-Na had met Tom Galt when he'd reported Willow missing. Ming-Na was still typing. "And a Tarrant?" appeared on Jake's screen.

She didn't know Tarrant. "10-4," Jake typed. "Tnx. Stnd by. 2 mins."

By the time he reached the squad room, he'd figured out what to do. Nodding to Tarrant, he approached the Galts. As he entered, they'd been on the couch, and then stood, bumping into each other.

"Come with me." He'd pointed them toward the victim room. Then he turned to Tarrant. "Five minutes," he said. He read the impatience on Tarrant's face before the guy wiped it off.

"Certainly," Tarrant told him.

He'd made Jake wait two days ago. Now the waiting was on the other foot.

But Jake would never have predicted what he was hearing now. Yes, Willow had seen what happened. But victim Avery Morgan was not an informant. Though they refused to discuss it further, the Galts admitted *they* were the ones hiding their past. And now, as Willow haltingly explained, those secrets had compelled her to keep another secret. Until her conscience, and her husband, changed her mind.

"I saw her hit the water," Willow said, eyes focused behind him, as if a script were written on the wall. "I couldn't see it all, but then, the dog was barking, I could only see him running, part of the way. Then she—Avery— didn't get out of the pool. Not that I saw. And then another person was there. A woman, with curly white hair—all I could see, I'm so sorry but that's all I could see. I didn't see Avery again. Then I thought, maybe she got out, but I hadn't seen it. But then, the dog kept barking, and barking, and then . . ."

Popcorn. Jake's gut twisted, remembering. Popcorn, now permanently renamed Rocco, had been officially "relocated" to DeLuca's house. *Witness protection, K-9 version,* D had said. Rocco could be there to greet D when he came home. If he came home.

"It's fine, Mrs. Galt. Take your time," Jake said. He had to focus.

"Willow doesn't exactly know what happened," her husband said. "But she did see—"

"A woman, with curly white hair," Willow repeated. "I turned away, expecting to see Avery get out of the pool. I knew she didn't like the water, she'd told me that. She laughed that it was a waste her house had a pool. But she'd fallen in, and I expected . . ." Tears came to her eyes. "If I'd have called sooner, maybe she could have been rescued."

Jake didn't answer right away. No use to make this woman more miserable than she was. "Drownings happen very quickly," Jake said. Weak, but all he had. The truth.

"I know," Willow said.

"Would you recognize the woman?" Jake asked. "Do you know who she is?"

"She doesn't know," Tom Galt answered.

"Mrs. Galt?"

"Maybe." She almost whispered the answer. "Maybe I'd recognize her. But I cannot testify. I can't, I can't, I—"

"Detective Brogan." Tom Galt stepped in front of his wife, as if Jake might yank her away. "As she says, it would be impossible for us to—"

"Sir?" Jake interrupted. The Galts' voices had grown more taut, more terrified. He had to stop this escalation of fear. "We're simply talking now. Okay? Your wife did nothing wrong. So, Mrs. Galt? The woman with white hair. She didn't help Ms. Morgan?"

This was a quagmire. A fricking law enforcement morass, where the law was about to get in the way of justice.

It wasn't illegal not to help a person in trouble. If a person jumped off a bridge, a bystander wasn't required to leap in and try to save them. You didn't—legally—have to yank a suicide off the train tracks. Swim out to rescue a person in a rip current. Or save Avery Morgan from drowning in her backyard pool. It was only a crime if the "bystander" had a duty, like a parent, to help them. Or. If they actively *caused* the danger. Jake didn't want to put words in this woman's mouth. But he had to ask.

"Willow? Do you know if the woman pushed her? Even in fun?"

"Am I in trouble for not calling nine-one-one sooner?" she asked.

Jake knew the answer to that, too, and though it might help the Galts, it wouldn't help him bring the white-haired woman to justice.

"No." Jake shook his head. "In Massachusetts, there's no legal requirement for most eyewitnesses to report anything but certain specified crimes—murder, attempted murder, armed robbery, rape. And in those cases, you'd be fined, not sent to prison. So again. Did Avery Morgan fall into the pool? Or did the woman push her?"

EDWARD TARRANT

Cooling his heels. *Waiting for Godot.* Stranded in a Kafka novel. Edward, refusing to sit on that disgusting couch in the homicide reception area, might have worn a pathway in the carpet outside the homicide squad's office by now. He'd passed the time by mentally listing the ways he'd been "disrespected," as the students often complained. Three times, perhaps more, he'd considered simply leaving this place, abandoning his idea, and allowing law enforcement, such as it was, to fend for its arrogant self.

But the specter of those harpies—those students, those women, those obsessive hoarders amassing their so-called evidence of his activities— forced him to swallow his pride and self-respect. He had to make this one last move to ensure his continued freedom and autonomy.

Many, he was certain, had prevailed through worse. Patton, and Mac-Arthur, and Churchill, suffered trials and unfair condemnation, dispar-agement from a public that did not understand the responsibilities of a leader. That the rules, so simply printed on paper, were not, in real life, as clear-cut as they appeared. That someone, someone with authority and experience, with the heightened knowledge of the exigencies of reality, had to sometimes make a decision that—

"Mr. Tarrant?" The girl's voice from the reception desk.

He masked his impatience. "Yes?"

"Detective Brogan will see you now."

That couple had not emerged, so perhaps there was a back exit. No matter. The receptionist stood, waving him—no respect here whatsoever—to follow her to a door marked only "A." She opened it to reveal a long metal table. Dingy linoleum floor. A fake plant, leaves dust-coated off-green, listing in one corner. Hardly welcoming, but then, it was most likely frequented by criminals. Of which he was most assuredly not one.

Detective Jake Brogan, in one of two folding metal chairs, stood as Edward entered. His sidekick, DeBuca, something along those lines, was not to be seen.

"Thank you for your patience." Brogan pointed him to the other chair. It screeched across the linoleum, fingernails on chalkboard. "What can I do for you?"

"It's what I can do for you," Tarrant began. "In the matter of Avery Morgan's death."

"I see," Brogan said.

"I've acquired some new information," he said.

"We can use all the help we can get," Brogan said. "And?"

"Well, that's the . . . quandary," Edward began. This would be the delicate part. To say enough, but not too much. "That's the . . . dilemma, if you will."

"I understand 'quandary,'" Brogan said. "Harvard, Class of 2000."

"I see," Edward said. Brogan did not look as interested as he'd hoped. But the cop would be interested soon. "Let me begin by outlining to you the responsibilities and jurisdiction of a person in my position."

He laid out, piece by piece, his role, the students and families who had come to him, the network—he'd chosen the word carefully—of helpful students who'd report to him when they heard about infractions or rulebreaking. "It works, in a way, like your network of confidential informants. They help me, I help them."

Edward smiled; they were two of a kind. "A distasteful but necessary part of our lives, correct?"

"Go on," Brogan said.

"Sadly . . ." Edward took a mental deep breath. This was the moment he had to set the hook. "Sadly, young Trey Welliver was the, shall we say, helper? Who informed me of Avery Morgan's death. And when you arrested him, I thought that made sense," he lied. "In a disturbing way, certainly, but made sense. Trey Welliver had—well, I can say no more about that. But suffice it to say he was not the most well-behaved young man, especially when it came to his relationships with young women. In fact, I'd been working with him, and his family, to make sure some questionable . . . 'activities' he'd been involved in with those young women would not come to the attention of the—"

"Are you covering up rape, Mr. Tarrant?" Brogan's eyes had narrowed. "As you know, in some circumstances it can be a crime not to report that."

"I understand. Completely." Edward had to get on with this part of his presentation. "But I was not a witness, nor did I have direct knowledge of what really happened. I assure you of that. Which brings me to what I want to tell you."

Brogan tapped a toe of his loafer on the linoleum, a pen in one hand and a notebook in the other. "I'm listening," he said.

Edward could almost feel the room getting smaller, more oppressive. The tattered beige wallpaper, the wheezing ventilation, the water-stained ceiling. But this was not the moment to be faint of heart.

"It appears that a few female students have now decided they are unhappy with the way I handled some of their concerns," Edward said. "But if you and I can discuss those cases, say, together, including a way to en sure that the young women are satisfied with my handling of their . . . issues . . ."

The detective was in full frown now. Maybe he wasn't used to negotiating, Edward thought. Which meant Edward had better get to the point. Some people would rather one just laid it on the table.

"Trey Welliver did not kill Avery Morgan," he said.

Ha. And there he had him. Brogan's face changed, certainly. Exactly the reaction he was hoping for.

"Exactly," Edward said. "And not only that. The real killer confessed to me. And if we can work something out vis-à-vis my—well, the situation I described? Then I can give you everything you need to know about Ms. Morgan's death."

Brogan nodded, then stood, fiddling with the zipper on his leather jacket, yanking it up, then pulling it down.

Edward waited. Happy to wait. Happy to let this dullard cop think it through. This could only be good news in the making. So wonderfully ironic that all his admonitions to students to stay silent, keep quiet, say nothing, had brought him to this pivotal moment where he'd saved his own career, his own marriage, his own reputation, his own, yes, life—by telling.

62

JAKE BROGAN

"What young women?" Jake yanked his zipper one last time. Which reminded him of Jane. Which reminded him that the young woman she'd brought to the hospital had indicated exactly the same thing, that Trey Welliver was not guilty of murder. Was she—what was her name?—one of the young women this pompous Tarrant was talking about?

"I'm sure that's impossible for me to say." Tarrant shook his head as he refused. "As you and I first discussed when you came to visit me at Adams Bay, the strictures of privacy prevent me from giving you names."

"Ah," Jake said.

"But I *can* give you the name of Avery Morgan's killer." Tarrant leaned forward, elbows on pin-striped knees, a gold watch glinting from under his starched cuff. "And I can tell you this, before we even have our . . . agreement. It isn't Trey Welliver. You have arrested the wrong man. Embarrassing, no? To have an innocent person in custody? And I can tell you exactly who called you about him."

"Funny," Jake said. This guy was a piece of work. "I was just talking to a person who wondered about their responsibility to tell the police if they know something terrible has happened. And about their responsibility to try to rescue the person, or, if that's impossible, to report the situation."

Jake tried to gauge this guy's reaction. So far, simply calculating. Wary.

"D'you know, Mr. Tarrant," Jake went on, deciding to push him a

SAY NO MORE   365

little, "most people are not required to do so? You don't have to, say, pull a drowning person out of a swimming pool. If they die, even if you're right there, it's not your fault. Legally, at least."

Tarrant raised an eyebrow, didn't respond. The guy was no idiot. He had to understand Jake was going somewhere with this.

"Thought you might want to know that," Jake went on. "But in addition, I'm hearing that these students feel you failed—neglected? You choose the word—to report something that happened to them. For whatever reason. And that you convinced *them* not to discuss it or report it as well."

Tarrant nodded. "That's part of it."

"I'm also hearing that you want to trade information about Avery Morgan's death for some sort of leniency? About some action you fear might be taken by these disgruntled students?"

"Precisely," Tarrant said. "You help me, I'll help you."

Jake stood, smiling, making his expression as pleasant as he possibly could. "Mr. Tarrant?" he said.

"Yes?"

"No. Not a chance in hell."

Tarrant rose to his feet, facing Jake, silent. Jake watched the man's fists clench, his chest rise and fall, his yellow foulard tie adjusting to the slight movement. Tarrant's chin came up, his shoulders squared.

"But I have proof!"

"Thank you so much, Mr. Tarrant." Jake got to the office door in two quick steps, opened it. Possibly a bit too dramatically, enjoying Tarrant's bewildered expression.

But Jake had all he needed about Avery Morgan's death from the Galts. Tarrant would be required to corroborate it, or face possible obstruction charges. What a mistake, to let on he knew what happened. And to think Jake would consider such a deal. Jake's ace in the hole was Tarrant's sidekick, Sasha Vogelby. The curly-white-haired Sasha Vogelby. Who, Jake predicted, was about to become very unhappy. And who knew what information that woman would offer to trade?

Tarrant strode through the open doorway. When Jake turned to follow, Tarrant stopped. Stood, stock still, on the middle of the reception room carpet.

There, at the door to the homicide reception area, was Jane. And beside her, the young woman she'd brought to the hospital.

Tarrant whirled, faced Jake again.

"You bastard," he snapped. "You set me up."

ISABEL RUSSO

You bastard, Isabel thought, though she wouldn't say it out loud. Was this why Jane had insisted they come here? Seemed like Jane knew this detective—more than "knew." She'd heard them on the phone in the hospital closet. *I love you*, he'd said. She'd heard him, and seen the worry and fear in Jane's eyes.

"This is unacceptable!" Tarrant turned to her, his face a mask of scorn. *"You?"*

He seemed smaller to her now, standing in this bleak reception room, no longer enhanced by the trappings of his opulent office. And certainly unhappy to see her. Well, yeah, she was pretty unhappy, too.

"This?" Tarrant hissed at her, pointing a forefinger. "You send your little friends to my office to threaten me? And now you're following me? Here?"

Little friends? Isabel hadn't heard from Manderley and the others. Had they gone to Tarrant's office while she was trapped at the hospital?

"Mr. Tarrant? Remember me? Jane Ryland, from Channel 2," Jane was saying. "Isabel tells me she talked with you about what happened to her."

"Happened?" Detective Brogan asked. Seemed like he and Jane were secretly communicating.

"Right, Isabel?" Jane said. "I'm sure Detective Brogan would like to hear about that encounter directly from you. If you're comfortable with it."

And here she was, and here was the moment. Curtain up, almost, on her new life. The moment she'd imagined, in so many ways, since May, May twenty-first to be exact. Today she'd come here, with Jane, to tell this Detective Brogan she knew Trey Welliver wasn't guilty of murder. But he *was* guilty of something else. And now Jane was asking her if she was comfortable revealing that. Isabel had not been comfortable with anything since May, May twenty-first. But heck—hell yes, she was comfortable now.

"Trey Welliver raped me." Isabel heard the words coming out of her mouth, strong and confident, words she'd never thought she'd say again, not to anyone.

She took a step toward Tarrant.

"I told you, and *told* you, and you said you would help me. But you didn't do one thing. Not. One. Thing. Except to order me, and my mother, to keep quiet about it. And she sent you money! All the families did!"

"I never—that is simply not true." Tarrant rolled his eyes at the detective like she wasn't even there. "This young woman is clearly—"

The detective held up a hand, stopping Tarrant. "Is it true that you knew or even suspected that Ms.—"

"Russo," Jane said.

"Russo had been raped by Trey Welliver? And that you did not report it?"

"I want a lawyer," Tarrant said.

"I hear that a lot," Detective Brogan said. He took a pair of handcuffs from his back pocket. Jane moved closer to Isabel, put one hand on her shoulder. Isabel felt like she was in a movie.

"Edward Tarrant." Detective Brogan's voice sounded formal, almost hard. "You're under arrest for obstruction of justice. Misprision of felony. You knew about Trey Welliver. You didn't tell. Actively didn't tell. That's a crime. Not to mention potential extortion. But that's for the district attorney's office to handle."

"And I'm not the only one." Isabel moved away from Jane. She had to do this on her own, had to take center stage. Tarrant had to hear this, every word. "And we're not being quiet anymore. There's Elaine, and Rochelle. And Manderley kept a record of all of it. You told all of us to keep quiet. Not to report it. Our parents, too."

"I assume those are the students with 'issues' you mentioned," the detective said. He seemed really angry. Isabel had never seen such a wonderfully angry face. "It's prison time, separately, for each incident, Mr. Tarrant. Just so you know. You'll have plenty of time to do the math."

"Bullshit," Tarrant said. "I'll wait for my lawyer to rake your absurd case over the coals, but here's what *you* might want to know, Detective. I'm only an administrator, not a mandated reporter, as I am sure you are aware. And I didn't witness any 'rapes.' Therefore I'm not responsible to report them. You have no case. Nothing."

"Tell that to a judge," Detective Brogan said. "I'm sure they'll be delighted to hear it."

"Is that true?" Isabel whispered to Jane. But Jane was on her phone, maybe texting in the story, or looking up the law. Jane was so cool, Isabel thought, working even while all this was going on.

"You're going to be humiliated in front of everyone now, Miss Russo." Tarrant narrowed his eyes at her, stumbling once with his arms behind his back as the detective led him toward the door. "Everyone will know. Everyone. And your poor mother will be devastated. You silly, stupid, fucking bitches. All of you."

"That's enough," Detective Brogan said. "But thank you for the corroboration of your cover-up. And sorry, Ms. Russo, for the inappropriate language."

"I can take it." Isabel stood taller, the sound of her own words, her own voice, somehow strengthening her resolve. She wished she had thought to use her cell phone to take video of it all, just as Jane had taught her in the hospital parking lot. It was crazy, right? Here she was, telling the police Trey was *guilty* of something—when she'd come here to report that he was *innocent* of something else.

The detective and the hideous Tarrant headed for a door in the back of the office. Isabel wondered when she'd see Tarrant again. She hoped never. Unless it was in the headlines.

"Detective Brogan?" Jane was clicking her phone, like she was sending something. "We'll stand by here, okay? Isabel has more to tell you."

63

JANE RYLAND

"Hang up, Fee," Jane said as she arrived at her office door and saw Fiola on the phone. Whoever Fee was talking to could wait. Jane waved her cell, trying to get her producer's attention. "You'll want to see this."

"Hang on, Jane," Fiola replied. She tucked her phone between her cheek and shoulder and clicked into her e-mail. "One second."

Jane turned to Isabel, shrugging. "Sorry," she whispered. "I know this is hard for you."

"Not anymore," Isabel told her. "It's okay. Or, it will be." She sighed, so deeply her shoulders rose, then fell.

Not in defeat, Jane knew. In change. In hope. As she'd watched Tarrant being led away, Jane thought she could almost see Isabel come back to life. And when—brave young woman—she'd then told Jake the whole story of her assault by Trey Welliver and the ensuing cover-up by Edward Tarrant, and then her calendared alibi for Trey's whereabouts, Jane had watched the color return to Isabel's cheeks, and the fire to her eyes.

Trey was still in custody. Before Jane and Isabel left the police department, Jake had whispered a promise to describe to Jane his next encounter—the delicious moment when he'd get to tell Welliver's attorney his client was being cleared of murder, but charged with rape.

Edward Tarrant's future was a legal snafu. Jake had called Jane a few moments earlier with that disturbing reality. Tarrant's cynical recitation of the law had been correct: In Massachusetts, there was no legal requirement to report a rape unless you had witnessed it. And under federal law, a school administrator was not required to convey information about a reported rape to law enforcement officials.

"So Tarrant's done nothing legally wrong?" Jane had asked him as she and Isabel arrived at Channel 2. She'd watched Isabel's face fall as she heard Jane's end of the phone conversation. "I can't believe that. Like you said, obstruction? Or how about blackmail? He'd told Isabel's mother that if she ever—"

"Yeah," Jake had said. "Interesting that he knew those particular laws so well, right? We'll hold the creep as long as we can. The students were obviously drinking alcohol in that poolside video at Avery Morgan's house. If we can prove he was there, knew they were under twenty-one, even provided the stuff, we may be able to get him on that. The DA's focused on the underage-drinking thing, big-time, and you know McCusker's a pit bull. But the law is the law. And being a slime-bucket jerk is not illegal. We'll have to see."

They'd *all* have to see. For Isabel it would be a difficult road, pitted with obstacles, and questions, and scrutiny. Isabel had not chosen what happened to her in the past, but she could try to choose her future, and Jane predicted she could handle the journey. Jane and Fiola, and the SAFE women, would all be there to help.

"One step at a time," Jane said out loud.

Fiola had finally hung up the phone.

"Huh?" Fiola said. "Anyway. Wait till you see what I have in my e-mail."

"Great," Jane said, "but I just sent you one, too. Open it."

Fiola clicked her mouse, twice, and a ping signaled the end of the download. The video clip Jane had sent her was only about three minutes long.

"You bastard!" the video began.

"That's Edward Tarrant." Fiola paused the screen, turned to Jane. "What is this? Where? What's the deal?"

"Oh!" Isabel clamped a hand on Jane's arm. "You taped it on your phone! I thought of it, too, but too late."

"Doing my job." Jane leaned down, clicked Fiola's mouse to play the rest.

Even though the video was shaky—Jane had tried to hide her cell phone—there was the homicide squad waiting room, and the fuming and obscene Tarrant, and Jake putting him in handcuffs, and his arrest for obstruction of justice.

"Wow," Fiola said. "Remember how smarmy that guy was when we tried to interview him? But I'd never have thought—I mean, he's the school's Title Nine coordinator. He's supposed to make sure all assault complaints are investigated, if the students want. Not to talk them out of it. Ugh. Disgusting."

She clicked off Jane's video, opened another file. "And, now, you look. At this."

Jane stepped closer to Fee's monitor, felt Isabel close behind her. Cell phone video, obviously, starting with a flare of light from a window behind whoever was the subject. Taken by an amateur, Jane couldn't help thinking. The voices, though, were clear.

"We've come to chat with you." A woman's voice. "About what you're doing to us."

"That's Manderley!" Isabel pointed to the screen. "And that's Tarrant's office. How'd you—"

"Watch," Fiola said. She turned her screen so Jane could get a better view.

"Holy . . ." Jane's voice trailed off as she listened, watched the women of SAFE confront Edward Tarrant, watched them defy him with their irrefutable knowledge of his manipulation of their lives.

"He threw the notebook out the sixteenth-floor window—can you believe it?" Fiola said. "I can't help it. Sorry, Isabel, I know I shouldn't laugh. But it's just so freaking perfect."

"Bad news, though," Jane said. "We can't use any of it on TV."

"Why not?" Isabel looked like she was about to cry. "Why?"

"Yeah, well, here's the deal. What we did in the hospital parking lot is fair game," Jane explained. "That's a public place. But this other stuff,

shot in Tarrant's private office? Without his knowledge? And at the police department? Under state law, we can't put it on the air."

"What if you don't use the sound?" Isabel asked. "How about then?"

"Nope," Jane said. She paused, regretting, imagining how great their
documentary might have been. The good the videos could have done, revealing Tarrant for the manipulating creep he clearly was.

The three women stared at the last frame. Slam-dunk devastating.
And all completely illegal.

"Jane?" Fiola said. "I know it's unorthodox. But I bet the cops would
love to see this."

Jane blew out a breath. Why was there always this conflict? She could
not give Jake this video. That was precisely the line she could not cross.
This whole thing had started with her stating her principles, refusing
to help the DA's office. Then being forced to do just that. And regretting
the hell out of it. She couldn't now suddenly decide to hand over video to
the cops.

"No way, Fee," Jane said. "We simply can't."

"*I* can, though," Isabel interjected. "Right? I'll talk to Manderley and
everyone. They'd do it in a flash."

"Because even if what Tarrant did is not technically illegal—" Fiola
said.

"It's all about the cover-up," Jane finished the sentence. "He threatened
Isabel and the others. Told them they'd be faced with humiliation, and
public embarrassment, and infinite disgrace. But when school officials
hear about this? And the faculty? And parents? And other students? Seems
like that's exactly what'll happen to Mr. Tarrant himself."

"*Vincerò*," Isabel said.

64

JANE RYLAND

"Okay, so yeah, you arrested Sasha Vogelby. But she as much as confessed!" Jane said, yanking open her front door before Jake's key had a chance to turn in the lock. Before he took a whole step into her apartment, she continued the conversation where they'd left off half an hour earlier, as if they'd never stopped talking. "She *did* confess. Isn't that what you said? How can they nail *you* for that?"

She kissed him, hard, then handed him a beer. Friday night—he didn't have to go to work tomorrow. And that was the problem they now faced. He'd broken the news to her on the phone, but she'd demanded he come talk about it in person. Instantly, if not sooner.

The August night was softly dark, and she opened her windows to catch the end-of-season breeze. No matter what the calendar said, the night had a touch of September. Anyone who understood Boston would feel the change.

She followed Jake into the living room, knowing she should give him a chance to answer, but this whole thing was incomprehensible. "Not that you need any more ammo, but Vogelby turned on Tarrant to save herself, right? So you nailed this, sweetheart."

She planted her fists on her hips, too infuriated to sit down. "They should be giving you a promotion, instead of—"

"I'm just gonna collapse for a minute, okay?" Jake said. "Then I'll tell you the whole ridiculous thing."

Jane couldn't believe it. And Jake looked so sad. But there was something else she didn't understand. "Can I ask you, before we talk about the other thing? Even though Vogelby was jealous of Avery Morgan, wasn't she required to—didn't she *have* to—save Avery from drowning? She was right there!"

"Nope." Jake took a sip of beer, put the bottle on the coffee table. "Not legally. Morally, that's her own problem. But all Willow Galt saw was Avery *falling* into the water. And then Vogelby walking away."

"Yow." Jane plopped onto the couch, scooting Coda's furry body aside. "That's so chillingly tragic. Like Tarrant wasn't required by law to report the rapes—since he didn't see them."

"Kind of, yeah," Jake said. Coda resettled into Jake's lap, swirling her tail. Jake wasn't much of a cat person, and Coda reminded him of that as often as she could. "They're quite the duo. Vogelby admitted she was jealous of Avery. Over her closeness with Tarrant, over the attention she got, over Avery's job and position. She admitted she watched Avery trip on one of Popcorn's toys, a yellow ball. She said Avery fell into the pool and got the wind knocked out of her. Told us she thought Avery was just 'pretending' to struggle. Being 'dramatic.' Said she didn't believe Avery would actually drown."

Jane pictured it, remembering the party video, the happily smiling Avery Morgan. Could her death have been an accident? "Did you believe that?"

"Well, it's possible. I guess. But pretty early on, you'd have to comprehend your friend was not playacting, wouldn't you? When I confronted her with that—and with the likelihood that she realized Avery would drown and be out of her life if she simply walked away—Vogelby panicked. Figured she was in deep trouble. To save herself, she offered to trade information about Tarrant's cover-ups and extortion. It was her idea to call us pretending to rat out Trey Welliver—but she insists Tarrant was complicit."

"Jake? About Tarrant. Being complicit." Jane thought about that video again. And what Isabel had told her. "I know when Trey Welliver must have drugged Isabel. At a party in May, by Avery's pool. And Tarrant was *there!*

Isabel saw him. Hey. She even showed us a—" She skidded to a halt. Could she tell Jake about the video?

"A video. Yeah." Jake toasted her with his beer. "You're not the only one with sources, hon. But your Isabel corroborates Tarrant was there? Nice. Very, very nice." He took a sip. "Very helpful. The DA can use that juicy tidbit for leverage while Tarrant and Vogelby and their lawyers battle to see who can rat out the other first."

"So much for true love," Jane said. "And their reputations."

"Yeah. Whatever happens in court, or not, Tarrant and Vogelby are about to get hit with a firestorm of public scorn, not to mention job-ending wrath from their bosses."

"Speaking of job-ending. And wrath." Jane could not believe what had happened. Jake was a good guy, an unassailably good guy. But *he* was the one being punished? "I'm so—excuse me—*pissed*! How could Super-intendent Kearney do that to you?"

"I know." Jake's voice was weary as he leaned forward, peeled off his leather jacket and tossed it on the wing chair. Coda, spooked, shot him a disapproving look. "But insubordination, you know? Disobeying direct orders?"

He sat, chin in hands, looking as close to depressed as Jane had ever seen him.

"But I get it." Jake looked at the floor as he talked. "Kearney had no choice. I'm guilty. I screwed up. He ordered me not to go into Grady's room, but I did it anyway. Now T'shombe Pereira's gonna get promoted. Good for him. Shitty for me. But the world is not always fair."

"You of all people." Jane, infuriated, wondered if there was anything she could do. But there wasn't. "And it all worked perfectly! Can you—"

Jane's phone buzzed, vibrating against the glass coffee table. Caller ID said "Isabel." She pushed the "accept" button. "Isabel?"

"I'm in the hospital," Isabel said.

"What?" Jane stood, her heart twisting. "Why? What happened?"

"Oh, no." Isabel's laugh came as a surprise. "I'm *at* the hospital. At BCH. With, you know. Grady. Visiting."

"You're at the hospital visiting Grady?" Jane said the whole thing out loud for Jake's benefit.

"What?" Jake said.

Jane put up a forefinger. *Hang on.*

"We talked about . . . everything," she said. "And he says Detective Brogan should find out who paid for the pizza and beer."

"Who paid for the pizza and beer?" Jane was confused.

"What?" Jake said. He came closer to Jane, leaned in. She tilted the phone so he could hear, too.

"Yeah," Isabel went on. "What he delivered that night at Avery's. He says it's on a credit card. Tarrant's."

Jake raised a fist. "Got you," he whispered.

"I'll tell him," Jane said. Grady and Isabel had clearly put two and two together. Her and Jake. "Are you okay? And Grady?"

"He told me he's leaving town," Isabel said. "I'm glad I got to say goodbye." She paused, cleared her throat. "He's almost well. And he's starting over, he says. I guess that's what I'll do, too."

"Do not do anything without telling me, Isabel," Jane said. "You're a rock star. A performer. Do *not* run away. I'm serious. You're graduating, right?"

"I won't. I will. Graduate, I mean. And if there's a trial, I'll testify against Trey. I gave the district attorney my calendar and file, though, and the SAFEs are giving him the creep list, so she says maybe that'll convince him to plead guilty. And then, well, I'll be fine," Isabel said. "And, Jane?"

"Yes?"

"Thank you. You're a rock star, too."

Jake gestured her back to the couch as she hung up. "I heard that, and you're both right. Both rock stars. Now, thanks to Grady's final performance as CI, we'll nail Tarrant for buying alcohol for underage kids. By the way, Grady's going into witness protection. Though *I* didn't tell you that."

"Think Isabel's going with him?" Jane leaned against her end of the couch. "I kind of hope not. She's got a great career ahead of her."

"If she does?" Jake said. "We'll never know."

They sat as they always did, facing each other with legs parallel, her toes kneading his thigh. She took a sip of her Cabernet, gauging the infinite sorrow in her dear Jake's face. Suspended from the force. With pay, but suspended. Because he'd made a decision to save Grady. He'd succeeded. And then gotten punished for it.

"Wouldn't that be a relief?" Jane asked. "To hide away, like Grady? Go someplace no one can find you? Now that Fiola and I have the Tarrant stuff, and Isabel, and the SAFE women, we'll be finished with the documentary in two weeks or so. . . ." She saw him smile, thank goodness. "I know, it's impossible."

But what *was* possible? Jane twisted her hair away from her face, tried to decide what to say. "Thing is . . ."

"What?" Jake said.

"I'm not sure the deal with Channel 2 is gonna work." Jane took a last sip. No more secrets. "Marsh was . . . critical. Of how I 'handled' telling you about baby-face Rourke Devane, and how I knew who he was. He thought I'd crossed the line. I hadn't, not at all! But even though I was telling the truth, the total truth, he never fully believed me."

Jane set her empty wineglass on the coffee table, then shifted position, putting her head on Jake's shoulder, both of them stretched out on the couch, toes sandwiched together. Coda, suddenly made of rubber, adjusted position, putting half of her body on each of them. Jane felt Coda's purr, and Jake's rising and falling chest beneath her.

What if he weren't a cop and she weren't a reporter? What would they do, where would they go? So many things tied them to their worlds. Family. Work—including Fiola, who, barriers lowering, finally shared her own college trauma, a vodka-fueled frat-party assault she'd never reported. Friends—DeLuca, who she prayed would recover. Mortgages. Insurance. Pets.

Coda looked up, blinked at her, as if she knew Jane was contemplating change.

"You think we could pull it off?" Jake murmured into her hair.

"I know how the police department works, know every place they'd check. And you're the queen of disguise, as you so often tell me."

A new life. Someplace completely different. Was that a fantasy, colored by wine and stress and the reality of the sometimes-unfair world they battled over every day? Or could they actually go?

"I have something for you," Jake said. He shifted on the couch, pulled something from his pocket. Held it up.

A scrap of paper. A heart, and the letter J. The note she'd left on his cruiser.

"I've kept this in my pocket, almost gave it to you in that hospital closet," he said. "What if we'd lost each other?"

Jane's fingers intertwined with Jake's. Gramma Brogan's diamond twinkled in the dimming light.

"Shhh," she said. In one move, she twisted over, their faces now barely inches apart. "Let's talk about it later."

ACKNOWLEDGMENTS

Unending gratitude to:

Kristin Sevick, my brilliant, hilarious, and gracious editor. Thank you—you championed this from day one. The remarkable team at Forge Books: the incomparable Linda Quinton, indefatigable Alexis Saarela, and copy editor Tom Cherwin who (hilariously) noticed everything, thank you. Another wow of a cover—my story fully realized—from Seth Lerner. Desirae Friesen and Bess Cozby, I am so grateful. Brian Heller, my champion. Bob Werner, I am so grateful! The inspirational Tom Doherty, leader of us all. What a terrifically smart and unfailingly supportive team. I am so thrilled to be part of it. Thank you.

Lisa Gallagher, a wow of an agent, a true goddess and visionary, who changed my life and continues to do so.

Francesca Coltrera, the astonishingly skilled independent editor, who lets me believe all the good ideas are mine. Editor Chris Roerden, whose care and skill and commitment made such a difference. Editor Ramona DeFelice Long—your insights are incomparable. You all are incredibly talented. I am lucky to know you—and even luckier to work with you.

The artistry and savvy of Maddee James, Jen Forbus, Charlie Anctil, Erin Mitchell, Mary Zanor, Kaitlyn Buscone, and Mary-Liz Murray.

The inspiration of John Lescroart, Lisa Unger, Tess Gerritsen, Mary Higgins Clark, and Reed Farrel Coleman. Big special thanks to Jeffery Deaver, who guided me so graciously.

Sue Grafton. And Lisa Scottoline. And Lee Child. Words fail me. (I know, a first.)

My darling posse at Sisters in Crime, and the dear Guppies. Thank you. Mystery Writers of America, you rock. Facebook pals, thanks for the grammar guidance, character names, and enthusiasm.

My amazing blog partners. Long may we write. Love you, Jungle Reds sisters, and you too, dear Femmes Fatales.

To the brave and powerful women who shared their stories, and who, as promised, will remain nameless. You are changing the world. I hope I got it right.

My dear friends Laura DiSilverio, Mary Schwager, Paula Munier, and Katherine Hall Page; and my darling sister, Nancy Landman.

Dad—who loves every moment of this. And Mom. Missing you.

And Jonathan, of course, who never complained about all the carry-out salmon.

Do you see your name in this book? Some very generous souls—hi, Ashley Masse!—allowed their names to be used in return for an auction donation to charity. To retain the magic, I will let the rest of you find yourselves.

Keep in touch okay?

www.HankPhillippiRyan.com
www.jungleredwriters.com
www.femmesfatales.tyepepad.com